"I think we could be f[...] Good ones."

"Friends," Cullen repeated.

"You don't want to be friends?"

Pushing the stroller down the long paved road that wound through the ranch, he gave her another sidelong glance. "Platonic friends?"

She fought a blush. *Duh.* "What other kind is there?"

He gave her a sexy look. "Come on. Don't act like you're that surprised something more might be in our future. You felt that kiss as much as I did the other night."

She gaped. "So we have chemistry! It doesn't mean we have to act on it."

"Doesn't mean we can't, either."

Bridgett huffed. "Am I going to be fending you off?"

He mugged right back at her. "Am I going to be fending *you* off?"

She couldn't help it, she laughed. "How did we even get on this subject?" she drawled, her voice every bit as goading as his had been.

He put a hand around her waist and tugged her against him. Then leaned over and whispered in her ear, "You were feeling me out on our...situation."

The Cowboy's Surprise

Cathy Gillen Thacker & Ali Olson

Previously published as *The Texas Cowboy's Baby Rescue*
and *The Bull Rider's Twin Trouble*

HARLEQUIN® MUST♥DOGS

ISBN-13: 978-1-335-69095-1

The Cowboy's Surprise

Copyright © 2019 by Harlequin Books S.A.

First published as The Texas Cowboy's Baby Rescue by Harlequin Books in 2018 and The Bull Rider's Twin Trouble by Harlequin Books in 2018.

The publisher acknowledges the copyright holders of the individual works as follows:

The Texas Cowboy's Baby Rescue
Copyright © 2018 by Cathy Gillen Thacker

The Bull Rider's Twin Trouble
Copyright © 2018 by Mary Olson

Recycling programs for this product may not exist in your area.

Printed in U.S.A.

www.Harlequin.com

CONTENTS

Cathy Gillen Thacker is married and a mother of three. She and her husband spent eighteen years in Texas and now reside in North Carolina. Her mysteries, romantic comedies and heartwarming family stories have made numerous appearances on bestseller lists, but her best reward, she says, is knowing one of her books made someone's day a little brighter. A popular Harlequin author for many years, she loves telling passionate stories with happy endings and thinks nothing beats a good romance and a hot cup of tea! You can visit Cathy's website, cathygillenthacker.com, for more information on her upcoming and previously published books, recipes and a list of her favorite things.

Books by Cathy Gillen Thacker

Harlequin Western Romance

Texas Legacies: The Lockharts

A Texas Soldier's Family
A Texas Cowboy's Christmas
The Texas Valentine Twins
Wanted: Texas Daddy
A Texas Soldier's Christmas

Harlequin American Romance

McCabe Multiples

Runaway Lone Star Bride
Lone Star Christmas
Lone Star Valentine
Lone Star Daddy
Lone Star Baby
Lone Star Twins

Visit the Author Profile page
at Harlequin.com for more titles.

THE TEXAS COWBOY'S BABY RESCUE

Cathy Gillen Thacker

Chapter 1

It was the day, Bridgett Monroe liked to say, that changed *everything*. She was on her way to work, same as always, when a puppy galloped out of the predawn shadows and dashed in front of her small SUV.

She slammed on the brakes, barely missing him, then watched as the mutt pranced around her vehicle, barking at her with ferocious urgency before looping back in front of her once again. The adorable beagle/golden retriever mix was splattered with dried mud and burrs, and dragging a tie-out chain and stake behind him.

Clearly, if she didn't do something, he was going to get hit.

Afraid to move her vehicle at all lest the two of them collide, Bridgett shoved her car into Park, turned on the emergency blinkers and got out.

"Hey there, little guy," she urged softly, kneeling down in front of the pup and holding out her arms in an attempt to coax him out of the path of her vehicle. "Why don't you come see me?"

He stared at her with liquid brown eyes, thinking.

"I won't hurt you, I promise. I just want to be your friend." Bridgett reached out to rescue the runaway pet.

To no avail. He eluded her grasp, jumped swiftly back out of reach and let out another commanding bark.

Tossing his floppy ears in the direction he wanted her to go, he headed on up the block, still dragging the tie-out chain and stake behind him. Periodically he looked back to see if she was following him.

Worried about what would happen if she left him to his own devices, Bridgett headed up the street after him. The cute little mutt let out a happy woof, raced over several lawns and crossed the street. He waited for her to catch up, then darted past a few more houses, out of the residential area into historic downtown Laramie, Texas, and behind the fire station.

The bays were empty, which meant the crew was out on an emergency run.

Too bad, Bridgett thought, as she stopped just short of the tall brick building. She could have used some help lassoing this frisky pup. Frowning, she glanced at her watch again, debating how much time she could really afford to devote to this when she had a car still parked in the middle of the street two blocks away, and patients in the hospital N-ICU who needed her, too.

And that was when she became aware of a whoosh of frantic activity as the pup dashed up to her once again, caught the leg of her nursing uniform pants between his teeth and pulled ferociously.

Determined, it seemed, to have her continue to follow him.

Curious, she did, the leg of her scrubs clamped in his jaws as he led her along the side of the big brick fire station. Over to a...*fairly large cardboard box*?

The pup let go abruptly and sat down next to the shipping carton, panting loudly. He stared up at her as if he expected her to know exactly what to do.

Taking a deep, bracing breath, Bridgett leaned over, cautiously opened up the loosely folded flaps and felt her heart stall with a mixture of shock and disbelief. "Oh, puppy," she whispered in startled dismay as she sank to her knees and reached inside. "No wonder you needed my help!"

Eleven hours later, the rugged Texas rancher who had been systematically avoiding all of Bridgett's calls and messages strode purposefully onto the maternity and pediatric floor of Laramie Community Hospital.

She wasn't surprised that the notoriously unsentimental rancher appeared to have come straight from the range. His short, curly, espresso-brown hair still bore the marks of the Resistol in his hand, his handsome face the burn of the spring wind and sun.

Nor was she surprised that he would want to have this conversation in person, rather than over the phone.

What she wasn't prepared for was the way her heart was suddenly pounding.

It's not as if he's all that much older. He'd only been five years ahead of her in school.

Or more successful. Professionally, both were at the top of their game. Although, she had to admit, given his rising success as a cattle breeder and land owner, he was likely a far sight wealthier.

Not that he flaunted that, either, she realized on a sigh as her knees went all wobbly. He was a man's man, through and through. The dusty leather boots on his feet were well broken in. And though there was nothing unique or expensive about his rumpled chambray shirt, it still cloaked his broad shoulders and muscular chest as if it was custom-made, and his faded Wranglers did equally showstopping things to his sinewy lower half.

Oblivious to the forbidden nature of her thoughts, Cullen McCabe slammed to a halt just short of her. His dark brows lowered like thunderclouds over mesmerizing navy blue eyes.

Her breath caught in her chest.

"Is this an April Fool's joke?" he demanded gruffly.

Feeling a little angry about how this all had transpired, too, she gestured at the infant slumbering on the other side of the nursery's glass window. The adorable newborn had a strikingly handsome face, ruddy skin, short and curly espresso brown hair and gorgeous blue eyes.

Just like the man standing in front of her!

She tilted her head back to better look into Cullen's face. "Does this look like a joke, McCabe?" Because it sure wasn't one to her! Or any of the emergency personnel who had been summoned to the scene of the abandonment.

Their eyes clashed, held for an interminably long moment. Cullen looked back at the Plexiglass infant bed, lingering on the tag attached to the front of it, marked Robby Reid McCabe?

His dark brow furrowed. "Why is there a question mark at the end of the name?"

Was he really going to play her and everyone else for a fool? Bridgett folded her arms in front of her. "Because we're not entirely sure of the foundling's identity."

"Okay, then…" He jabbed a thumb at his sternum. "What do I have to do with this baby? Other than the fact we apparently share the same middle and last names?"

Bridgett reached into the pocket of her scrubs and withdrew the rumpled envelope. "This was left beside the fire station along with the child. The infant was in a cardboard box, and the puppy—who had upended his tie-out chain—led me to him."

Cullen gave her another long, wary look. With a scowl, he opened the envelope, pulled out the typewritten paper and read out loud, "Cullen, I know you never planned to have a family or get married, and I understand that, maybe more than you could ever know, but please be the daddy little Robby deserves. And take wonderful care of his puppy, Riot, too."

Reacting a little like he had landed smack-dab in the center of some crazy reality TV show, like the one his cousin Brad McCabe had famously been on years ago, Cullen looked around suspiciously. Just as she might have in his situation.

To no avail. The only cameras were the security ones

the hospital employed. "I don't see a puppy," he gritted out.

Aware she wouldn't have believed it, either, had it not
actually happened to her that very morning, Bridgett
returned wryly, "Oh, believe me, Riot was here." Wiggling and jumping around like crazy.

Cullen shoved a hand through his hair. "In the hospital?" His glare radiated swiftly increasing disbelief.

Bridgett flushed. That little irregularity could get
her in a whole mess of hot water. Yet what choice had
she had at the time?

Aware he radiated an intoxicatingly masculine blend
of sun, horse and man, she stepped back. "It was just
temporarily. My twin sister, Bess, came and took him
to my apartment until you could get here to claim him."

"And the baby," Cullen added in disbelief.

"Actually," Bridgett told him, "because of the way all
this went down, that is going to take a few days. And
that's assuming you want Robby and Riot." She held
up a hand before Cullen could interrupt. "If you don't,
then social services is already working on a solution."

He stared at her, then the Plexiglas infant bed, then
back at her. "You really found this infant next to the
fire station *in a cardboard shipping box*?"

Bridgett nodded as her heart cramped in her chest
once again.

"I really did," she said softly, stepping a little closer.
"Why else would I have tracked down your cell phone
number and left ten messages over the course of the
last eleven hours?"

Cullen fell silent once again and just shook his head.

Bridgett had an idea how he felt. She'd had most of her shift to deal with this, and she still couldn't get over both the miracle and the horror of it.

She had to keep reminding herself that despite the fact the several-days-old Robby Reid McCabe had been swaddled in a disposable diaper and a man's old chambray shirt, and his knotted umbilical cord was still attached when he was found, he really was okay.

And that was as much a godsend as the fact that she had been in the right place at the right time, for once in her life.

As Cullen stepped closer to the glass and gave the baby another long, intent look, Bridgett inched nearer and stared up at him. At six foot four, he towered over her five feet seven inches. Quietly, she explained, "Robby was apparently surrendered under the Texas Safe Haven law. Or attempted to be, anyway."

Cullen swung back to Bridgett, all imposing, capable male. "What's that?"

"Any infant sixty days old or younger can be surrendered—safely and legally—at any fire station, freestanding emergency medical care center, EMT station or hospital in Texas, but they are supposed to be left with an employee. Not just dropped off and left in the care of a dog who was staked nearby. Although, to Riot's credit, he did do a good job of insuring that Robby got quick aid."

Cullen rested a shoulder against the glass and folded his arms against his broad chest. "You found him?"

She nodded. "Fortunately, the baby was sleeping. From the looks of it, little Robby didn't even seem to know he had been abandoned. So he couldn't have been there very long at all." Thank heaven.

Cullen's expression radiated all the compassion Bridgett had hoped to see. "I'm sorry to hear that." He stepped forward, inundating her with the mint fragrance of his breath. His voice dropped another notch as his eyes met and held hers. "But unfortunately, I don't have any connection to this baby."

"Sure about that?"

He frowned at her. "I think I would know if I had conceived a child with someone."

"Not necessarily," she countered. Not if he hadn't been told.

Briefly, a resentment that seemed to go far deeper than the situation they were in flickered in his gaze.

He braced both hands on his waist, lowered his face to hers and spoke in a low masculine tone that sent a thrill down her spine. "I think I would know if I had slept with someone in the last ten or eleven months." He paused to let his curt declaration sink in. "I haven't."

Neither had she, ironically enough. Although she hadn't ever really been interested in having sex simply for the sake of having sex. She wanted it to mean something, the way it had with Aaron.

She wasn't sure a man as unsentimental as Cullen would feel the same. For him it might only be about satisfying a need as basic as eating and sleeping.

Studying her, he scoffed. "Obviously, you don't believe me."

Bridgett shrugged, aware this was becoming way too personal, too fast. "It's not up to me to believe you or not," she returned lightly as Mitzy Martin, Laramie County's premiere social worker, walked up to join them, sheaf of papers in hand.

Not sure if they knew each other, Bridgett made introductions.

Laramie County Sheriff's Deputy Dan McCabe—one of Cullen's younger brothers—strode up to join them, too.

"Let's take this into a conference room," Mitzy said, leading the way down the hall.

Once the door was shut behind them, all four moved to take seats at the table. The windowless space was tight, especially with two big, strapping men in it, and Bridgett had to work to keep from brushing shoulders and legs with Cullen.

"Why are you here?" Cullen asked his brother.

Dan sent his older brother a sympathetic glance. "I volunteered due to the sensitive nature of the situation."

Cullen nodded his understanding, but he did not look happy. Briefly, he repeated what he had already told Bridgett, then asked in the same gruff tone he'd used with her, "Is there any way I can prove this baby isn't mine?"

Bridgett called on her training to answer what was essentially a medical question. "Not without the mother's DNA."

"So, until then?" he pressed.

Mitzy's answer was brisk. "Robby is going into foster care."

Bridgett's heart squeezed in her chest. Aware she was about to learn of an even more important decision, she looked at her friend hopefully. "Was my request granted?"

With a staying lift of her hand, Mitzy allowed, "Temporarily. As long as you understand that this child is not, and may not ever be, available for adoption."

Bridgett thought about the emotional connection she had already forged with the infant. The reservations she'd had up to now, about opening herself up to further heartache, faded completely. "I can handle it," she vowed to one and all. "Furthermore, I'll do as the note requested and take Riot, too."

Cullen would have figured the social worker would be happy to hear that, since it meant her job here was done. Instead, Mitzy Martin looked as stressed as Bridgett Monroe had when he'd arrived at the hospital to confront her.

She leaned forward. "Are you sure, Bridgett? Up to now you've adamantly refused to consider fostering any child not available for adoption because you have a hard enough time saying goodbye to the babies in N-ICU and didn't think you could do it in your personal life, too." She reached over to take her friend's hand. "And I get that. We all do."

So, Bridgett Monroe had a heart as soft as her fair skin and bare pink lips. Cullen couldn't say he was surprised. Any more than he was surprised about his reaction to her. Stubborn, feisty women always turned him on.

"This is different," Bridgett said, color flooding her face.

"How?" Cullen asked, an answering heat welling up deep inside him.

"I know it sounds crazy...but I think I was meant to find these two."

It was all Cullen could do not to groan. The last thing he needed was another overly sentimental woman in his life. Even on the periphery. Yes, she was graceful and feminine. Pretty in that girl-next-door way, with her glossy, rich brown hair, delicate features and long-lashed pine-green eyes. She wore a long-sleeved white T-shirt beneath the blue hospital scrubs that seemed to emphasize, rather than hide, her svelte curves and long legs.

But she was also an emotional firebrand—at least, when it came to him. Jumping to conclusions. Pulling him in. Then shutting him out, just as quick.

He did not need those kinds of ups and downs.

Especially not now.

Mitzy and Dan exchanged a wary glance.

"Unfortunately, Bridgett," the social worker put in gently, "even if what you say is true, that this was all destined to happen the way it did, it doesn't mean your chances of fostering then adopting a baby on your own have changed. At least, as far as the department goes."

Cullen watched as disappointment glimmered in Bridgett's eyes.

Gently, Mitzy continued. "The district supervisor and the local family court judge who hears these cases want infants who are in search of permanent placement in a stable, *two-parent* home."

"But for every rule or policy there's always an exception that can be made, especially in special circumstances like these," Bridgett persisted resolutely.

"Yes." Mitzy chose her words carefully. "But I wouldn't count on that happening, long term."

Except Bridgett was, Cullen noted in concern.

With a sigh, Mitzy continued, "They're willing to make an allowance for Robby *temporarily* because you're a nurse and Robby is just a few days old with health issues that may or may not crop up, but—"

"Whoa," Cullen put in. "If there is any kind of risk, why not keep the baby in the hospital?"

Bridgett swung around, her elbow nudging his rib in the process. "Because the few problems he had upon admission have been treated. Hence, there's no reason to keep him here."

"So—" Mitzy looked at Dan "—unless there has been any further news on the law enforcement front…?"

Dan shook his head. "Sadly, not yet. But the Laramie County sheriff's department has sent information requests to all the hospitals, clinics and urgent care facilities in the state."

Cullen's gut tightened at the thought of all the people who would hear his name tied to this heartbreaking situation. The assumptions they would make about his character, and by default, the McCabe family, could be catastrophic.

He couldn't believe he was doing it again, bringing shame upon those closest to him.

"Is this going to be on the news?" he asked tensely.

"No," Mitzy said. "We don't want to scare off the birth mother if she does change her mind in the next few days and wants to come forward and reclaim her child."

Looking as shocked and horrified as Cullen felt, just

considering the possibility. Bridgett cut in, "Would the Department of Child and Family Services really allow that to happen?"

Mitzy paused. "It's hard to say. There could be mitigating circumstances behind the mother's actions."

"Like what?" Cullen bit out, not surprised to find himself siding with Bridgett on this.

"Like she's suffering from postpartum depression and isn't thinking clearly," Mitzy suggested.

"The note she left with the baby seemed pretty clear-cut to me," Cullen said.

"In any case, we're all aware there has to be much more to this story than we know thus far," Mitzy explained. "So law enforcement and the medical community are all on alert for a woman coming in, having just given birth but without a baby to show for it. If anything the least bit suspicious occurs, we'll hear about it, pronto. And go from there."

Bridgett sat back in her chair, looking dejected again.

Cullen could imagine how the dedicated N-ICU nurse felt.

She'd found the abandoned infant and puppy, and the idea of giving Riot and Robby back to someone who had been unhappy or unbalanced enough to leave a baby alone in a cardboard box with only a puppy to guard it had to rankle.

It sure as hell did him.

"So, if you're sure this is what you want, Bridgett, even knowing it's only temporary…" Mitzy began.

Bridgett's expression turned fierce. "I am."

"And what about you?" Mitzy turned to Cullen.

Not sure what the social worker was asking, Cullen shrugged. "I just told Bridgett. There's no way on earth that Robby is my baby."

To his frustration, Mitzy looked as skeptical of that as Bridgett and his younger brother had. "Can you tell us who might *want to assign* paternity to you, then?" Mitzy asked.

Suddenly, all eyes were upon him once again. Cullen thought a long moment, then, unable to come up with anything, shook his head.

Mitzy pulled a pen from her bag, perfectly calm. Matter-of-fact. "So you're formally surrendering all claim to this infant, then?" She brought out another piece of paper.

Was he?

Cullen hadn't expected to do anything except come to the hospital, straighten out the situation and leave. However, seeing the newborn infant, reading the note, changed things. Made him feel that he just might be involved here.

How, exactly, he didn't know yet.

But he was a McCabe, as well as a Reid.

And unlike the Reids, McCabes did not shirk their obligations, familial or otherwise. So he was going to have to see this calamity through to its resolution.

Aware what Bridgett Monroe probably wanted him to say, so the way would be clear for her, he paused, then finally said, "No."

His younger brother Dan looked on approvingly, while sharp disappointment showed on Bridgett's pretty face.

Mitzy simply waited.

Cullen inhaled deeply, then directed his remarks to everyone in the room. "Someone left the puppy and the baby for me. Like it or not, that makes them my responsibility. At least until their real family is found or permanent arrangements can be made to give them a good home. So I'd like to keep tabs on the child while he's being fostered. Meet the dog." Who might have more of a connection to him than anyone except his brother yet knew.

Mitzy turned. "Bridgett? Is this going to be okay with you? Because if you'd rather your first ward be a child who has already been released for adoption, I would completely understand. And so would everyone else at the department."

For the first time since he'd laid eyes on her, Cullen saw Bridgett falter. She turned to glance at the papers that would make her the baby's temporary foster mother and, for a second, looked so vulnerable he couldn't help but feel for her. Pushing aside the temptation to take her in his arms and comfort her, he swallowed hard, reminding himself this situation was complicated enough as it was.

Bridgett drew herself up, raised her chin and looked Mitzy straight in the eye. "I can handle this," she vowed.

Could she? Cullen wondered.

Chapter 2

"You really don't have to walk us to my SUV," Bridgett said half an hour later, as she got ready to go.

Cullen was clearly skeptical. "You're saying you could easily manage all this on your own?"

Bridgett looked at the messenger bag she took to work, the diaper bag filled with emergency essentials, and the swaddled infant she was about to pick up. He had a point. It was a lot.

"Okay." She handed him both bags and her vehicle keys, then gently picked up little Robby.

She'd handled hundreds of newborns in her career. Cuddled and given medical aid and taken care of their emotional needs for as long as they were in the N-ICU.

But this was different. It had been from the first moment she'd gathered the little infant in her arms.

She felt connected to this child, heart and soul.

As if she were already his mother.

"But that's all the help we need," Bridgett continued firmly. "Once I get to my apartment and you meet the puppy, to see if that sparks anything, I'll be able to handle it from there."

The only problem, she noted ten minutes later as she pulled up in front of her nondescript brick apartment building and saw a furious man pacing outside, was that she still had a few more wrinkles to iron out.

Cullen emerged from his pickup truck. He nodded at the short and stocky man storming their way. "Who's that?"

Her heart sank as she stepped from the driver's seat and faced off with the man who had just been peering in her apartment windows. "My landlord, Amos Stone."

The gray-haired man marched closer. "Miss Monroe! Do you have *a dog* in your apartment?"

Too late, Bridgett realized she should have found another emergency solution that morning. One that hadn't involved spiriting a dog who'd had no place in the hospital to yet another place he was absolutely forbidden to be. She fixed the building's owner with her most winning smile. "I can explain."

Her landlord did not think so. "Your lease explicitly says *no pets of any kind* allowed. Ever."

"I know." Bridgett reached into the car to gather Robby in her arms. "But—"

"No buts," the older man huffed. "You're out of here! Effective immediately."

Cullen stepped forward. "Surely there's some middle ground here," he beseeched cordially, on her behalf.

Amos Stone glared. "Nope. Twenty-four hours to get everything out, or I start formal eviction proceedings. And that mangy mutt goes right this instant. Or I call animal control to take him for you!" He stomped off.

Able to hear the barking from inside her unit, Bridgett handed Robby over to Cullen, then hurried to unlock her front door. What she saw, as the pup barreled toward her and leaped into her arms, was even more dismaying.

Riot had pushed aside the temporary barrier she'd set up between her small galley kitchen and the rest of the unit. He'd wreaked havoc throughout the apartment, knocking pillows off the sofa and upending plants, lamps and a basket of clean laundry. He'd also had several accidents on the wood floor.

Apparently being left alone had stressed the poor little guy out.

But now that the puppy was in her arms again, he was quiet, cuddly and clearly exhausted.

Cullen stood beside her, a drowsy Robby held against his broad chest. He looked around, surveying the damage. "What next?" he said.

Outside the window, she saw her landlord standing next to his car, phone to his ear. She headed outside again, to her vehicle, and Cullen followed. "Mr. Stone is probably on the phone with animal control right now. So we need to get Riot out of here."

Cullen inclined his head toward the slumbering infant. "Want to switch?"

"Um...let's not rock the boat just yet."

Especially since Robby looked as if he were in baby nirvana. She nodded at the safety seat that had been installed in the backseat of her SUV. "If you can settle Robby back in that, I'll hand off Riot to you and then get the baby strapped in."

Cullen did as she asked and then took the dog from her. "Where do you want the pup?" he asked.

Good question. To have Riot on the loose while she was driving and Robby was strapped in a car seat did not seem like a good idea.

Cullen understood her indecision. "Why don't I put him in my truck and drive him wherever you're going next?"

If only she knew where that was, Bridgett thought, opening the door on the driver's side to let the pleasant spring breeze circulate through the interior of the car. For the next few minutes, they remained next to her SUV while she scrolled through the hotel listings on her phone and made a few quick calls.

"Any luck?" Cullen asked, after the third.

Disappointed, Bridgett shook her head. "None of the inns in the county allow pets."

Still holding the puppy against his chest, he used the index finger to tilt his hat a little higher on his forehead. "Doesn't your family own a ranch?"

"The Triple Canyon. My younger brother, Nick, and his wife, Sage, live there now, but they're currently putting a commercial kitchen in the ranch house so Sage can do the majority of the baking for her café-bistro on the premises. So they are at Sage's old one-bedroom in town with their two kids for the next three months."

He squinted down at her thoughtfully. "What about your twin sister?"

"Bess lives in the same building I do."

"So that's out."

"Right."

He studied her. "There's no one else in the area you could call upon in an emergency? Other family?"

Yes and no, Bridgett thought. "I've got two more siblings. My older brother, Gavin, and Violet and their two kids live in a shotgun house here in town that is already bursting at the seams. And my sister Erin and Mac are living in the Panhandle now, with their brood, so although they *would* take me in, I can't leave the county with Robby until everything is straightened out."

He edged close enough that she could smell the soap and sun-warmed-leather scent of him. "Friends, then?"

"The ones who live in houses all have kids and pets of their own, and the ones who don't live in apartments."

Cullen shrugged. "You could board the puppy at the vet clinic in town temporarily or turn him over to the animal shelter."

"No!" The force of her response stunned them both.

Bridgett drew in a bolstering breath. "If it hadn't been for Riot's determination to get my attention, I never would have known Robby had been abandoned at the fire station. Who knows how long it would have been before he'd been rescued? Plus, the note specifically said the mother wanted the two of them to stay together. I intend to honor that."

"Do you even know anything about caring for a dog?"

Irked by his doubt, she tilted her chin at him. "No. But I'm sure I can learn. I just made an offer on a house, so all I need is a short-term solution that will hold us until I move."

He regarded her with new respect. "You're buying a home?"

Apparently, real estate was a language they both spoke. She nodded, forcing herself to relax. "An adorable little bungalow here in town. I'm just waiting for my mortgage application to be approved. Which unfortunately rules out renting another place. No one's going to want me in and out for just a couple of weeks."

"Well, since you are clearly out of options..." Cullen gave an affable shrug. "You could bring Robby and Riot to the Western Cross."

Bridgett blinked. "Stay with you? At your ranch?"

He nodded.

She crossed her arms and glared up at him. "Why would you want to do that?" she blurted out.

He regarded her calmly. "To fulfill my moral obligation, and to preserve my reputation and that of the McCabe family, of course."

Cullen could see it wasn't the explanation Bridgett wanted. Which was too bad, because the blunt truth was the only reason he was prepared to give. "I've got a virtual cattle auction coming up in ten days. My first at the Western Cross ranch. If people think I am unreliable on any level, they're not going to buy livestock from me. So it's to my advantage, and yours, to get this resolved as soon as possible. And maybe if we're all together I'll be able to more quickly figure out who would have wanted me to be responsible for all this."

"Makes sense. I guess."

He continued looking her in the eye. "I also don't want to embarrass Frank and Rachel or any of the rest of my family." Thanks to his mom, and the way she had selfishly kept his paternity a secret, for years, so she wouldn't have to share him, they had already been through enough.

Bridgett went still, for a moment giving him a glimpse of the woman she was, at heart. "You call your parents by their first names?"

His attention drifted to her mouth. "Rachel is my stepmom. And Frank didn't come into my life until I was sixteen."

She bit her lip, her gaze glued to him. "That explains the Rachel. But Frank…?"

He shrugged, wishing he could table the urge to take down her hair and run his fingers through the thick, silky waves. "I never got the hang of calling him Dad."

She moved closer. "Did he want you to call him Dad?"

"We never discussed it," he said curtly. And he sure wasn't going to dissect his tumultuous early years with the nosy nurse in front of him. "So," he said, bringing the conversation back around to the current trouble at hand. "Are you going to take me up on my offer or not?"

She looked down at the baby, who was beginning to stir, and sighed. "I'm not sure if I'll stay the night or not, but I'll follow you out there, assess the situation and then figure out what I'm going to do."

Not exactly a yes. But likely the closest he would get.

He gave her the address to put into her navigation system in case they got separated, and then they took off. Twenty minutes later, they were turning beneath the archway to the Western Cross ranch. Both sets of vehicle headlamps swept over the live oaks lining the drive, the fenced pastures filled with cattle and the cluster of brand-new state-of-the-art barns and stables. Finally, he drew up in front of the ranch house and parked behind the Laramie Animal Clinic van.

His good friend, and recent widow, Sara Anderson stepped out. It was hard to tell whether the pale, drawn hue of her face was due to grief over the sudden loss of her soldier husband or the nausea associated with the first trimester of pregnancy. But he appreciated her willingness to help them out today.

He picked up Riot and met her in the middle of the circular drive. "Thanks for coming," he said.

The willowy blonde smiled, kind-hearted as always. "No problem." Sara studied Riot with a clinician's unerring eye, stroked him beneath the chin. "This the little runaway?"

"It is." And though it had been years since he had held one, Cullen experienced the lure of a puppy all over again.

Bridgett parked and got out, too, a fussy baby Robby in her arms. Cullen made introductions. "Sara Anderson, Bridgett Monroe. Sara's a neighboring rancher and the veterinarian who sees to all of my cattle and horses."

Bridgett nodded. "Sara and I talked at the county's High School Career Fair last fall. And we also both volunteer at the West Texas Warriors Assistance nonprofit."

"Ah, then no introduction necessary." Indeed, the two women looked surprisingly chummy. He hadn't thought about them being friends. But then, he didn't spend a lot of time socializing with anyone outside the cattle business.

Sara moved an electronic wand over the pup, between his shoulders and neck and from side to side. Then over the rest of his body.

"Anything?" Cullen asked.

"No." Sara frowned. "I thought he might be a little too young for a microchip, but I wanted to be certain. There were no tags on his collar?"

"No."

"That's too bad. I'd like to know more about him." She opened up the back of her van and pulled out a medium-sized plastic crate with a metal-grill door. "The food, dishes and leash you requested are all in there. You're also going to need to make sure he gets started on all his vaccinations, ASAP."

"I'll make an appointment."

"Good." Sara grinned, tossing Cullen a bottle of puppy shampoo. "And you might want to give him a bath while you're at it."

Grinning, Cullen caught the bottle with one hand. "Thanks, Sara."

Sara paused to greet little Robby, who was wide-eyed and squirmy. "Bridgett? Good luck with the baby.

I heard about the situation." She frowned, shaking her head. "I hope you get to keep him."

Abruptly looking like she might burst into tears at any moment, Bridgett nodded. "I want what's best for them both," she said thickly, the strain of the day showing on her pretty face. "And I appreciate your help with Riot."

"It was my pleasure," Sara said with a warm smile. "And if you need anything else, just ask." Then she climbed back into her van, gave a parting wave and took off.

Silence hung heavy between them as they stood there together, cradling puppy and baby.

Bridgett looked up, wordlessly scanning the compact century old farmhouse, whatever she was thinking at that moment as much a mystery to him as the emotion resonating in her dulcet tones.

"So, this is where you live," she said.

Chapter 3

"For the last ten and a half months, it has been," Cullen admitted as they moved inside.

He hit a button on the keypad by the door, and the place lit up. "And before that?" Bridgett prodded, trying to recall what she'd heard.

He led her through the foyer and shut the door behind them. "Oklahoma, for two years."

They were standing close. Almost too close. Bridgett swung around to face him, stepping back a pace in the process. She was acutely aware she really didn't know much about Frank McCabe's eldest son at all—and she wanted to know more, because of the situation they were in. Noting he looked as inherently masculine as he smelled—like sun and soap and leather—she searched the rugged planes of his face. "And prior to that, where were you?"

The grooves on either side of his sensual lips deepened. "Colorado for eighteen months, Nebraska for four years."

"Nebraska. Wow, you must have really liked it there."

He studied her, as if trying to decide how much farther he wanted this discussion to go. "It's the second-largest cattle-producing state in the country, and I had two different ranches. A small one in the north for about twenty-six months, a larger one in the south, for about the same amount of time."

"Which you purchased after starting out here, correct?" Her feminine instincts on full alert, she pushed on, curious to hear about the time he'd spent outside of Laramie County. "Somewhere in the Panhandle?"

His gaze roved her upturned face. He looked at her for a long beat. "How do you know that?"

She flushed under his intense scrutiny. "My sister Erin and her husband, Mac, mentioned it when they moved up there for his work."

He continued holding her gaze for a brief but electrifying moment that swiftly had her tingling all over. "Hmm."

"Mac said you were a rancher to watch."

Cullen shifted the exhausted puppy in his arms, cradling it to his broad chest. "I don't think Wheeler was too fond of me back then," he pointed out. "I outbid him on a property he wanted for his wind energy turbines."

Bridgett grinned. "I'm sure Mac forgave you." If there was one thing her brother-in-law respected, it was business acumen and skill.

A wave of unexpected contentment flowing through her, she snuggled the sleepy Robby, breathing in his sweet baby scent. "Speaking of family, though, yours must be happy to have you back in Texas again."

His expression darkened and the corners of his lips slanted downward. "They are."

"Are you?" Curiosity won out over caution yet again.

"For the moment."

Which meant what? He had one foot out the door? Was getting ready to bolt again?

Not that it was any of her business what his future plans were. Once the current mystery was solved, anyway. She knew what her future was—it was right here in Laramie County with Robby and Riot.

"So." Bridgett forced herself to concentrate on their surroundings. She inclined her head toward the front two rooms of the thousand-square-foot first floor. The one on the right sported a wall of what appeared to be security monitors showing various areas of the ranch, while the other room was outfitted with a large, masculine mahogany desk, a comfortable chair, built in bookshelves and sleek computer equipment. Framed diplomas and awards adorned the whitewashed wood-paneled walls. "I gather this is where you do all the Western Cross ranch office work."

"Yep. And there's never any shortage of it." He moved forward, leading the way past an iron-railed staircase to the living room in the rear, which also had an open layout. She paused to admire the rustic fireplace, a big comfy sofa and the state-of-the-art entertainment center.

After getting a cursory glimpse at the pristine eat-in kitchen, she followed him to a screened-in porch, complete with cushioned furniture and a chain-hung swing. It overlooked a stone patio and built-in barbecue grill as well as an impressive view of the ranch.

"This, I am guessing, is where you hang out when you're not working." She tried not to think about how intimate it would be, sharing such a cozy space, and failed. "And maybe entertain." She pushed the words through the abrupt tightness of her throat.

He swung back to face her, looking as intrigued by her as she was by him. "Yes to the first. No to the latter."

Good heavens, her pulse was pounding. She moved slightly away. Pretended to stare out the windows at the fields beyond.

She spun back to face him, pretending a tranquility she couldn't begin to feel. "You don't entertain?"

Gesturing for her to follow, he moved back inside toward the centrally located staircase. "I give tours of the ranch to business associates by request. That's it." He paused on the first stair. "Why? Is that a high priority for you?"

"Not really. I've been spending all my time these days working extra shifts so I could save up enough for the down payment on a house. Which I have finally done."

Upstairs were three modestly decorated bedrooms, decked out in the same masculine gray-and-white color scheme as the rest of the home, and a full bath off the hall featuring a single pedestal sink, a private water closet and a tiled bathtub/shower combo big enough for a man of his size. "So, what do you think?" He shifted a restless Riot a little higher in his arms. "Will you-all be comfortable here tonight?"

In terms of creature comforts? Yes. In terms of having him sleeping just down the hall from her? Not so much. Yet what choice did she have? She had to make do until she had a better solution worked out.

"Absolutely. If you're sure it's going to be okay with you, too?"

He looked at her a long moment. A myriad of emotions came and went on his ruggedly handsome face. "We'll make it work," he said cryptically. And in that moment, as they headed back downstairs, she knew they would.

While Bridgett carried the baby and the diaper bag into the family room, Cullen headed outside with the puppy.

Thirty minutes later, she and Robby found them on the screened-in porch. The freshly bathed Riot was getting a rubdown with a towel and she smiled. "He has a lot more white fur than I realized."

"Yeah, I thought he was mostly brown, too." Laugh lines appeared at the corners of his eyes. "Guess a lot of it was mud. Robby okay?"

Trying not to think how easily she and Cullen meshed in the mom and dad roles, she nodded. "He took his bottle like a champ. Now all he has to do is burp a time or two, and I'll be able to put him down again."

Cullen brought two stainless steel bowls of food and water over and set them in front of where Riot was leashed to the railing.

The puppy stared at both.

"I know you have to be hungry," Cullen said, kneeling down to pet the mutt's head.

Riot still didn't touch the food.

Cullen took some kibble into his hand and offered it that way.

Riot hesitated, then inched closer, nudging Cullen's palm and finally eating a few small pieces. Cullen offered the bowl again, but when the pup once again refused, he was forced to go back to the hand-feeding method.

"Are all puppies that fussy?" she asked, walking back and forth, gently patting Robby on the back.

"I wouldn't know. I only had the one when I was a kid."

Bridgett caught the low note of emotion in his voice. "What happened to him?"

"He died at age nine. Cancer."

Clearly, Cullen still missed him. "You never got another?"

Another shake of his head. "Initially, I wasn't in a position where I could get another dog. After that—" he shrugged "—I was too busy ranching."

Robby gazed over at Cullen, mesmerized by the low timbre of his voice. As was she. "Too busy?" she asked lightly, inclining her head at Riot. "Or too leery of giving your heart away to another little cutie like this?"

Cullen's head came up. As he exhaled, his broad shoulders tensed, then relaxed. "Too busy fixing up ranches, adding to my herd and moving from place to place."

"How big a spread do you want?" she asked, edging closer.

Cullen set the empty bowl aside, then led the still-leashed Riot over to the grass. "Minimum, ten thousand acres and a couple thousand head of cattle."

"Maximum?"

He shrugged. "Frank has fifty thousand acres on the Bar M."

"You'd like to equal your family's ranch?"

He nodded, solemn now. "Yeah, I would."

There was something oddly sentimental about following in his father's footsteps that way. Especially coming from such an unsentimental man. She looked out at the fenced acres, all of them spring-green and lush after plentiful March rains. "How many acres do you have here?"

Noting Riot had finished his business, Cullen praised him and patted him on the head. "Four thousand."

"So you have a way to go." She watched the puppy and man amble back onto the patio.

"I'll get there," he said confidently.

She'd bet he would.

In fact, she'd bet he would get just about anything he wanted. Good thing it wasn't her.

Bridgett and Cullen had dinner together and got the baby and puppy settled, then Cullen excused himself to go check on one of his prize bulls. Bridgett used the momentary quiet to hit the shower and change into a pair of light gray yoga pants and a long-sleeved light blue T-shirt.

That done, she settled on her bed and began making a to-do list for the following day, including all the notifications she had to take care of that very evening. Two and a half hours later, she was still working on the last and most important one. Aware Robby would be waking again soon, and would need to be fed when he did, she headed back down to the kitchen.

Cullen was seated at the kitchen table, laptop in front of him and what appeared to be business materials all around him. To her surprise, he appeared to have had a shower, too. But he had put on jeans and a black body-hugging T-shirt that let her know just how taut and muscular his body was. Clearly, he didn't sleep in jeans. Those were for her benefit, just like her yoga pants, instead of pj bottoms, were for his. She wondered if he slept in that shirt or went bare chested. Not that she should be conjuring up a mental image of him in boxers or briefs in the first place.

Her pulse kicking up a notch, Bridgett remained in the portal. Her face bare of all makeup, her freshly shampooed hair spilling about her shoulders in damp waves, she felt oddly defenseless. The situation suddenly way too intimate.

"Okay if I come in long enough to warm up a bottle?" she asked lightly.

He glanced up from the laptop in front of him, his gaze raking lightly over her from head to toe. Sensual lips curved into a ghost of a smile, he encouraged her to come in with a tilt of his handsome head. "*Mi casa* is you-all's *casa…*"

Temporarily, Bridgett reminded herself. Very temporarily.

She could not share close quarters with a man she found this attractive. Not for long, anyway. Not without something ridiculously sexy and impulsive happening.

"Not for much longer if the solution I have been working on all evening comes to fruition."

Was that disappointment she saw etched on his handsome face?

He got up, suddenly. Went to the fridge, got a bottle of water, then held the door open for her so she could help herself, too. "How are things going up there?" His voice was low, polite.

She moved past to retrieve a premade bottle of formula, being careful not to touch him. She inhaled the clean, soapy scent of him. The minty smell of toothpaste. He hadn't shaved and the evening beard shadowing his face gave him an even more ruggedly masculine air.

Aware she hadn't answered his question yet, she smiled. "Both little fellas are still sleeping, but Robby should be waking up soon for another feeding, so I figured I would get ahead of the game and warm the bottle."

He tilted his head, his gaze drifting over her lazily, creating little sparks of awareness. "Before all hell breaks loose," he guessed.

Because she had no bottle warmer—yet—she filled a bowl with hot water and set the bottle in it. "I haven't noticed anything being out of control this evening." She adapted a militant stance. "If you discount the tiff with my landlord."

He flashed a teasing grin. "That's because, for the most part, there's been two of us and two of them."

It was so true she didn't want to think—or was it worry?—about that. Adopting the confident, cheerful air she usually used to tackle the problems in life, she asked, "What time do you usually get up and out of here in the morning?"

"Before dawn, usually, but tomorrow I'm planning to hang around here and do office work, at least initially." Seeing her unease, he murmured, "I also usually grab breakfast with the guys at the bunkhouse, but I could cook you breakfast." He shrugged. "If that will help you out."

There was a limit to how far she wanted his gallant involvement to extend. The vibe between them was far too personal already. "Or we could each cook our own," she said pleasantly. Another spark of tension flickered between them, and she felt her breath catch in her throat.

"Independent, hmm?"

She swallowed hard, then shot back firmly, "Like you're not."

He chuckled, a deep rumbling low in his throat. Then he slowly ravished her with his gaze, as if he found her completely irresistible. "Is that why you wanted to adopt a baby on your own?"

Trying not to think how physically attracted she was to him, too, Bridgett checked the formula on the inside of her wrist. Still cool. She added more hot water to the bowl and set the bottle back inside.

"I never said that solo adopting was my first choice." Intimacy shimmered between them as he took up a station opposite her. The brooding look was back on his face. "But you're doing it?"

She leaned back against the counter, her hands braced on either side of her, not sure why his opinion mattered so much.

She sighed, figuring it wouldn't hurt to confide this much. "Only because I stupidly gave up the one shot I had at a happy family life."

His brow quirked and he shifted closer.

Which didn't mean she had to explain further. But, for reasons she couldn't understand, she wanted him to know. "I was in love with a fourth-year medical student while I was in nursing school. He was headed back to Utah, where he was from, to do his residency, and he wanted us to get married before he left, start having kids right away. I still had another two semesters to go and I wasn't ready. But Aaron saw no reason to wait if we loved each other. So he gave me an ultimatum." Refusing the crazy urge to take refuge in Cullen's strong arms and rest her head against his broad chest, she continued. "Thinking he would become more reasonable over time, I refused."

Dark gaze skimming hers intently, he moved closer still. "Didn't work out?"

Her heartbeat quickened at the unexpected compassion in his low tone. "He married someone else within a few months of our breakup."

"Still married?"

Bridgett nodded. "Happily. They have six kids and another on the way." Six kids who could have been hers.

His brow knotted. "Wow."

"Yeah."

Silence fell between them.

"Still wishing it was you?"

Not the way he thought.

"Not really," she replied honestly. "I wouldn't want to leave my family, be that far away from Texas." She locked eyes with Cullen, not ashamed to admit it. "But I do regret giving up my one shot at marriage, especially knowing it might never come again."

His expression guarded, he said, "You're selling yourself short."

Finding his low, grumbling voice a bit too determined—and too full of sexual promise for comfort—she returned, "How do you know?" Who was he to give her advice on her love life or lack thereof? "Especially since you're not known to be the most sentimental guy around!"

Ooh, she should not have said that. But he was goading her. Making her feel foolish in the way he kept looking at her.

He came close and, if she was not mistaken, looked very much like he wanted to make love with her then and there. A wicked grin deepened the crinkles around his navy eyes.

She felt as if she'd just waved a red flag in front of a bull.

"You think not?" he prodded.

Bridgett huffed. "I do." Knowing it was a dangerous proposition to have him that close to her—because she did desire him more than anyone who had come before—she moved away. Feeling hot color flush her cheeks, she enunciated as clearly as possible, "I also know that, unlike you, I believe very strongly in destiny or fate or whatever you want to call it. And that destiny brought Riot and Robby—"

He prowled toward her. "And me."

Ignoring the fierce sense that he was about to put the moves on her, she stubbornly finished her sentence. "Into my life. So if this is what's meant to be for me, I'll take it."

In one smooth motion, he took her all the way into his arms. Pressed her against him in a way that left her reeling and lowered his lips to hers. "So will I," he said.

In inviting her to stay, Cullen hadn't meant to do anything but clear his own reputation and help Bridgett out. He hadn't figured what it would be like to have her, and the baby and puppy, in his home. Or how much he would quickly come to admire her fierce desire to help others, even as she shortchanged herself.

Was it possible she really had no idea how beautiful and desirable she was? How worthy of having?

It seemed so. And that was something he couldn't let stand unchallenged, as all thoughts of being a gentleman fled. She had to know how captivating she was. So he did what he'd been wanting to do since they had first caught sight of each other; he kissed her. Kissed her to discover how soft and supple and sweet-tasting her lips were. Kissed her to fulfill a yearning deep inside him that he hadn't known existed.

And, most of all, he kissed her to show her that they could simply enjoy each other without the false illusion of love or emotional promises that would most likely end up being short-term.

But he was the one who was surprised. Because this kiss, holding her like this, didn't feel like any normal clinch. It felt different. Unique. *Amazingly* unique, as it turned out.

And who was the naive fool now?

Bridgett had known from the moment that she walked into the kitchen, hours after dinner, that a kiss, a touch, an embrace, something might be coming. It was in the way he looked at her. The way she felt when she looked at him.

It was in the leftover adrenaline still sizzling non-stop in her veins. In the building emotions and after-effects of this crazy, crazy day. Of having her dreams start to come true, but not. Of realizing she *still* wanted it all. Maybe could have it all. If only she could find the right man.

She never would have imagined it could be Cullen Reid McCabe. But then, she had never really imagined kissing him. Now that she had, well, suffice it to say her whole world had turned upside down.

Which was why it was a very good thing when a short, loud, high-pitched cry split the silence of the ranch house. Followed by a single urgent bark.

Destiny once again, Bridgett thought, pulling away from the sexy cowboy who held her in his arms. But this time it was telling her *not* to go down this particular path.

Chapter 4

"So, he kissed you?" Bess asked the next morning at Bridgett's apartment.

"Shh!" She cast a look over her shoulder at the guys helping her move out. "Yes."

Her sister grinned. "Did you kiss him back?"

"What does that matter?" she whispered, flushing. Unfortunately, yes, she had kissed him back! For way too long a time! "It was obviously a mistake."

Bess grinned again. "Sure about that? From what I've seen, he's very sexy. Well regarded in the community. Single and obviously interested in you. *And the baby.*" She taped shut another box. "And where is Riot, anyway?"

"With Cullen. He took him to work in his truck." Bridgett selected the clothes she needed to take with

her when she left versus those that were going into storage. "Well, the puppy couldn't be here, obviously, after
what happened yesterday with the landlord, and *quit*
looking at me like that!"

Bess chuckled. "What is it they say? Life happens
while you were making other plans. Well, while you
were trying, rather unsuccessfully, I might add, to adopt
a child on your own, a baby and a puppy and a kind,
great-looking cowboy all drop in your lap!"

Bridgett thought about what a great and gallant thing
it was that Cullen was doing. Not just inviting her to
stay with him at his ranch but helping her out with both
infant and puppy, too. She looked at her sister. "It's almost crazy spooky, isn't it?"

"*Fated* is the word you're looking for."

Bridgett paused. "It may seem that way."

"I'm telling you…it most definitely is." Bess pointed
at the well-dressed Realtor coming up the walk. "Oh,
and speaking of fate…"

Bridgett met Jeanne Phipps at the door. "Did you get
the answer from the sellers?"

"Yes." Jeanne flashed a regretful half smile. "Unfortunately, Bridgett, it's not the one you want to hear."

"What's wrong?" Cullen asked, coming through the
ranch house door at five that evening.

Bridgett eased the sleeping Robby into the carrier sitting on the kitchen island, strapped him in and
brought him into the adjacent family room. "What do
you mean?" She knelt down to greet an equally tuck-
ered-out Riot.

He nuzzled her palm, licked it once and then went into the back of his crate and promptly fell asleep.

"You look like you just lost your best friend." Cullen strode over to the kitchen sink, rolled up his sleeves and washed his arms up to the elbows.

She waited until he'd grabbed a towel and then moved in to wash up, too. "Not exactly," she murmured.

"Then what, exactly?"

She drew a deep breath. "My plan to be out of here— maybe as soon as this evening—fizzled. At least temporarily."

He kept his eyes locked with hers.

"The house I have put an offer on is currently empty. I was hoping the owners would allow me to rent it from them until I can close on the property. They told my Realtor, Jeanne Phipps, they would consider it, but only after all the inspections are done and my mortgage application is approved."

"How long do you think that will take?"

"Three, four weeks minimum. Which means I have to come up with a new plan to get us out of here."

"Maybe not," he corrected with a smile.

She regarded him quizzically.

"You could continue to stay here."

She pressed a hand against her trembling lips and drew a deep, bolstering breath. "After what happened last night?"

He leaned close enough for her to inhale the brisk fragrance of sun and man. "What happened last night?"

She gave him a droll look. He gave her one back.

Ignoring the warmth of his body so close to hers, she reminded wryly, "You kissed me."

His mouth quirked in masculine satisfaction. "And you kissed me back."

Boy, had she ever. In fact, she had spent the night dreaming about it. She scowled in renewed embarrassment. "We can't do that."

He threw his arm around her shoulders and gave them a companionable hug. "Why not?"

Tingling everywhere he touched and everywhere he didn't, she averted her glance. "My life is complicated enough as it is."

He tucked a hand beneath her chin and guided her face back to his. "News flash, Bridgett. It's always going to be complicated." His deep voice sent another thrill soaring through her. "That doesn't mean you can't enjoy yourself."

"Is that what we were doing?" Her throat was thick with emotion. "Simply enjoying ourselves?" Because to her it felt as if they had been on the brink of much, much more.

He brushed his thumb across her cheek, then dropped his hand at the sound of a car coming up the drive. He went to window, looked out. Swore.

Her pulse jumped again. "Who is it?"

"My folks." He grimaced.

"Want me to make myself scarce?"

He caught her wrist before she could escape. "Nope. There's a chance—a remote one—your being here will help them censor their remarks."

"If I didn't know better, I'd think you were scared of them, Cullen Reid McCabe."

He shoved his hands through his hair. "In awe, maybe. And you'd be damned right." He swung open the front door before they had a chance to ring the bell and wake the little ones. "Hey. Frank. Rachel. You-all know Bridgett?"

As always, the handsome couple radiated warmth and good cheer. The petite blonde Rachel smiled. In a cardigan set, skirt and heels, a strand of pearls around her neck, she looked as if she had come straight from her work as a tax attorney. Frank's jeans, shirt and vest indicated he had left his work on the ranch. "Actually, we know her entire family," Rachel said. A long, awkward pause followed.

Cullen nodded at the picnic hamper in his dad's hand and the long wicker basket stuffed with baby things in his stepmother's. "What do you have there?"

"We heard about what happened," Rachel said gently, "and we brought by some dinner and a few baby items to help out in the interim."

It was a nice gesture. Or would have been, Bridgett thought, if Cullen obviously didn't resent the interference.

Frank frowned as Cullen ushered them inside. "We were disappointed you didn't call us to tell us about the situation yourself."

With a sober nod, he relieved his father of the basket of food and carried it back to the kitchen. "How'd you hear?"

His dad glanced into the family room where baby

and puppy were sleeping. "I think the question is who *didn't* call to let us know about the note left with the baby."

Ouch, Bridgett thought as she took the Moses basket from Rachel with a grateful smile.

"Can we see the baby?" Rachel asked eagerly.

Cullen tensed. "If you promise not to wake either of them."

Who was sounding like a daddy now? Bridgett wondered.

Everyone tiptoed toward the baby carrier.

Robby was sound asleep. He'd worked one arm out of the swaddling—it rested on the center of his chest. A blue knit cap covered most of his dark curly hair. His cheeks were slightly pink, his bow-shaped lips pursed. He was the epitome of sweetness and innocence.

On the floor opposite the Pack 'n Play, Riot was curled up in his crate, eyes closed, chin resting on a stuffed toy. He, too, was slumbering away.

"Adorable," Rachel whispered approvingly.

For Frank, the emotions seemed more complex.

They trooped back out of the family room. Cullen grabbed four bottles of sparkling water from the fridge and ushered everyone out onto the screened-in back porch, leaving the door to the kitchen open so they could hear.

Everyone sat.

He waited.

"I'm just going to be blunt," Frank said, looking at his eldest son. "Rachel and I both understand why you might have felt awkward about coming to us with this.

It had to have been a shock, finding out about Robby the way you did. But surely you'd know that I would understand, better than anyone, what it's like to get news like this after the fact."

Cullen held up a staying hand. "Before you continue, you both should know, he's not mine."

Frank and Rachel exchanged concerned looks.

Finally, his stepmom cleared her throat and said kindly, "What we're trying to tell you, Cullen, is that it would be okay, if he was. A McCabe is a McCabe. Part of our family, no matter how they come into it. Whether it's by marriage."

"Or illegitimacy?" Cullen challenged.

Frank leveled Cullen with a disappointed look.

Silence fell once again, more awkward and fraught with emotion than ever.

Finally, Cullen bit out, "Have you talked to Dan?"

Frank nodded. "He said attempts are being made to find the mother, but without her DNA, the child's true parentage may never be known. And that would be a shame, son. For everyone."

His words hung in the air, simultaneously an indictment and a plea to come clean.

Uncomfortable, Bridgett rose. "I really don't think I should be here for this."

Cullen put a hand on her shoulder. "This concerns you, too."

Not wanting to contribute to what increasingly felt like an emotional melee, Bridgett eased back into the chair.

Cullen turned back to Frank and Rachel. "I am not

dissembling when I tell you and everyone else the child could not possibly be mine. Obviously, I've been tapped to be the responsible party. Why, I have no clue. *Yet*. But I will figure this out. And when I do—" he turned back to his parents and finished heavily "—you-all will be the first to know."

"Are you okay?" Bridgett asked, short minutes later, after his father and stepmother had left.

His broad shoulders flexed against the soft chambray of his shirt. Exasperation colored his low tone, resentment his eyes. "What do you think?"

Knowing that he needed her support, whether he realized it or not, she ignored his curt reply. "You really don't have any idea who did this, do you?"

An awkward silence fell. "You're *just now* figuring this out?"

Hating the fact he thought she had betrayed him in some way, she gave in to impulse and caught his arm before he could turn away. "I can see why the accusation—never mind an anonymous one—would be upsetting, Cullen." The hard curve of his biceps warmed beneath her fingertips. "But I can also see it goes much deeper than that."

He didn't take his eyes off her. "Let me guess," he muttered. "You want to talk about my illegitimacy, too."

She blinked, taken aback. Dropped her grasp and moved away. "Were you born illegitimately?"

"You don't know?"

"How would I?" When he'd been a junior in high

school, she'd been in sixth grade. Way too young to hear that kind of talk.

His dark brow furrowed. "I thought everyone in the county knew."

"Obviously they don't," she returned, equally blunt, "or I would have heard about it."

A skeptical silence fell.

She folded her arms in front of her. "All I do know is that you're Frank's son, conceived several years before he married Rachel, and you came to live with him after your mother died when you were a teenager. That you were here for almost two years, went off to college, lived elsewhere for most of the last decade and then came back."

His eyes held hers for a long, discomfiting moment.

Ignoring the fluttering in her middle, she trod even closer. "I had no idea your mother and father were not married when you were born, but really, Cullen, in this day and age, is that such a big deal?" After all, she was attempting to adopt as a single parent! There were plenty of families where the parents were divorced, too.

Jaw set, he spun away and strode toward the front of the house where his office was. "It is a huge deal, even in this day and age to have 'unknown father' on your birth certificate."

Okay, she thought, reeling at the implications. Maybe that was a little different. She watched him check the security screens, find nothing amiss. "Are you saying your mom didn't *know* who sired you?"

Cullen dropped down into his desk chair, deep frown lines bracketing his mouth. "No. She knew. She just didn't want anyone else to know that she had a child by one of the Texas McCabes."

Bridgett leaned against the front of his desk, facing him, and took a moment to absorb that. Her denim-clad thigh almost touching his, she peered at him closely. "So, what *did* she tell you then?"

He rocked back in his chair, long legs stretched out in front of him, looking sexy as all get-out. "Nothing— except that it wasn't important who my biological father was. She was parent enough."

"And that was a problem because...?"

"She refused to accept the shame in the continued public perception that she 'had no idea' who her baby daddy was, and instead, cast herself as the lead in some romantic, ongoing stage play of life." He shook his head in obvious regret. "Raising me on her own was all part of the drama and the angst."

"She made you feel like a burden?"

"It wasn't her intention. But it was definitely the outcome." His expression didn't change in the slightest, yet there was something in his eyes. Some small glimmer of sorrow. "My mother worked as a ranch-house chef. She never had a problem getting jobs, because she was very talented. But she never stayed in one more than a year or so, because by then her romance of the moment would have fizzled out, and she would need a fresh start and move on."

Bridgett began to see how this had all played out for Cullen. "Taking you with her."

He gave a terse nod. "To another small, rural town, often in yet another state, where I would again have to register for school." His lips thinned in frustrated re-membrance. "And to do that, I would have to provide my formal birth certificate. The administrators would see I had 'no known father.' My mother would tackle the subject head-on. Treat it as a joke and wear it as a badge of honor."

Gently, Bridgett said, "That must have been difficult for you to deal with at such a young age."

Cullen accepted her empathy with a downward slant of his mouth and a harsh exhalation of breath. "Pity was the most common reaction." He shook his head sadly, recalling, "I just felt embarrassed and degraded. To the point I begged my mother to tell me the truth."

The pain in his eyes matched his voice.

"I wanted her to get the name on the birth certificate and be done with it. I even promised her I would never contact my father." He walked to the windows over-looking the front of the house, then paced to another window, another view. "I just didn't want to go through the rest of my life wondering who I was, where I came from. But—" he spun around and flung out a hand "—she wouldn't budge."

Bridgett's heart broke for him. Yet she had to ask, as she edged closer yet again. "Is it possible she really didn't know?"

Cullen shook his head, certain. "No. She was very much a one-man woman for as long as she was with someone. That was part of her own moral code. And, besides, I knew her. I could see that she knew my fa-ther's identity. She just wasn't going to tell me."

Bridgett stood opposite him, her shoulder braced

against the window. She hadn't expected him to reveal this much about himself. Now that he had, it had opened up the floodgates of emotion within her, too. "Then how did you end up with Frank?" she asked curiously.

"My mom died in a car accident when I was fifteen. I was put in foster care for about a year, which was a horrendous experience, mostly because I was so angry about the fact that now I was never going to know who my dad really was or have the chance to meet him."

He exhaled. "Luckily, I had a social worker who understood how torn up I was about that, so she got a detective on the local police force to help. He used my birth records and my mother's work history to figure out where she had been employed when I was conceived." He grimaced. "From there, he found out she'd had a romantic relationship with Frank McCabe that lasted almost a year."

She studied the sober lines of his handsome face. Thought about the hell he'd been put through, not just after he'd been orphaned, but throughout his entire childhood.

"Frank apparently wanted to get married. Mom didn't, so they broke up, and she took off for parts unknown."

She listened empathetically, unsure how to help. Cullen's eyes took on a stormy hue. "A couple years after that, Frank married Rachel and no one ever gave my mom another thought. Until the social worker told Frank her suspicions."

"How did you verify it?"

"I had some belongings of my mom's. A hairbrush

still had some of her hair in it. So they used that and Frank's DNA to determine I was their child." His manner guarded, he continued, "Frank immediately brought me to Texas. Rachel welcomed me as part of the family. And so did my five half siblings."

She shot him a commiserating look, guessing, "No one in Laramie made you feel demeaned…?"

"Of course not." He straightened and moved away from the window. "I was part of the legendary Texas McCabes. But they wouldn't have, even if I hadn't been from a well-known Texas family," he said gruffly. "Laramie isn't that kind of place."

"No. It's not." It was why she loved it so.

"Here, it's all about neighbor helping neighbor," he continued. "Everyone feeling like family, even if there isn't an actual biological connection."

"That's why I'll never leave here. Because it was that kind of community support after my own parents died when I was in middle school that helped me move on." He nodded and she touched his arm gently, feeling the kinship between them grow. "Is that why you came back to Laramie County? Because you wanted to live in a warm and welcoming place again?"

Was he perhaps more sentimental and idealistic than he wanted to admit? Was it possible they could connect on that level, too? Because if so…

Unfortunately, he hesitated just a second too long for comfort. Finally, he said, "My family all wanted me here."

Bridgett's heart sank as she read the reluctance in his expression. "But *you* didn't really *want* to come back home, did you?"

* * *

Cullen wasn't sure how to answer that. Not in a way a woman like Bridgett would understand, anyway. Finally, he said, "I hoped being with my dad and his family—as an adult, this time—would give me the kind of peace I've never had. Instead, it just feels like I'm waiting for the other shoe to drop. Something to happen. Some evidence that I am just as much my heartless, irresponsible, overly sentimental mom as I am my strong, hardworking, responsible father."

Bridgett let out a slow breath, the warm understanding in her eyes a balm to his soul. "And now it's happened. With this baby and this puppy."

Keeping his gaze meshed with hers, he confided ruefully, "On the surface, at least to other people, including Frank and Rachel and the rest of the McCabes, it would certainly seem so." He leaned in closer. "Which is why I have to find out who Robby's real parents are. Otherwise…"

Bridgett stared at him unhappily. "I'll convince DCFS that I'm the right mom for Robby and Riot, and foster-adopt them and they'll both be loved and cared for and have an amazingly happy life?"

He regretted the angry flush in her cheeks. "I know it hurts you to hear this." He captured her wrist before she could turn away. "But it's true. Robby will never be as happy as he could be unless the mystery is solved and he knows who he is, what his past is and why his mother or father—or whoever it was—left him and Riot at the fire station to be given into my care." He gave a ragged sigh. "And you won't be happy, either, if you and Robby and Riot have to live the way I have all my life, just waiting for the truth to finally come along and blow your life to smithereens."

Her silky skin warmed beneath his touch. She pulled away and threw up her hands in frustration. "But if that happens, Cullen, and you do find out who surrendered him so heartlessly and irresponsibly, I could end up losing Robby and Riot forever."

"Or end up keeping them forever," he pointed out sagely, looking deep into her eyes. "Either way, Bridgett, for all our sakes, we have to do whatever it takes to discover the truth."

Chapter 5

"The Monroe family wants to do something for you-all. We're just not sure what's appropriate," Bridgett's older sister, Erin, said later that evening.

Bridgett pushed the speaker button on her cell phone. With Cullen out on the ranch, prepping the Western Cross barns for the upcoming video tour in advance of the virtual cattle auction, and Robby and Riot both snoozing peacefully in the next room, she was free to talk to the closest thing she had to a mom these days.

"I know. And I appreciate it." If she'd come by a baby the traditional way, there would have been showers and parties galore to celebrate.

"I'm mailing some of my boys' old newborn clothing, and a few toys. Plus a few new things. Sleepers, T-shirts, booties, knit caps."

Tears blurred Bridgett's eyes. "Thank you," she managed. "It will really help."

Gently, Erin continued, "Mac and I were surprised not to see anything about the foundling on the news."

Bridgett saw Cullen's pickup truck coming down the lane toward the ranch house. She turned away from the window, relaying what she had initially been stunned to learn, too. "The authorities don't publicly announce any infants turned over via the Texas Safe Haven law. The assurance of privacy—for both baby and parent— is what keeps the program going." And little ones who might not otherwise be well cared for, safe.

"So, when will they know if the child has any other family willing to claim him?"

Bridgett's heart twisted in her chest at the thought of losing the little boy she was quickly coming to think of as her very own. "I'm not sure." She explained everything currently being done, the lack of results thus far.

Erin paused. "How long do you get to foster Robby?"

Bridgett tensed at the worry in her sibling's voice. "Another twelve days, until the DCFS makes its recommendation to the court."

"Well, if you need any character references…"

"I'm hoping my care will speak volumes. And make me the exception to the rule." Bridgett looked up to see Cullen standing in the portal. They hadn't parted well after their last discussion. She had to get her thoughts in order.

Struggling not to notice how good he looked with the blue chambray of his shirt bringing out the deep navy of his eyes, she fastened her gaze on the strong column of his throat and the tufts of curly espresso-colored hair visible in the open collar of his shirt.

When she felt composed enough, she returned her glance to his. His eyes lit up in the way they always did when he wanted her full attention and knew he had it.

Aware they had to find a way to make peace, even when they didn't agree on something, she flashed him a brisk, businesslike smile and said, "Listen, Erin, I have to go…"

Cullen hadn't known what kind of reception he would get upon returning to the ranch house. Bridgett hadn't exactly been happy with him when he'd left. But there was no helping it. He'd had to be honest with her about his intention of doing everything possible to discover Robby and Riot's real family. Even as Bridgett worked to keep them with her.

Fortunately, that was a bridge they didn't need to cross quite yet. It was enough right now to take things as they had been, an hour or two or three at a time.

He went to the sink to wash up. "Sara Anderson called. She's going to be over tomorrow to certify the health of the herd for the virtual auction. She suggested she do the puppy physical at the same time."

Finished, he grabbed a towel and turned back to her, noting how pretty Bridgett looked in a buttercup-yellow Western shirt and jeans. "I wasn't sure if you'd want to be there…"

Bridgett lit up at the mention of the puppy they had both quickly come to adore. "I do."

"It'll be later in the day. Not sure exactly what time."

Kneeling down to the cushion where Riot dozed, he smiled at the pup's sleepy-eyed glance and affectionately patted his head. Then he moved to the Moses basket on the sofa table where the swaddled newborn slept, while Bridgett went about measuring powdered formula into the bottles she had lined up on the countertop.

"How was Riot this evening?" he asked casually, savoring the sweet intimacy of the situation.

She slanted him a contented smile. "I don't know what the two of you did when you were out on the ranch today, but he's pooped." She moved down the line, adding filtered water as she went. "He slept the entire time you were gone."

"Good." Cullen nodded, and inched closer to the slumbering child. Touching Robby's cheek with the back of his hand, he felt the fragile warmth of his skin.

He watched as Bridgett finished and put the baby bottles into the fridge.

He remembered kissing her, right here, right about this time, the evening before. Knew he had to do something—*anything*—to distract himself. Not sure why this felt so much like a date that wasn't going particularly well, he said, "I'm guessing you already had dinner?"

She wiped down the counters where she had been working, dropped the disposable cleaning cloth into the trash. "Around seven."

She was definitely the model of efficiency. Another thing they had in common. "How was it?"

She swung back to face him, her soft lips twisted into an aloof smile. "You're in for a treat. Rachel's chicken tortilla casserole was fantastic."

Could this get any more awkward?

"Rachel's a great cook." He took the containers his stepmother had brought over earlier out of the fridge. "She's always bringing food by for me and dropping it off." He spooned a generous amount onto his plate. "That's where last night's meatloaf dinner came from, too."

Bridgett moved to the other side of the island. Her slender hands folded in front of her, she perched on the edge of a stool. Drew a breath that raised and lowered the shapely lines of her breasts. "Sounds nice."

"Yeah. It is." He covered his plate with waxed paper and put it into the microwave to heat. "She says she's forgotten how to cook for fewer than a dozen people and has to do something with all the excess."

Bridgett twisted the length of her hair and put it back up into a clip. "Not buying it?"

Aware he liked her glossy dark brown hair up as much as down, he shrugged.

"I think she just likes an excuse to drop by and see her kids."

The corners of her luscious lips curved up. "You included."

Cullen nodded.

And if he stood here much longer, talking with her about the intimate details of his life while she looked so sexy and beautiful, he'd end up kissing her again. Still waiting on the microwave to finish, he opened the fridge and pulled out an icy-cold beer and the green salad.

In the Moses basket, Robbie began to fidget and fuss a little in his struggle to wake up. "I think I'll take him upstairs to feed him and get him ready for bed," she said.

He couldn't blame her for wanting an exit.

The situation between them was making him want family, too, and not just any family. And that couldn't be good for any of them, given how this was likely to end.

The evening before, Bridgett had been cool to Cullen. The next morning, Cullen was polite but distant to her. And though the new caution with each other was probably wise, she still didn't like the way it felt. As if they were erecting artificial barriers around their hearts.

It couldn't be good for Riot and Robby, either. They seemed to sense the underlying tension between the two adults caring for them and were a little more fussy than usual. Not surprisingly, the little ones' cantankerous moods ended when the four of them split up for the day. Riot went off with Cullen, accompanying him on ranch work, while Robbie stayed at the ranch house with her.

Bridgett worried about what it would be like when they met up again, but luckily, at the end of the day, they had Sara Anderson's cheerful professional presence and the puppy's exam to distract them.

"Word around town is that little Riot here is a dead ringer for a stray you took in as a kid. Which is funny because I never knew you had a puppy *also called Riot* in the past," Sara Anderson said, lifting the new Riot onto the scale to weigh him.

Neither had Bridgett.

And even more curious…why hadn't Cullen mentioned this to her? He'd said he had one dog as a kid.

He hadn't said that dog had been named Riot. And that was a pretty big deal, having a stray show up that was named after the dog he'd had in his youth.

Although he certainly did not owe her an explanation, deep down she felt a little betrayed he hadn't confided in her.

Cullen looked equally unhappy about the fact this part of the story was also now public knowledge. Frowning, he folded his arms and moved closer to the ongoing exam. "Who'd you hear that from?" he asked Sara.

The veterinarian listened to Riot's heart and lungs with a stethoscope. "I think it might have been my receptionist, who heard it from your little sister."

Cullen groaned. As well he might, Bridgett thought. Lulu McCabe was a chatterbox and then some.

"I don't know how Lulu'd know of any physical resemblance between the two," Cullen muttered.

Bridgett tilted her head, perplexed.

He frowned. "I never showed the photos of my late dog to anyone here."

"But your entire family knew about the pet," Bridgett ascertained.

He nodded.

"What did Riot Senior look like?" Bridgett asked.

"He was a black, brown and white German shepherd, chocolate Lab, collie mix."

"So, in reality there isn't much physical similarity between the two Riots, aside from the color of their coats," Bridgett surmised, wondering what the connection was.

"Correct, since Riot Junior appears to be all beagle

and golden retriever," Sara remarked as she examined his eyes, ears and nose.

Cullen raised his brows. "How can you tell?"

Sara looked at the mutt's mouth and teeth. "The shape of his face and eyes, the long snout. The floppy ears. Silky coat and tail…"

Bridgett sighed dreamily. "He is cute."

"Definitely," Sara agreed, palpating the puppy's abdomen and lymph nodes.

"And very sweet," Bridgett continued. Hearing Robby fuss, she went to get him.

"Maybe the two of you should start a fan club," Cullen teased.

"Or a new breed," Sara Anderson suggested, grinning as Bridgett rejoined them. "One that will win Grand Champion at the dog shows every time."

United by the puppy, they all smiled.

"Why haven't you ever mentioned you like dogs?" Sara asked Cullen.

He watched her give the vaccinations. "It wasn't a big deal. I like all animals."

Except it was a big deal, given how quickly he had bonded with the mutt, Bridgett thought. As quickly as she had bonded with Robby.

"Well, all I can say is that this one seemed attached to your hip when you strode up here. How many days has it been now?" Sara prodded.

Shrugging, Cullen replied, "Three and a half days."

Three and a half days that were changing their lives, Bridgett thought.

Three and a half days to tell her how much she knew

about the Cullen behind the mask of gruff chivalry and how much she didn't.

"How old is the puppy?" Bridgett asked.

Sara made a few notes on the chart. "He still has all his baby teeth, so I'm guessing around twelve weeks. Do you want to microchip in case he gets lost again?"

"*Yes*," Bridgett and Cullen said, unexpectedly in unison.

Sara smiled at them. "Okay, that can be done in the office if you schedule an appointment. In the meantime, you're going to want to get some tags on him. Or a collar with his contact information."

"I've already ordered both," Cullen said, stunning Bridgett yet again. "They should be delivered in the next day or so. What?" He mugged at their astonished looks. "I'm efficient."

Sara smiled tenderly at the little mutt and scratched him behind the ears. "Well, I hope you get to keep him—if he doesn't already have a family, and I'm guessing not, or we would have seen posters up for him as well as calls to the shelters in the last week. The Fire Department faxed his photo around, too. In any case, I think you should get a dog for yourself, McCabe. Better yet—" Sara winked "—you can train one of my therapy dogs."

Culled squinted. "I thought those were only for military vets."

"Not all of our wounded warriors can train their own companion dogs. Some need their service animals trained for them. Which is where you would come in."

Cullen promised readily. "I'll see what I can do to help out with that, after the auction."

"Good. Bridgett, nice to see you again. We need to spend more time together. Catch up. Get to know each other all over again. High school was a loooong time ago."

Bridgett laughed. "No kidding."

Vet bag in hand, Sara headed for the door.

When they were alone again, Bridgett turned to Cullen. "Why didn't you tell me both dogs were named Riot?"

Cullen had figured she wouldn't be happy about the oversight. "I was hoping to figure out what the link was, first."

"And have you?"

He worked to contain his frustration. "No. But when I eventually do, I promise you'll be the first to know."

To his surprise, Bridgett looked appeased.

Infant in her arms, she walked with him out into the yard, standing nearby while the leashed Riot did what he had to do. She turned to him, her eyes full of questions. "I'd really like to see some photos of the original Riot."

The last time he'd reminisced over his deceased family pet, it had stirred up a grief that nagged at him for days. "I'm not really sure where they are," Cullen fibbed.

"If you come across any, then…"

He nodded, promising nothing. Together, they walked inside the ranch house. Turning her attention back to the baby in her arms, she said, "Hey, little fella, you have one damp diaper." She put him down on the changing pad atop the sofa, unsnapped his sleeper and opened up the soiled diaper.

Cullen winced at the ugly yellow stump emerging from the center of Robby's little tummy. "Is he okay?" he asked in alarm.

Bridgett cleaned the area gently. "This is the umbilical cord."

"Is it supposed to look like that?"

Her nursing background coming into play, Bridgett sent him a reassuring glance. "Yes. It takes ten days to three weeks for it to heal completely and fall off. And just so you're prepared—during that time it will go from yellow to brown to black."

He exhaled, still watching intently, still keeping his distance. "You know, this could be a problem. How little you know about babies and how little I know about dogs."

He settled Riot on his dog cushion and watched her put a fresh diaper on Robby. "What are you suggesting?"

"That we switch for a while."

Cullen would have thought she was joking, save for the serious look on her face as she finished dressing Robby and then put him in his Moses basket. "How about you give him a bottle and rock him for a while, and I'll take Riot for a walk."

"Why would we want to do that when this is all working so well?"

Her chin jerked up. "Because we're living on a ranch

miles from town, and you're my backup with Robby and I'm yours with Riot."

"Exactly. Backup." His gaze moved over her silky-soft lips before returning to focus on the tumult in her pretty green eyes. "The likelihood of either of us needing to do the other's job is almost nil."

"*Almost* being the operative word." She looked at him for a long, quelling moment then propped her hands on her hips. "Look, I didn't mention it, because I thought I would be long gone by now, but, because the three of us—" she made a sweeping motion with one hand "—are staying here at your very kind invitation, I'm *forced* to make a case to social services that this situation *really is* best for the baby. Plus, you said you wanted to be responsible."

He caught the hint of accusation in her low tone. Wishing he could kiss her again, without fear of driving her away, he retorted equably, "And I do."

"So?" she challenged with a tilt of her pretty head. "What's the big deal, then?"

He was competent on the ranch, in the kitchen and the bedroom, but this…spending time with her and the baby…threw him for a loop. She was still staring at him like he was the most perplexing person on Earth.

He exhaled and said matter-of-factly, "The big deal is I don't know anything about babies, never mind an infant that was just born a few days ago."

Bridgett adapted a defiant stance. "Actually, Robby is at least a week old now. So far as we can tell, anyway."

For a moment, they both fell silent again. Cullen tried not to be bummed about the fact that they might never know specifically where or when Robby had been born. He thought it had been tough growing up without a named dad. Not having knowledge of *either* parent would really leave a kid rudderless.

His protective instincts escalated. "He's still way too young to be left alone with a novice."

She wrinkled her nose. "You might have a point."

"I always have a point."

She laughed softly. "Okay." She tried again. "How about I heat the bottle and then we sit together on the porch swing. You can feed Robby while I talk you through it, and then we'll take everyone on a walk. You can push the convertible stroller, and I'll handle the leash, and you can instruct me on the proper way to do that." She flashed him a wry smile. "So I'm not being dragged along the way I have every time I've tried to take Riot somewhere by myself."

It was a reasonable request. One, in the end, he couldn't refuse.

Although Bridgett had taught a lot of new moms and dads how to handle a newborn baby, she hadn't ever instructed someone she was attracted to. However, she sort of liked the idea of Cullen turning to her, even if it was just for information.

Sitting close enough to him to be able to reach out and help, if needed, she inhaled the brisk masculine scent of his hair and skin as she watched Cullen gingerly hold Robby in both his big hands.

"Support his head and neck." She put her hands beneath Cullen's, to help guide him, trying not to notice how strong and masculine he felt. "Snuggle Robby in one arm and cradle him against your chest. Keep his head a little higher than his body. Yes, like that." Her pulse racing, she handed over the bottle of warmed formula. "Now, offer the bottle. When he feels the nipple against his lips he'll know what to do."

She flushed at the unintended double entendre. Shook her head. "Sorry. That was…"

Successfully following her instructions, Cullen said, "True?" Mischief glimmered in his eyes. So he was feeling the sexual awareness, too!

His flirtatious gibe sent a shiver of awareness spiraling through her. It was a good thing they were well chaperoned. Otherwise, who knew what might happen between them? She pretended an aloofness she couldn't begin to feel. "Ha, ha."

His sexy grin widened. "I aim to amuse and be helpful, too."

Which could be a problem, Bridgett thought, rolling her eyes. Since she already had been wondering what it might be like to kiss him just one more time. Luckily, they had tasks ahead of them that would prevent just that from happening.

"So, what next?" Cullen asked, as Robby drank hungrily.

Exactly what you think. We proceed, oh, so cautiously. And try not to kiss again—never mind be tempted to recklessly make love!

Tamping down her rising desire, Bridgett turned her full attention back to the baby, then continued in the soft, encouraging tone she used with all new parents.

"You're going to want to feed him an ounce. Two at most, then stop and burp him, so he doesn't get too much air in his tummy."

Cullen watched the baby feed with a surprising air of contentment. "We wouldn't want that," he cooed softly, smiling as Robby tapped his hand against the side of the bottle.

"No," Bridgett agreed, acutely aware of what a good daddy Cullen would make. Even if he didn't yet know it. "We wouldn't…"

For another minute or so, they sat in silence. Savoring the wonder of the moment, the peace that could be had when caring for new life. Was this what it would be like if they had been Robby's parents? All Bridgett knew for certain was that something about this whole situation was more magical and alluring than anything she had ever felt before.

Cullen seemed introspective, too.

Finally, he took the bottle away, checked and saw that about an ounce and a half of formula had been ingested. He handed her the bottle, then shifted Robby upright against his shoulder, in the same way she knew he had seen her do.

The sight of the big, strapping cowboy holding the fragile infant with so much awkward tenderness was almost her undoing. Again, she talked Cullen through the basics of burping. He patted Robby's back gently until a resounding belch filled the air.

Cullen chuckled, impressed by the man-size effort. "Do I feed him again?"

"Yes."

He shifted Robby with a little more confidence this time, nestled him in his strong arm and held him against his chest.

"Know what to do?"

"Feed. Burp. Repeat."

"You've got it, cowboy." Bridgett eased away from him, realizing she had been sitting way too close on the swing.

Her heart swelling with all she was feeling, she watched as a big silver pickup truck came up the lane. "Are you expecting someone?"

"No. You?"

Bridgett shook her head. The luxury vehicle came to a halt, and the local Cattleman's Association president stepped out. Bridgett half expected Cullen to shift the baby to her arms. Instead, he nodded at their guest. "Let him know we're back here," he said.

Bridgett stepped off the screened-in porch. "Hey, Sam!" she called to one of the biggest supporters of the hospital fund-raiser every year.

Kirkland waved and strode toward them. His glance cut to Cullen, who still didn't let go of the baby. He held his hat against his chest. "Hope this isn't a bad time."

Seeing Robby had taken another ounce of formula, Cullen shifted him to his shoulder to burp. "What's up?"

"I'm just checking to see if there's anything the association can do to support your upcoming virtual auction."

Cullen used the corner of the burp cloth to dab at the milk bubbles appearing on the corners of Robby's lips. "Vouch for the quality of my breeding program if anyone asks."

Sam cut a glance toward Bridgett. Cullen gave the other rancher a look indicating he should continue.

"Actually, we already have had a number of calls the past few days, with questions about your cattle operation," Sam said.

Cullen frowned. "Which doesn't usually happen."

Sam grimaced. "Not to someone of your reputation who is auctioning off purebred Hotlander cattle, no."

A tense silence fell. Cullen exhaled heavily, even as he kept right on feeding Robby. "It's about the baby and the puppy…"

Sam cleared his throat. "Well…you know. People talk. And character counts."

Cullen squinted at their guest. "And people wonder why I'm still denying what they feel is obvious?"

Sam Kirkland sidestepped that landmine. "Look, all I'm saying is that if you want to delay your sale until things settle down, no one would fault you for it."

"No." Cullen stood, gently handing Robby to Bridgett then squaring off with their guest. "I've got nothing to hide. Nothing to feel ashamed about. And I'll be damned if I'm going to act like I do."

Chapter 6

"You're sure you still want to go on a walk?" Bridgett asked short minutes later, after a drowsy and content Robby had been strapped into his convertible stroller.

Cullen snapped the leash onto Riot's collar. "That was our deal." He flexed his brawny shoulders, the motion as careless as his attitude. "You teach me. I teach you…"

"But after what just happened. With Sam Kirkland…"

He shrugged, as if the inquiries into his trustworthiness were of no consequence. "It's a nice afternoon for a walk and everyone is cooperating."

"Well, maybe it will help dissipate the steam coming out of your ears."

To her frustration, he didn't even crack a smile. He

was back to being the grim, testy rancher who had come
striding toward her in the hospital. He inhaled a long
breath that expanded the impressive musculature of his
chest and drew her attention to his washboard abs. "I
know you mean well, Bridgett, but you don't need to
be concerned about me."

"Really?" She toed off her flats, sat to slip on some
boot socks then stretched out one leg at a time to pull
on her favorite peacock-blue cowgirl boots. "Because
you sure look like you need some emotional support."

Something flickered in his expression at that. Annoy-
ance at having been thought to need anything or anyone,
probably. "Is that what this is?" he asked in surprise.

Bridgett was suddenly stunned to realize how much
she was beginning to care for him. "Isn't that what
you've been giving *me* the past few days?"

His glance lingered on the bare skin of her upper
calves between the boots and the hem of her denim skirt
before moving over her fitted shirt to her face. He escorted the puppy to the other side of the threshold, then
held the door for her. She gently pushed the stroller out.

Showered but unshaved, wearing a dark green canvas shirt and jeans, he was every inch the indomitable
Texan. He sent her a level look, showing her how to
situate Riot at her left side and hold the leash with two
hands across her body. "I hadn't really thought about it."

Their fingertips brushed as he released her.

"Well, I have." Determined to get through to him,
she ignored the new heat in her skin and said in a ca-
joling voice, "I think we could be friends, Cullen Mc-
Cabe. Good ones."

"Friends," Cullen repeated. He came closer, his expression that of a lion stalking his prey.

Her heart did a funny little twist inside her chest. Needing a little space to compose herself, she moved herself and Riot to the other side of the stroller. "You don't want to be friends?"

Pushing the stroller down the long paved road that wound through the ranch, he gave her another sidelong glance. His expression didn't change in the slightest. Yet there was something, a small glimmer of bemusement, in his blue eyes. "Platonic friends?"

She fought a blush. Duh. "What other kind is there?"

He gave her a seductive look. "Come on. Don't act like you're that surprised something more might be in our future. You felt that kiss as much as I did, the other night."

"So we have chemistry! It doesn't mean we have to act on it."

He slowed his pace to better accommodate hers. "Doesn't mean we can't, either." He gave her the sensual once over, his gaze returning to linger on her lips.

Wishing she didn't want to kiss him as much as she did, Bridgett huffed responsibly. "Am I going to be fending you off?"

Chuckling mischievously, he shot right back at her. "Am I going to be fending *you* off?"

She couldn't help it, his tone was so playful, she laughed. "How did we even get on this subject?" she drawled, her voice every bit as exasperated as his had been.

The warm spring breeze wafted through their hair

and blew across their bodies. He put a hand around her waist and tugged her against him. Then he leaned over and whispered in her ear. "You were feeling me out on our…situation."

The unyielding imprint of his strong, hard body had her nipples tingling and pressing against her shirt. "Really?" she groaned, but she didn't move away. "You had to use that term?"

He met her gaze, his eyes dark and heated. "Can't help it," he teased in a way that made all rational thinking cease. Releasing a soft exhalation of breath, he cupped her face and rubbed his thumb across her cheek before dropping to explore the shape of her lower lip. "I like seeing you all spunky and indignant." Reluctantly, he let her go as the four of them continued on their stroll. "It brings a real sparkle to your eyes."

She had the strong impression he had been about to kiss her again and still might. "For someone who is unsentimental, you can certainly be a handful." She lifted a warning finger. "And don't even think about going down that verbal path…"

He grinned. "Whatever the lady wants…" He made a motion as if he was zipping his lips, locking them tight and throwing away the key.

They walked some more in silence, enjoying the day, each other. With conversation momentarily halted, Riot pulled ahead. Grateful for the much-needed diversion, Bridgett concentrated on her task. As did Cullen.

"Try varying your pace a little." He reached over to show her exactly how much pressure to exert on the leash. "You want Riot to be following you, not the other way around." He watched with masculine satisfaction as she did it on her own. A mixture of pleasure and unmet need rolled through her.

"That's it. Yeah. Nice."

She could imagine him giving her the same low, deep-throated encouragement in bed.

Cautioning herself not to wear her heart on her sleeve, she slanted him a look and broke the tension with a joke. "Are you talking to me or the dog?"

He waggled his brows. "Both."

Bridgett had never imagined he could be so playful. He was always so serious and businesslike. At least, around her. She wondered what else about him she had yet to see. "So, how come you're not married?" She blurted the first question that came to mind.

He slanted her a reluctant look. She wasn't surprised he didn't want to answer. Still, she pushed on. "You already know all about my romantic past." How she had given up her one shot at love and marriage and family. "What's your story, cowboy?"

"I'm single."

"Have you ever been married?"

He looked out at the pastures with a brooding expression. "Nope."

"Engaged?"

He bent to adjust the canopy around the still-sleeping Robby. "I was close a couple of years ago."

This hurt. Why, she couldn't say. "What happened?"

He continued grimly. "I brought her home for a weekend to meet my family."

The suspense was killing Bridgett. "And?"

His hands tightened on the handle. "She found out I was only half McCabe."

It was all Bridgett could do to keep walking. "So…?"

He finally turned to look at her. Their glances locked and they shared another moment of tingling awareness, an emotional connection Bridgett did not expect. "Theresa found that concerning. She thought that might affect my future inheritance."

Bridgett blinked. "She really said that?"

"She really did," Cullen reflected sadly. "Anyway, her interest in me cooled really quickly after that, but she was very interested in getting to know a couple of my brothers, so…when we got back to Oklahoma, I told her I didn't stand to inherit anything from Frank."

"Is that true?" It didn't sound like the McCabes she knew!

"No, but not too long after that she asked to start dating other people."

Because there were not going to be any large sums of money. *Nice.* Curious, Bridgett studied the rugged lines of his handsome profile. "*Did* she go after your brothers?"

Cullen smirked. If he was still heartbroken, Bridgett noted, he wasn't showing it. "Apparently she sent some pretty friendly private messages via social media. I'm not sure what my brothers said to her."

Hopefully they'd told her to take a hike!

"All I know is she has been incommunicado with my family and out of my life."

He appeared relieved. Bridgett couldn't blame him. "And there's been no one serious since then?"

"That *was* true," he said very quietly, gazing into her eyes.

Bridgett took a bolstering breath and forced herself to hold his gaze with the same calm, quiet deliberation he was holding hers. "Until?" she asked, her heart doing cartwheels in her chest.

His smile slowly widened.

She had the gut feeling he was about to kiss her again. And she knew, wise or not, she was going to kiss him back. Or would have, had Riot not chosen that particular instant to give out a short little bark at something in front of them.

Turning to check on her charge, Bridgett gasped at the unfolding calamity.

"You sure you're okay?" Cullen asked twenty minutes later, walking into the upstairs bathroom, first-aid kit in hand. "Riot really dragged you through the brush."

Bridgett placed her foot on the edge of the tub so she could better see the scrapes she was tending to. They covered her calves, knees and lower thighs. Being careful to keep the hem of her denim skirt modestly down, she addressed each jagged cut with a cotton ball dipped in a numbing cleanser/antiseptic. "Note, though, I did not let go of the leash!"

"No, you didn't." Cullen handed her the tube of antibiotic cream from the first-aid kit. "And your fierce grip on him kept Riot from landing his first wild game." He stepped back slightly to give her room to work. Arms folded across his chest, he lingered in the portal of the smallish, old-fashioned bathroom. "Though I'm not sure what he would have done had he caught that squirrel."

"Me, either." They both laughed.

Their eyes met, held. "Well, he's certainly tuckered out now," Bridgett said softly.

"He is."

She straightened, aware all over again how much taller he was. How smoking hot. It didn't matter what time of day or night, or how he was dressed, whenever she looked into his eyes, felt that fierce magnetic pull, she wanted him.

It was crazy.

It was real.

It was....destiny?

Oblivious to the lusty nature of her thoughts, he leaned closer. Reached up and plucked a leaf from her hair with the same smitten look she had seen other men give their wives in the maternity ward. Her hand went up automatically. "Do I have anything else in there?"

Another lift of his impossibly wide shoulders. He shook his head mutely, his gaze still locked on hers. Her pulse skittered. Awareness grew. "Cullen..."

"I know," he told her gently threading the fingers of both hands through her hair and lowering his head. He gazed at her as if she were the most desirable woman in the entire world. "I'm feeling it, too."

The next thing she knew, his lips were on hers. Her arms were around his neck. The kiss—if you could call it just a kiss!—was more incredible than the first had been. With a low moan of appreciation, she pushed all the way against him, drinking in the heat and masculine feel of his hard physique. Her knees went weak, her lips opened to the dizzying pressure of his. Their tongues tangled as surely as their hearts. The next thing she knew, he was dancing her backward to the room at the end of the hall that held his king-size bed.

All it would have taken was one hand pressed against the center of his chest. One hint of dissent. She could have put on the brakes.

She didn't.

The truth was, he was as much her fate as Robby and Riot. And she was his. This was all meant to be. And she was determined to enjoy every single moment of it.

"You smell so good." He buried his face in her hair.

Arousal swept through her, more potent than before.

She kissed his neck. "So do you. Like sunshine and spring…"

He chuckled softly then dropped a string of kisses down the nape of her neck, across her cheek, up her jaw, then hovered over her lips. Passion roared through her, fierce as a tornado, as he pressed her lower half to his. She surged against him, softness to hardness. He kissed her, even more amorously this time. She could feel the strong, steady thrumming of his heart, beating in rhythm with hers. Lower still, there was a tingling need.

She melted against him. And they kissed and kissed and kissed. Until there wasn't any place she would rather be. He was hot and powerful and male. And he wanted her as much as she wanted him.

Although he'd known the time would come, Cullen hadn't expected to make love to Bridgett just yet.

He had planned to get to know her, spend quality time with her. After solving the mystery of why the puppy and baby had been left to him.

But that was before she had looked at him with such tender devotion. She had been alone a long time, too. Yet he needed to know she was all in before they took this any further. He caught her face in his hands and searched her eyes. "You're sure?"

"Very."

His glance fell to the nipples protruding through her top. He unbuttoned her blouse, unfastened her bra. Found the curves, the tips, the valley in between her breasts until she shuddered in response.

"You're so damn beautiful," he rasped, kissing her again, desire exploding in liquid heat.

She unbuttoned his shirt and palmed the contours of his chest. Lower still, she unzipped his jeans. Her hand closed over him as he reached beneath her skirt and divested her of her panties. He shifted her against the bureau and slid a knee between her thighs. She moved her weight onto it, building the pleasure even as he determined to make their lovemaking last. His mouth slid over her neck, dragging against the skin, and he felt her erotic little shiver. She whimpered in frustration, her body straining all the more, before abruptly finding the release she'd clearly been wanting.

Her head fell to his shoulder. He held her until her shudders stopped then finished undressing her and moved her to the bed.

He found a condom, stripped down and joined her. She slid her hands down his sides, to his hips. He grinned as she arched up to kiss him again. "Now, where were we...?" he murmured roughly.

Impatience glimmered in her pretty eyes. She nipped his shoulder. "I want you in me."

All too ready to oblige, he eased his hands beneath her. Her muscles trembled, tensed, as he settled between her thighs, his hips nudging hers apart.

Her hands rubbed his shoulders, stroked against his chest. They kissed again, their bodies immersed in friction, in need, in sweet, all-encompassing heat. He couldn't get enough of her as he slowly, erotically slid home, and she rose up to meet him, answering each fierce, deliberate thrust and intoxicating kiss. Until there was no more holding back, for either of them. It was all hot, out-of-control kisses and reckless daring and want and need. Until finally satisfaction came. Roaring through them both. And they collapsed, spent and shaking, in the warm protective embrace of each other's arms.

Bridgett wasn't sure how long it took her to catch her breath after they finally rocketed into oblivion. She did know she'd never been made love to like that. Like she was the most precious woman on Earth.

She did know she'd loved it. Every steamy moment of it. And that left her feeling surprisingly unsettled.

She wasn't supposed to be having a romance here. She was supposed to be figuring out a way to prove she was the best—the only—mother for little Robby. She was supposed to be solving her housing situation fast so she could get out of here and regain her usual level-headedness, gosh darn it.

Ignoring her first instinct—which was to stay here, wrapped in his arms—she pushed against his chest and murmured, "Um… Cullen?"

Sleepy-eyed, content, he lay back against the pillows. Sensing she wanted her physical space, he reluctantly folded his arms behind his head. "Yes… Bridgett?" he echoed in a low teasing tone that had her wanting to make love to him again.

She reached for her panties and slipped into them, then her bra. To her embarrassment, he was still watching, enjoying the show. "I don't think we should do this again."

To her frustration, he did not look the least bit surprised. Or offended. He grinned at her good-naturedly. "Okay, we can make love in your bed next time."

"That is not what I meant!"

He sighed, sat up and reached for his boxer briefs. "Yeah. I know," he grumbled.

Ignoring the reckless warmth spiraling through her, Bridgett pushed aside the desire and held her ground. "I have a lot to get straightened out here. I can't afford to be sidetracked by a passionate interlude!"

He nodded. Tugged on his jeans. Zipped up his fly. Fastened his belt. Serious now, he asked, "What can I do to help?"

By the time they were fully dressed, Robby was awake, ready for his next feeding. Needing a little time to compose herself, she stayed upstairs to change his diaper, while Cullen went down to heat another bottle in the electric warmer his stepmother had brought over for them.

He got the puppy out of his crate and fed him, too. Then he glanced at her cell phone, which was blinking.

"Looks like you've got some messages. I'll finish burping Robby if you want to check on that."

Bridgett sent him a grateful glance. "Thanks." Maybe they could go back to being team players, after all.

She read her message. "Excuse me while I make a call. The bank is long closed. But the loan officer processing my mortgage application is a friend, so…maybe it's some good news."

Except, Bridgett swiftly found out, it wasn't.

"Everything okay?" Cullen asked when she finally hung up.

Turbulent emotions tautened her pretty features. "The bank wants to know if I intend to take a maternity leave to care for Robby."

He followed her into the kitchen and watched as she poured herself a lemonade. "And obviously you do."

"I'm on vacation for the next couple of weeks, so I'm still getting paid. But if I can overcome the obstacles and get approved to foster-adopt Robby I am entitled to family leave for six months." In a low voice, she added, "Unfortunately, that's unpaid, and I can only qualify for the loan if I am working at the time the mortgage is processed."

He summed up her dilemma, "So you'd have to close on the property before your vacation is up."

"Which I've just been told is impossible."

"Or go back to work until you do." His heart went out to her. "Sounds like you're between a rock and a hard place."

She sipped her lemonade. "Yep."

Wishing he could help her in some way, he studied the sober set of her soft lips. "What are you going to do?"

She straightened defiantly. "Talk to my Realtor again and see if there is some way I can convince the sellers to rent to me for the next six months, until I can get approved and close the deal."

More determined than ever, she went off.

A flurry of phone calls followed over the next few hours. And by the time she finally hung up, for what appeared the last time, it was clear from her dejected expression that she was in worse straits than before.

His eyes asked the question.

"The sellers won't budge," she informed him miserably. "They are living in a hotel in their new city, and they can't buy their new house unless they close on their old one, so if I can't get approved our deal is off. They're willing to return half of my earnest money, but that is the best they can do."

He took her hand. "I'm sorry."

"So am I. It was a great house. It would have been perfect for the three of us."

Not, Cullen thought, as perfect as the Western Cross ranch, for the four of them. But sensing she did not want to hear that just now, especially since there was still no guarantee someone else wouldn't show up to claim the baby, he said, instead, "You could always try for a private loan via promissory note."

Bridgett shook her head. "I don't want to lean on my siblings."

"I'm not talking about your siblings." He waited until she looked at him. "I'm talking about me."

Chapter 7

Bridgett stared at him, sure she couldn't have heard right.

"You want to loan me money."

Cullen reached up and stroked her cheek as tenderly as he'd made love to her. "You're good for it, darlin'. Or, if you prefer, I could buy the property outright, rent to you now, and you could purchase it from me later."

Aware her life had taken another surreal turn, she blinked, not sure whether she should be grateful or insulted. Mostly she was just stunned. "You're unbelievable, you know that?"

More to the point, how and when had she ever given him the impression that she was the type of woman who would depend on a man *monetarily*?

His gaze drifted over her face. "I don't see what is so

shocking." Moving away, he rummaged around in the fridge and brought out a container of pizza dough and a bag of shredded mozzarella cheese. "You need a place of your own to live, if you're to have the best chance of being chosen to foster-adopt Robby. And right now you don't have one, except for this ranch, which you don't seem to think is going to be an acceptable home—in the minds of those making the decision, anyway."

She moved to the other side of the island, to give him room to work. "It's not the ranch. It's the arrangement. What it might seem to imply."

He set the oven to preheat then rolled the dough out onto a baking sheet. "What goes on between you and me, Bridgett, is between you and me."

The walls around his heart were as impenetrable as ever, yet there was no mistaking the sexual undertone in his low voice. Disappointment lanced her heart. "You're saying there are strings attached?"

It was his turn to look surprised. Nixing the allegation with a shake of his head, he lightly touched her forearm. "No strings."

Thank heaven!

"I am saying I'd like to make love to you again." He paused to let his words sink in. "I'm not going to lie about that. And judging by the fireworks in the bedroom, I think you want the same thing."

She did. That was the hell of it. She worked to keep her tone nonchalant. "I also need to prove that I can stand on my own two feet. Take care of myself and a baby and a dog without relying on the kindness of family and friends to do so."

That hit a chord. He opened a jar of pizza sauce, and spread it over the dough. "My mom used to say the same."

Not surprised he was as adept in the kitchen as he was everywhere else, Bridgett set her elbow on the counter and rested her chin on her hand. "And?"

"It was never true. Everywhere we went, there were people who reached out to help." He sprinkled shredded mozzarella onto the pizza, then added sliced pepperoni and precooked sausage. "Other moms who watched me when I was sick, so she could still go to work. Cowboys who taught me to ride and rope and took me out on the ranch to work right alongside them when I was out of school."

Salivating, she watched him slide their dinner into the oven to bake. "Is that how you became interested in ranching?"

He grabbed two light beers and came to sit next to her. "I loved being outdoors. Working the land, caring for the cattle. Being my own man."

Their knees touched as he swung toward her. "As long as we're on the subject…" He flashed her a sexy grin. "How did you decide to become a nurse?"

"I've just always loved taking care of people. My twin sister, Bess, feels the same. Nursing was the one career that made sense."

He tapped the neck of her bottle with his. "You have a lot to offer a child, Bridgett. Riot, too. With Mitzy's help, the people in the department will see that."

"I hope so." She didn't know what she would do if she lost the opportunity to be Robby's mother.

* * *

They ate a quick dinner together. Bridgett shooed him off while she did the dishes, since he had cooked. And Cullen spent the rest of the evening answering questions to potential buyers about the Hotlander cattle he was putting up for auction, both by phone and on email. By the time he was finished it was midnight. Robby and Riot had long ago been put to bed for the night, and Bridgett was in the guest room, door shut. He passed by, saw from the arc of yellow light coming out from under the door the lamp was still on. He wanted to ask if everything was okay, but aware of all she had been through and was still dealing with, forced himself to respect her privacy.

The rest of the night passed uneventfully. He tossed and turned for a while, wishing he'd taken her back to his room for another bout of hot lovemaking, but knew he was treading on dangerous territory. Finally, he drifted off into a restless sleep. He came downstairs at 6:00 a.m. the following morning. Bridgett was already up and dressed.

"Need me to do anything before I head out?" he asked, hoping she'd say yes.

She gave him a sweetly contented look that made him want to make love to her all over again. "No. Everyone's been fed, changed and/or taken outside."

Noting the scrapes on her legs looked better, he nodded at the Mason jar in her hand. "What are you eating?"

She licked the back of the spoon. "Overnight oatmeal."

He moved closer, inhaling her lavender lotion scent. "What?"

She smiled at him as if sharing space like this was the most natural thing in the world. "You mix it with milk and other stuff and let it set overnight in the fridge." She waved an airy hand. "I made extra, if you want to try it. One has bananas, yogurt and pecans. Another one has fresh peach, almonds and coconut. And there's a blueberry, raspberry and blackberry one, too. Take your pick."

"Where'd you learn to do this?"

Her eyes lit up as she savored another bite. "Nursing school. We were encouraged to eat healthy to keep going." She shifted slightly, so he could get into the fridge. "The classes, studying and long shifts left little time to cook. So Bess and I figured out how to do as much as possible ahead so we could grab something from the fridge and go."

He chose the one with the bananas and took a place standing next to her.

The cereal was creamy, crunchy and sweet. "It's good." He took another bite. "Almost like a breakfast dessert."

From his infant seat, Robby looked around with interest. Bridgett picked up her phone and, adjusting the seat so the light coming in from the windows was just right, took a couple of quick photos. He couldn't blame her. The kid was adorable.

Not to be outdone, Riot—who had been lounging on his dog cushion—came closer, his tail wagging. Bridgett knelt down and took some photos of him, too.

Without warning, she turned the cell's camera lens toward Cullen and popped off a few more of him eating breakfast. "What are you doing?"

"Gathering photos for Robby's baby book." She gestured to the island counter, showing him the embossed white leather album with Baby's First Year written in gold leaf across the front.

It looked expensive. And it was still in the original protective wrapping.

He studied her loosely flowing hair and pink cheeks. "Where and when did you get this?"

Bridgett beamed. "At the baby boutique in town, when I first decided to foster-adopt. I knew getting a baby could happen suddenly, so I wanted to be ready."

That made sense, knowing how sentimental she was. Starting it now—when she was far from being awarded permanent custody—did not.

He put his empty dishes in the dishwasher. Turning back to her, he clamped his arms across his chest. "Why are you doing this?"

Her chin took on the stubborn tilt he was beginning to know so well. "So, no matter what happens to him, Robby will know that he was loved his very first days." She jerked in a quavering breath. "It won't just be the story of how he was found in a cardboard shipping box with only a little puppy to watch over him." Her voice caught. It was a moment before she could go on. "Though I'm hoping he never learns that part."

Cullen's heart clutched. "Me, too."

Next to the album was an open file folder. It held the

fostering paperwork along with the note that Robby had been found with. "You're planning to put that in, too?"

Bridgett stiffened in indignation. "This letter proves that his mother loved him and wanted the best for him." She studied him, scowling. "I can see you don't approve. You think that I shouldn't be doing this at all, at least, not now," she guessed in obvious disappointment.

"I think you're setting yourself up to be terribly hurt if this dream of raising Robby as your own child all goes south." Which it still could.

Bridgett glared at him resentfully. "Don't you think if Robby and Riot had any other family who wanted to keep them, that family would certainly have realized the two were missing by now and be looking for them?"

Cullen didn't know how to respond, except to say, "You would certainly hope so."

Fortunately, in the meantime, there were things he could do to protect them all.

"Hey," Cullen said, to his brother Dan, later the same afternoon. "I'm glad you could take the time to meet with me."

Dan stepped out of his patrol car. "I was headed in this direction, anyway. What's up?"

Cullen took the tack off his horse and led him into the stable. "I'm worried about Bridgett."

His brother lounged in the center aisle. "Taking care of a baby and a puppy—and putting up with you—too much for her?"

Cullen made sure his horse had fresh water and then shut the stall door. "Ha, ha."

Dan accompanied him to the tack room. "You are a handful. According to Mom, all of us kids are."

Except he wasn't one of Rachel's kids, Cullen thought, putting the saddle away.

He was a stepson.

Not that Rachel treated him any differently. In fact, she treated him like he was her biological son, too.

Aware this wasn't something he could discuss with his law-enforcement half brother, Cullen sobered. "Bridgett thinks it's destiny that she was the one who found Robby and Riot."

As far as he was concerned, whimsical thinking like that only brought trouble.

Dan shrugged and walked back out into the sunshine with him. "Maybe it was."

"She's got her heart set on adopting them both and being their mom. She's even making a baby book."

Dan leaned up against the pasture fence. "You're worried someone is going to come and claim him?"

"Or maybe won't now—only to show up later when her heart is really involved. Which is why we have to solve as much of the mystery as we can, as soon as we can."

"You've got some more ideas on how to go about this?"

Cullen nodded. "Do you remember me talking about the original Riot?"

His brother squinted. "You mean, aside from that one time, the first year you were with us?"

It had been an awful, awkward, emotional conversation, with him fighting back tears. Cullen bit down his embarrassment. "Yeah."

"No. You've never mentioned him since. Or anything the least bit personal to you."

"Exactly," Cullen said, knowing it to be true. "Yet someone—who left the baby and named their puppy after mine—knows about him. They must, because that's not a common dog name. And that's gotten me to thinking. I vaguely recall telling a few stories about my Riot to a group of people at some point during the last year."

Dan straightened. "Seriously?"

"It wasn't anything I'd planned. The subject of dogs came up and someone asked me point-blank if I'd ever had one. Before I knew it, I was talking about the virtues of having a dog, as a boy, on the various cattle ranches where my mom and I lived. How he made every new place immediately seem like home."

Dan rubbed his jaw. "Wow. I think that's the most I've ever heard you talk about anything but cattle ranching."

Cullen gave the other man a deadpan look. "I was hoping you might be able to help me figure out where or when this soliloquy of mine happened."

Dan shrugged. "I don't know. Sounds like a gathering that was at least semi-social."

"Yeah." *But where? And when?*

"You think figuring this out will lead you to who left the baby?"

"It's possible. One thing is for sure," Cullen admitted worriedly, "I'm not sure Bridgett will recover if she loses Robby and Riot."

Nor was it likely she'd want to spend a lot of time hanging out with him. Or at the Western Cross, given the painful memories that would likely generate. He'd be nothing but a reminder of all she'd lost.

Dan studied him. "What about you? How are you going to feel if someone comes forward to claim them?"

Bummed. He'd gotten used to having the baby and puppy around. Bridgett, too. Bridgett *especially*. Aware his brother was still waiting for his answer, Cullen adopted a poker face. "I'll be fine."

Dan studied him in disappointment. "Robby's really not your kid?"

Cullen wondered how many times he would have to repeat this. "Really not." But he was beginning to wish they were his family. Not one to dwell on things he could not change, however, he pushed on. "Anyway, that's the second reason I called you. I wanted to find out if there were any updates on the search."

"Actually—" Dan brightened "—there are."

Dan only wanted to go over it once, so they went up to the ranch house. Bridgett was in the kitchen, typing away madly on her laptop computer. Robby was sleeping in his Moses basket nearby. The smell of still-brewing coffee and home-baked cookies filled the room. Additional baked goods lined the counter. "More gifts of food?" he asked, stepping inside.

Bridgett smiled happily, still typing. "And baby and puppy things. It's tradition, when there's a newborn or new pet in the house."

He was beginning to see that.

A constant influx of unexpected visitors was not something he usually liked. On the other hand, their generosity made going into town—for some of the very things that had been dropped off—an avoidable chore. With the virtual auction coming up, he was glad not to have to spend the extra time commuting back and forth.

Not sure what he was interrupting, Cullen asked, "Is this an okay time to talk?"

Bridgett saw his brother, in uniform, come in after him. She closed her laptop and gestured for the two men to help themselves to a late-afternoon treat. "Sure. I was just filling out more bank paperwork."

With a nod of thanks, Cullen and Dan helped themselves to cookies. "I thought that was a closed avenue."

"The local bank is," she said, taking a peanut-butter cookie for herself. "I'm trying one of those online services that promise to provide a loan to *every kind* of borrower."

Or, at least, take your application fee and squash your hopes, Cullen thought.

Bridgett continued cheerfully, "They've promised an answer within forty-eight to seventy-two hours, provided I give them all the necessary documentation. The sellers agreed to give me one more try to obtain financing, so I'm going for it."

She walked across the room to the Moses basket, tenderly checked on Robby. Seeing he was starting to wake, she checked her watch then went to get a bottle of formula from the fridge.

"What's up?" She tossed the words over her shoulder, giving Cullen a fine view of her slender waist and delectable backside. She was beautiful in a nurse's uniform, but she also looked damn fine in jeans and a form-fitting red knit shirt that clung to her midriff and buttoned up the front.

Too fine for him not to want her.

Apparently oblivious to his amorous thoughts, Dan leaned against the counter, arms folded in front of him. He looked at them both seriously. "I wanted to update you both on the progress of the investigation thus far. We dusted the shipping box the baby was found in and came up with fourteen different sets of fingerprints. None of them matched anything in the integrated fingerprint identification system."

"What kind of box was it, anyway?" Cullen asked, aware he'd never actually seen it.

Bridgett gave the name of a popular internet shipping company.

Cullen watched her set the bottle in the electric warmer that Rachel had thoughtfully brought over the previous day. "Did it have an address label?" he asked.

"Yes," Dan confirmed.

Bridgett nodded. "But both the address and tracking numbers had been marked through with permanent black ink."

Cullen felt a stab of disappointment. He wanted to get this mystery cleared up, so they could all move forward, unencumbered, a permanent home for Robby and Riot and Bridgett decided upon.

"There's no way to uncover what was beneath?" Realizing the coffee had finally finished brewing, he gave his brother a mug then poured two more. His fingers grazed the silky softness of Bridgett's as he handed hers over. Fueling memories of their passionate lovemaking the day before and furthering his desire to bring them closer yet, in ways that went far beyond this situation they found themselves in.

Dan answered Cullen's question matter-of-factly. "We sent it to the crime lab for analysis. They said they would do their best but weren't encouraging."

"What about the clinics and hospitals?" Bridgett asked, stirring some cream into her coffee, her soft pink lips taking on an even more serious curve. "Anything there?"

"Nothing yet," Dan admitted candidly, "but we're still hopeful."

Bridgett nodded, sipping her coffee as she and Dan exchanged knowing looks. Cullen felt like the odd man out. She explained. "We know by the way the entire umbilical cord was left hanging that Robby was not born with any medical personnel present. Otherwise, that would have been handled much differently. So his mother could have similar post-birth problems that would have compelled her to seek medical help."

"So, why not put out the news about what happened and publically encourage her to come in for the proper medical care she needs?"

"Because that would likely have the opposite effect and could keep her in hiding," Bridgett said firmly.

Dan drained his mug. "The department agrees. The best thing to do is stay the course. Plus, we're starting to get a few tips."

"Like…?" Cullen prodded.

"An elderly resident on Spring Street noticed a car moving slowly down her street around three thirty in the morning, a few hours before Robby was found."

"Were you able to track down the car?"

"She didn't have her glasses on, so she didn't get a color, make or model. Or even part of a license plate number."

"That's disappointing," Bridgett interjected. "But did anyone else see anything?"

Dan nodded. "A few blocks over from there, a young mother, up nursing her baby, thought she heard excited teenage voices and maybe a dog barking outside around 4:00 a.m. Because it was April Fool's Day, she wondered if they were attempting to get an early start and prank someone before school started. By the time she had finished nursing and went to the window, though, there was no one there. No evidence of any prank she could see."

"And that's it?" Cullen asked.

"So far. But we've quietly put the word out in the neighborhoods surrounding the fire station as well as all the high schools in the area. So if there is more information to be had," Dan promised, "I'm sure we'll get it shortly."

As his brother left, Cullen's phone rang. He paused before moving to answer it, ready to let the machine take it. Then he asked Bridgett, "Need any help?"

Bridgett took Robby from the Moses basket and nestled the cooing baby close. "I've got this," she said softly. "You just take care of business. Your office phone has been ringing off the hook all day."

"Thanks." Cullen strode to the front of the house.

By the time he returned, forty-five minutes later, Bridgett was putting a sleeping Robby back down.

Regret welled within him. He had hoped to be able to hold the baby a little bit, before he went back to sleep. How crazy was that? If he didn't watch it, he would be as attached to Robby as Bridgett was. Her heart wouldn't be the only one that was broken if the birth mother or her family did suddenly show up to claim him.

Finished with the baby, she grabbed the leash off the hook by the back door and clipped it to Riot's collar. Wordlessly she led the puppy outdoors. Cullen followed as Riot sniffed and circled, looking for the perfect patch of grass.

"You are such a good puppy!" she praised as Riot relieved himself, all the while gazing up at her adoringly.

"Someone has been reading about dog training."

"Competition. I want to get as good as you are with him."

And he wanted to up his game where the baby was concerned. Even if they didn't get to keep Robby. Because this experience had made him realize he did want a family someday. Actually, his wish was a little more specific than that. He wanted *this* family. Foolish or not.

Being careful not to stray out of earshot of the house, Bridgett walked Riot to another patch of grass, pausing to send Cullen a concerned glance. "Is everything okay?"

"All the phone calls? Yeah. People have been pre-registering for the virtual cattle auction online. They have a lot of questions."

"I meant about what your brother Dan had to say."

"Oh." He exhaled. Funny how well she could read him after such a short period of time. "I'm just frustrated," he admitted, pursing his lips.

A mirthful sparkle appeared in her eyes.

He tilted his head. "Not that kind of frustrated," he muttered, edging closer. Although, if she kept looking at him with that same sweet innocence, he might soon be.

"Good to know," she said softly, her gaze remaining playful while her cheeks turned the same pink as when they made love.

His body reacted at the memory.

He longed to kiss her. But with them standing outside, the dog on the leash, he wouldn't be able to give the embrace the time and attention he wanted. And when he kissed her again, and he *would* kiss her, he wanted to be able to take his time about it. Give her the care she deserved.

Aware she was still waiting, he cleared his throat. "It's driving me crazy, trying to figure out how Riot Junior is connected to Riot Senior and me."

"I'm sure it will come to you eventually."

Would it? he wondered, his frustration returning. It hadn't so far.

"Maybe if you had some photos to look at, it might jog your memory." She snapped her fingers. "Oh, right. You don't know where they are. Do you?"

Chapter 8

Bridgett had grown up with two brothers, so she recognized masculine evasion when she saw it. And she had caught Cullen Reid McCabe red-handed.

He offered a sexy half smile, making her feel more beautiful and womanly than anyone ever had. "It's not that I don't know where they are, exactly. I do. They're in a storage locker in Laramie."

Bridgett forced herself to concentrate on the mystery they were trying to solve, not what she wished would happen between her and Cullen. Again. "EZ Time Storage Lockers?"

His glance roved her slowly. He seemed to be contemplating how to bring them closer than they already were. She thrilled at the notion.

"The one and only."

Reminding herself to keep her guard up, lest they further complicate an already ridiculously complex and emotional situation, she step back a pace. "That's where I put my stuff when I had to move out of my apartment."

He took her hand in his, letting her know with a look and a touch they had nothing to be wary about. They were adult enough to handle whatever happened next, with Robby and Riot. And most especially, the two of them.

Tightening his fingers around hers, he drew her closer still. His voice dropped to a sexy rasp. "Guess that makes us neighbors there, as well as temporary housemates."

"And friends?" she clarified, before she could stop herself.

He gave her a thoughtful once-over. His steady regard gentled. "At the very least."

She glanced up at the ruggedly handsome contours of his face, appreciating his strength and determination as well as his indomitable spirit. The way he made her feel as if she were no longer in a waiting-mode, but suddenly living every moment of her life to the fullest. Yet so much of him was still a mystery to her. She needed to know more, before she could allow herself to get any closer to him. She needed him to want to tell her. "So what's the problem in running over there—besides the fact it will take us about thirty minutes?"

He shrugged, disengaging their linked fingers, maddeningly reserved once again. "I can't just walk in and walk back out." He tucked his thumbs in the belt loops on either side of his fly. "I'm going to have to hunt through a bunch of old moving boxes to find them."

Her turn to shrug. "That's fine with me."

"It'll be a pain," he predicted.

They took Riot back inside. She went straight to the sink and washed her hands. "Won't it be worth it, though, if looking at old photos jogs your memory in some way?"

His grimace let her know that this was a trip down memory lane he did not want to take. "You have no idea how disorganized and dusty it is in there."

She propped her hands on her hips. With a tilt of her head, she surveyed him up and down. "Are you a secret packrat?" she teased, in an attempt to lessen his reluctance.

He stroked his chin with his thumb and index fingers. "Could be," he drawled, sizing her up right back. "You never know about us Texas cowboys."

"But you will go, right?"

He exhaled. "Right."

Aware she had almost finished her online mortgage application and had until midnight to send it in, Bridgett bypassed her computer and went to get her bag and phone. When those were ready to go, she started packing a diaper bag.

Still mulling over his reluctance, she remarked, "From the look of things here, I thought you were one of those super organized, everything in its place kind of guys."

Another shrug. "Kind of had to be."

"Because those were the rules, growing up?"

The distant look in his eyes faded. "No. My mom was laid-back in that respect." He smiled, remembering, "She always let me keep my room as messy and full of mementos as I wanted it to be. It was foster care that changed me. Taught me to leave as small a footprint as possible, if I wanted to stay under the radar. And I did."

She thought about how miserable that must have been for him. Working to keep the pity out of her voice, she said, "And when you moved to Laramie?"

His eyes shuttered. "It seemed like a good idea to keep that habit."

"Just in case...?"

His lips thinned. "Frank and Rachel decided I was more trouble than I was worth."

"Oh, Cullen," she said softly.

He moved away before she could comfort him. "But as you can see," he said over his shoulder, striding into his office to turn off his own computers, "everything worked out."

Had it?

It seemed like there was still a barrier between Cullen and the rest of his McCabe family, just as there was between him and her.

The walls guarding his heart were starting to come down, at least between the two of them. But they had a long way to go if they were ever going to be more than temporary housemates and one-time lovers.

"Well, I must say you have amazing organizational talents," Bridgett continued lightly in an attempt to get the conversation back on safer ground.

He moved away from his desk and spread his hands

wide. "I can't take all the credit for how good this place looks. My half sister, Lulu, helped me move in. She's very particular in how she likes things decorated and arranged. All I do to keep it looking this way is put everything back in its preassigned place."

"Do you have a housekeeper?" She hadn't seen one thus far.

He shook his head.

She studied him in surprise. "You keep this place this tidy all on your own?"

"Yes, I do."

Wow. "You are way too humble, cowboy."

One brow went up.

Laying a hand across her chest in true Texas-belle fashion, Bridgett drawled, "You are a woman's dream man."

He chuckled, as she'd meant him to. "Because I can cook and clean?"

She shook her head and let out a low laugh. "And so many other things."

"You'll have to show me just how dreamy I am, sometime." He leaned in to kiss her, sweetly, tenderly.

On impulse, she kissed him back. His kiss was every bit as magical as it had been before, and her body jolted from the sheer bliss of it. She heard herself make a sound of pure pleasure and opened her mouth to the pressure of his, aware she hadn't made out like this, like kissing was an end in and of itself, since she didn't know when.

Satisfaction emanated from him, too. With the flat of his hand against her spine, he pressed her closer, until her skin sizzled and her nipples budded against the hardness of his chest.

Her knees went weak.

And still he kissed her, until she was tingling all over and so dizzy she could barely stand, until desire unfurled like a ribbon inside her and her thighs were trembling.

And she knew, unless they stopped—now—they'd never make it to the storage locker.

Reluctantly, she pressed a hand to the center of his chest. He drew back, content, yet wanting more. And, as she looked up at him, she wondered how he could not be aware just how gorgeous a guy he was. With his chiseled features, thick, curly dark hair, navy blue eyes and tall muscled body, he was masculine perfection come to life. Physically, anyway. Emotionally they still had some barriers to take down, and connections to build. But they were working on it. For the moment, that was enough.

Bridgett and Cullen dropped off the baby with her sister-in-law, Violet, and made plans to join her and her brother Gavin later for dinner. That accomplished, they proceeded to EZ Time Storage Lockers.

"You weren't kidding. This is a bit of a mess," Bridgett remarked in surprise as they walked into the nine by twelve foot temperature-controlled room. The lights overhead came on automatically when the door was opened. Wanting privacy, Bridgett shut the door to the interior corridor behind them.

"Yeah, I've never gotten around to organizing things."

Because it was too painful?

Bridgett could understand that.

Cullen walked past a flowered sofa and wing chair. Past a dining table and four chairs. Twin and double beds, two bureaus, a nightstand and a coffee table.

It was, Bridgett thought, a sad summary of a life.

He approached the stack of thirty or so boxes. Exhaled roughly. "Plus, it wasn't a stellar packing job, by any means. I was lucky the social worker assigned to me after my mom died made sure everything we had, in the home we were living in, was put in storage for me until I came of age and could decide what I wanted to do with it."

"Have you been through it at all?"

He shook his head, his expression conveying how much he had been dreading it.

Squaring his broad shoulders, Cullen demonstrated he was up to the task. "No time like the present."

Twenty minutes later, they had opened up all of the cartons. A lot of them held linens and women's clothing. There were a few boyish toys that Robby might one day enjoy, as well as a very out-of-date video game system. "This might be worth something if it still works."

A corner of his mouth crooked up. "Maybe as a museum piece."

And, finally, they found a cloth-covered box of photos.

She handed it to him.

He made his way back to the sofa and sat down. Motioned for her to join him. She dragged the coffee table over so they could sit with their feet up. "You sure you don't want to do this alone?" She knew how an image, long unseen, could catch you like an arrow through the heart. "'Cause my storage unit is just one row over, and I could also use a few things."

He patted the place right next to him. "Sit. I know you're curious. This way I won't have to do it twice."

She plopped down next to him, then abruptly stopped, staring at the butchered pictures. "What happened to these?" she asked, aghast.

He sighed at the oddly cropped photos. "My mom did it. She was all about the Boyfriend of the Moment. When he eventually failed to become her Prince Charming, and they all did, she couldn't bear any reminders, so she cut them out of the photos."

Noting that, even as a kid, Cullen had been tall and good-looking, already growing into the ruggedly masculine man he would become, Bridgett quipped, "Apparently that was in the days *before* photoshopping became popular?"

He grinned, sharing in the black humor. "Actually, I think my mom rather enjoyed erasing them that way."

Bridgett could imagine it had all been very dramatic. And undoubtedly quite upsetting for Cullen, when he was a kid. She reached over and took his hand, offering wordless comfort. "How did you feel about it?"

The reserve back in his expression, he set a stack of butchered childhood photos aside. "I wish she'd had some pictures taken of just the two of us, so we could have kept those and tossed out the rest."

"It definitely would have been a lot simpler," Bridgett agreed gently.

And less melodramatic.

He exhaled, accepting the past for what it was. "But that wasn't the way she worked, so…" He sat back, propping his feet on the coffee table in front of them.

She got comfortable, putting her feet up, too. "Did you like the men she dated?" Because if he hadn't, that would have really been awful.

He stretched his arm along the back of the sofa and protectively curved a strong arm about her shoulders. He lowered his voice to a husky murmur that did nothing to lessen the impact of his warm, sexy touch.

"Most of them were really nice. Kind. All of them cowboys on the various ranches where she worked as a chef. They all took me under their wing, even the gruff ones." He looked down at her as, feeling a wave of compassion for him, she nestled in the curve of his body. "I think they felt sorry for me, not having a dad, having a mom who was more interested in her love life than her child."

That had to have stung.

He reached out and smoothed a strand of her hair. "So whenever we inevitably left the ranch where we'd been living, it was usually harder for me to say good-bye to everyone than it was for my mom."

No wonder he worked so hard to keep from forging ties that might hurt if they one day had to be broken. With a sigh, she snuggled in even closer. "I'm sorry."

He nodded, the muscles of his powerful chest straining against the soft blue chambray of his shirt.

"So where did Riot Senior come in?" she asked, as their eyes met, and everything around them began to fade.

He smiled affectionately, recalling. "I was six the night he showed up on our doorstep in the snow, on Christmas Eve, begging to be let in."

She could imagine the joy he'd felt. It was probably one of the highlights of his youth. She swallowed around the growing knot of emotion in her throat. "Did your mom put him there?" she asked, knowing she wasn't the only one who needed kissing and holding and loving.

"She said it was Santa. I think it was Buck, her boy-friend at the time. He was always saying every boy should have a dog."

She met his wry smile. "But your mom let you keep him."

"I don't think she had a lot of choice." He removed his arm from her shoulders and thumbed through the few photos of him and his dog, a big, long-haired black, brown and white mutt. "I was completely in love with the little fella. Buck taught me how to care for him and train him."

"He sounds like a great guy."

Cullen nodded fondly, "He would have made a great dad for me. But Mom got tired of him. Said he wasn't romantic enough and moved us on. Again. But this time, I got to take Riot Senior with me, so it wasn't so bad."

"Did you ever stay in touch with Buck?"

His gaze narrowed and Bridgett felt her heart break for him all over again. "No. Buck and Mom both thought it would be better if we all made a clean break, so we did."

Bridgett ached to ease his pain.

"You don't think that Buck could be responsible for the new puppy in some way?"

"Actually, the thought crossed my mind. So I did some checking on my own and found out he died of a heart attack five years ago at the same ranch where he had always worked."

Bridgett shared his sadness. For a moment, they fell silent. Finally, she asked, "And there's no one else? No other ex-boyfriend of your mom's who would have given you a puppy and a baby?"

"No. No one."

She reached over and covered his hand with her own, both their hands resting on his muscular thigh. "It's too bad you didn't know about Frank sooner," Bridgett observed eventually. She turned to look him in the eye. "It seems like that would have made your childhood so much better."

"But I didn't," he confided quietly. "And we can't go back, Bridgett, and redo the past, much as we might want to. We can only go forward."

And, given the intent way he was suddenly looking at her, she realized on a quick inhalation of breath, going forward meant one thing.

She had hoped to wait until her situation was more settled before they did this again.

However, the way he had opened up his heart to her, the way he looked at her now, so full of yearning, changed all that. He was inviting her in, and the truth was, she wanted in. Already all of her senses were in overdrive and he hadn't even kissed her yet.

He leaned in and her lips parted. He pressed a light kiss to one corner of her mouth, and then another to the other side. Trembling with pleasure, she wreathed her arms about his neck. Their breaths mingled. And then his mouth was moving over hers, creating frissions of delight. His hands were beneath her blouse, cupping the weight of her breasts, teasing the taut nipples with his thumbs. And still they kissed, tongues and lips tangling, the caresses hot and hard, slow and soft, again and again and again, until making out felt like the most intimate thing they could ever do.

Heavens, the man knew how to kiss! How to make her want him. Not just like this, but in every other way, too...

"Not here," he whispered finally, lifting his head.

She was too far gone to stop. Too far gone to *want* to stop. "Yes, here," she insisted, just as fiercely, shifting so they were both prone on the sofa.

Giving in to the passion flooding them both, he tugged off her jeans and panties. She divested him of his. And then his hands and mouth began a downward journey. She fisted her hands in his hair, afraid he would stop. He didn't. Not until she was shuddering with sensation and crying out his name. And then he was moving again, swiftly now, finding the condom, rolling it on.

Feelings sweeping through her, she wrapped her arms and legs around him, urging him home. And when he entered her, thrusting into her, long and slow, taking her to a whole new level of need, he made her feel so utterly…taken. And that was what she wanted, too. So much.

She was his. He was hers.

And still they kissed as he brought them closer and closer, making her moan and cry out, until she lost track of where he ended and she began. All she knew was that everything around her was lost in the hot, intensely erotic pull of the two of them, the inevitable ascent to ecstasy and the slower, softer, oh so satisfying fall back.

As the aftershocks faded, Cullen went still, waiting to see what Bridgett would do. She didn't pull away from him, the way she had the first time they'd made love. She didn't snuggle closer, either. He wasn't surprised about that. She was an elusive woman.

Still holding her in his arms, he pressed a kiss to her temple. "So," he prodded finally, knowing their situation was complicated. But complicated was okay when it led to results like this. He just had to convince her of that. He shifted so he could see her face. "Was that a pity move, on your part?"

She lifted her head so he could gaze into her pretty green eyes. "You mean did I make love to you because I felt sorry for you?" Her voice was filled with surprise.

Not sure it mattered to him if she had—since it had brought them closer—he sifted his hand reassuringly through the silky mane of her hair. "Did you?" he asked curiously.

She shifted against him, and he felt himself grow hard again. Rolling onto her side, she spread her hands across his chest. "I definitely felt for you and what you'd been through."

He knew that. He had noticed her compassion.

"I also felt closer to you, because you trust me enough to confide in me that way."

He grinned. "So, is this the part where you tell me that now I've seen your pictures, you will show me yours?"

She regarded him with wide-eyed interest, both surprised and pleased. "You want to see my family albums? What ones I have, anyway?"

"Only fair." He wanted to know what she had been like as a child, before he moved to Laramie, Texas. That was unusual, too. Generally, he liked to stay in the here and now. Not think about the past. Or the future. But with her, he wanted to know everything.

Smiling, Bridgett extricated herself. She reached for her clothes and shimmied into her bra and panties. "They're in the storage locker with my stuff."

He lay back, watching, while she put on her blouse and her jeans. Damn, she was beautiful. Kind. Smart, and every kind of wonderful, too.

"I know right where they are, so I can slip over to my rental unit and get them. We won't have time to go through them right now, though. We're already close to being late for dinner with Violet and Gavin."

Reluctantly, he rose and began to dress. Doing what a guy always did when he was interested in a woman. Try to nail down their next time together, before the current interlude ended. "Later, then?" he made her promise.

Bridgett grinned, nodding. "It's a date."

Chapter 9

It's a date. Why had she said that? Bridgett chastised herself silently. She and Cullen were not dating. Sleeping together, yes, but dating? If she didn't want him to think she was one of those women who would hook up with a guy once or twice and then be ready to move in with him permanently, she would have to be more careful.

He sent her a sideways glance. "Stop beating yourself up."

"For what?"

"Showing me your feelings."

Bridgett ducked her head and rummaged around for her boots. "I didn't."

"Yes, you did," he said, giving her a frankly admiring glance. "And unless you want your brother and sister-in-law to see 'em, too, you better apply a little more lip gloss and run a brush through your hair."

Bridgett rushed to her shoulder bag, to find a mirror. "I really look that ravished?"

He shrugged. "To me you do."

Bridgett opened a small compact of blusher and groaned. She did look all...tousled. In fact, her skin seemed to be glowing from the inside out. Same as the rest of her. "I knew you were trouble the moment I met you," she grumbled teasingly.

He extracted a comb from his wallet and tidied up, too. "Right back at you, kid."

Short minutes later, they were on their way.

Gavin had just arrived home. As soon as greetings were given, Bridgett rushed over to see Robby, who was in his cozy little infant carrier, sleeping peacefully. "How has he been?"

Violet smiled. "He was a little dreamboat."

"He is a very cute kid," Gavin agreed, as they all sat down to dinner. "I can see why you're so attached to him, Bridgett."

Bridgett helped herself to some salad. "But you're worried."

"He's not actually up for adoption. Is he?" Gavin paused and looked at Cullen. "Is he even going to be?"

Cullen held her brother's level, assessing gaze with one of his own. "If you're asking...he is not my baby."

Biologically, anyway, Bridgett thought. It seemed emotionally the two had already bonded.

"And yet you've stepped in," Gavin said, his voice hard.

Cullen passed the breadbasket. "It's the right thing

to do. In fact—" he met her brother's gaze equably
"—I would help care for Robby and Riot even if they
hadn't been left with a note, charging me with the responsibility."

Bridgett knew Cullen well enough now to realize
how true that was. He might act all tough and gruff on
the outside sometimes, especially around those who
might be seeking to take advantage, but inside he was
kind and big hearted. Tender and loving to a fault. The
perfect father for Robby and Riot.

The perfect husband for her?

Now who was jumping the gun? she thought, hanging her head. For a moment, everyone ate their salad
in awkward silence.

Finally, Violet looked at Cullen, one McCabe to another, interjecting kindly. "We went through something
similar with our first child, Ava."

Glad to have the focus off her and Cullen, Bridgett
explained what had happened while Cullen was living out of state. "Gavin and Violet were named legal
guardians of a premature infant whose mother died in
childbirth. They hardly knew each other at the time."

Violet took Gavin's hand. The love between them was
palpable. "It was while taking care of little Ava, seeing her through her medical crisis, that we fell in love."

Gavin squeezed his doctor wife's hand affectionately,
then started on his lasagna. "Circumstances were a little
different, though. Since from the very beginning you
and I knew we could adopt Ava, if we chose."

"If we passed social service's home study," Violet
amended.

Happily, that wasn't a problem here. "I've already passed mine," Bridgett said. "Two years ago, when I was approved to foster-adopt."

Violet looked at Cullen. "Is that something you're interested in doing?" she asked.

Cullen continued devouring his pasta. "Never gave it any thought until now."

Bridgett was sure that was true.

"What about marriage?" Gavin asked. "Are you interested in that?"

Bridgett winced. This was nothing new. She knew Gavin felt it was his duty as the male head of the family to protect all three of his sisters. But there was no way she was letting Gavin chase Cullen away, the way he had every man he thought might potentially hurt her. There was simply too much at stake. He needed to back off.

The two men continued staring each other down. "I might be inclined to get hitched, if the right woman came along," Cullen shot back evenly.

Gavin stared back at him, waiting it seemed for a declaration that never came.

Which meant what? Bridgett wondered.

Cullen wasn't really serious about her? Or he was, but—like most strong, silent men— didn't feel the need to explain himself?

There was no clue from the impassive look on his handsome face.

Nothing that Gavin could jump on, either.

The rest of the meal was eaten in tense silence, and stilted small talk. Unable to stand the disquiet any longer, Bridgett thanked them both for a lovely meal, as did Cullen, and begged off, right after dessert.

"I am so sorry," Bridgett moaned as they drove away, short minutes later.

"Why?" Cullen asked, his muscular frame filling the interior of the pickup truck. That time of night, there wasn't a lot of traffic, and he went through one green light, then another. "They love you. They want what is best for you. They just don't think it is me."

Bridgett straightened. "Pull over."

His brow furrowed. "What?"

Bridgett pointed to an empty parking lot, next to an office building on the outskirts of town. "Pull over! I want you to look me in the eye when I say this." She waited until he had complied before she continued. "My family doesn't know what is best for me, Cullen. I get to decide that."

He met her gaze wryly, his eyes dark and heated. "Really? And what have you decided?"

"That we do not have to decide anything right now," she said firmly. She waved a hand. "Beyond, of course, figuring out how I am going to get my living conditions straightened out before the foster placement decision on Robby and Riot."

His big body relaxed. He reached over to take her hand. "What can I do to help?"

"Take care of Robby and Riot while I finish my on-line mortgage application this evening?"

"I'm on it," he assured her. "No problem."

And it wasn't.

Until just before midnight, seconds after her application had been emailed in. He was sitting on the sofa, his cheek pressed against the top of Robby's head, Riot curled up at his feet. He had the pictures of his first dog spread across his lap.

She eased down next to them. Then turned so she could sit kitty-corner to him. "Any luck remembering?"

Frustration curved the corners of his lips. "No. I talk to so many groups of people. Potential buyers who come for a tour of the ranch. Cattlemen's meetings around the state..."

"And don't forget the career fair at the high school," Bridgett interjected helpfully. "You and I were both present for that."

Cullen's brow furrowed. "Actually, I didn't just visit Laramie County High School. I spoke at two in San Angelo last fall, as well. In fact, I've done them wherever I lived."

A mixture of hope and dread sparked inside Bridgett. "You think that might have been where you discussed Riot?"

"Maybe. I mean the conversations with business people tend to stay on track. With high school kids, looking to choose their life's work, the conversations can go all over the place. And I do mean all over the place!"

Bridgett grinned ruefully. "I know what you mean. I was once asked if the best way to marry a handsome doctor was to become a nurse or a physician. Which one did I think would give a girl a better chance?"

Cullen winced. "What'd you say?"

"That I wouldn't know because I wanted to marry for love, not profession."

Approval shone in his eyes. "Good call."

"What about you?" Bridgett asked curiously, loving the intimacy that sprung up between them. "What was your weirdest question?"

"Boxers or briefs. Definitely the most uncomfortable."

"What did you say?"

He made a comical face. "Next question!"

Bridgett laughed softly. "Can't say I blame you."

Robby sighed in his sleep. Cullen snuggled the infant closer and bussed the top of his little head.

They looked so sweet together, so right, it nearly broke Bridgett's heart.

Oblivious to the tenderness welling up inside her, Cullen continued, "It's par for the course—a lot of teenage girls show up to hear the cowboys speak. But they also want to know things like if it's lonely on a ranch. Do we have to work all the time, or do we still have time for fun? Is it a good place to raise kids? Things like that."

"So, maybe…that is where you talked about Riot."

He nodded in agreement, still mulling over the possibilities. "But at which high school? And when?"

Bridgett had no idea.

She did know, however, that her life had just gotten more precarious than ever.

Cullen called Dan first thing the next morning to let him know what he and Bridgett were thinking.

"Well?" Bridgett asked anxiously when he hung up the phone. She stepped away from the breakfast she was cooking.

"Dan said he doesn't think it was Laramie High, because he's already talked to the principal and guidance counselors there, and they haven't had any girls get pregnant. But he'll call the two other high schools in San Angelo, where I spoke. See what he can find out."

She sauntered nearer, hands in her pockets. She had dried her hair after her shower that morning, leaving it long and loose and straight. But he liked it tousled and wavy, too. "How long does he think that will take?" she asked quietly.

He wrapped his arm about her shoulders, and she turned toward him, the warm abundance of her breasts brushing his chest. He pushed away the urge to explore her soft, womanly curves. "A couple of days, minimum. Everyone in the area is out for the week, on spring break, which includes the administrators."

She bit her lip, sighed and rested her head against his shoulder. "So it will be next week before we hear anything."

He pressed a kiss into her hair. "Most likely."

"I guess that's good news and bad news. Good, in that it gives us more time with Robby and Riot. Bad—" her eyes suddenly shimmered with unexpected tears "—in that if this lead does take us to Robby's birth mother, it could also mean the situation is about to get a lot more complicated." After giving the scrambled eggs another stir, she set down the spatula, looking all the more anxious. "Making my chances of foster-adopting Robby and Riot a lot more improbable."

He paused, surprised she had voiced a negative thought out loud. Up to now, she had been resolute in her view that this would all work out in her favor. Guilt came at him, swift and hard. It was because of him, somehow, that she was going through this. If it didn't work out, he would likely be to blame.

Watching her wipe her lashes with the pads of her index fingers, he stepped closer. "Are you going to be able to do this? Give the baby and puppy up if it comes to that?"

Embarrassed by the show of emotion, she turned away. "Are you?"

He caught her by the shoulders and spun her back to face him. "I'm serious, Bridgett."

"So am I." She stalked to the oven and removed a pan of fluffy, golden-brown biscuits. Then she piled freshly prepared sausage patties onto a serving platter. He helped her by doing the same with the scrambled eggs.

She set the dishes on the island, then went back to the cupboard to get out plates and utensils. "Do you honestly think that Robby would be better off with someone who would leave him in a cardboard box, with only a well-intentioned puppy to guard him, instead of with me?"

Her lower lip trembled.

She sloshed juice over the sides of the glasses, then set the pitcher down in frustration, looking at him. "I want you to be able to clear your name, Cullen. I know how important that is to you. But after that," she said fiercely, unable to contain her emotions any longer, "I want what's best for Robby and for Riot. And that means keeping them *with us*." She started, as astonished as he was at what she had let slip out. "Well, of course, I mean me."

She circled the island and slipped onto a stool.

"You know what I'm trying to say here," Bridgett amended hastily.

Yes, Cullen thought, *I do, because I have been thinking and wishing and hoping for the very same thing. Even though I know it's not likely to happen.*

Sighing, he sat down to eat, too. "I think you're right to be concerned. You could be in for a fight, when it comes to custody of the baby and the puppy, particularly if Robby has blood relatives who don't know about him yet and do want to raise him."

"Should kin with blood ties always win out?"

Cullen fed her a forkful of egg. "Not necessarily, not in my view. But to the court, it could be the deciding factor."

She huffed in frustration. "But don't you think that if help from the birth mother's family were readily available that Robby's birth mother would have already gone to them, given the baby and puppy over, instead of acting in such a desperate manner?"

"It had to be very hard for the birth mother, leaving Robby and Riot the way she did, even if she thought I would follow through on the written request, claim them and keep them safe and happy."

They were silent, brooding.

Bridgett broke a biscuit in half. "Or maybe the birth mother just wasn't thinking straight and underestimated her family. And they do want Robby." Her voice broke. "And Cullen, if that's the case…"

He slanted her a brief, consoling look. "Then the court will decide what is best for him, and you'll deal with whatever their decision is. Because in the end, Bridgett, you only want one thing. Same as me."

"What is best for Robby and Riot," she surmised on a heartfelt sigh.

He nodded as a contemplative silence fell.

He reached over and squeezed her hand, doing his best to comfort her. "In the meantime, you can still do everything possible to bolster your argument that a change in DCFS policy, regarding placement of newborns, is warranted. At least in your case."

She looked deep into his eyes, hanging on to his every word.

"For starters, this isn't a whim on your part. You've gone through the entire vetting process and been waiting to foster-adopt for some time now."

Bridgett brightened. "So I should use that?"

He luxuriated in the silky feel of her palm. "As well as the fact that your work as an N-ICU nurse gives you an expertise on caring for infants that few have."

Bridgett bit her lip. "That's true, but…" Her shoulders slumped. "There's still the fact I'm not married or even engaged to be."

"Maybe you don't need to be," he told her gruffly, although he was already privately wishing that would change. "You have a large and loving extended family who stand ready to help you with whatever you need."

She stood. "That's true."

Using his leverage on her hand, he drew her closer still and wrapped his arms around her. She was gorgeous and courageous and vulnerable, and he wanted to help her achieve her heart's desire more than he had ever imagined he could.

He gazed down at her tenderly. "If you present a detailed plan for caring for Robby, demonstrate to DCFS and the court how much he will benefit with you as his mommy, and reassure them that he'll never lack a loving support network of family and friends, like me, who stand ready to assist you-all.... Well, there's no way they'll be able to deny you."

Who knew he was such a cheerleader?

Bridgett splayed her hands across his chest. "You'll really be there for us?" she marveled softly. "Not just temporarily?" Her voice caught unexpectedly. "But long term?"

He brought her in for a close, comforting hug. "To support you?" he rasped, feeling abruptly emotional, too. *And help and care for you?* He savored her feminine strength. "You bet."

It wasn't what Cullen wanted, of course. To be stuck, standing on the sidelines, cheering Bridgett on. He wanted to find a way move the foster-adopt process along, get approved and get his name on the petition for custody, too.

Only the knowledge that he would be slowing down the entire process and hindering her chances to get anything resolved quickly, if he acted on his reckless desire, kept him from doing it.

Figuring, however, that he could support her behind the scenes, he called the local San Angelo newspapers. Asked if they had any photos from the high school career fairs the previous fall that hadn't been printed in the paper.

Turned out they did.

He could view them, but he'd have to go there in person. He got in the truck and headed for San Angelo.

Chapter 10

The next few days passed swiftly. Cullen was busy prepping for the Western Cross cattle auction; Bridgett was busy marshalling her family. All four of her siblings had provided letters of recommendation, as well as detailed lists of things they could do to help her—like babysitting and grocery shopping, even laundry.

Yet she and Cullen found time to be together every night. Eating dinner. Walking Riot. Getting Robby ready for bed and giving him his last snuggle of the evening. They didn't always do all of it as one unit. And they hadn't made love since her brother Gavin had given Cullen the third degree about what his intentions toward her might be. And successfully infused Cullen with guilt.

But he still looked at her like he wanted her and

treated her with gallant kindness and concern. And they always did enough to make them feel like family. And that, Bridgett knew, was dangerous. Given all that could still go wrong.

But she tried not to think about all the what-ifs, lest she start to go crazy with worry. It was enough to appreciate what they had with each other in the here and now...

"So, what do you think little fella?" Bridgett cooed to the infant in her arms, aware she had never in her life felt this content. "Do you think we should stay up a little longer and watch the sun rise or head on back upstairs and try to catch a little more shut-eye?"

Robby looked up at her adoringly. He opened his mouth, releasing a milk bubble that hovered between his rosebud lips, then yawned.

Bridgett figured, what the heck, why not stay on the back porch a few more minutes? It would give her a chance to see Cullen before he headed out, to start the ranch work with the rest of the hired hands. With the sale only four days away, there was a lot of last-minute stuff to be done.

Behind her, she heard the sound of a door opening and closing. Cullen strode out, Riot beside him.

She was still in her pajamas and robe, he was already in jeans and a work shirt and boots. He hadn't yet shaved and the stubble gave him a rugged, sexy look. "There you are," he said. "I woke up and your room was empty."

Memories of the way he had kissed her the last time they had made love sent a burning flame throughout her entire body.

Bridgett forced herself to quell the flames. He had listened to her brother's common-sense warning and taken a step back. She knew she should be sensible and do the same.

She leaned down to pet Riot, who wagged his tail gleefully. "We were trying to be quiet."

Something hot and sensual shimmered in his eyes. "How long have you been up?"

Wondering how he could look so good early in the day, Bridgett wrinkled her nose. "Since four."

Cullen took care of the dog's needs then ambled over and took a place beside Bridgett and Robby on the porch swing. "He wouldn't go back to sleep?"

Bridgett could have shifted over to give him a little more room but, liking the way her body bumped up against his, decided to remain in the strong, reassuring curve of his big frame. "He was a little restless. I think he had a little more air in his tummy than usual. It wasn't colic exactly, but…"

"Is that serious in a baby?"

Bridgett knew colic could be deadly for horses and cattle.

As she turned her head to gaze up at him, her cheek brushed his chin. "It can be sometimes. This wasn't. He just needed to be soothed and held upright."

Cullen looked like he wanted to kiss her again. She knew, because she wanted to kiss him, too.

"Good thing you're a nurse." His voice was low, gravelly.

She savored the emotion welling in her heart. Wag-gling her brows, she quipped, "And an increasingly skillful mom."

"That you are, darlin'." He grinned, more than willing to give credit where it was due.

Another moment of quiet contentment and suppressed sexual need passed between them.

Bridgett cleared her throat. Aware that Robby wasn't the only one who needed to be cared for. "Speaking of not sleeping," she prodded softly, "you were up awfully late last night." He'd disappeared right after dinner to check on a few things and still been hard at work in the office downstairs when she turned off her lamp at midnight.

"Yeah."

To her frustration, although they had shared a lot over the past week, nothing else was forthcoming.

"Everything proceeding okay with the presale?" she asked, wanting to help if she could. After all, he'd done so much for her.

He hesitated a moment too long. "Pretty much."

"I'd like to hear about it."

When, again, he said nothing else, she handed Robby to him. "Here. Snuggling with him will make you feel better."

He grinned, cradling the infant against his chest like a pro. "Always does." He bussed the top of Robby's head.

"So what gives?" Bridgett watched Riot—who also bore a look of concern for Cullen—curled up on the dog blanket opposite them. His silky head on his paws, he continued watching them all. Robby looked up at Cullen, too.

With such an intent audience, he finally confided with a sigh, "Over the course of the past couple of days, five potential customers have pulled out of the virtual auction."

"Is that usual?"

"No. Once someone has taken the trouble to get all the information, register as a buyer for the sale and provide a bank guarantee that funds are immediately available, they rarely withdraw."

"Did they say why?"

Another grimace. "No."

"Do you think it has to do with all the rumors?"

"Not sure what else it could be."

"People have to know you would never turn your back on a biological child!" He was far too honorable a man for that! Look how he had stepped up thus far.

"A McCabe wouldn't." He turned to give her a hard look. "A Reid might."

Angry heat welled in her chest and she stiffened. "You were *not* responsible for what your mother did to you and Frank."

"I know that." Cullen exhaled wearily. "You know that." He shook his head. "But some people think blood ties tell character, and face it…" Still cuddling Robby tenderly, he said, "…one half of mine is suspect."

Another silence fell.

Finally, Bridgett said, "I'm sorry."

"It's okay."

Except it wasn't. Not at all.

"How much of an impact will this have?" she asked gently.

"I should still be able to sell all my stock," he answered. "Purebred Hotlander cattle are in high demand."

"Why is that?"

"A number of reasons." Seeing that Robby had fallen asleep, he moved to put the baby down in the Moses basket then returned to her side. "They breed extremely well, even during a drought. The longevity of the females is very good, their udder quality outstanding, their calves are very uniform and they crossbreed well.

"Plus, the cattle producers I sell my cows and bulls to can either crossbreed their own Brangus, Braford, Beefmaster and Santa Gertrudis to mine. Or work to achieve an entire herd of purebred Hotlander cattle of their own, as I have."

Aware how cozy and domestic this all felt, cuddling next to him on the porch swing, she smiled. "So it's a win-win."

He nodded, his eyes warming as he talked about a subject he loved. "As well as a substantial investment, given the cost of Hotlander bulls and cows."

Bridgett frowned, steering them back to the problem. "Do you think all the unsubstantiated gossip will affect your bottom line?"

"Not in the end," he answered, leaning over to kiss her temple, "because if I don't get the price I want, I'll hold on and try again later."

Bridgett snuggled against him. "Wouldn't that cause a lot of talk, too?"

Another nod. "But it would be a mistake to allow the part of the herd I'm selling to go for a lower-than-usual price and have that affect future demand and profit, so…" He shrugged his broad shoulders again. "We'll see what develops."

In more than one way, Bridgett thought, as silence fell.

Knowing what she was hoping for—an ending that had all four of them as a family—she reached over and took his hand. "Well, if it helps, you weren't the only one who got bad news last night." His eyes met hers and she drew a deep breath, aware she needed him in this moment, as much as he needed her. "The online mortgage company let me know that they are turning down my request for a mortgage, too."

He did not look surprised. "I'm sorry, sweetheart."

"Yeah, me, too." She released a pensive sigh. "They said to try back in six months, once I go back to work and things are settled, and I would likely have no issue getting approved for a mortgage."

"But the house you wanted…" He shared her disappointment.

"Will be put back on the market as soon as our two Realtors read their email. I notified them last night, before I went to bed."

His gaze narrowed protectively. "You know, my offer to help you out financially still stands."

When he was potentially about to have financial woes of his own? When she had her own family standing by, ready to help her in that regard, if only she could bring herself to let them?

No, life was getting far too complicated as it was. There were decisions to be made, but not today. Not about that. Pushing aside the mixture of gratitude and attraction mingling deep inside her, Bridgett asked cheerfully, "How about I continue to just take you up on your offer of a place to stay, for now?"

He clasped her shoulders warmly, said with the gruff affection she was beginning to know so well, "You and Robby and Riot are welcome here as long as you want, you know that."

The next thing she knew he had shifted her onto his lap. She wreathed her arms about his neck and shoulders, opened her mouth to the plundering pressure of his.

She'd never been one to focus on the here and now. To let a rush of emotion overwhelm her. Yet as sensation swept through her like a tsunami, followed by a tidal wave of yearning, she felt herself surrender to everything he wanted and needed.

And still he kissed her, as if he were in love with her, and would be for all time. As if he too felt that coming together like this was something special, that they were destined to be together like this. As a couple and as a family. And for now, she thought, as they continued to kiss and hold each other wonderingly, it was enough. It had to be.

"I come bearing food! Is now a good time?"

Bridgett grinned at Rachel McCabe. Cullen's stepmother was wearing skinny jeans and a long sunflower-yellow tunic. She also had a pencil stuck in her upswept hair—all signs it had been a work-at-home-day for the renowned local tax attorney.

Bridgett ushered her in. "Now is a great time, especially given how much Cullen and I both love your cooking."

The older woman smiled. "He said that?"

Bridgett relieved Rachel of her burden. "He doesn't have to. I can tell by the way he inhales whatever you bring." She inclined her head at the covered dishes on the tray. "What's on the menu tonight?"

Rachel followed her through the house. "Old-fashioned pot roast, mashed potatoes and string beans."

Glad for some female company, Bridgett grinned. "My mouth is already watering."

Rachel walked into the kitchen. She eyed the platters of cookies, muffins and various home-baked breads and fruit baskets. "Seems like I'm not the only one feeding my son these days."

Bridgett slid Rachel's gifts into the fridge. "You know how it is with new babies. Everyone wants to bring the family food." She shrugged. "Not that we're a family, but…"

"I know what you mean."

An awkward silence fell. Sensing Rachel wanted to chat, Bridgett asked, "Would you like to stay for a glass of iced tea?"

"Do you have time? I don't want to intrude."

"I'd appreciate the adult company." They peeked in on Robby and Riot, who were both sleeping, then took a seat at the kitchen island.

"I'm guessing Cullen is out on the ranch."

Having his stepmother here reminded Bridgett how much she missed her own mother. She poured tea for both of them, then set out sugar, some sliced lemon and a plate of oatmeal cookies. "He and the hired hands are sorting the cattle being put up for auction, moving them to different pastures."

Rachel nodded. "How are you doing?"

Bridgett warmed at the maternal concern. "Good. Between the baby and the puppy…" *and my thing for Cullen* "…I don't seem to have enough hours in the day, though."

"You'll get used to it."

Bridgett got up to retrieve a bunch of red grapes. "How did you manage with such a big family?"

Rachel helped herself to some fruit. "Everyone pitched in, doing chores. Lending a hand. Which was the only way I could have managed to work while they were growing up."

"You've always been a tax lawyer?"

Rachel smiled. "I have. In fact, that's how Frank and I met. Starting out, he tried to do it all, but didn't quite have a handle on how he should set up the ranch business at the Bar M. An LLC, S Corp. or straight corporation. At some point he tried all three—badly. Made a real mess of things, as far as the revenue agents were concerned. Hired me to straighten it all out. Sparks flew—because he was a McCabe and McCabes are brought up to make their own way—and he did not want to listen to me."

Bridgett could imagine. "Yet you prevailed."

"We fell in love, married and had six kids."

Six. Not five. Maybe it was rude, but she had to ask. "You consider Cullen yours?"

Rachel stiffened. "Do you consider Robby yours?"

Okay, that was a mistake. "Yes."

"But…?" the older woman prodded.

Given permission to delve further, Bridgett asked,

"Is there any difference in carrying a baby inside you and giving birth as opposed to simply being presented with a child, one day?"

Rachel relaxed. "None," she said gently. "If anything, sometimes I think I love Cullen more because of the shape he was in when he came to us at sixteen. He's still getting over the tumult of his early years." Her gaze narrowed. "How is he doing with all this?"

It was a lot, both women knew. To be publicly assumed guilty of something you knew you hadn't done. Bridgett shrugged. She was close to Cullen and getting closer every day, but there was still a lot separating them, a lot he had yet to reveal. But what she did know, she liked, or maybe more to the point, loved. "He's mystified. Frustrated. A bit overwhelmed. More than anything, he wants to know the truth. Not just for himself, but for Robby."

Rachel sipped her tea. "Because he's sure his true parentage will be an issue in the future for Robby, like it was with him."

"Yes." And though Bridgett had told herself repeatedly it didn't matter, as long as Robby had a family who loved him, she worried about the ramifications of his never finding out where he came from or why he had been abandoned. That would be a lot to carry, and she didn't want Robby to suffer the way Cullen had.

"What about you?" Rachel asked gently. "Do you want to find this woman—or not?"

Bridgett bit her lip. "I'm not sure. Depends when you ask me. Sometimes I do, so I won't have this uncertainty hanging over us, and sometimes I don't because it could turn out that Robby has blood family who want him, and in court, biological ties trump all. Unless there's a concrete reason for them not to," she amended, "like addiction or abuse, and that would be a bad situation."

"I'm guessing Cullen is worried about what the social services and courts will eventually do, too."

Given how much he had bonded with baby Robby and Riot? Bridgett saw no reason not to admit it. "Yes, he is." She sighed and shook her head. "And then, on top of all that, having the potential buyers unexpectedly pull out of the auction..."

Rachel sat up straighter. "Wait. Could you repeat that?"

Briefly, Bridgett explained what had happened.

"Do you know which customers?" Rachel asked, brow furrowing.

"No."

"Or how many?"

"He said five this morning. There are still another fifteen bidding. At least, that was what he told me when he left earlier."

"That's good." Rachel finished her tea. She went for one last look at the sleeping baby, then tiptoed back out of the family room. "You'll call us if you need anything?" She stepped in to give Bridgett a hug.

Basking in the knowledge of what a wonderful mother Rachel was, Bridgett nodded. "I will."

When Cullen came in several hours later, she was gently dabbing baby oil onto Robby's scalp and working it through his silky dark curls.

Cullen sauntered closer, a bemused smile curving

his sensual lips. He paused to greet her with a warm embrace, then bent down to kiss Robby, too. "Shouldn't you be using hair gel, instead of baby oil, if you want our boy to be all styling?"

Our boy. How nice that sounded, Bridgett thought wistfully. If only it were already true. She demonstrated with the oil-soaked cotton ball. "I'm softening the cradle cap on the top of his head."

"The...what?"

"See the little crust starting to form?" She pointed out the yellow skin. "Especially in the soft spot? This is cradle cap. Most new babies get it at some point during their first year."

"Should we be worried?" He went to the sink to wash up then ambled closer, still drying his hands on a paper towel.

"No." She used a soft-bristled baby brush to loosen the flakes, then combed them out of his hair.

He leaned in close, watching. "Are you just going to leave that in there?"

"No." She suddenly felt the overwhelming urge to kiss him again. "I'm going to wash it out while I give him his sponge bath. Want to help?"

His gave roved her upturned face before returning to her eyes. "You don't think I'll mess it up?"

"I won't let you mess it up," she promised with a smile.

"Okay then." He rolled up the sleeves on his shirt to above the elbow. "Let's do this."

Bridgett had already laid out a thick towel on the kitchen island. She settled Robby in the middle of it and poured a little warm water from the pitcher into a bowl.

She added a squirt of soothing lavender-scented baby wash and, one hand still on Robby's chest to keep him from rolling off, dampened the washcloth.

"Wouldn't it be simpler to put him in a baby bath tub?"

Wanting Cullen to be as good at this as she was, she unsnapped the sleeper and removed Robby's damp diaper. "We will, as soon as the cord falls off."

Cullen watched as she quickly and methodically washed Robby thoroughly, from front to back. Then she swabbed the navel area with a small amount of rubbing alcohol, wrapped the infant in a towel and handed him to Cullen. "The shampoo is going to be a little trickier."

"What are we going to do?" he asked solemnly.

"You're going to hold him in your arms, yep, just like that, with his neck fully supported and his head slightly over the crook of your elbow. I'm going to dampen his hair with a little bit of water and then add some shampoo." She worked as she talked. "And then I'll lather his scalp."

The scent of lavender baby shampoo enveloped them. Cullen made a funny face at their tiny charge and was rewarded with wide-eyed wonder. "He seems to like it," he reflected proudly.

"I think he likes being held."

Cullen chuckled and continued cuddling Robby tenderly. "Don't we all," he rumbled, just loud enough for her to hear.

His low, sexy voice generated a tsunami of need deep inside her. Not daring to look him in the eye, Bridgett *tsked*. "Okay, cowboy, let's stay on task."

"Hear that, Robby? Your mommy wants us to get serious here."

Mommy.

How she liked the sound of that.

Daddy, too.

Ignoring the way her nipples were tingling, Bridgett instructed casually, "If you sort of hold him over the basin, I'll rinse his head with the water in the pitcher. And then we'll be all done."

And, a minute later, they were.

Bridgett already had Robby's clothes all laid out, so she diapered him and put on a clean baby-blue sleeper. A matching knit cap went on his head. "Is there some reason you always have him wearing a hat?" Cullen asked when she gave him the baby to hold again.

"Newborn infants can get chilled easily. Covering their heads helps keep in the body heat."

"Ahhh."

It was hard to say who of the three of them was happier in that moment, as he moved in closer, so their sides were touching in an electrified line. Warmth exuded from the rock-hard muscles of his body. And she felt a melting sensation in her middle, completely at odds with the easy emotional territory she was attempting to stake out. She slanted Cullen a glance. Amazed at how at quickly and fiercely she had come to want him in her life. "We could get you and Riot matching caps, if you like."

He favored her with a sexy half smile, his eyes roving her face. "Actually, I think we should all wear matching caps." He bent over to kiss her temple. "One for all. All for one."

Another thrill swept through her. Were they about to

take their relationship to another level? "Like the four musketeers," she surmised softly.

Cullen nodded, serious now. Then he paused, and turned so she could see Robby's face. "Hey, will you look at that?" he whispered, his brawny shoulder nudging hers slightly in the process. He looked as proud as any daddy in the newborn nursery. "The little cowpoke's asleep already."

"Bath time usually tuckers him out." Bridgett transferred him from Cullen's arms to his little bed, whispering, "We should put him down while he's still sleeping."

Cullen stood for one last long, tender look at the child they were quickly coming to think of as *their* son. "How long will he be out?"

"At least two hours." Riot, too, was passed out in his crate. "So, if you want, we can have a relaxing adults-only dinner."

Not a date.

But sort of like a date. Even though it would be experienced at home.

"Actually..." Cullen wrapped his hands around her waist, suddenly all hot, possessive male. "I had something much more pleasurable in mind."

Chapter 11

Bridgett saw the kiss coming and it was everything she had expected it would be. And everything she hadn't. It was soft and warm and unbearably seductive. Pure happiness soaring through her, she wound her arms about his neck and opened her mouth to the unerring pressure of his. Luxuriating in the scent of him, so brisk and familiar and masculine, she murmured, "I thought we were taking a break from this kind of intimacy."

He touched her cheek. "I wanted to give you a chance to reconsider, if that was what you wanted."

"Because of what Gavin implied during his third degree?" That Cullen was not to be trusted and did *not* have her best interests at heart, only his own?

"No, because of what I know to be true," Cullen corrected, stroking a hand through her hair. "That you're not, and never have been, a reckless person. Romantic? Hell, yes. Passionate in going after what you want? Absolutely. But the type to rush headfirst into anything? Especially with me…under these circumstances? No." He exhaled heavily, holding her gaze. "That's not you, Bridgett Monroe."

"Until now," Bridgett whispered, touched by his need to protect her, even as he let her know with a look and a touch and a kiss he still desired her. And when the time was right, intended to have her again.

Fortunately for the both of them, that time was tonight.

He held her by the shoulders as she rose on tiptoe and pressed her mouth to his, suggesting caution once again. "We can just hang out together, Bridgett. Make out a little."

"Oh, we'll do that all right," she promised, sliding her hands over the sinewy hardness of his chest. Pausing only to turn on the baby monitor, another gift, she took him by the hand and led him up the stairs, to the guest room, this time. "As well as so much more."

Determined to have all of him, she unbuttoned his shirt and pulled it off. Worked similar magic on his boots and pants. And, oops, there went his briefs, too.

"What's gotten into you?" he rasped, the twinkle in his navy blue eyes intensifying.

Enjoying what she was doing to him as much as he apparently liked her doing it, Bridgett sat back on the bed, admiring everything her quick work had uncovered. Glowing, golden skin. Smooth muscle. Enticing tufts of curly dark hair that spread across his chest and arrowed downward, delineating the goody trail. Nice broad shoulders. Not to mention long, powerful legs and strong arms.

She could sit here in front of him, just looking and admiring, all night long. As he noticed the depth of her enjoyment, his own pleasure grew.

Bridgett smiled, aware he was still waiting for her to reply. Her gaze shifted to his. "I made up my mind to stop putting off till tomorrow what I could enjoy right now. Tonight. And to that end..." She switched places with him, so he was on the bed. Still fully clothed herself, she dropped to her knees and captured the male essence of him with both hands, sculpting and caressing the hard, velvety-hot length.

"Whoa..." He groaned with arousal as she touched him with lips and tongue and teeth. "Getting a little ahead of you, here..."

No kidding, Bridgett thought. "That's okay," she breathed, as her nipples beaded and ached, and the damp throbbing between her legs intensified. She wanted to burn away the anxiety she felt over everything that might happen next. Concentrate on all that was good and right. And this, she thought on a blissful sigh, was the way to do it.

Cullen had been thinking about making love to Bridgett again for days now. Because the problems that could keep them apart fell away when they were kissing and touching and driving each other wild and they were only dealing with what they wanted, what they felt.

And what he wanted most was her—in his home, in his bed, in his heart.

Not about to let her push him to the finish line without her, he curved his hands around her shoulders and drew her up to face him. "You, too," he said, undressing her, an item of clothing at a time. "I want to look at you."

Excitement building inside him, he stroked the silky texture of her skin, charting the hills and valleys as well as the plains in between. Her body shuddered beneath his questing fingertips, and he put all he wanted and needed, all he felt, into another searing kiss. He wanted to be everything to her, and he sensed, as he drew her down onto the bed, she wanted to be everything to him, too.

Feeling the yearning pouring out of her, he cupped the soft weight of her breasts in his hands and bent his head, loving her with his lips and mouth and tongue. She clung to him wordlessly, arching her back, opening herself up to him completely.

Shifting her onto her side, he pressed his body against hers, kissing her ceaselessly, until she was in a frenzy of wanting, her need making a low sound in the back of her throat. Until there was only the pulsing of her body, and his, only the wonder and affection in their hearts.

Her breath hitched as he found a condom and rolled it on. Her body trembled as he filled her. Yielding to him with the sweet surrender of a woman who was fated to be his, she clasped his shoulders as he kissed her and possessed her, again and again. Adrenaline rushed. Pleasure built and spiraled.

He slid his hands beneath her, lifting her, diving deep. Taking, as she gave, and giving her more in return. Until, together, they soared toward a completion more stunning and fulfilling than he had ever imagined possible.

And he knew this was what he wanted. Not just for now, but for all time.

"It's crazy," Bridgett said, as they snuggled together afterward, in no hurry to get up to eat dinner, "how much my life has changed in just a little over a week."

He loved the way she felt, holding him close, the silken warmth of her sprawled over his chest. "Mine, too." He ran a hand lovingly down her hip. "But there's no arguing that it's been for the better."

"For all of us." Bridgett smiled, and they made love again, slowly, thoroughly, tenderly this time, finishing just as Robby woke and started to fuss. Downstairs, Riot yelped from his crate, signaling he, too, needed attention.

Ready to tend to their more familial—but just as emotionally satisfying—duties, Cullen rose. "I'll put a bottle in the warmer, then feed Riot and take him out. Or…" He paused, thinking he might have assumed too much, taking charge so readily. "I could do the diaper." At least, he thought he could. "And you could do the other."

Looking tousled and well loved, she slipped into his shirt and headed for the stairs. "I like your first plan better."

Relieved, he winked. "Ah, teamwork. Nothing like

it." He could help birth a calf blindfolded, but the fragility of a newborn infant still sometimes stymied him.

Riot was a little frisky after sleeping for so long, so Cullen snapped a leash on him and walked him down to the barn and back. When they walked in, he was disappointed to see Bridgett dressed in jeans, a T-shirt and bright blue moccasins. Her hair had been brushed into order and twisted atop her head, but there was no denying the flush in her cheeks or the plump kiss-swollen set of her lips.

"I kind of liked the way you looked in just my shirt."

She laughed, looking as contented as he felt. "If you behave, cowboy, you might be able to see me in it again before the night is through."

"Good." He ambled closer, drinking in the fresh lavender and baby powder scent of her. "'Cause I have plenty of them, you know. Dark denim, light blue denim, stonewashed denim..."

She mugged at him comically. "Tan and dark green canvas. And lots of blue chambray, too."

"Why, Ms. Bridgett..." He did his best imitation of a romantic comedy hero. "Have you been memorizing my wardrobe?"

Her eyes darkened affectionately. "Actually," she slid her hands up to his shoulders and rose on tiptoe, kissing him, "I might have been memorizing a lot of things about you."

They kissed again, but aware duties waited, reluctantly drew apart. "You must be starved," she murmured finally.

"You, too. And I am. But I need to do one thing first. Check my business email."

She stepped back, still studying him. "To make sure no one else has dropped out of the sale?"

"That. And…it's usual to have a lot of last-minute questions coming in."

Relaxing, she waved him on. "Go ahead then. I'll start warming up the dinner your stepmother brought for us."

Cullen nodded then paused in the doorway, memorizing that moment, savoring the sensation of just how happy he was. He had never imagined life on the ranch could be like this. Up until now, he had always felt there was something lacking. At first, a father of his own. Then, after his mother died, parents or family of any kind. After that gap had been filled, he'd lamented the lack of a woman he could keep company with and make love to. Now he had that, and all he wanted was for Bridgett and Robby and Riot to stay.

Even as the logical side of him knew they were living a fairy tale right now. That reality could come crashing down on all of them at any second. And if it did, Bridgett might not want anything further to do with him.

"Cullen?" she said softly, giving him an intent look. "Everything okay?"

He shook himself. "More than okay, darlin'," he promised. And right now, he told himself, he was good with that.

"Good news, I take it?" Bridgett set the warmed food on the kitchen island. She took in the day's growth of beard and the flush of sun on his rugged, chiseled face. It seemed impossible he could appear even sexier now than when he'd been making love to her, but he did.

Cullen slipped onto a stool beside her, the happy gleam in his eyes at odds with his solemn tone. "Amazing, actually."

"Well, don't leave me in suspense! Tell me."

He handed her a serving bowl with exaggerated chivalry. "Two more local buyers dropped out."

She paused, a spoonful of mashed potatoes in midscoop. "And that's good?"

He flashed her a lopsided smile. "One of the biggest buyers in Nebraska—Dirk Cartwright of the Cartwright Ranch—has signed up to participate in the virtual auction in a big way."

She poured gravy over her potatoes. "Do you know Dirk?"

He nodded as they begin to serve themselves the pot roast. "They bought a few calves from me when I was living there. If I were to sell even a hundred Hotlander cattle to him, it would launch me into the big time."

"Congratulations."

He turned his gaze to hers. "Let's not get ahead of ourselves. This auction isn't over yet."

Bridgett tried not to read anything into the easy affection in his blue eyes, never mind how comfortable and intimate this all felt. "But if he did…"

His eyes glimmered. "It would mean I'd finally made Frank proud."

Bridgett ruminated on that. "He seems that way already."

Cullen made a seesawing motion, with his hand. "When he was my age, he already had ten thousand of the fifty thousand acres he owns now."

Bridgett looked at him. "You've mentioned that before. Is that really what you want? That size ranch?" Because it could mean—would probably mean—leaving Laramie County, maybe even Texas.

He finished his string beans. "I'd be happy with that."

Would he? Bridgett studied him, her appetite suddenly fading. "But you want more?" she guessed.

For a moment she thought he wouldn't answer. That she'd delved into an area that was just too personal. Which sort of stung. She was beginning to think they had gotten to a point where there was nothing they couldn't share with each other.

His expression pensive, he turned to her, his knees brushing her thigh. "Have you always been a neonatal intensive care nurse?"

"No." Skin tingling, she swung around to face him. Now both their knees were touching. "I started in pediatrics."

He touched her hand, tracing each knuckle in turn. "Why did you move into N-ICU? Isn't it a lot harder, emotionally? Dealing with all those preemies, who might not make it?"

Bridgett inhaled, aware they were now traipsing into territory *she* might not want to discuss. Her appetite fading even more, she admitted, "It's very hard to take care of little ones who have so much stacked against them."

She paused, her lower lip quivering as she thought

about the premature infants they'd lost over the years. With the rapid advances that had taken place in medicine, there weren't nearly so many tragic losses these days, but sometimes, a baby who had been getting better slowly, day by day, hour by hour, would suddenly take a turn for a worse. Their heart would fail. They'd stop breathing or develop an inoperable clot. And that was wrenching. Not just for the family, but for all the doctors, nurses and support staff who worked tirelessly to help them thrive.

She clasped Cullen's hand tightly. "It's why I didn't think I could bear to foster a child not available for adoption." Her voice caught. "The thought of eventually having to let the child go, perhaps even returning to circumstances that were a lot less loving and stable than what I could offer, just slayed me."

"And yet you are." He gave her an admiring glance that meant more to her than any compliment she'd ever received.

"Because every instinct in me tells me that this is still our destiny. That I'm going to get to keep Robby and Riot. Otherwise, you're right." She inhaled a shuddering breath. "I never would have done this." *I never would have gotten to know you and fallen so hard and fast for you.*

Pausing, she sat back and withdrew her hand. "But what does my fostering to adopt have to do with the size of ranch you would like to have?"

Once again, she could see she had touched on something extremely personal.

He chose his words carefully. "Part of it is that the

bigger the ranch and the bigger the herd, the more financial security I have." He went back to eating his dinner. "Given the way I grew up, with us moving every year or so, that was something in my early life that was sorely lacking."

She touched his arm. "I'm sorry you went through that."

He leaned down to kiss her fingers. "Hey, darlin', don't be. It's part of what nurtured my ambition." He straightened lazily so they could go back to eating. "The other reason I want to keep on expanding is that I'm easily bored."

She certainly didn't want him feeling that way!

"Building and improving my ranching operation is how I keep myself challenged, professionally." Half his mouth tilted in a sexy smile. "I like learning new things and putting that knowledge to use."

A thrill went through her as she thought about other ways that inclination could be put to use. "Hmm, learning new things," she echoed facetiously. "Putting that knowledge to use."

He ran his knee along the outside of her thigh. "You betcha."

She thrilled at the amorous look in his eyes. "Is it only on the ranch, cowboy?"

Already up off the stool, he mirrored her inviting tone. "How long do we have before we're back on baby and puppy duty?"

She took his hand. "A couple of hours."

He drew her to her feet. "Plenty of time for me to demonstrate just what an avid student I am."

Talk about a way to while away an evening! It was all she could do not to swoon. Bridgett wrapped her arms about his neck. "You think?"

Kissing her, he plucked her off her feet. "Let me show you."

They made love again, took care of their little ones, slept, woke and then made love again just before dawn. They ate breakfast in shifts, between feeding, burping and cuddling Robby, and walking and feeding Riot. But it was okay; all the activity had a decidedly family feel to it.

At least, it did until Dan McCabe and Mitzy Martin showed up just as Cullen was about to head out to tend cattle with his hired hands.

Bridgett's heart sank in her chest. It was clear from the looks on their faces they had news of some sort. Probably not good.

"I'm glad we caught you," Mitzy, who was in full social worker mode, said.

Dan's manner was official, as well. "We told you-all the sheriff's department would keep you updated, so we wanted to let you know we were able to get the rest of the photographs—the ones that remain unpublished— from the freelance photographer who took them."

Realizing she was the only adult in the room who wasn't up to speed on what was being discussed, Bridgett turned to Cullen. Matter-of-factly, he explained, "I went to the San Angelo newspaper earlier in the week. I thought they might have pictures from the high school career fairs that I attended there—that hadn't been printed in the newspapers. But when I explained to them why I wanted them, they said they would only speak to law enforcement or someone from social services."

"So Mitzy and I went over yesterday afternoon, talked to the freelance photographer hired to capture both events and explained the situation," Dan continued. "He understood we are doing our best to protect the privacy and health of the birth mother, and keep her from being spooked into running, assuming she already hasn't. He cooperated without a warrant. Gave me copies of every photo he took of Cullen speaking to the groups at both high schools."

"We're hoping you will recognize someone," Mitzy said.

There were some thirty black-and-white photographs in all. They spread them out over the kitchen island.

It didn't take long before Cullen identified a trio of students. "These three girls sitting in the front row. They were the ones quizzing me about ranch life and Riot Senior, and they also asked about my marital status and whether I thought I'd ever have a family someday, and so on."

Mitzy gaped in surprise. "That must have been some Q&A."

Cullen exhaled heavily. "Yeah. They were the final group I spoke to that day."

"You're sure this was them," Dan asked.

"Now that I see them again, absolutely." Cullen pointed to the girl in the middle. She was very tall and thin, and had long, curly dark hair, as thick and unruly as Robby's—and Cullen's, for that matter. She was wearing loose, unattractive clothing and had an intent, almost worried look on her face. "She seemed to be taking the lead. I remember thinking at one point that it was almost like she was interviewing me for a job."

"Maybe she was," Dan said with a beleaguered sigh, abruptly sounding more younger brother than deputy. "Like…adoptive daddy?"

"So you think…?" Bridgett pressed.

Cullen scrubbed a hand over his face. "Dan's right. This all fits. If it wasn't the dark-haired girl or one of her girlfriends who left the baby, they probably know who did."

"I can't believe we're going to have to wait until Monday to find out the identity of those students," Bridgett lamented when Mitzy and Dan had left, promising to call as soon as they had more news on the baby-mama front. "That's three whole days of wondering and worrying!"

"Maybe it's a good thing. The virtual auction is tomorrow."

Saturday morning.

Cullen continued, "I'd prefer the sale be over with before we have to deal with whatever is coming next."

He had a point there, Bridgett conceded. It would be awful to be getting news regarding Robby's biological mother in the midst of the most important business transaction of Cullen's fiscal year. And there was something else…

Drawing a deep breath, she moved closer. "Why didn't you tell me about any of this?"

Cullen shrugged, to her deep disappointment, once

again shutting her out. "I didn't want you to worry about something that might not yield anything. As it initially didn't. You had enough to deal with between the mortgage and the baby and trying to get chosen to foster-adopt." His eyes gleamed. "I was trying to protect you. It's what a man does for his woman."

His woman. Bridgett gulped. "You're saying…?"

"That you're my woman? Hell, yes. What did you think? That this was casual for me? It's not, Bridgett. It never has been." His eyes closed to half-mast. "It never will be." Slowly, he lowered his head and cradled her face in his big, rough hands.

"For me, either," Bridgett whispered back, her heart pounding in her chest.

The raw affection in his embrace made her catch her breath. This time there was nothing easy about his kiss. It was hot, persuasive, hungry. She kissed him back, in much the same way, knowing that, once the sale was over the next morning, they would have the rest of the weekend to enjoy. But would it be their last—as the makeshift family neither she nor Cullen had ever imagined would come about?

Bridgett didn't know.

Wasn't sure she *wanted* to know.

Fiercely, she splayed her hands over the hardness of his chest and drew back. "That was a pretty passionate sentiment, cowboy."

He ran a hand down her spine, positioning her even more securely against him. "You got that, right, sweetheart."

She sighed blissfully, luxuriating in his heat and his

strength. "And here I thought you didn't have a romantic bone in your body."

"I never thought I did." Confident as ever, he ran his hands through her hair and kissed her again, even more thoroughly this time. "Until you showed me otherwise."

Chapter 12

"Three minutes!" Bridgett exclaimed in stunned amazement Saturday morning. It seemed like he had just gone into his home office to monitor the virtual auction, and now he was telling her it was over?

"I got top dollar," Cullen told her proudly. "Way more than I expected."

"Who-all bought them?" Bridgett continued folding laundry.

"The Cartwright Ranch."

"That big outfit in Nebraska?"

Cullen nodded. "Dirk outbid everyone, pushed the price up to a level none of the Texas ranchers could compete with."

Bridgett stood and threw her arms around his neck. "Congratulations."

Grinning, he hugged her back. "Thanks."

"Is it always so fast?"

He joined her on the sofa. "The process has been getting speedier. The first time I did this, it took most of the day to sell them all. Last year, it took me about an hour to sell the entire group."

She took the cell phone out of her hip pocket. "We should call your folks."

His hand covered hers. "Why?"

Stunned by his reluctance, when just seconds before he had been bursting with joy, she turned her palm up to clasp his and tried again. "We should let them know you had a record sale. Heck, we should invite them all over. Have a party to celebrate."

His dark eyes shuttered. He stood and walked away. "Ah, I don't think so."

She followed him into the kitchen. "Why not?" She knew for a fact that the McCabe clan was as big as the Monroe's on family gatherings.

He shrugged and pulled a jug of orange juice out of the fridge. "I just don't think it's a good idea."

Still puzzling over his attitude, she moved closer. "Do you think they won't be happy for you?"

"No." He poured two glasses, recapped the bottle and set it back in the fridge, his expression as careful as his words. "They will be."

O-kay. She lounged with her back against the island, accepting the glass he gave her. Stymied, she studied him over the rim. "Do you think they will expect that you should have gotten a higher return?"

He downed his drink in one long thirsty draught.

Set it aside. "Hell, no. What I got was damn near amazing," he stated firmly. "More than I ever could have anticipated."

"Then what is it?" she asked softly, needing and wanting to understand him. "What's keeping you from wanting to share this very good news with your family?"

"I just think it might be something better done a few weeks from now."

His tone was so vague. "This has something to do with the implied accusation against you, doesn't it?"

"You're right." His lips took on a determined slant. "I'll feel a lot more comfortable facing my family after my name is cleared."

She tried not to notice how handsome he was in a new pair of jeans and canvas shirt that brought out the navy in his eyes. He had also shaved closely that morning. "I think you're underestimating them."

He sighed and sent her a piercing glance. "I think you're underestimating how much I want to enjoy our time together." His eyes met and held hers. "So, what do you say," he drawled, "we focus on that and forget everything else—especially business—for the rest of the day?"

An hour later, the four of them were enjoying a picnic lunch at the Triple Canyon. "So this is where you had your family parties, growing up?"

There were several picnic tables and an open air pavilion at the end of a gravel lane, high atop a rocky ridge. The area was windy and cool, and had a spectacular view of the rocky canyons, wildflower meadows and winding streams that comprised the thousand-acre ranch.

"Except," Bridgett pointed out, "we didn't have the wind turbines along the fence line then."

"It's beautiful."

"And private."

"The little ones like it." Robby was in a BabyBjorn. He had just finished his bottle and was happily nestled against the solid warmth of Cullen's chest. Riot was leashed to one of the tables in the center of the pavilion and was alternately chewing on a couple of dog toys, watching the two of them and looking out onto the amazing vista beyond.

"We all still come here a lot." Bridgett doled out the grilled chicken sandwiches, chips and fruit they'd hastily packed. "Sometimes as a group, sometimes individually."

"I can see why." He uncapped a thermos of hot coffee. "It's a great place for a picnic."

"Especially on a day like today." When they had so much to celebrate, so much at risk...

They lingered over their meal, talking about matters big and small. Finally, Cullen said, "Want to take a selfie, for Robby's baby book?"

Not too long ago, he'd been warning her against getting prematurely attached. Now—to the immense surprise of both of them—his heart was in play, too.

Bridgett smiled. "Why not? I definitely want to remember this."

Bridgett set Riot on her lap. Cullen turned sideways,

so they could see the profile of Robby in his BabyBjorn, sleeping with his head resting on Cullen's chest. They put their heads together, and with his arm outstretched, he took the picture with his phone.

"One more…"

They grinned. Riot—impatient now—let out a happy bark.

Together, they walked the area around the pavilion, found a field of bluebonnets, and—like every other young family in Texas that time of year—took another couple of selfies against a backdrop of wildflowers.

"Speaking of photos," Cullen remarked as they headed back up to the picnic pavilion. "You were going to show me your childhood photos."

"My albums are back at the ranch house, but I've got some of them on my social media pages." She accessed them on her phone.

He studied the photo of her mom, dad and all her siblings. It was the last photo taken of all of them together.

Cullen studied the picture with a wistful gaze. "You look like you were a happy family."

Bridgett nodded, poignant emotion filling her heart as Cullen transferred Robby and the BabyBjorn to her and they settled at a picnic table once again. "We were, until my mom and dad died suddenly in a car crash, and then it was sad chaos for a long time afterward."

He wrapped his arm around her shoulders and brought her—and Robby—into the curve of his body. "How come?"

"My older sister, Erin, was married with three small children. G.W., her husband at the time, was a geologist for an oil company and traveled constantly. My older brother—grumpy old Gavin—was in med school, so he wasn't around a lot to help out."

"Sounds…stressful."

"It was. We sold all the cattle my dad had been running on the ranch. But we still had the Western-wear store in town—Monroe's—that had been in our family for generation to run. So Erin was managing that and the custom boot-making business that went along with it."

"Sounds even harder."

"Then her daughter, Angelica, got seriously ill. G.W. couldn't handle it and checked out. Literally and figuratively. Two years later, when Angelica died at just six, they divorced. Meanwhile, Erin was raising Bess and me, and even though we were teens at the time, we tried to do everything we could to pitch in to help out around the house and also help her look after our baby brother, Nick, who was only ten when our parents passed."

"Sounds unimaginably rough."

"It was. Anyway, we stopped taking group photos after my parents died because it was so hard anyway, without Mom and Dad, and doing that just made us miss them more acutely. So, suffice it to say, there's a big gap in my family photo history. But…" She brightened, glad to have of it all out there, at long last. "I do have these pictures from nursing school."

She thumbed through a couple of dozen pictures on her phone. "I still didn't really want to memorialize anything, but my fellow nursing students took photos of me whether I wanted them to or not, so there are a fair number of them. Including a lot of me and Bess."

"Does this have anything to do with why you resisted getting married right out of college?"

"Ah, perceptive, cowboy."

He waited. Sensing there was more.

She knew that as long as she was baring her soul, she might as well tell him everything—the good, the bad and the ugly. "Yeah. In retrospect, I know it's self-ish, but back then, all I could think was that when my parents passed I was just at the age where I would have started dating, and I had to step in and help Erin out with chores and babysitting her kids as well as my younger brother."

She let it all out in a rush, as her emotions soared out of control. "And then there wasn't enough money, and we all had to put ourselves through college, so Bess and I were always working and going to school, and I felt like I never got the freedom to go out and have fun and do as I please like most of my peers."

"Anyone in your position would have felt the same way, sweetheart," he said softly.

"Maybe, maybe not," she acknowledged. "Anyway…" She stopped and shook her head, comforted by the depth of understanding in Cullen's mesmerizing blue eyes. "The thought of marrying someone I wasn't sure I felt deeply enough about to make a lifelong commitment to….and having a ton of kids right away… seemed like a death sentence."

"Interesting." He tugged tenderly on a lock of her

hair. "When you talked about your ex before, you didn't say you didn't love him."

And she hadn't, for a very good reason. Bridgett gathered her courage and looked deep into Cullen's eyes. "That was because I didn't know what life-changing love was then." *I hadn't found Robby or Riot or spent time with you.* "I know now."

It was Cullen's turn to feel trapped. Not by all that he felt about Bridgett—which he welcomed—but by what he couldn't say just yet.

Not without rushing her into something neither of them was quite ready for. Especially with so much still unresolved. "I'm sorry that you had such a hard time." He leaned down to buss her temple.

She turned slightly and kissed the underside of his jaw. "Right back at you, cowboy." She sighed, still snuggling close, and glanced up at him wryly. "Sounds like the high school years were not particularly good for either of us."

"Maybe it will be different for Robby." He hoped.

Bridgett smiled.

Cullen's phone chimed with a text message from Frank McCabe. Great news on the auction! You've got everyone buzzing. Want to get together to celebrate?

Cullen paused, then punched in a return message. Sounds good. Couple weeks?

A long pause. Let us know where and when.

Bridgett read the exchange. "That was nice."

Cullen nodded, his expression inscrutable.

She studied him, perplexed, able to feel the wall

around his heart going back up. "You don't think it was sincere?" she asked.

"It was."

"Then what's the problem…?"

He shrugged and put his phone away. "Things have just never been that comfortable between us."

"Maybe if you tried harder?" she suggested gently. "Went through that door that he just opened for you?"

Clenching his jaw, Cullen gazed out at the canyons, and Bridgett had never felt more removed from him. She curved her fingers around his forearm. "Look, I know it's none of my business," she pushed on with difficulty. "I just know that if I had another day or hour or minute with my folks, I wouldn't waste it. I'd embrace it with everything I had."

Another terse nod in response.

She could tell by the way he was still studying the wind farm in the distant part of the ranch that he thought she didn't—couldn't—understand.

And maybe she didn't.

Maybe, ever the sentimental fool, she was only seeing what she wanted to see. Not what really was, between him and the McCabes.

One thing was for certain, he did not appreciate what she had said, no matter how well-intentioned it had been.

Cullen was relieved when Bridgett let the subject of his family drop and spent the rest of the day going back to their original plan—which was to celebrate his big win. And it *was* a huge success.

So much so that he felt he might finally be in a financial position to think about settling down. Getting married. Having a family. And there was only one woman he had in mind for that course of action.

Aware it was way too soon to be thinking or talking that way, however, he concentrated on having fun. They went into town for dinner and ate at one of the outside tables along the sidewalk so that Robby could hang out in his stroller while a leashed Riot lounged at their feet.

The next day, however, work called. He had 500 head of cattle that had been sold to be separated into smaller, manageable groups and moved to pastures closer to ranch roads.

He came in at dark that evening, exhausted, and was welcomed with a nice hot dinner that Bridgett had made. A nighttime walk with Riot and cuddling with Robby followed that, and bedtime meant sweet and tender lovemaking with Bridgett.

The next morning brought more of the same.

He paused before heading out. Bridgett looked gorgeous, her hair all tousled, cheeks still pink with sleep. "You going to be okay alone today?"

She smiled, amused. "I think I can manage, cowboy."

"Mitzy… Dan…the search."

She heaved a big sigh. "I haven't forgotten it's Monday and they are headed to the high school to try and identify the three girls. I've just been trying not to think about it."

"Good plan."

She looked so vulnerable.

"You know, you could always call in reinforcements for Riot and Robby, and saddle up."

She wrinkled her nose. "What makes you think I know how to herd cattle?"

"You said your dad raised cattle until you were fourteen…"

"Fine. So I might know a thing or two about herding. And your point is?"

"Thought you might enjoy a change of scenery." He sat down on the edge of the bed and enveloped her in a hug. Anything to keep her from worrying too much.

She splayed her hands across his chest. Her eyes were all soft and misty. "Maybe one day," she promised softly. "Today, I'm going to be all mom."

He couldn't blame her for wanting to cherish every second. "I'll have my cell phone with me. If you hear anything…"

"I'll call. Promise."

He brought her close for another hug. He breathed in the womanly scent of her. "You're going to get the family you want, sweetheart."

She drew back, her lower lip quivering, no longer the ultraconfident Bridgett he'd clashed with in the hospital nursery. "How do you know?" she whispered.

Easy. He buried his face in the fragrant softness of her hair. "Because I am personally going to see to it."

One way or another she would have a baby and puppy to love, a husband who cherished her, and a place for them all to call home.

And when that happened, they would both know what true contentment was.

* * *

For Bridgett, the day went on forever. She hated when life spiraled out of her control. The way it had when her parents died. The way it was now. The only help for that was activity focused on someone else.

And that someone was Cullen.

He had done so much for her and Robby and Riot.

Been so kind and selfless and downright heroic.

She knew she owed him, big time. She also realized there was one thing she could do for him, and she hoped that would be just as meaningful. So she worked on arranging it all day long, via phone calls, texts and emails. And by late afternoon her big thank-you to him was all set.

And still there was no word from the sheriff's department or social services.

Finally, just as Cullen was coming in from the range at five in the evening, Mitzy stopped by. The social worker looked as frustrated as Bridgett felt. "No news?" she guessed.

Mitzy set her bag down. "We were able to ID all three girls. Sherri and Dawn are still students at the high school in San Angelo. The tall one—with the dark curly hair, Marie Griffin—dropped out in January, said she hadn't been getting along with her parents and was going off to live with her grandmother in Tulsa."

"And…?"

"Dan checked. Her grandmother died last summer."

Bridgett's heart lurched in her chest. "So, where is she?"

Cullen moved in, simultaneously taking her hand and pushing her onto the closest seat—a kitchen stool.

The social worker frowned. "We don't know. Dan's trying to track Mr. and Mrs. Griffin down now. I got their phone numbers from the school, too. We're both leaving messages all over the place. If we don't have any luck, we'll ask the two other girls, but records show they have been in school with only a couple intermittent absences, due to illness, this semester, so I'm not sure if they will be able to tell us anything or not."

"Do school officials think Marie Griffin might have been pregnant?" Cullen asked.

"The guidance counselor wasn't sure. She just recalled her looking both stressed and relieved the day Marie came in to say she was leaving."

"The time frame fits," Cullen said.

Mitzy nodded. "It does. Although no one at the school recalls Marie dating anyone there. She was a pretty quiet seventeen-year-old. Actually, she's eighteen now. She had a birthday last month."

"So now what?" Bridgett asked, beginning to feel her life spiraling out of control again.

Mitzy sighed. "We let Dan do his job. I'll do mine. As soon as we learn anything else, we'll contact you. In the meantime, stay put. Stay calm. And Bridgett?" She paused, beaming her approval. "The new plan for your living arrangements is likely to go over *much better* with the department heads at DCFS and the family court judge."

Chapter 13

New plan? What new plan? Cullen wondered. He stayed inside with Robby and Riot while Bridgett walked the social worker out. When she came back in, he noticed her face was flushed with emotion. He didn't know whether to feel concerned for her welfare or betrayed. The truth was, he felt a little of both. "What was Mitzy talking about?"

"You know I have my meeting with the social services department on Thursday afternoon, to talk about Robby's placement." Bridgett was chipper, as always, when things were going her way.

"I knew it was this week. I don't think you had told me when, though."

In the laundry room, the washer dinged, signaling the cycle had finished. She spun around and headed for the small space, leaving him to follow. "Well, it could still be moved up or back, depending on what happens with Marie Griffin, and so on. But I was only initially allowed to foster Robby because his health was uncertain and I was an approved foster mother who was also a registered nurse, and an N-ICU, one at that."

He lounged against the door, giving her room to work. "I remember."

"Luckily, Robby has been healthy."

He let his gaze rove from the satisfied curve of her soft lips to her sparkling green eyes. "His umbilical cord hasn't fallen off yet."

"Actually, it did. This morning. In his diaper."

Aware she was awaiting his reaction to such momentous new parent news, he said, "Oh."

"So…" Bridgett bent to take the clothes from the dryer and drop them into an empty laundry basket "…from the standpoint of his health, anyway, there is no more reason why he would need to be placed with me, specifically."

He tore his eyes from the enticing way her knee-length cotton skirt hugged her slender hips and her cotton blouse her breasts as she moved the damp baby clothes from washer to dryer.

"Except he loves you and is used to you, and I'm damn sure, thinks of you as his mommy."

"And you his daddy." She shut the door and leaned across the top of the machine to set the dials and switch it on. Swinging back to him, she leaned up against the machine, her hands braced on either side of her. "But we both know that could—maybe will—change." Her mouth took on a sober line.

A tense silence fell.

"What does Mitzy have to say about all this?"

"She's going to support me in my request to continue beyond the approved two-week period and foster-adopt," she informed him. "But I need to have all my ducks in a row. Including and especially the housing issue."

"I told you. You can continue to stay here as long as you like. You all can."

Briefly, gratitude shone in her eyes. "I know." Her soft lips took on a new, troubled slant. "But... Mitzy feels that because you and I have no longstanding commitment to each, other than the one we have forged the last twelve days or so, coupled with the fact that I have decided to take a full maternity leave from the hospital...and lost the house I was applying for a mortgage for...that I need to have a more solid housing plan in place."

"And now you have one?" he asked, with a great deal more equanimity than he felt.

"Yes, we do," she answered with a nod. "My twin, Bess, and I are going to buy a house together. We were both planning on purchasing our own homes, individually, but we could just as easily pool our funds and buy a bigger place to accommodate all of us right now. And we could stagger our work schedules so that there would always be one of us there for Robby. Hence, he wouldn't need to go into day care at all!"

It was a great solution. One DCFS would have trouble finding fault in. The only one not served well by it was him. He swallowed his hurt and anger and forced himself to be the Texas gentleman he had been raised to be. "How long is all that going to take?"

"Well, that's the rub." Reaching up, Bridgett undid the clasp holding her hair up on the back of her head. She clipped it to the open neckline of her blouse. "Bess and I haven't started looking yet, and we'd have to find a place and go through the whole mortgage process."

With a beleaguered sigh, she ran her fingers through the silky strands, combing them into place. "So, in the interim, Robby and Riot and I would need a place to stay."

She retwisted her hair and knotted it on the back of her head again. "Nick and Sage have invited us to bunk with them at the Triple Canyon as soon as the remodeling is complete, in another month. In the meantime..."

Her eyes lifted to his and a muscle ticked in his jaw as he listened in silence.

"...Sage's mother, Lucille Lockhart, has said we could all move out to the guest quarters on her Circle H ranch—a six bath, six bedroom bunkhouse with full kitchen and living area. As well as staff at our disposable, should we need it."

She sounded really happy and relieved about all of this. Which begged the question—did she really not know how bereft the new arrangement would leave him?

He forced himself to do what she was doing, and focus on the welfare of their two little charges. "Seems like you have it all figured out."

She studied him, intuitive as always. "You're upset. Or maybe insulted?"

He definitely felt burned by the way she had left him out of the equation. No question. Although maybe he shouldn't. She'd made it clear from the start that her fling with him, as well as her lodging here, was only a temporary solution to a very long-term problem.

She caught his hand in hers. "Please tell me what's on your mind."

The feel of her smooth skin touching his brought only partial comfort. He shrugged and tried to summon up what little gallantry he seemed to have left. "I'm just wondering if I should read anything into this."

She blinked. "What do you mean?"

With a disgruntled frown, he stepped back. "It's interesting that you will buy a property with your sister, but not allow me to buy you the house that you wanted in town, and rent it back to you, thereby eliminating all these complicated financial and domestic arrangements." *That are going to take you and Riot and Robby away from the Western Cross and away from me.*

She leaned back against the washer and looked up at him. "It's not the help I'm rejecting. It's the way it might look to outsiders."

Unsure what she meant, he waited.

"I guess if we are able to locate the biological mother and get proof the baby isn't yours, then that part of the scandal goes away and anything you do would be viewed as noble. If we don't..." She flushed and shook her head in silent remonstration. "Then, as you said, people are always going to wonder."

Reluctantly, he had to admit to himself that she had a point.

"And if you buy a home to house the kid—and his caretaker—in, people will *really* wonder. It will fuel the talk. It'll hurt your reputation. And my chances to foster-adopt."

Unfortunately, Cullen had to admit, that was true, too.

Her eyes shone. "It will also make it look like I can't do this as a single parent." Her low tone took on a defiant edge. "When we both know I can. I just need a little help to get started, since this was all so sudden. And my family, the whole Monroe clan, and even Lucille Lockhart—my brother's mother-in-law—will be here to back me up. Now and in the future. You yourself have promised me the same."

He certainly had.

Glad she had taken his offer to heart, he listened quietly as she continued.

"As you pointed out, that is a very powerful statement to make on my behalf. Mitzy agrees. She thinks her supervisors and the family court judge will, too. In fact, with this new plan and all the concrete ways my siblings have vowed to help me, she thinks I now have a real shot to foster-adopt Robby."

Cullen could see how much this meant to her.

Worse, he felt like the world's biggest jackass for making this more about him and their new romance than the two little ones they should be looking out for.

"Of course, it goes without saying—" Bridgett choked up "—I want you to be a part of our lives, even after we move out." She waved a hasty hand, amending in a low, strangled voice. "If that's what you want, of course."

He took her in his arms, holding her close. "Of course it's what I want, sweetheart." He buried his face in the intoxicating lavender fragrance of her hair. "Never ever doubt that, okay?"

"O-kay." She sniffled. "I'm sorry I didn't tell you. I just…" She gulped and went on, voice even more wobbly. "I wasn't sure how you'd take it."

He drew back. "Badly?"

She laughed, as he meant her to. But her smile trembled as tears glistened in her eyes.

And suddenly he knew her moving out was going to be every bit as difficult for her as it was for him. "I'll miss you," he rasped. "When you go." *If you go.* He was still working on a plan to keep her here. And not just temporarily.

"I'll miss you, too." She hugged him back.

He lowered his head and delivered a tender kiss. "But let's not get ahead of ourselves here. You-all aren't gone yet."

That night, after they put the little ones to bed, they made love again. He laid claim to her lips and body as he wanted to lay claim to her heart and soul. And this time, when they came together in shattering sensation, he knew—even if she didn't, yet—that there was no going back for either of them. She belonged to him, and he to her, and that was the way it was always going to be. Together, they would have the passionate relationship

and family they had both always wanted. Whether she—
and Robby and Riot—moved out temporarily or not.

Bridgett had known that Cullen wouldn't be happy
about her news. She had also known he was practical
enough to understand why she had to lean on her family more than him right now.

The sexy, tender way he'd made love to her the night
before had proved it.

She'd returned the gesture by putting all the hope
she felt for their future into her lovemaking, too. Hence,
they both woke up in a fine mood. Which was a good
thing. Tuesday was going to be a big day. "The trucks
are here." Bridgett marveled at the sight shortly after
dawn.

One after another, the cattle haulers and Cartwright
Ranch trucks rumbled up the road.

His expression now all business, Cullen watched a
late model luxury pickup park close to the ranch house.
"And so is Dirk Cartwright." He grabbed his hat from
the hook by the door and settled it on his head.

Bridgett resisted the urge to kiss Cullen goodbye, the
way a wife did when she sent her husband off to work,
and contented herself with one last long look, instead.
"I didn't realize he was coming here, too." She followed
him to the door.

"A purchase this big?" Cullen flashed a smile. He
bent his head and briefly captured her lips. "He's going
to want to check on the herd in person."

While Bridgett and the baby watched from the window, Cullen met the snowy-haired rancher outside.

The hardy six-foot cattleman vigorously shook Cullen's hand. The two set off.

All morning long, both the Western Cross and Cartwright Ranch crews worked fiercely. One by one the big semi cattle haulers and the Cartwright Ranch pickup trucks drove away.

At one point, the two men left, too.

When Cullen returned, he was alone and looking a little shell-shocked. Bridgett met him at the door. "Are you okay?"

Noting all was quiet, Cullen took her by the hand and led her back onto the front porch so they could talk. "Dirk Cartwright made me an incredible, unexpected offer. He wants to sell me the Cartwright Ranch."

Bridgett did a double take. "In Nebraska?"

Cullen nodded and sat down the steps, overlooking the ranch. "Sixty-five thousand acres. Five thousand head of cattle."

Bridgett settled beside him. "That's more than your dad has, isn't it?"

He nodded.

She turned slightly to face him, her bent knee nudging his muscular thigh. "Can you afford it?"

He grinned. "Here's the miraculous part." He leaned forward in a confidence-inspiring pose, forearms on his thighs. "Dirk Cartwright wants me to move there *now* and begin managing the operation. And buy in incrementally, year by year, until I own it all a decade from now."

A front was moving in, turning the late-afternoon

sky a dark blue-gray. Bridgett shivered in the newly cool air. "You'd sell the place here?"

Cullen nodded, seeming oblivious to the damp, chilly air. "I'd have to. But it wouldn't be a problem. Jeanne Phipps has told me more than once she could sell any property I renovate."

Bridgett folded her arms in front of her to cover up the pearling of her nipples and wished she'd thought to put on a sweater. "You wouldn't flip the Cartwright place?"

"No." His voice was casual. "It's state-of-the-art already. I'd probably change the name once I owned it, though."

Her heart skidded to a halt, then took up an erratic beat. She perched on the edge of the top step. "So, are you going to take him up on his offer?"

Even though he had just been talking like the decision were already made—at least on some level—Cullen seemed brought up short by her assumption. He turned to her, dark brow furrowed. "I don't know. I can barely wrap my head around it right now." He paused to study her in concern. "This upsets you?"

What could she say to that that would be true and wouldn't hurt him? After all, he had supported her through so much, worked side by side with her to see she achieved her dreams. Which, even now, weren't quite within reach. Even if they soon would be.

Scolding herself for her selfishness, she straightened. "No, of course not. I'm proud of you, Cullen."

And she was. She was just sad for herself. Because once again, she was involved with a man who had dreams that were right for him and not for her. She feigned an enthusiasm she couldn't begin to feel. "How long do you have?" she asked brightly.

"Dirk Cartwright told me to take a couple of weeks to think about it." He shook his head. "I don't think it will take that long to make a decision, though."

Bridgett knew what she hoped it would be.

The phone rang. He looked at his caller ID. "It's Dan." He picked up and put the call on speakerphone so Bridgett could hear. "Hey, little brother. Got some news for us?"

"As a matter of fact," Dan said gruffly, his voice coming out loud and clear, "I do. We still haven't been able to locate either Marie Griffin or her parents but we *did* talk to the neighbors at their home in San Angelo."

Bridgett tensed.

Cullen put his arm around her.

"And?" he prodded.

Dan continued, "They said Mr. and Mrs. Griffin aren't exactly model parents. In fact, they've complained for years about how the burden of having a child in their teens cramped their style. When they came into a small inheritance late last fall, they quit their jobs and put their home on the market. It sold around Valentine's Day. They stored what few belongings they decided to keep, then took off to backpack across every mountain range in America."

Cullen asked, "Did their daughter go with them?"

"No. According to her parents, she took off in January to start living her own life. Which they had expected her to do, anyway, as soon as she was eighteen. The fact she left a little earlier than that was not a surprise to her folks. They said she was always independent to a fault."

"Independent or neglected?" Bridgett murmured.

Dan exhaled. "From the sound of it, a little of both. Anyway, no one has seen any of the Griffins in several months. Although we do have the parents' cell phone numbers and we are still trying to get in touch with them."

"What about Marie?" Cullen asked. "Does she have a cell phone?"

Dan exhaled. "No one knows. What they do know is that the parents refused to pay for one. Said whatever Marie had, she had to earn."

"So we still have no idea where Marie is?" Cullen asked, sounding impatient once again.

"None. We had the school guidance counselor call in her friends, Sherri and Dawn, today. She asked them if they had any info on their friend. They both said no."

Noting how nervous Bridgett was getting, Cullen wrapped his arm even more tightly about her shoulders. "Did the counselor believe them?" he asked.

Dan scoffed. "Not for a red-hot minute. So Mitzy and I are going to the school to talk to them tomorrow afternoon. The school asked that their parents be there, too, so that was as soon as we could arrange it."

"You'll let us know?"

"We will." Dan paused. "And since Bridgett is there with you, on to a more cheerful note—when is the party starting?"

Chapter 14

"Party?" Cullen rolled to his feet as a bevy of vehicles came down the lane.

"Actually…" Bridgett winced, standing, too, and wishing she'd had a moment to prepare Cullen for the celebration she had planned. "The McCabes are already arriving en masse." It was Cullen she hadn't exactly expected to be here yet.

"Great! Be there in fifteen."

Cullen turned to her, an unreadable expression on his face. Without warning, they were back to the first day in the hospital corridor with him not trusting her one bit. "Bridgett? What's going on?" he ground out.

Too late, she realized she'd made a huge mistake. "Surprise!" she said weakly.

He wheeled around and strode across the porch and

back into the ranch house. Fury emanated from every pore. "Who-all did you invite?"

She struggled to keep up with him. "Frank and Rachel. Your five siblings."

He drummed his fingers on the kitchen island. "Anyone else?"

"Ah...no." She hadn't been quite sure how this was going to go, so she hadn't wanted an audience if it turned out to be unbearably awkward.

He exhaled heavily. Abruptly looking as if he had the whole world on his shoulders. "I wish you hadn't done this," he said.

Right now, so did she. "Too late," she offered brightly, as Robby, alert to the new tension in the ranch house, began to fuss. Bridgett went to get the baby. Riot, who'd been sleeping on his cushion, got up, went into the very back of his crate and settled there, watchful.

Rachel and Frank came through the back door, bearing food and beverages. "Congratulations!" Rachel said, stopping to kiss Cullen on the cheek. "We're so glad you agreed to have a party now!"

Except he hadn't agreed, Bridgett thought, observing her lover's smile. He hadn't known anything about it. And clearly would have vetoed it wholeheartedly if he had.

Rachel set cellophane-covered trays of oven-ready enchiladas down. She turned back to Cullen to give him another big hug. "We are so proud of you! Selling out the entire group in three minutes!"

Finally, Cullen began to relax. He couldn't help but smile at his stepmother's warm approval. "It was something, all right."

"A record for the Western Cross!" Frank stepped up to shake his eldest son's hand.

Matt McCabe came in. The military vet had been uncharacteristically joyless since returning from Afghanistan several months prior. Still, he managed a respectful smile as he put down the beer and sodas he carried and strode over to give Cullen a high five. "Way to go, man."

"Thanks," Cullen said.

Jack McCabe came in, carrying big take-out containers of Mexican rice and beans. The orthopedic surgeon had his two-, three-and four-year-old daughters—and their fifty-year-old nanny—in tow. Tragically widowed almost two years ago, he was being chased by hordes of women but had vowed far and wide to remain single for the rest of his life.

He set the offerings on the counter, next to the enchiladas, held out his hand to Cullen. "You've got my respect, brother."

Cullen nodded. He dipped his head toward Jack's brood. "Right back at you."

Businessman Chase McCabe came in, carrying a brand-new fine leather saddle from his manufacturing firm in one hand and a boxed cake in the other. He set the cake down and handed the saddle to Cullen. "Proud of you, man. And now that you're such a big shot, maybe you could test this out for me and let me know what you think."

"Thanks." Cullen shook his hand, practically beaming now. "I will."

Beginning to relax—it looked like this hastily ar-

ranged family get-together might work out, after all—
Bridgett grinned, too.

Cullen's baby sister, Lulu McCabe, breezed through
the door carrying a big bag of fresh flour tortillas from
the Mexican bakery in town and a bottle of honey from
her own hives. She set both down on the counter, then
turned to hug Cullen and offer her congratulations.
"And to celebrate," she finished happily, "I've got everything we need for sopaipillas!"

Last but not least, Dan came in, still in his sheriff's
deputy uniform, carrying a big bag of freshly made restaurant tortilla chips and salsas. "Way to go!" He took
Cullen by the shoulder, brought him in close and shook
his hand. "You've turned Western Cross into one fine
ranch, brother!"

Unable to keep quiet any longer, Bridgett burst in,
"You don't know the half of it! You should hear about
the offer he just got!"

Thunderstruck, Cullen turned to her.

"What?" Rachel buzzed, excited, too.

Cullen seemed at a loss as to how to begin to tell them.
Bridgett helped him along. "Dirk Cartwright was just
here. He offered Cullen a stake in his Nebraska ranch."

The only one in the room who did not look surprised
by the revelation was Frank McCabe. "What kind of
stake?" his father asked.

Briefly, Cullen explained what he had already told
Bridgett. With a lot less enthusiasm this time.

"So, you'd have to pull up stakes and leave here?"
Rachel asked, clearly upset by the notion.

Her husband turned to her. "It's an offer of a lifetime, honey. I think he has to at least consider it."

"Well, I disagree," Lulu said, going to stand beside her brother. She wrapped an arm about his waist and grinned up at him. "I like having you here. I don't care what anyone in town has been saying!"

Tensing, Chase warned, "Lulu…"

"What?" The ebullient beekeeper turned around. "We're not going to talk about the elephant in the room? We have to! Sorry, Bridgett, but we have to discuss this."

Bridgett agreed. Cullen needed to know—directly from them—how much his family supported him.

Quietly, the nanny caught Jack's eye and ushered his children out to the back porch to play.

With the young audience gone, Lulu continued, "Personally, I think all the rumors were starting to force the price of your cattle down, even drive some potential buyers out entirely. Thank heaven Cartwright came along and saved the day with his bid. Talk about perfect timing!"

"It was, wasn't it," Cullen said. To Bridgett's dismay, his cold, peremptory tone had everyone in the room staring and going silent. "The only question is," Cullen continued with sad resignation, "how did Dirk Cartwright happen to do just that?"

Cullen wasn't surprised no one answered. Only his father seemed to know where he was going with this. Heart aching, he strode forward to confront the man whose respect he most wanted. The bitterness of all the years spent elsewhere clogged his throat. Reduced once again to the black sheep, illegitimate son, he rasped, "Tell me. How much did you have to pay Cartwright to offer me a job elsewhere?"

Rachel gasped, her hand flying to her throat.

Frank's gaze narrowed in steely warning. "Careful, son."

Cullen knew he should keep his feelings to himself, the way he had for years now. This once, however, he couldn't do it. Maybe because he had worked his ass off to earn his father's love and respect, only to have this brick wall between them remain.

Able to feel Bridgett quaking beside him, he kept his eyes locked with Frank's. Then he shook his head and shrugged off the soul-deep disappointment. "I understand why you'd want me gone. I'm nothing but a reminder of a time, with my mother, you to want to forget."

"You don't know what I want to remember and what I don't," Frank returned.

"Ah, maybe we should leave," Dan cut in uncomfortably.

"Nope," Frank said, his hard, uncompromising gaze still locked with Cullen's. "Everyone stay. We're having this out here and now."

Rachel, Lulu and Bridgett all eased onto the padded island stools. The men remained standing at various places along the counters.

Frank looked at Cullen, for once not about to mince words, either. "I loved my time with your mother. I would have married her, had she been willing. And I certainly would have stepped up from the get-go had I known she was carrying my child. But I didn't and we can't change that. All we can do is move forward with the love we should have had all along."

His eyes glistened as his voice grew hoarse. "And I do love you, Cullen. Every bit as much as I love my five other children and Rachel. You are a part of this family," he continued sternly. "You always will be. I know you've felt you never really belonged here, but you're wrong. You do."

Cullen stared at his dad, clearly taken aback by the emotional declaration.

"Would I go out of my way to help you succeed in business?" He shook his head. "That answer is more complicated."

Frank paused again, "If you came to me, asking for help, which you haven't, none of you have, I would consider it. But mostly," he continued, putting his arm around his wife, "I expect every single one of you to make your own way, the way Rachel and I did, and the way your mother apparently did, too, Cullen."

Cullen paused, accepting that.

Frank continued resolutely, "It is not the result that impresses me." He shrugged. "It never has been. It's the effort." He looked at all six of his children. "I want to know that whatever you decide to do, you've given it your best effort."

Silence fell.

Cullen continued to look at his father and Frank stared right back, a telltale glimmer in his gaze. Cullen felt his own eyes welling. Bridgett was tearing up, too. And they weren't the only ones.

Guilt spread through him, along with the relief.

Smiling, he realized, he wasn't being forced out. No one here wanted him to go.

Especially and including the remarkable woman who had arranged the festivities.

"Now—" Frank scrubbed a hand over his face, a smile spreading "—last I heard, we had a celebration happening here..."

"I made a horse's ass out of myself, didn't I?" Cullen sighed, hours after everyone had finally left.

"Yes. But you and your dad hugged and made up, and everyone else was finally able to breathe a sigh of relief—because you both did say all that—and nothing happened except everyone finally knew what he and you were both thinking and feeling."

Fine lines appeared at the corners of his eyes, and he smiled. "It's funny. I never knew he loved me. He never said it. Until tonight."

Bridgett snuggled in the curve of his body, loving his warmth and his strength. "Maybe he didn't think he needed to. Maybe he thought you knew."

He slid his thumbs beneath her chin and raised her face to his. "You've got a point, darlin'," he told her tenderly. "None of us go around saying we love each other all the time, yet...we feel it...even when we're not physically together."

Bridgett turned her head slightly and kissed the center of Cullen's palm. "It's the same with my sibs."

They stood in the kitchen, locked in each other's arms, both baby and puppy contentedly sleeping in their beds.

Looking pretty relaxed and happy, too, Cullen exhaled and looked around. "It was a good party, wasn't it?"

"It was," Bridgett murmured.

The food had been a stellar impromptu Mexican feast. The hot sopaipillas, covered with confectioner's sugar and drizzled with homemade honey, had been the crowning glory.

Everyone had helped clean up, then gone home well fed and happy. The goodbye hugs had been long and fierce and genuine.

No one had commented further on the proposition Cullen had received. But Bridgett thought she knew what they all felt. Unable to stand the suspense any longer, she asked impulsively, "What are you going to do about the offer Dirk Cartwright made?" *Please don't tell me you're packing up and moving to Nebraska.*

Cullen exhaled, his expression maddeningly inscrutable. "Honestly? I don't know yet. I have to think about it."

It was what she had thought he would say, given the scope of the opportunity. Still, Bridgett could not deny she was disappointed.

He turned, backing her up against the counter. Caging her in with his arms on either side of her, he slanted his head over hers and lowered his mouth to hers. The kiss was an explosion of tenderness and heat, longing and fulfillment.

She knew he wasn't in love with her, but when they were together like this, she felt loved. Warm and safe. She felt secure in her life in a way she had never felt before.

They made their way to the bedroom and undressed each other in the moonlight. They kissed and stroked and caressed until she thought she would melt from the inside out. He reached into the nightstand and found a condom. She sheathed him, protecting them both.

Her eyes drifted shut as he parted her thighs and settled between them. Cupping her bottom, he lifted her toward him. Sliding home. Going deeper, and deeper still, until pleasure flooded her in fierce, unchecked waves. And then there was no more holding back. She shifted, so she was straddling his hips, her moan of ecstasy mingling with his.

And still he kissed her, taking her, the delicious glide in. And out. And back in...

He laid claim to her as no one ever had before. Kissing her breasts. Diving deep. Incoherent, she let her head fall back. Gave herself over to him and the feelings gathering deep inside her.

She'd thought she could separate love and desire. Make love with him without being *in love* with him.

She'd been wrong. He made her feel like a complete family was within her reach. That it was okay to want... everything. As long as it was with him. And, heaven help her, she did.

Wednesday afternoon, Mitzy summoned them to the Social Services office in San Angelo. The teenage girls were not being cooperative. It was Mitzy's hope Bridgett and Cullen might be able to help get the information they needed, so of course they agreed to go.

She and Cullen were silent on the drive, each of them wrapped in their own thoughts.

Finally, they walked into the building together. They

signed in at the reception desk and made their way to the appropriate conference room, Bridgett carrying Robby and Cullen leading Riot.

Around the large table were the two teenagers, their parents, Dan and Mitzy. Sherri and Dawn both looked mutinous. And guilty.

"As you can see," Mitzy observed kindly, indicating the baby and puppy with a tilt of her head, "Robby and Riot are both fine."

Dan added with law enforcement practicality, "But it's been a hard road for Bridgett, the nurse who found the baby and the puppy, and Cullen, the man who was charged with caring for them."

Actually, it hadn't been much of a burden at all.

It was not knowing what was going to happen next that was tearing her heart apart, Bridgett thought anxiously.

The girls couldn't take their eyes off the baby or the puppy.

They looked incredibly relieved, yet somehow awestruck.

The way Mitzy was looking at her, silently beseeching her to take the lead, Bridgett knew it was up to her to somehow find a way to reach them and get them talking.

So, using the same approach she used with the parents of her tiny patients at the hospital N-ICU, she started with the truth.

"We're worried about Marie," Bridgett stated matter-of-factly, cuddling Robby close. "When a woman gives birth, she needs proper care during her pregnancy, the actual birth and the aftermath. If the mother doesn't get it at any one of those stages, there are a multitude of complications that can occur, some of them even life threatening. Plus, there are the emotional aspects of giving birth and surrendering a child to be dealt with."

She turned to Cullen.

He weighed in. "If you've helped her…we know you were too young to be thrust into this situation. That you stepped up, anyway, and did the best you could in a very difficult situation. And we want you to know we're all grateful." Cullen looked Sherri and Dawn in the eye. "Everyone last one of us."

Mitzy and Dan backed this up.

Bridgett pressed on emotionally. "But we still need to find Marie. Make sure she is okay."

"Can't she just go to a doctor anywhere?" Sherri asked belligerently.

"Why would she need to do it here—assuming she did have anything to do with this, anyway?" Dawn added hastily.

Firmly, Bridgett explained. "Because time is of the essence if Marie does have any kind of postpartum health problems."

Sherri bit her lip. "What would that look like?"

Bridgett listed the most obvious. "Fever. Flu-like symptoms. Soreness around the area of the birth canal. Menstrual-type bleeding that goes on and on…"

Sherri and Dawn both paled. Dawn said, "You're a nurse. Can't you help her?"

Bridgett was trying. "She really should be seen by an obstetrician."

Cullen cut in, "I think it might help Marie to physically see Robby and Riot, and know they are all right, too."

"Bottom line," Bridgett said, knowing it was the right thing to do, even as it cost her dearly. "Marie needs to know she still has options." Even as her heart was breaking, she paused to let the weight of her words sink in. "That nothing has been set in stone. She had no support system prior to this. We can and will give her that."

Whether through social services, or her—and perhaps Cullen's—own largesse, if need be.

"Then..." Bridgett took another deep breath, and pushed the words through the ache in her throat. "When Marie's had time to really think about it and consider, she can decide with an open heart and open mind what she wants to do. Give the baby and puppy over for adoption. Or—" It was all she could do not to break into sobs herself as she prepared to give up what she wanted so dearly in order to do what her heart was telling her was the right and decent thing. "Or receive a lot of help—and there is a lot of that out there—and keep them."

Because, as much as Bridgett wanted to keep Robby and Riot, she was not going to do it at another woman's expense. Not under these horrific circumstances.

Sherri and Dawn looked at each other. "You'd really do that for her?" Dawn asked in amazement. Staring at her as if she were an angel just sent down from heaven.

Bridgett thought of Robby, who was so sweet, so innocent and untouched by all this. And Cullen, who'd suffered because he hadn't known his biological father for so long. And Marie, who apparently had grown up a burden to her own parents, feeling unwanted and un-supported. And probably unloved, as well.

Robby might not care now who had given birth to him. But one day he would. He'd want to know where he came from and why his birth mother had given him away. And though it would be difficult to face, in the long run it would be better for all involved if they used every avenue available to them to help his mother, the way they had helped him and his puppy companion. They all needed to know where—and with whom—Robby and Riot really and truly belonged.

Otherwise they'd always wonder. Always feel guilty. Always feel like maybe they hadn't done enough for everyone involved—and should have.

Bridgett looked at Mitzy, Dan and Cullen, the parents of the teens, the girls themselves.

They were staring at her as if they couldn't believe her unselfishness.

She knew she had surprised them. She had surprised herself. She hadn't thought she had it in her to love and possibly let go.

She'd just found out she did.

Heaven help her, heaven help Cullen, she did.

Chapter 15

An hour later, they finally had the news they had been waiting for. The two teens had confirmed what everyone else had long suspected, that Cullen was not related to Robby biologically in any way. And Marie Griffin had been found at Dawn's family's vacation home on Lake Laramie.

Cullen and Bridgett left the family crisis center and made their way to the Laramie Community Hospital, where the teenage mother had been taken. Mitzy Martin arrived just ahead of them and was there to greet them. Bridgett had called Violet and Gavin, and they'd taken Robby and Riot to their home nearby.

"How is she?" Bridgett asked, her nurse's training kicking in.

Mitzy had just spoken with the ER doctor. "Dehydrated. Suffering from a mild pelvic infection. A few days in the hospital with some IV fluids and antibiotics and she should be okay."

Bridgett and Cullen breathed a mutual sigh of relief.

In full social-worker mode, Mitzy escorted them to the second floor. "I filled Marie in about the two of you taking care of Robby and Riot. She asked to speak to you both. So if you-all are okay with that...?"

Bridgett looked at Cullen, unsure where the latest developments left the two of them, since his name had now been cleared. "Do you want to do this together?"

"Wouldn't have it any other way," he said gruffly.

He took her hand and gave it a hard, reassuring squeeze. Their gazes meshed and they took a simultaneous breath, then walked in.

Marie Griffin was sitting up in a hospital bed, an IV in her arm. Her long, curly brown hair was drawn into a low ponytail. Clad in a hospital gown, covers pulled up to her waist, she looked pale and anxious. And so very young and vulnerable.

Mitzy Martin made introductions then eased away from the bed so Cullen and Bridgett could step in.

Marie swallowed. "I guess you remember me?"

Cullen nodded. "You and your friends were at the high school Career Fair in San Angelo last fall."

Marie flashed a wan, grateful smile. "You came to talk to us about ranching and what it meant to you. How you moved around a lot when you were a kid, but even when you felt your dog, Riot, was your only friend, you were always able to find something worthwhile and satisfying to do on the ranch."

"You asked a lot of questions."

Marie sighed wistfully. "I always wanted to live on a ranch. Work with horses. Maybe cattle, too. I just couldn't figure out a way to make it happen." She knitted her hands together.

Bridgett saw her nails were bitten to the quick.

"But I knew I was going to have to do something since all the rest of my dreams had just gone bust." In a halting voice, she told them about the clandestine romance she'd had with a boy she'd met at a weekend-long concert in Houston the previous summer. By the time she realized he had been lying to her about everything, including his name and phone number, he had disappeared and she was pregnant. Unable to turn to her parents, she'd gone to a couple of her girlfriends for help.

"I had a lot of time to think about who I wanted to give my kid to when he or she was born, and I kept going back to Cullen. He seemed so good and kind. And he sort of looked like the baby daddy, too." She released a quavering breath. "And then, when Riot showed up on my doorstep, just a tiny shivering little thing last February, I thought of the stray dog that Cullen found when he was a kid. It seemed like a huge sign. So my girlfriends and I figured out a plan to take them both to the Laramie fire station and leave them for Cullen."

"Except I found them," Bridgett put in.

"I know. We saw. We were hiding a short distance away, just to make sure that Robby and Riot got found. When they did, we went back to the lake house."

"Where you've been ever since," Cullen said gently.

Tears shining in her eyes, Marie nodded.

Bridgett took her hand. "You don't have to run any-more. Cullen and I will be here to see that you and Robby and Riot get everything you need."

"You mean that?" Marie's lower lip trembled.

Bridgett looked at Cullen. He nodded in solidarity. "We do."

"I just have one question."

They waited.

Marie's chin quivered. She regarded Bridgett soberly. "Mitzy told me that you've been fostering them. I know you've been taking great care of both Robby and Riot, on Cullen's ranch, and that Cullen has been helping out a lot, too. But...do you think you could ever love them? The way I can't? The way really great parents always do?"

Bridgett nodded, her heart bursting wide open. "Oh, honey, I already do." She bit her lip, trying hard not to cry. "I have since the start."

Marie turned. "What about you, Cullen?"

His eyes filled with emotion. He closed his fist and tapped the region over his heart in the age-old sign of love and solidarity. "They're right here, kid," he finally said in a rusty-sounding voice. "They always will be." He paused. "No matter what happens."

He was doing the decent thing, just as Bridgett had. Giving the troubled teen an emotional out from a deci-sion she'd made under extreme duress. Bridgett appre-ciated his valor. Knew it was the right thing to do, even as she mourned their own potential loss. But wasn't that what being a parent was all about? Caring for your children, then letting them go, when life demanded it?

Marie paused, looking uncertain and conflicted again. "I don't know if I still have any rights, but… would all of you…" She burst into tears, then turned to Mitzy, too. "Would it be okay for me to see them again?" She dabbed at her eyes. "Because I feel like I really need to be with them, at least one more time."

A part of Bridgett had always known it was possible that whoever had left Robby and Riot in such distress would have a change of heart. Resurface. Ask for a second chance.

Experiencing it, however, was more numbing and heartrending than even she'd expected.

Cullen seemed awfully quiet, too, as they picked up Robby and Riot and drove back to the ranch.

"Are you okay?" Cullen asked finally, as they neared the Western Cross. His large hands gripped the steering wheel. "Because you don't have to be the one to take Riot and Robby to the hospital to visit Marie tomorrow. Mitzy and I can do it."

Why put off the inevitable? Especially if this was where fate was leading them.

"No." Bridgett girded her heart. "I think it's important Marie see them—now that she's in a place she can get the help she would need to keep them." Help that a few weeks ago the runaway teen didn't think was even possible. She swallowed. "I don't want to bail—just because things might not go my way. I owe it to everyone to see this through." That was what being a foster mother was about. Loving, and then doing what was right for everyone in the end, even if it was agonizing for her.

She slanted Cullen a glance. He seemed to fill the cab.

"I feel that way, too," he admitted, reaching over to take her hand in a grip that was as strong and reassuring as ever.

Bridgett drew from his courage. "In any case, we have at least one more night with them. I'd really like to savor it."

And they did. Having what could very well be their last "family" dinner out on the back porch. Taking both puppy and baby for a long walk around the Western Cross. Lingering over the nightly bedtime routine.

Meeting up in the master bedroom, when Riot and Robby were both sound asleep, to make love one last, bittersweet time. At least, that was the way she saw it. Cullen, however, had other ideas.

"This is our destiny, Bridgett," he told her, holding her close.

The irony of the situation was not lost on her. Nor should it be on him. She flushed as her emotions rose. "Let's not romanticize this, Cullen. If this path to family closes, another one will open up."

"I'll make sure it does," he promised, his expression suddenly one of concern. "But sometimes in life you have to let things play out the way they're meant to." Even though waiting was the hardest part.

They made love throughout the night, and the next day took both puppy and baby to the hospital. The visit was a pleasant one. As they convened in the rooftop solarium, Marie asked a ton of questions about both Robby and Riot. She petted the puppy and held the baby briefly, then turned both back over to Bridgett and Cullen, watching the way they interacted with each other.

In between subsequent visits over the next couple of days, she met privately with Mitzy, and a psychologist and counselor.

Finally, Marie was well enough to be released.

And she made her decision.

Mitzy made the trip out to the Western Cross to tell Bridgett and Cullen the news. "Marie wants the two of you to adopt Robby and keep Riot."

Bridgett did a double take. Relieved and yet… "Together?"

"Marie has thought about it and thinks two loving parents would be way better than just one."

Obviously drawing on his own childhood difficulties, Cullen said gruffly, "Can't disagree with her there."

Although Bridgett knew that was true, the last thing she wanted to do was back Cullen into a corner, the way her ex had once tried to force her into something she'd wanted in the long run but wasn't ready for at that moment.

Determined to give him an out, the same way she had given Marie one, she pointed out quietly, "But we're not married."

Mitzy shot back, "Are you going to be?"

Put on the spot, Bridgett flushed and shrugged. She couldn't quite look Cullen in the eye. "I don't even know how to answer that," she mumbled finally.

Neither, apparently, did Cullen, judging by his silence.

Mitzy continued, "Because it would make a difference with the court, if you are. In any case, Marie is prepared to surrender all rights to the baby and the puppy as long as one or both of you follow through on your promise to care for the child. So we can put your wish to become mutually responsible in the same petition or separate ones. Or go back to the original plan and just let Bridgett foster-adopt on her own."

"And in the meantime?" Cullen asked.

"Formally," Mitzy explained, "Robby and Riot remain with Bridgett, since she is the approved foster mother."

Bridgett cleared her throat. All along she had been prepared for everything but this—figuring out what exactly she and Cullen meant to each other.

Was it real?

Or was it an infatuation—at least on his part—generated by the way they had been playing house? "Do I have leeway about where I care for them while I figure everything out?" Bridgett asked.

"Yes." Mitzy smiled. "You can stay at the Western Cross, if that works for all of you. Or move in with family. In the department's eyes, you've more than proven yourself a stellar foster parent, Bridgett, so really, it's up to you."

Except it wasn't.

Because if she wanted to stay, she would be putting Cullen on the spot.

His own emotions under wraps, Cullen asked, "What

about the foster-adoption? If I ask to be included in that, is the court going to approve my request?"

"If you were married to Bridgett? Both petitioning to formally adopt? Yes, it would be a sure thing. Especially, Cullen, since you are one of the McCabes and Bridgett is a Monroe, to whom family is all."

"Except…" Bridgett hated to point it out, yet again. "Cullen and I aren't married." They weren't technically even dating!

A heavy silence fell between them as the implications of all that was at stake hung in the air.

Finally, Cullen asked, "What happens in regard to the baby's biological father?"

Mitzy frowned. "There were ten thousand people at that music festival in Houston. Even if she had a picture of the father—which she apparently does not—she doesn't have his real name or phone number. There's no way to track him down."

So Robby would never know the identity of his biological father, Bridgett realized, as Cullen hadn't for so many years.

"What will the birth certificate say?" Cullen asked.

"That the father is unknown. Until he is formally adopted," Mitzy admitted. "Then, if Robby has an adoptive father, the birth certificate can be legally changed to reflect that."

Reason enough, Bridgett thought, knowing Cullen's gallant, loving and caring heart, for him to go forward. And while that might be—probably was—the right thing to do for Robby, was it the right thing to do for the two of them? Especially if their relationship was based on friendship and passion rather than love? It was one thing to carry on an affair, with no real ties holding them down or back. Another, to find themselves boxed in by circumstances beyond their control.

Her breath hitched. They'd been so focused on solving the mystery, clearing Cullen's name and caring for Robby and Riot, she and Cullen hadn't given any thought to their relationship in the long term. All he had said, when pressed, was that he wanted to concentrate on the "here and now."

Not wanting to find out that it was mutual loneliness plus crisis propelling them together, she swallowed, focusing on things that were easier for her to deal with emotionally. "What about Marie? What is going to happen to her?"

Mitzy sighed sadly. "She was right about her parents. We finally tracked them down. And they want nothing to do with Marie or her problems. So she is going to a girls' ranch in North Texas for the next two years. She's very excited about it. She's going to be able to work with horses, finish high school and get the counseling and group therapy she needs to recover from her ordeal, as well as start community college. They'll help her get loans and scholarships."

"Will she stay in touch?"

"She's open to it, eventually, if you are. Right now, though, she wants to concentrate on getting her life together." Mitzy gathered up her things. "Look, I know you need to think about all of this. Talk it over. Obviously it is a big decision, so I want you to take your time."

Cullen turned to Bridgett as Mitzy drove down the

lane. He seemed as relieved as she was fraught with anxiety. "Congratulations, Mom."

Not sure whether she should say "Congratulations Dad!" or not, Bridgett held up a staying hand. Her feelings an incredible jumbled-up mess, she countered in a low, strangled voice, "Let's not go there just yet."

He released an impatient breath. "Why not?"

"I don't want to jinx it. There are still so many things that could go wrong."

"Not if we get married. Then it sounds like it will be a slam dunk."

Bridgett's mouth opened in an O of surprise. "What did you say?"

"You heard Mitzy. Getting approved won't be a problem if we get married."

"For the baby?"

"And the puppy. And us," he retorted cheerfully. "We make a great team, Bridgett. The last few weeks have shown us that."

Her overwhelming need for him to be happy remained intact. He would not be, if he never experienced the kind of all-encompassing love she still wanted. Not that their relationship would immediately crash and burn. They'd probably be fine for a while. But then one of two things would happen. He'd either realize he had settled, in marrying her, or he'd fall in love with someone else and be torn between what he had already promised and what he wanted and needed. Either way, they'd be miserable and brokenhearted. Robby and Riot would suffer, too. The way he had suffered when his mother had split up with Buck.

Resolved to limit the damage as much as she could, she reminded him of all the success that still lay ahead for him. "You have an offer to buy a huge ranch in Nebraska."

He stared at her, looking every bit as blindsided as she felt when he had offered to marry her in order to give Robby a daddy and make the foster-adoption go smoother.

"So?" The happiness left his eyes. In its place, something hard and forbidding took over.

Her throat ached almost as much as her heart. "So, if we were to get married you would have to stay here, with us."

He stepped back and ran his hands through his hair. "I thought that was what you'd want," he snapped, looking confused.

Her eyes burning, she replied warily. "Not if it makes you feel trapped. I was nearly forced into marriage with Aaron because he wanted to have kids right away. It was a miserable experience. Having lived it, I can't put anyone else through it."

He stared at her in mounting disappointment. "So you're saying that clinching the adoption is the *only* reason you'd marry me."

Hurt he would think she was saying this because she had no regard for his feelings, she stepped forward and countered, as calmly as possible, "I'm saying it's not enough reason to rush into anything. I can petition to adopt right away without slowing things down. You can petition, too, if you decide not to go to Nebraska, and go through the home study and the background checks and all of that."

"And if I don't go. Would you and Robby and Riot stay here with me or live elsewhere?"

Talk about a loaded question!

She shrugged, feeling every bit as boxed in as he. Like they needed to take a step back. Give each other a little time to breathe. Think about what they each really felt. "I'd move in with Bess." Hopefully, temporarily. "The point is, if you do decide to stay and foster-adopt with me, we could still see each other all the time—without actually living together."

His face was a bland, polite mask. "You don't have any doubts about taking on Robby and Riot?"

"No, of course not." Where was he going with this?

He folded his arms in front of him, all too ready to judge her. Unfairly. "But you do have doubts about hitching your wagon to mine."

"No, but I'm saying this has all happened awfully fast for you, Cullen. I've been on the foster-adopt list for the last two years. For you, even the idea of parenthood and sharing your life with anyone is all brand-new. When the novelty wears off and reality hits, and you have to decide whether to keep flipping ranches and expanding your horizons or staying here, waiting for the right land to open up, you may not be so happy."

He looked at her, incredulous. "So it's all on me."

Defiantly, she held her ground. "Why are you twisting everything I say?"

He caught her by the shoulders. "Because I think my

issues have nothing to do with your reluctance to marry me." Hurt and resentment underscored his low tone.

Blinking back tears, she splayed her hands across his chest, holding him at bay. "Then what does?"

He stared at her as if she was a stranger. "Your notions of destiny. Of finding a romance so big it will never fade."

She inhaled sharply, not about to mislead him. "I admit I want what three of my siblings have and my parents had," she said stiffly. "What my twin and I still lack. A relationship that is so strong and so right it will last a lifetime."

He gave her a slow, critical once-over. "And you don't think we have that."

I might if you'd ever once said you loved me, she thought miserably. Or could love me. Or were falling in love with me.

But you haven't. So...

She wrested herself from his arms as hot, stinging tears raced down her face. "I know you desire me, Cullen." She swallowed around the increasing ache in her throat. "I know we work well together and we can have fun together, and we even want the same things for Riot and Robby, but...*is that enough*?" Could it ever be?

Anger flared in his navy blue eyes. "Obviously not for you." He spun away from her.

"Where are you going?" she cried, aware this could easily blow up into something neither of them wanted.

Grimacing, he tossed the words over his shoulder. "Out. To clear my head."

Her pulse took on a rapid staccato beat as the loving

home they'd built over the last two weeks quickly devolved into the last place she would ever want to be. A place that was attractive and orderly on the surface, but chaotic and numbing underneath. Swiftly, she closed the distance between them. "You're leaving us?"

"No," he said, in the same take-no-prisoners voice he had used on her that first day in the hospital corridor, when he thought she'd been playing a very bad joke on him. "I made a commitment to Robby and to Riot, to keep them in my heart and always take care of them," he said softly but firmly. "I'm not reneging on that."

Her heart broke. "Just me."

For a long moment, she thought he was going to say something, but he didn't. He merely drew an equalizing breath. "We'll find a way to coparent. To have a friendly, cordial relationship. But given the way you feel about me and what we've had…" He paused and shook his head in silent remonstration, a look that went deeper than any hurt she had ever sustained. "It's clear to me now that the two of us building upon anything more than that is just not going to be possible." And on that note, he walked out, shutting the door behind him.

Shattering her heart in the process.

Chapter 16

"I've been showing you houses all afternoon that would be fantastic for you and your family, and you haven't liked any of them," Jeanne Phipps complained, several days later.

Bess grinned. "I'm beginning to think she doesn't really want to leave that ranch she is living on."

Bridgett pushed Robby in his stroller around the landscaped backyard. Past the outdoor playset with the toddler-size slide, and the baby swing that would be just perfect in a few months.

"Don't start, you two."

She didn't know why she couldn't imagine living here, even with her twin as her housemate—but she just couldn't. "We'll find the place. Eventually." Although nothing she had seen thus far had even come close to

the home she was still living in—albeit in a slightly es-
tranged way—with Cullen.

Jeanne assessed Bridgett's inner tumult with a glance.
"How about I let the two of you talk before we see any
other properties on the list? I have a few calls to make,
anyway." She strode off, her high heels clicking on the
pavers.

The back gate snapped shut.

Bess sat down on one of the wicker chairs on the
patio. The leashed Riot dropped down beside her. "Why
don't you just admit what's going on with you?"

Too restless to sit down, Bridgett kept rolling the
contentedly sleeping Robby back and forth. "And what
would that be?"

"You regret turning down Cullen's marriage pro-
posal."

Regret didn't begin to cover it. Not a second went by
without her wishing she could have followed her heart
and said yes. Instead of listening to her head.

Miserably, she countered, "He doesn't love me, Bess.
Not in the all-encompassing way you need to love someone you marry and intend to spend a lifetime with."

"Could have fooled me. And everyone else who has
seen the two of you together.'"

"Me, too, for a while, anyway." Until there at the
end he'd shown what he was really thinking and feeling. Or *not* feeling.

"Cullen is a man of his word, Bess. When this whole
thing started, we made a deal. I would do everything I
could to help him preserve his good name and not bring
shame on the McCabe family."

"By letting him help you with Robby and Riot, even though they weren't his."

"Right. And, in turn, he promised to do everything within his power to help me get approved to foster-adopt Robby and Riot. Suggesting we marry was just a way to expedite that process and ensure the outcome."

Bess scoffed. "It had nothing to do with how much he has come to care for you and Robby and Riot?"

"We're friends."

Bess lifted a brow.

"And lovers."

Another pause.

"And we have successfully coparented."

Bess petted Riot. "So, what else do you need to be happy?"

Bridgett sighed. "In the long run? A lot more."

"You don't think it's destiny?"

That was the hell of it; the emotional side of her still did. The intellectual side of her did not.

Bridgett drew a deep breath. "The crisis brought us together, Bess. Not knowing what was going to happen with Robby and Riot, or where they came from. Struggling to care for them together intensified all that." *Gave us a false sense of intimacy that I sentimentally interpreted as way more than that.* "And now..." She swallowed, unable to continue.

"Now what?" Bess pressed.

Bridgett stiffened her spine. "He was very clear when this whole situation arose that the only reason he was participating was out of honor and responsibility." He hadn't seen the situation as their destiny. Or been looking to get married. Or have kids—the way she had for some time now.

"So?" Bess squinted over at her. "That's admirable in a way that only adds to his allure. Not every guy I know would have stepped up the way he did."

Anguished tears stung Bridgett's eyes. "Don't you think I know that?" He'd kindly offered them his home and his help, and to a certain extent, anyway, his heart…

"Then what's the problem?" her sister persisted.

Knotting her hands together, Bridgett struggled to explain, "Cullen is a McCabe. He still wants to do the right thing. And the right thing in his mind, the easy thing that would make everyone happy—at least in the short term—is for him to marry me. And for us to live together like a real family."

Bess arched a brow in Bridgett's direction. "Like the real family you've been the last few weeks?"

It had been a fairy tale. But fairy tales did not last. Any more than relationships forged in crises did. She couldn't bear to see their happiness deteriorate bit by bit as cold reality returned. "I can't take advantage of his generosity." And that's what she would be doing. So she had to be as noble now, as he had been.

"I see." Bess regarded her gravely. "So you'll break his heart, instead."

Bridgett flushed.

Silence fell.

Bess stood to square off with her. "Have you told him how you feel?"

"Yes."

Bess grasped her forearms. "I mean really, sis. Deep down."

Bridgett jerked her arms free. Unable to bear the scrutiny, she walked away. "I told you. I don't want to back him into a corner." The way her ex had once tried to pressure her into doing something she wasn't convinced she wanted, never mind was actually ready for...

"So what's the alternative?" Bess threw up her hands in frustration. "Live a lie?"

Stubbornly, Bridgett tried to hold on to what she could. "It's not like Cullen and I are giving up everything," she argued.

"Isn't it?"

Bridgett moved the stroller closer, spoke softly so as not to disturb the sleeping infant. "We're on the verge of being friends now. Coparents, if the court and Department of Children and Family Services agree." Or, at least, they were trying to accomplish all that. Since their falling out, their interactions were excruciatingly polite. Stilted. And while she hoped the awkwardness would ease, over time, she could not guarantee it.

Bess looked as disappointed as Bridgett felt. "Are you telling me you'd be happy with that?"

"No, but..." Bridgett shrugged and dug in all the harder. "I was prepared to be happy with a whole lot less when I signed up to foster-adopt as a single mom."

Her twin looked at her long and hard. "Maybe," Bess said softly, "that's always been the problem."

"A little lonely around here?"

Cullen turned to see his stepmother, Rachel, striding toward him. He turned away from the fence post he had been repairing. "Always is when I auction off a big part of my herd." That would change in a few weeks, when the new crop of Hotlander calves were born. Then life would be busy again. Almost as busy as it had been when he and Bridgett and the baby and Riot were a team.

Though not as happy...

Not anywhere near as happy...

"That's not what I'm talking about." Rachel strode closer, scolding. "And you know it, Cullen McCabe!"

Obviously, she'd heard that Bridgett was off looking at houses again. Not that he hoped she would find anything. Because until she did, she and the baby and the puppy would be staying right there on the ranch with him. And though they weren't exactly getting along famously—at least, not in the intimate way they once had—it was still good to have them nearby. Comforting, almost. If you could overlook their almost unbearably fake cordiality, anyway.

"You forgot the Reid." He pointed out the omission of his middle name in an effort to change the subject.

"Yes, I did!" Rachel shot back fiercely, surprising him. "Although I wouldn't have—if I thought you were as proud of being a Reid as you are of being a McCabe." She strode even closer, her boots digging into the manicured grass. The empathy he'd come to expect from her lit her eyes. "It made sense when you first came to live with us. You'd always been a Reid and then, suddenly, with the truth about your paternity discovered, you were a McCabe, too."

That had been a rocky time.

Rachel studied him with a lawyer's assessing gaze. "But now the use of both surnames just seems to drag you down. Make you feel fifty percent McCabe, fifty percent Reid, instead of one hundred percent McCabe and one hundred percent Reid."

Hadn't she just hit the nail on the head, he ruminated sagely. Cullen shrugged, embarrassed to find his mother's selfishness and his illegitimacy could still embarrass him. "I think it's understandable why I don't quite fit in anywhere," he muttered. At least, he hadn't. Until Bridgett and Robby and Riot came along and made a home with him. Then, for a short while, at the Western Cross, he had.

He went back to stringing barbed wire. "Not the way the rest of my half siblings do."

Rachel stood next to the section he was repairing. She folded her arms in front of her. "Do you think your feelings about yourself would have been different if Frank had known you as his son from the beginning? That your life would have been better, somehow?"

An honest question deserved an honest answer. "For me? Probably. I don't know how it would have been for you and him, given the fact that the two of you were newlyweds and my mom not really the sharing type."

Rachel nodded in understanding. "In any case, we can't change what was."

"I know that."

Her expression softening, she reached out to touch his arm. "Then why do you keep punishing yourself?"

He ignored the brief, familial touch. "I'm not."

"You let Bridgett and Robby and Riot go without a fight," she pointed out gently, stepping back.

They hadn't actually left yet. But they would, as soon as Bridgett found a place, and then life as they knew it really would be over. Cullen met his stepmother's steady glance, squared his shoulders. "It was what Bridgett wanted."

Rachel seemed skeptical. "Sure about that?"

Unfortunately, he was. "I suggested we get married," Cullen stated tersely. "And instead of saying yes, as I had hoped, she said there was no reason to rush into anything."

"She could have a point, given how fast everything has happened."

If it were only that, Cullen would have agreed. Figuring he had done enough for one day, he began packing up his tools. "She also wants to continue on with a solo adoption rather than refile completely so I can join her."

Rachel's brows lifted at his terse tone. "She's opposed to you becoming Robby's legal father?"

He strode back over to his pickup. "No. She just wants it to happen separately from her petition to foster-adopt."

Rachel followed. "Because she doesn't trust you to be around?"

Because she wants some big wildly romantic love that he had failed to give her.

And if she couldn't have that, she would prefer to go on romantically unattached. As a single mother. As friends. And nothing more.

"Something like that," he fibbed.

Rachel watched him pull off his work gloves. "Is that

the way you feel? Like you want to move on? Maybe take that tremendous opportunity in Nebraska?"

Even though it felt like he was being pushed away with both hands, leaving was the last thing on his mind. And that was weird, Cullen acknowledged silently. Usually, in a situation like this, he would have already been packed and on his way to his next ranch to flip. Or, in this case, to the Cartwright Ranch in Nebraska to take advantage of what was still a very big opportunity.

Something about the way his stepmom was looking at him, however, tempted him to respond more candidly than usual.

He dropped the toolbox into the bed of his truck. Tossed the excess barbed wire in after that. "The truth?"

Rachel flashed an encouraging grin. "Nothing but."

Taking her up on her offer of a shoulder to lean on, he confessed, "The whole thing has left me feeling blindsided."

She nodded, to her credit, not at all surprised. "Completely understandable."

He exhaled wearily. "And I'm lonely as hell." He bit down on a curse as soon as the words were out of his mouth. Had he actually said that aloud? He guessed he had.

Rachel rocked back on the heels of her cowgirl boots, looking more ranch wife, now, than attorney. "I figured as much." She stopped to search his face. "But that's the way you've always been, isn't it?"

He didn't answer. Didn't have to. This woman who had breezed into his life without a prayer of taking his deceased mother's place knew his heart like nobody else. Always had, always would. Rachel edged closer. To his shock, tears suddenly blurred her eyes. "I blame myself for that, you know," she said thickly.

He stared. "Why?" He reached inside his truck and retrieved a box of tissues, handed them over. "You welcomed me with open arms when not many women in your place would have."

Rachel took several and blotted her eyes. "I also did you a terrible disservice." She shook her head in obvious regret. "When you first came to us, with that impenetrable shield of politeness, this obvious determination not to be a bother to anyone, your dad wanted to tear it down. *Force* you to tackle the difficulties and become a McCabe from the get-go."

Sounded like Frank.

It was also the way he would have treated any of his five other kids.

Rachel blew her nose. "But I wouldn't let him," she confessed, distraught. "I told him how overwhelmed I had been when I first married into the iconic Texas McCabe clan. How I had only become family bit by bit, and because of all you had been through, he needed to give you the *room* to absorb it all, on your own terms, in your own time."

The overwhelming emotion in her low voice had his own throat tightening. "You were right," he told her hoarsely, knowing how fragile he had been, how afraid he'd been of losing what he had left of the only life he had ever known—and his late mother.

But, on the other hand, if Frank had done that—treated him just like his siblings, instead of with kid gloves, maybe there wouldn't have been such a feeling of apartness all these years.

Rachel touched his forearm gently. "Actually," she corrected, practical and empathetic as ever, "your dad and I both were right in our approach. He should have pushed you more, made you see that he did care deeply about you, had from the very first moment he found out about you. In fact, in some ways, I think he and I both loved you more than your siblings at that stage because we hadn't been given the chance to know you earlier. So we were making up for lost time." She teared up again. "I just wish you had seen that."

He wrapped his arms around her, pulling her in like the family he had always wanted her to be. "I knew it, Rachel. I felt it." Deep in his soul and his heart.

She hugged him back with maternal ferocity. Then shifted back far enough to allege sadly, pragmatically, "You just didn't return the emotions."

Feeling the moment turn awkward again, Cullen dropped his arms. "I did." He studied her wary expression. "I just…didn't trust it. For my mom, love—romantic love, family love, love of friends—it all always faded." The way Bridgett's had apparently diminished for him.

Rachel shook her head. "From what I know, you are probably right about your mother's love for everyone else, but not about what she felt for you, Cullen. I'm betting that was incredibly fierce from beginning to end. Otherwise, she wouldn't have taken such pains to have you with her all those years. She wouldn't have been afraid to share you with the rest of your kin."

Rachel paused to let him absorb what she was saying.

When she was certain it had registered, she took both his hands tightly in hers. "If your mother hadn't loved you with all her heart, Cullen, she could have left you with your dad at any time. She knew that. But she didn't. Instead, she made the best life she could for you."

She had, at that.

"Yes, it was a mistake, keeping you and your dad apart, but you have each other now." Rachel sniffed again and continued in a low, quavering voice. "And that counts for a heck of a lot, doesn't it?"

"It does." Knowing this had to be said, and said now, Cullen pushed the rusty-sounding words out. "And Rachel? Just for the record? As long as we're being clear here?" He looked her in the eye. "You mean an awful lot to me, too."

Her eyes shone.

They were silent.

She embraced him fiercely. "I want you to be happy and fulfilled, Cullen. And the only way that is ever going to happen," she warned, "is if you stop holding back and seize the opportunity in front of you. Talk to your dad, Cullen. Start letting him be there for you the way he has always wanted to be. And after that? Open up your heart to Bridgett, too."

They talked a little more, then Rachel left. Buoyed by her pep talk, Cullen returned to the ranch house, and began to prepare for what he was determined would be the most important evening of his life thus far.

He had just finished seasoning a couple of porterhouse steaks, when he got the text from Bridgett. Headed back to the ranch. Finally know what our next steps should be.

Our next steps.

He wasn't sure what that meant, given that she intended to leave the Western Cross as soon as possible. Had she found a place? Decided to take Lucille Lockhart up on her offer, after all, and made a move-out plan she wanted to share with him? Or was she simply speaking in temporary generalities?

Hoping it was the latter, he poured premade salad into a bowl, put a couple of Idaho potatoes into the oven to bake and made sure there was charcoal in the grill. He had wine, too. Although he wasn't sure she would want any.

Finished, he stepped out onto the front porch to wait for the little group he'd come to think of as his family. It wasn't long before he saw Bridgett's SUV coming up the drive. He walked out to help her, but only she emerged from the vehicle. He shoved aside his fear that this really was the end for them, and forced a welcoming smile. "Where are Robby and Riot?"

"In town, with my family. I told them I'd pick them up later, after we'd talked."

Looked like he had one last chance to make things right. He damn well was not going to squander it. He escorted her away from the SUV. "Before you begin, I have some things to say to you, too."

Suddenly, she looked as apprehensive as he felt. "Okay," she said softly, setting down her bag and taking a place on the front steps of the ranch house. "I'm listening."

He settled next to her. "The last few days have given me a lot of time to think." She turned to him, her gaze intent, giving him courage. "I've realized some things about myself." He forced himself to go on with un-flinching honesty. "My flipping ranches was more than just a way to amass the cash I needed to build a cattle-breeding business for myself. It was also a way to con-tinually cut ties and keep from putting down roots. Just the way my mom did when I was growing up."

It hadn't brought them happiness, in either case.

Bridgett studied him with keen understanding. "And yet you succumbed to family pressure and came back to Laramie, anyway," she pointed out softly, covering his hand with her own.

"I wanted to belong here," he admitted, weaving his fingers through the slender grip of hers. "I just didn't know how to make things better with my dad and the rest of the family. But you're right." He grimaced at the rusty sound of his voice. "Deep down, I hoped buying a ranch and setting up a cow-calf operation here would earn me the approval I craved from Frank and Rachel and the others."

He exhaled.

"Unfortunately, the Western Cross was no more a real home to me than any of the other places I have lived." With a rueful grin, he admitted, "Until you and Robby and Riot moved in. Then it became the place I'd always wanted and dreamed of having." *The place where we all belonged*.

"I thought it was perfect, too, not just for you, but for all of us," Bridgett confided softly, meeting his eyes. "At least—" her lower lip took on a disappointed slant "—until you got that big offer to sell out and move to Nebraska."

"About that." He tightened his grip on her hand. "I

formally turned it down the day we found Marie Griffin. I just didn't have a chance to tell you. And then, with everything going on… I wasn't sure it mattered. But it does now," he told her firmly. "I want to put down roots in Laramie County. I want to be here with you and Robby and Riot."

She wanted to believe him; he could see that.

"What about your dream of owning as many acres as your dad does?" she asked in a low, quavering voice.

"That can still happen right here in Texas. If I'm patient, and I promise you I will be."

Her slender shoulders relaxed.

She looked over at him, her cheeks flushing self-consciously. "Now, on to why *I* wanted to talk to *you* about next steps."

He tensed, his heart thudding in his chest. This could be bad or this could be good.

"You aren't the only one who has done a lot of soul-searching. First, I've redefined what home is to me. When I met you, I thought all I needed was to buy that perfect little bungalow I had my eye on." Still holding his gaze, she bit her lip and plunged on. "But I've realized home isn't comprised of the right-sized walls and a sturdy roof over your head. Or even the much valued fenced-in back yard with playset that I was convinced I would need to please DCFS. It's a place where you feel safe and warm and loved. And that," she said, her voice breaking slightly, "can be anywhere we hang our hats."

We…

Did she mean all four of them?

Or was she speaking metaphorically?

Her expression was so serious and intent, he had no clue.

She took another deep breath. Plunged on. "Second, I think the real reason I've been so hung up on destiny all this time is because I haven't wanted to be responsible for my own happiness." She shook her head in heartfelt regret. "I wanted bliss to magically fall into my lap, like a twist of fate, and until it did—" she took another shuddering breath "—I had made up my mind not to pursue anything but safe bets."

She reached over and squeezed his hand. "I didn't want to be involved with anything that had even the tiniest potential to hurt me. It's why I felt I couldn't foster a child unless it was available to adopt."

He could understand that, now that he had faced the possibility of loving a family he considered his only to lose them.

Her hand tightened on his. "I knew chances were slim to none of that happening, given the long waiting lists and the fact I was single and had no experience fostering, but I thought if I waited long enough, that would magically happen, anyway."

He tucked an errant lock of hair behind her ear. "Except for one thing, Bridgett. You did find Robby and Riot. And the note left with them led you to me." *And all of that to us.*

"That was definitely a life-changing miracle."

He nodded in agreement.

Her soul laid bare, she continued confiding. "But again, I didn't know as much about myself as I thought I did. Because the experience with Marie taught me I could be more selfless than I ever imagined." For a silent moment she searched his eyes. "It helped me realize that love comes in all sorts of ways. You just have to be open to it. And that's what I want, Cullen."

She stood, drawing him to his feet, too, and splayed her arms across his chest. "I want this ranch that has come to make us all feel so safe and loved and cared for, be home to all of us." Her lower lip trembled and tears filled her eyes. "I want love—with you. Family love. Passionate love. The love that comes between two friends. And two parents. And two people." Her voice quavered with all the affection he had ever wanted to receive. "Two people who one day just might not be able to live without each other."

The tentative, hopeful note in her voice filled him with joy unlike anything he had ever felt. "I think we've already reached that point," he admitted gruffly, pulling her all the way into his arms and holding her close. "That's what I was waiting here to tell you. I finally know where I belong and with whom." No longer afraid, he took the final leap and laid bare his heart and soul, too. "I love you, Bridgett, with every fiber of my being. And I'm never, ever going to stop."

She flung her arms about his neck. Tears glittered on her eyelashes and spilled down her face. "Oh, Cullen, I love you, too. So much."

Her heartfelt confession filled him with warmth and tenderness. He paused to kiss her, again and again, her face cupped in his hands. As long as they were spilling all, he had to be completely honest with her. "I know you said you didn't want to get married." *At least, not right now.*

She silenced him with an index finger against his lips. "I fibbed. I do. Very much."

"I do, too." The peace he'd wanted stealing through his heart, he warned, "But I want to do it when we both agree we are ready and the time is right."

She grinned. "Right back at you, cowboy."

Their most important next step tentatively agreed upon, they kissed. Tenderly at first, then with more and more passion. Until there was no longer any denying not just their physical need, but this life they were building together.

Blindly, they found their way inside the ranch house. Still kissing, traversed the stairs, and made love in the cozy comfort of his bed. Afterward, they clung together, savoring the closeness, yet knowing another very important decision had to be made.

"Cullen?" Bridgett prompted softly.

"Hmm?" Knowing he had never been happier, he buried his face in her hair, drinking in her unique fragrance.

"About Robby and Riot."

He drew back, heart pounding.

"I've changed my mind about that. I want us to foster-adopt them together so we can continue to be the real family we were meant to be, right from the start. With absolutely no interruption."

Another dream come true. Soberly he told her, "I want that, too."

She hugged him fiercely, the joy flowing between them, tangible. "Then it looks like we will be calling DCFS first thing tomorrow and amending that adoption petition, after all."

Epilogue

April 1, one year later

Cullen watched as Bridgett paused at the edge of the bandstand that had been set up on the Western Cross ranch lawn. Gorgeous as could be in a red party dress and heels, their baby on her hip, their dog at his side, she turned to Cullen and murmured, "Hard to imagine so much could have happened in so little time, isn't it?"

And yet it had.

Savoring the happiness infusing every corner of his life, he grinned back at her. Winked. "Well, hang on, darlin', because the best is yet to come."

Her eyes lit up in the way he loved. "Promise?"

He nodded solemnly. "I do."

They locked gazes as readily as they had already

locked hearts. Knowing it was either proceed with the festivities or sweep her off to make love with her then and there, Cullen reined in his desire and caressed her cheek with the pad of his thumb. "So, what do you say, Mrs. McCabe? Ready to get this party started?"

She slipped her hand into his. "Let's do it, cowboy!" Together, they moved to the microphone at center stage and gazed at the circle of family and friends gathered in front of them.

As previously agreed, he talked first while caterers passed out glasses of champagne. "Bridgett and I want to thank you all for coming to help us celebrate the first anniversary of the miracle discovery that brought Bridgett and I and Robby and Riot all together." *And opened up our lives, and our hearts...*

Beside him, Bridgett wordlessly offered her support.

Ready to finally say all the things that needed to be said, he located the beaming matriarch and patriarch in this branch of the McCabe clan. "And first, in this very long list of people to whom we owe so much, I want to thank Mom and Dad. And, yes, I call Rachel and Frank that now, because they are both my parents and I love them both very much."

A ripple of appreciation went through the crowd. "To my brothers and sister, Dan, Jack, Matt, Lulu and Chase, for hanging in there and being my sibs even when I wasn't sure I needed any younger brothers, never mind a baby sister, in my life!"

Soft, knowing laughter followed.

When the hilarity died down, Cullen said, in all sincerity, "A special thanks to the entire Monroe clan, as well—" he paused to name them all in turn "—for welcoming me into their lives."

Emotional hoots followed.

Cullen looked over at the cowboys seated at the gingham-draped dinner tables. They were part of the Western Cross family, too. "I'd also like to thank everyone who helps me out on the ranch." He paused to list them.

"And Riot, the handsome mutt that accompanies me everywhere…and as all our wranglers can readily insist, has turned into one of the best darn cattle dogs who ever lived."

Hearing his name, Riot perked up and thumped his tail.

Cullen wrapped his free arm around Bridgett and brought her and their baby in close to his side. His voice turning as tender as his feelings, he continued his increasingly emotional toast. "I'd also like to thank Robby, who teaches me every day what it is to be a dad," he said, his voice cracking slightly. "And how spectacular it is to have a son."

He leaned over to buss the top of their little one's head. The one-year-old chortled happily and, a ham at heart, blew first Cullen and then his mommy affectionate, noisy kisses back, making everyone laugh.

Eyes misting, Cullen turned and looked deep into Bridgett's beautiful eyes. Knowing he could never say it often enough or well enough to convey all he felt, all he had discovered, he continued from the deepest recesses of his heart.

"And last, and most importantly of all, to my wife, Bridgett." He gazed lovingly down at her. "The woman who upended my life and stole my heart and showed me how to love with every fiber of my being," he managed, before his voice caught.

Taking a deep breath, he plunged on, reminiscing fondly, "All, mind you, while sharing with me the best three month courtship and nine months of marriage a couple could ever dream of having."

Tenderly, he lifted her face to his, and blotted the tears of happiness streaming down her face with the pad of his thumb.

Once again, they were completely in synch. "I adore you, sweetheart," he said gently.

Bridgett went up on tiptoe and kissed him. "Oh, Cullen, I adore you, too!"

Love flowed between them, fiercer than ever.

He bent his head and kissed her again while the baby let out a whoop of delight and Riot gave a jubilant woof. The family and friends gathered round laughed, cheered and clapped. But all Cullen could focus on was how right everything finally felt. How…there was no other word for it…*destined.*

Eventually he drew back, knowing deep in his soul that their lives were now the way they were always meant to be. Bridgett felt it, too, he could see it in the way she looked at him every hour of every day.

"And now—as we all get ready to lift our glasses—Bridgett has a few words of her own to say."

Her cheeks taking on a rosy maternal glow, Bridgett handed off Robby to him and stepped up to the microphone. Looking more angelic than ever, she declared, "Multiple births don't just run in the McCabe clan. Twins run in the Monroe family, too. And now," she declared joyously, to one and all, "Cullen and I are going to have a pair of babies simultaneously, too!"

Elated, Frank stood. So did Rachel. The McCabes and Monroes and their spouses all followed. Soon everyone was on their feet, cheering wildly, raising their glasses.

"To our family, which is getting bigger and happier and more fulfilling every day," Bridgett toasted.

"Amen to that!" someone shouted. Glasses clinked. People sipped.

"You've made all my dreams come true," Cullen said, cuddling their son and drawing her close once again.

Bridgett looked up at him adoringly. And kissed him one more time. "Mine, too, cowboy," she whispered back, snuggling close. "Mine, too..."

* * * * *

Ali Olson is a longtime resident of Las Vegas, Nevada, where she has been teaching English at the high school and college level for the past seven years. Ali has found a passion for writing sexy romance novels, both contemporary and historical, and is enthusiastic about her newly discovered career. She loves reading, writing and traveling with her husband and constant companion, Joe. She appreciates hearing from readers. Write to her at authoraliolson.com.

Books by Ali Olson

Harlequin Blaze

Her Sexy Vegas Cowboy
Her Sexy Texas Cowboy

Harlequin Western Romance

The Bull Rider's Twin Trouble
The Cowboy's Surprise Baby

Visit the Author Profile page at Harlequin.com.

THE BULL RIDER'S
TWIN TROUBLE

Ali Olson

For my siblings. To Claire, for her enthusiasm; to Alaina, for her love and support; and to Jerrod, because I think you'll be embarrassed having a romance novel dedicated to you and that amuses me.

Chapter 1

Brock McNeal breathed deeply, moving his body in time with the jumping, twisting animal beneath him, and counted the seconds. *Six...seven...eight.*

The whistle sounded and he jumped off the bucking bull as bullfighters surrounded them, rolling to his feet and away from the large animal.

Brock soaked in the roar of the crowd. It hadn't been a great ride, he knew, but he'd hung on to Big Tex, one of the wildest bulls he had ever faced, and the audience was showing their appreciation. He tipped his hat to them and slid a wink over to a group of buckle bunnies holding signs, their skintight clothing leaving little to the imagination.

He almost didn't hear the shouts behind him as he basked in the glow of the crowd, but eventually he registered that something was wrong in the ring. Before he could turn around, two thousand pounds of animal flesh and muscle slammed into Brock, pushing him to the ground.

A hoof slammed into the ground inches from his face, kicking dirt into his eyes. Brock lay still, waiting for the next hoof, the one that would break his arm, puncture a lung or crack his skull.

After another few seconds, he opened his eyes to see the sky above him. The bullfighters had pulled the stomping, twisting bull away and out of the ring. The audience was silent, waiting to see how injured he was.

Brock jumped to his feet, tossed another smile to the people noisily showing their approval and walked out of the ring to join the other riders, enjoying the feeling of adrenaline pounding through his veins.

After receiving congratulations from the pack of men, Brock set off toward his truck.

"You trying to get yourself killed?" a gruff voice demanded the moment Brock was alone.

He turned to find his uncle standing behind him, hands on his hips. He looked angrier than Brock had seen him in a long while.

Brock gave him what he hoped was a calming smile. "I'm fine, Uncle Joe. Not a scratch," he said, raising his hands for inspection, or possibly in surrender to his uncle's fury.

"That was dangerous, and *stupid*, Brock. You know not to hang around in the ring like that, especially not with a bull like Big Tex in there with you," Joe said, shaking his head. "Jeannie must be rolling in her grave right now. And what would Sarah say if she knew you were putting yourself at risk like that? My sisters would never forgive me if something happened to you. I'd be hounded in this world and the next."

Brock winced at the verbal assault. His mother had been dead for twenty years, since he was just a little boy, but it still bothered him to hear his uncle talk about her like that. And Brock knew that if his uncle said anything to Sarah, his ma, the woman who had raised him since his parents died, she would worry herself sick.

Uncle Joe seemed to realize he'd been harsh, and his expression softened. "You're lucky you survived today, you know."

Brock nodded, not saying anything. His uncle had been one of the best bull riders in his day, and it was only through his coaching that Brock had managed to turn it into a career.

"I don't know why I put up with you and your recklessness," Uncle Joe groused.

Brock stayed silent. His uncle always said things like that when he was angry, and Brock had learned it was best not to respond. Joe would keep coaching Brock as long as Brock wanted to ride, so there was no point fighting with the old man.

Joe seemed to have grumbled himself out on the matter, and he changed topics, to Brock's relief. "You're headin' home tonight, right? Sarah's been on my case about you going for a visit."

Brock nodded. "Ma's been especially persistent lately, so I'll be there for two weeks, until the next rodeo. Amy, Jose and Diego will be coming into town in the next couple of days, too."

It had been a long while since Brock had seen his adopted brothers and sister, and he was sure Ma was in a tizzy waiting for her kids to come home. Sarah and her husband, Howard, had treated Brock like their own child since he was eight years old, and his adopted siblings even longer. Even though they were technically his aunt and uncle, he never thought of them as anything but his parents.

Joe nodded. "Keep your nose clean and I'll see you at the rodeo."

Brock couldn't help but smile. He was pretty sure it would be impossible to get into any trouble in a one-stoplight town like Spring Valley, Texas.

His uncle seemed to know what he was thinking, because he pointed his finger at Brock's chest. "Don't give me any guff, boy. I don't know how you manage to get yourself in the scrapes you do, smart as you are."

Brock considered saying that what Uncle Joe considered "scrapes" usually involved other men from the rodeo, whom he'd met through Joe himself, but he kept his mouth shut. If he wasn't careful, he'd be there all night listening to a lecture.

Brock tipped his hat in silent promise to keep his nose clean, then he turned back to the parking lot. "I better get on the road. I'll tell Ma you said hi."

The older man nodded. "Take care of yourself and don't do anything foolish," he said before heading back toward the large arena, from which sound erupted as another cowboy tried for his chance at the purse.

Brock turned toward his truck, the silver behemoth glinting in the afternoon sun, just one of many in the parking lot, waves of heat floating above the sea of metal. It was still early enough that most of the audience and competitors wouldn't be leaving for another hour or more.

Normally he would have stayed to talk to the other cowboys, watch the last few rides, the closing ceremonies and possibly even the musical performance scheduled after the rodeo ended—and maybe get to know a few buckle bunnies while he was at it—then top the whole thing off with late-night drinks and planning the next big adventure with his friends. But he had a long drive ahead of him and he wanted to get to his parents' house before it was too late for a good meal, so he took one last look at the stadium behind him and opened the door to his truck, allowing the wave of pent-up heat to pass over him.

He wished he had his motorcycle with him so he could enjoy the sweeping curves of the mountain roads at top speeds, feel the rush of adrenaline and the wind at the same time. When he was on the circuit, though, it stayed in storage back in Dallas, so his truck would have to do. Anyway, if he rode up to Spring Valley on his bike, he'd get an earful from his ma, and he'd already had enough of that for one day.

He couldn't say he was happy about spending the weeks before his next rodeo in his tiny hometown, without much of a chance to prepare. He wanted to earn a spot at the NFR in Las Vegas, one of the toughest rodeos around, and Brock knew he couldn't take time off without hurting his chances.

But at least he was sure to get big servings of his ma's delicious country cooking, and he'd manage to find some way to keep himself sharp. Also, he could spend time helping Pop with the small riding school he ran on their property, though Brock knew that any insinuation that his dad was too old to do the work would earn him more than a stern talking-to.

Brock cranked the AC, steered out of the crowded parking lot and turned south toward Spring Valley.

As the sun disappeared behind the mountains surrounding the small town and ranches of Spring Valley, Brock turned off his truck's engine and stretched. The sprawling house in front of him looked cool and welcoming against the heat of the evening, and the unmistakable smell of horses and jasmine was so familiar that he would have known he was home even with his eyes closed. It was a smell that filled him with nostalgia and even a little longing. He'd always loved working on the ranch.

But that wasn't the life for him, he knew, though at times he wished it was. Rodeo life took a toll on a man, not just physically, but mentally. Moving from city to city, following the rodeo circuit, left Brock weary and glad for the short respite of a visit home, even if it made him itch for something more challenging, more dangerous, at the same time.

He saw the front door open and pulled the reins on his wayward thoughts as his ma came bustling out, her grin wide and her arms open. He climbed out of his truck and walked toward the woman who had cared for him so much of his life.

The frail-looking older woman pulled Brock into a hug so tight he could hardly breathe. He smiled at her. "You miss me?"

She swatted him on the shoulder. "Don't give me any attitude, boy. You've been gone too long and you know it. I oughta give your uncle Joe a piece of my mind. At least you didn't ride in here on that infernal motorcycle of yours," she said, shaking her head.

Before he could even attempt to respond, she continued, "Come in now, dinner should be ready in a few minutes. I made Howie wait until you got here. I knew my boy would be hungry."

Brock let Ma's words of reprimand and love wash over him as he followed her into the warmth and glow of home, smiling at how familiar it all was. Everything was just as it should be on McNeal Ranch.

The smell of fried chicken attacked his senses as soon as he crossed the threshold and his stomach growled in response. "You were right. I'm starving," he said, veering toward the kitchen and the delectable smells.

Before he reached his destination, however, his ma blocked his entrance. "Don't you go rummaging around in there. You'll need to wait 'til I'm finished with everything and we sit down at the table like civilized folks."

He stopped and heaved a theatrical sigh, hoping she might relent, but it seemed clear she wouldn't be swayed by pity. After another look at the determined set of her jaw, he shrugged. "Okay, okay, I'll go grab my things," he said, turning to head back out to his truck.

"Actually, I have a job for you to do," she said in a seemingly casual voice that didn't fool him for a second. Brock wondered if he would finally hear why she had been so insistent about him coming for a visit.

He raised his eyebrows and waited. In that same falsely casual tone, she said, "A sweet widow moved into the old Wilson place. Cassandra Stanford. She needs some help fixing up things around there. I told her my strong son would be happy to lend her a hand. You should go introduce yourself before we sit down to eat."

Brock was slightly disappointed. She just wanted him to do some work for an old widow? He had been expecting some bigger reason than that. His mother had been so pushy about him coming home, he'd half expected a mail-order bride to be waiting on the doorstep when he arrived. Maybe Ma had finally stopped trying to get her kids hitched and settled down, and was focusing her energy on helping her neighbor instead.

Brock doubted it, but for the time being, he was happy to be out of his ma's crosshairs. The last several times he'd been home, she had spent most of the time hinting about one girl or another from his high school, and she was always disappointed when he left for the circuit again without anything to show for her efforts.

Even if she had some plan for him during his stay, he was glad to see that she wasn't entirely consumed in her schemes. And it would be good for his ma to have a new friend nearby. Maybe they could knit together or something. Or, he shuddered to think, they could team up and become the town matchmakers.

He held in the smile that would lead to questions and another smack on the arm and gave Ma a kiss on her cheek. "Sure, I can help. I'll go introduce myself."

She grinned like the cat that ate the canary. "Don't rush yourself back. The chicken still has a ways to go."

Brock turned and headed back out the door he had walked through just a couple of minutes before, cutting through a paddock instead of heading out to the road. The Wilsons had been talking about moving for years, and he knew the place had fallen into disrepair as they got older. Why an old woman would want to take on the job was beyond him.

The walk was quick, and he hurried up the steps to the front porch of the neighboring home, noting the squeak of one of the steps and the white paint that was flaking off the house, showing the wood beneath.

There was plenty to do to make this place like new, if his first impression was any indication, but he knew it was a solid construction with good land. Part of him wished *he* had been the one to buy this property. Not that he had the money for this place. A middling rodeo cowboy didn't pull in enough for that kind of down payment. A National Finals cowboy might, though.

And it wasn't that likely he had even a chance of making it to Vegas if he spent the next two weeks painting and mending porch steps. He hoped the widow didn't expect him to be working there too often, or he'd be in a bit of a pickle. If Ma was so desperate to have him around, why would she give him a big job that might eat into all the time he had at home?

Brock brushed the question aside and turned his mind to the task at hand. He'd go through a short introduction and make his way back for his hot meal just as quickly as he could, then he'd make a plan as to how he should go about fixing up this place while leaving time to prepare for the next rodeo. He knocked.

After a few seconds, the door opened and any thought of food or rodeos disappeared. He stared, caught off-guard by the lovely woman who stood there, the warm glow of the lit room behind her enveloping her in almost a halo of light.

Her dark brown hair fell around her shoulders in a mass of curls, framing an open, sweet face and lips that promised more than just smiles for the guy lucky enough to get to kiss them. It was impossible to tell if her eyes were more brown or green, and he wanted to get near enough to get a better look. The blood in his veins moved faster just at the notion of being that close to her.

His ma's designs suddenly became clear: it wasn't the widow she had wanted him to meet, it was the beautiful lady standing before him. The widow's daughter, maybe?

He silently thanked his mother for her interfering ways as his eyes slid lower and took in more of the amazing view, noting how her jeans hugged her hips and the tied button-down shirt that accentuated her slim waist, giving just a peek of midriff. The top was unbuttoned low enough to give more than a suggestion of the breasts beneath.

Everything about her set him on fire. She was rather petite but didn't seem frail in the slightest despite her stature. She gave off an air of feistiness. Brock liked feisty.

Brock realized that he'd stood there without speaking for far too long, and brought his eyes back to hers. He suddenly felt a bit like an awkward teenager, not a grown man of nearly thirty. It took all his effort to arrange his face into a cool, confident smile. "Hello, ma'am," he said, putting on a slightly thicker drawl than usual. Ladies liked the Southern drawl. "I'm Brock McNeal. My folks live just over the way. They said Mrs. Stanford was in need of some help fixin' up this place, and I thought it best to come introduce myself."

A plan was already formulating in Brock's mind. Make nice to the old lady, get in good with the beautiful mystery woman, then ask her for a date. Easy enough. His only problem was that two weeks in town suddenly didn't seem near enough time if he could spend it enjoying her company.

The woman standing before him smiled. "Nice to meet you. Call me Cassie. Your mother was so sweet to offer your help. I really don't know how I would manage all of the work by myself."

Brock's mind shifted gears quickly. The widow wasn't some old woman at all. Which meant that Cassie was here all on her own. But was she mourning a recently lost husband? She didn't seem to be. Would it be wrong to ask her out?

Before he could come to a conclusion, there were noises behind her and two young boys shot into the doorway behind Cassie, their identical faces peering at him from behind Cassie's legs.

"Zach, Carter, say hello to Mr. McNeal. He'll be helping us fix up the place a bit," Cassie said.

Brock tried his hardest to keep the disappointment off his face, but he wasn't sure he succeeded.

Of course she had kids. There had to be something or his ma would've just come out and told him about her sneaky little plan. She knew well enough by now he didn't plan on having any children, and that meant no dating women with kids, either.

When the boys chirruped quiet hellos, he gave them a little wave before turning his attention back to their too-beautiful mother. "It was nice to meet you, but I better get back for dinner," he said.

Cassie seemed to sense his suddenly urgent need to leave; she nodded and said, "But I'll see you tomorrow and we can discuss the repairs?"

The almost desperate look in her eyes was too much. "Sure thing," he responded before turning away from the door, cursing his own bad luck.

Why did she have to be a mom?

Chapter 2

Cassie closed the door, trying not to show just how shaky she was feeling. She took in a large gulp of air, as if she hadn't breathed properly since first opening the door.

She put her hand to her chest, trying to calm the beating heart beneath. As soon as she did it, she realized her fingers were only touching bare skin and she groaned. She'd been unpacking boxes in the warm living room and had answered the door without realizing she was wearing a shirt that showed far more skin than she would have otherwise.

What must he have thought, to see her standing in the doorway showing off her stomach and chest like that?

Her mind went from zero to naughty in an instant, and it took all her effort to bring it back to being appropriately embarrassed.

"He's got big arms," Carter commented, oblivious to his mother's mental gymnastics.

Oh, she had noticed his arms. She had noticed every single inch of him, from the shaggy sun-kissed brown hair under a battered cowboy hat all the way to his scuffed boots. Her eyes had eaten him up like so much candy the moment she had seen him standing on her porch. But she wasn't planning on telling her four-year-old son that. "Hopefully he'll be strong enough to do things I can't do all on my own to get this ranch working," she said, trying to maintain her concentration on the tasks at hand.

"We'll help, too," Zach responded, a look of such sincerity on his young face that her heart—and eyes—welled up at the sight.

"I know you will," she answered, ruffling the boy's dark curls, trying to keep the worry out of her voice.

It had seemed like a great idea only a couple of months ago. Purchase a ranch, get out of the city and live the life she'd always wanted. It seemed so simple. But she hadn't expected everything to cost quite so much, and now here she was with a broken-down ranch that needed to make money, somehow, and she didn't have the faintest clue how to go about it.

She knew that once she got her small doctor's office going in the front room of the ranch house, she would be able to make ends meet, but finances would likely be tight for a while, and a running, profitable ranch would help give her a cushion. Instead, she was going to need to pour money into this place before she could hope to get much out of it.

Finding this ranch for sale when she so desperately wanted to leave Minneapolis had seemed like fate, and she'd jumped at the chance. Now, it seemed more like a crazy whim she'd acted on without thinking it through.

Mrs. McNeal's offer of a helpful son had been a gift from heaven, and she knew she could never turn down the assistance, even if the man on the doorstep made her think nothing but the most sinful of thoughts.

Cassie pictured the way he had been standing there looking her over, and she felt short of breath again. She had tried to behave as professionally as she could, despite the inclination to kiss this complete stranger. She was no longer a whimsical young woman who could give in to an impulse of that sort, no matter how strong.

It was more difficult than she'd like to admit, though. She did *not* look forward to seeing the man again, and she needed to keep her distance when those urges pushed her to do some very inappropriate things. If she had any choice, she would tell the neighbors she didn't require any help, after all. But she did, so there was nothing for it.

Cassie turned her thoughts back to her two sons, who were playing amid the boxes piled around the living room. "Time for bed," she told them, and they hopped up, racing for the bathroom.

Zach won, shutting the door in Carter's face. While he waited his turn, he went over to his mother and pulled on her arm. "Can you tell us the story about the time Dad saved the baby birds?" he asked, looking up to her with his large green eyes.

Cassie's heart squeezed tight. The boys idolized their

father and always wanted to hear stories about him. He had only been gone for six months, and she couldn't face tarnishing their perfect image of him, so she had kept telling them the good stories over and over, keeping the not-so-good ones to herself. To them, he was a kind-hearted police officer who had died in an unfortunate car crash. She wanted it to stay that way.

Zach and Carter were by far the biggest reason why she couldn't bring a man into her life. They weren't ready. Especially not for someone like this Mr. McNeal, who carried an air of recklessness about him.

If only that recklessness wasn't so damn enticing.

"Your new neighbor seems nice," Brock told his ma as he piled mashed potatoes onto his plate, trying to keep any hint of emotion out of his voice.

The old woman was terrible at hiding her exasperation. She had been so interested to hear what had happened that he was surprised she hadn't been hanging out a window with binoculars and some kind of long-distance microphone like in an old spy movie.

Well, it served her right to be on tenterhooks for a while, after that bit of meddling. Not that she shouldn't already know exactly how it went. She was well aware of his rule.

A bite of delicious fried chicken later, he felt he had tortured her enough.

"No kids, ma. You know that."

She gave an exaggerated sigh. "Brock, I can't understand what you have against children, particularly those two. They're sweet things. And being around them might do you, and them, some good. Howie, tell him," she said, swatting her husband on the arm.

The elderly man looked up from his food slowly, clearly unwilling to join the conversation. His gray mustache shifted from side to side as he chewed. After it was clear he was expected to make some sort of contribution, though, he nodded slightly. "Fine boys," he said.

Sarah looked triumphant, as if that settled everything.

Brock shrugged. "You know how I feel about raising kids. Between the rodeo circuit and the kind of life I live—"

His ma snorted, making her thoughts clear on *that* score. He plowed on, regardless.

"—I don't want the responsibility of children hanging over me every time I go rock climbing or hop on my motorcycle."

He didn't need to say any more. His adopted parents knew that he would never want to leave children without a father. When his parents had died…well, it wasn't something he would wish on anyone.

He turned his attention to his food, the air thick with unspoken words.

Still, if there was ever a woman who could make him consider breaking his "no kids" rule, it was this Cassie. Even then, the only type of relationship he was prepared to have with her would need to be something temporary, casual, especially when he'd be on the road again in another couple of weeks, and he doubted she would be okay with something like that. Not a widow with two young children.

It was best not to even start something, no matter how tempting the lady.

His ma shook her head at him. "Why you and your sister can't be happy with a nice calm life, I'll never know. With her always thousands of miles away and you doing reckless heaven-knows-what…at least your brothers don't try me like the two of you."

Brock bit his tongue, but he was sure Ma knew what he was thinking: what she called "reckless," he called fun, interesting, exciting.

"Where's Amy going after her visit?" he asked, hoping to change the subject.

"She said she needs to write an article about Morocco or something," Ma said, still glowering. "It's as if you two have a bet going to see who can make the last of my hairs gray the fastest."

Brock had to laugh at that. He'd never told Ma about the time the previous winter that he'd nearly snowboarded off a cliff face when a storm blew up around him, or a dozen other adventures he'd had in the last few years, but he could imagine her hair going pure white if she ever found out about it. He wondered if Amy had been keeping similar secrets from their ma.

The older woman harrumphed, but didn't say anything more on the subject, and for that he was grateful. They'd had the "When are you going to settle down?" conversation so many times that another run-through just sounded exhausting.

After eating, Brock climbed the stairs to his childhood room, too tired from the competition earlier in the day and the long ride home to think about much of anything. Before he went to sleep, however, the image of Cassie floated before his eyes, and he drifted off with a smile on his lips.

The next morning dawned hot and still, the sky quickly turning from soft lavender to a bright, cloudless blue. Cassie was awake but kept her eyes shut, not wanting to let go of the luxurious feeling that had come with whatever dream she had been having. Most of it had slipped away the moment she awoke, but she remembered one part of it with a vivid clarity: strong arms encircling her, holding her close to a warm muscular body.

She sighed and opened her bleary eyes, pulling herself off her bed, which was currently nothing more than a mattress and box spring on the floor. The time for dreaming was over, and that dream in particular had no place in her very busy day. She looked around the bedroom full of cartons, her eyes passing from the unfinished Ikea dresser to the headboard leaning against one wall, waiting to be attached to a bed frame she hadn't gotten around to putting together. She sighed again and started rummaging in one of the boxes for something to wear.

They had moved into the house two weeks before, but with the delays from the moving company and two raucous boys with no friends in town yet, she had hardly made a dent in the mounds of containers everywhere. Most of her time had simply been spent assessing what needed to be fixed and trying to organize the mass of paperwork the Wilsons left her about the property, none of which helped much.

What had she been thinking, buying this place and moving them all out here to chase some childish dream of hers? The thought had flitted through her mind over and over again since they'd arrived.

Without noticing, she had gotten to the bottom of the box of clothes, and her hand touched something silky. Curious, she pulled out whatever it was she'd found, promptly dropping it in surprise. The lingerie fell to the floor, a small pool of black silk and lace.

She didn't remember packing it, had even forgotten she'd ever purchased the thing. It was years ago now, when she was trying to keep her marriage afloat. It was a reminder that she had once hoped to have an exciting love life, the sort of thing she was now avoiding.

Cassie shook her head slightly and shoved the thing into the bottom of the box marked "Pajamas," then went back to picking something practical to wear. She pulled on jeans and a blouse, trying to forget the sexy black teddy, only to have the concerns about her new ranch rush back in on her.

She tried to make those thoughts go away, too. It was too late to second-guess her decision to put an offer on the ranch and sign the mortgage paperwork, so she might as well stop it and just look ahead to what needed to get done so their new home would run smoothly. Now that she'd have someone helping who might know a thing or two about how to do that, she felt hopeful about the progress that would be made.

If she could manage to keep her hands off him, of course.

She walked out of her depressingly cluttered room without looking at it again. That would need to wait until she dealt with more pressing matters, like when she could start seeing patients and figuring out how she could get the ranch to make money.

She let the worry drift to the back of her mind as she entered the living room, where Zach and Carter were using the piles of boxes and some blankets to make a fort. She smiled and crawled through the little door-way they had created using two kitchen chairs and a rug. Before she spent the day trying to be a doctor and a rancher, she could spend an hour being a mom to her two boys. That, at least, wasn't overwhelming.

They weren't very far along on their fort, however, when there was a knock on the door that made her heart sink. There was only one person who could be on the other side of that door, and despite how much she needed his help, she wasn't looking forward to seeing the handsome Mr. McNeal again, especially not after her dream from the night before. Zach jumped up, his head grazing the blanket that made the fort roof. "I'll get it!" he shouted, diving between the two chairs.

She listened to his quick footsteps and the squeak of the front door. When she heard the deep rumble of Brock McNeal's voice as he spoke to Zach, her face flushed. She steeled herself for a long day of pretending not to notice how attracted she was to him.

And how attracted he is to you, a little voice inside her added. Her mind drifted back to what hid in the bottom of her box of pajamas. She quelled all that immediately. Sure, she'd seen the way he had looked her over when she'd opened the door the previous night, but she had also seen the way his face fell when Zach and Carter joined her. She knew what that look meant, and it was enough to make her even more sure that she would keep her distance from this man.

If he wasn't interested in a woman with kids, well, it just made things that much easier. She took a deep breath, glanced down to make sure her shirt was more modest than yesterday and began trying to extricate herself from the tiny fort.

Brock followed the young boy into the home formerly owned by his old neighbors, Mr. and Mrs. Wilson, where he had played dozens of times as a kid. The house had a slightly dilapidated look about it, as if nobody had taken the time to keep it in good working order, but it was still clean and homey, the wallpaper and fixtures exactly as they had been twenty years before, and likely twenty years before that.

Though it was outdated and a little the worse for wear, it was of solid construction, a good home. He imagined there wouldn't be too much to do to get it up to snuff; hopefully the land was in a similar state and not too far gone to seed.

In the living room, the lovely woman of the evening before was crawling out of what was clearly a makeshift fort, her curly hair a messy tangle that hid half her face, her splendidly curved butt shown off in lovely detail.

How did she manage to make climbing out of a blanket fort sexy?

If he'd been out of sight, he would have smacked himself in the forehead to dislodge these wayward thoughts. It was clear to him that he'd need to help her as quickly as possible, and then keep his distance from this woman from then on out. If she got his heart pumping doing something so innocent, he needed to do everything in his power to protect himself.

She straightened up, looking even more deliciously tousled, and nodded to him with a small smile. "Thank you for coming, Mr. McNeal. I wasn't expecting you this early. I was just going to make some pancakes for the boys. Would you like some?"

Brock knew he should take the chance to get working while she was busy elsewhere, to ensure that he could concentrate on the manual labor without her nearby, but the thought of missing out on pancakes was disheartening. His ma was happy to make eggs and bacon but had never been one for pancakes—too sweet for a good start to the day, she'd always said. He forced himself to shake his head. "No, thanks, I already ate. I'll just get started on whatever you need me to do, if you don't mind."

Her mouth thinned a little and her cheeks blushed a light shade of pink. He realized that she really hadn't expected him yet, and she wasn't sure where he should start. She seemed to be at a loss for a moment.

Not that it was surprising she hadn't anticipated his early arrival. He'd woken at dawn, itching to get over there—to get started on all the work that needed to be done, he'd told himself. After all, two weeks wasn't much time, and he didn't want to leave his new neighbor in the lurch after he'd gone. So he'd headed over right after eating, without noticing exactly how early it was.

Brock decided that just because there was so much to do didn't mean there wasn't time for pancakes. "Actually, pancakes sound great. After all, there's probably enough work around here to burn off four breakfasts, I'm sure. And while you're at it, I'll take a look around to see what all there is to do, if that's all right?"

She nodded, looking relieved, and he immediately felt like he'd made the right choice. Plus, he would get to eat pancakes. That was a win-win.

"I'll go get them started. Please make yourself at home, Mr. McNeal."

"Call me Brock," he answered before she disappeared into the kitchen.

The moment she was gone, he looked around the room and started creating an inventory of everything that would need to be done to get the house in shape. Besides two warped window frames and the very faded wallpaper, the living room at least appeared in decent condition.

"Would you like to come in our fort?" one of the boys asked suddenly, poking his head out between two boxes.

Brock had forgotten he wasn't alone in the room. He gave the kid a small smile. "No, thanks," he said, not sure if there was anything else he was supposed to say.

It had been a long while since he'd spoken to anyone under the legal drinking age.

The other boy, identical to his brother, crawled out of the fort and moved to stand right next to Brock. Brock waited, wondering what the little boy was thinking. Finally, he spoke. "I'm Carter."

Brock nodded, wishing the child wasn't quite so close. He wasn't used to children and their lack of understanding about personal space. "Hi. I'm Brock," he answered.

Carter kept staring, as if waiting for Brock to say more, but he couldn't think of what else he should say.

"What are you doing?" the boy asked.

"I'm trying to figure out what we need to do to get this place fixed up," Brock answered.

Carter looked around the room. "Like what?"

Brock felt slightly relieved that the large hazel eyes were no longer staring at him in that intense way. He pointed out the windows, explaining about the frames.

"Momma tried to open those when we got here and couldn't," Carter commented. "What else is wrong?"

Brock shrugged. "I don't know. I just got here."

With that, Carter was off, pointing out every problem he had noticed since they'd moved there. Some, like the faint scratches on the wood floor from furniture being moved around, didn't concern Brock, but there were others that he added to the mental list he was making.

Soon, Brock and Carter had moved into the room the boys were sharing and Brock was examining the large wooden bunk bed the boys would use once, as Carter explained, it didn't wobble anymore. "Momma says the Wilson boys must have been pretty rowdy to break such a big piece of furniture," Carter said as Brock pulled on the top bunk and watched it sway precariously. Brock smiled, remembering exactly how "rowdy" the Wilson boys were. They had gotten Brock into quite a bit of trouble more than once when he was a kid.

Carter continued talking, as if he had no plans to stop anytime soon. "But it was free, so she said she would fix it and then we won't have to sleep on the floor no more."

"Anymore," said a voice from the doorway. The other brother, Zach, had joined them.

Brock nodded to him, then turned back to Carter. "It'll be easy to fix. A couple planks of wood and some nails will do it."

"There's some in the barn. Momma showed me."

Brock stood, ready to go find them, but Zach interrupted his thoughts. "Mom says food's ready, Mr. McNeal."

Before Brock could say anything, Carter jumped up and grabbed his hand. "We have to wash up before we eat. I'll show you." And with that, Brock was being pulled into a small bathroom and shown how to clean his hands properly.

Brock washed at the sink and followed Carter and Zach into the kitchen, where the boys jumped into chairs, both sitting on their feet so they could see over the table. The moment he was back in the same room as Cassie, the air felt warm and heavy, neither of which had anything to do with the cooking.

Brock tried not to let his eyes wander along the length of her legs as she stood by the stove, flipping the last pancakes on the griddle. The jeans she was wearing hugged her in all the right places, and a long study of them would just make things worse.

He was here to do a job, help a lady and her kids

out, and then he would get back to doing the things he did best. After all, his next big bull ride was coming up soon. It wouldn't do to start getting sidetracked by a mess of russet-colored hair and a pair of shapely legs. Or any of her other attributes he had noticed.

With difficulty, Brock pulled his eyes to the plate in the middle of the table piled high with flapjacks. The smell wafting from them was light and sweet, and they made his mouth water despite the large breakfast he'd already had. The boys had quickly grabbed a couple and begun dousing them in syrup, so he speared a few of his own with his fork.

Cassie came to the table, taking the only open seat, the one directly across from him. Now that she was close and in the bright light of the kitchen, he could see a dusting of freckles across her nose and the clear green-brown of her eyes. When she leaned forward to grab her own pile of pancakes, he quickly glanced away. There was too much to catch all of his male attention when she did that.

Thankfully, she soon sat back in her seat and he could actually savor the flavor of the pancakes he had shoved into his mouth in a desperate bid for a distraction.

She didn't seem to notice any of this and her attention remained focused on her children. "Did you both wash up before coming in and getting covered in syrup?" she asked.

Carter nodded as he licked some of the sticky sweetness off his forearm. "I showed Brock how to wash up, too," he said.

Cassie gave her son a warning look. "Don't be impolite. You can call him Mr. McNeal."

"It's fine," Brock cut in, not wanting Carter to get in trouble for his actions. "I told him he could call me that. I think the only person who has ever called me Mr. McNeal was my fourth-grade teacher, and that lady was plumb crazy."

Carter smiled at him. Brock couldn't help but smile back.

Cassie also seemed pleased, though she wasn't as obvious in her emotions as Carter was. "Well, now that that's settled," she said, "I was thinking we would start working in the library first, and then some of the fencing around the place, or maybe the barn. I want to get the ranch ready to hold horses."

He nodded, trying to keep his eyes on his plate instead of on her. Hopefully she would show him where to start and leave him to it, and he could lose himself in hard work and avoid this woman who set his blood on fire.

After she dumped the dishes in the sink, though, she looked at her two boys and said, "While we're moving things around, I'd like you to put your clothes into the drawers in your room. After that, you can work on your fort or play with your cars. Can you do that?"

So, she clearly wasn't planning on freeing him from her presence. If he hadn't been pleased that she was willing to get her hands dirty and help fix up the place, he would've been annoyed about spending even more time near her.

The boys nodded and raced into their room. Brock

was impressed that such young children could follow directions, but before he could comment, Cassie smiled at him and shook her head. "They'll probably throw everything in one drawer before getting sidetracked and playing with toys, but it'll keep them busy for a few minutes, at least."

Brock pictured himself doing just that as a kid and laughed. Her dry humor only made her prettier, which sobered him quickly. "So, you wanted to start in the Wilsons' old library?" he prompted.

Cassie nodded and walked out of the kitchen, beckoning at Brock to follow her. He took a deep breath and tried to ignore the well-formed bottom that swayed so enticingly before him.

Chapter 3

Cassie showed Brock into the small room off the living room that she hoped to turn into a doctor's office. Before she could start seeing patients, however, there was a lot to do.

The room had obviously been used as a library. The empty shelves lining the wall were of dark oak, making the entire space feel shady and somber. She imagined leather chairs and dusty volumes of old books giving it an air of class, but it didn't fit with the light, friendly tone she wanted to convey.

"Mr. Wilson was quite a reader," Brock commented, looking around the room. "I never understood why they lived on this ranch when he would have been much happier being a professor or something. What do you want to do with it?"

"I want to take out these shelves and make it into a

doctor's office," she started, ready to turn her dream into a reality.

"You're a doctor?" he asked, clearly surprised.

She nodded, waiting to see how he would react. Her husband, Hank, had always been negative about her choice to continue school instead of staying home with their young children, and even though he'd been gone for over six months, she still heard his disapproving words in her ears.

Brock gave her a sideways grin that turned her insides to mush. "You're full of surprises," he commented, and she couldn't stop the blush of pleasure that worked its way up to her ears. "Well, the town certainly needs a doctor. People are going to line up at your door. So I guess we should get this place ready."

Then he turned back to the room as if nothing had changed. Cassie's defenses lowered slightly as she accustomed herself to Brock's presence.

"Okay, so the shelves need to go," he said. "What do you need to make the room ready?"

With that, she was off, describing the room she had imagined. A small desk, some shelves to hold supplies, bright paint, a couple of chairs and an examination table. A happy place where she could help people.

Brock listened, nodding occasionally. When she finished, he stretched, his arms raised to the ceiling. Cassie tried not to stare at him, but it wasn't easy. "Let's get started, then," he said, moving farther into the room.

Soon they were grappling with the bookcases— heavy bulky things that, thankfully, took all her attention. With some difficulty, they managed to get the three large shelving units on their sides and slide each one out the door until they were lying in a row on the living room floor.

With those out, the room seemed much larger and brighter, and Cassie's heart lifted. She knew she could make it into everything she wanted. Then she realized there was one big problem that prevented her from doing more.

Brock seemed to sense her sudden change of mood. "You don't have paint yet, do you?"

Cassie shook her head, trying not to feel too disappointed.

"Then we'll need to get some. We can do that tomorrow morning, if you like. For now, on to the next thing," Brock announced, sidling out of the room.

Cassie could tell he wasn't going to let her sulk, and it made her smile. He was right, anyhow. There was too much to do to sit around just because she didn't have paint.

Back in the living room, they both looked at the shelves taking up most of the floor space. "I guess we could put two of these in my room and the other in Zach and Carter's," she said at last.

Brock moved into place to pick up one of the units and waited for her. Cassie couldn't believe how willing he was to haul them all over her house, without a word of protest. She silently thanked Brock's mother for having such a helpful son.

Soon all her thoughts and energy were once again absorbed by the task of lifting the heavy pieces of furniture, which they lugged down the hall.

Maneuvering the first one into her bedroom was a

bit of a challenge, but finally the shelf stood against the wall opposite her bed. If the room wasn't large, it might have looked hefty, but Cassie felt it fit nicely. She turned to Brock to see if he was ready to move the second one, and found him standing awkwardly near the doorway.

Then she realized that they were in her bedroom and she felt a flush creep up her neck at the memory of what lay at the bottom of her box of pajamas, only a couple of feet from where she was standing.

Brock cleared his throat and looked at her, but didn't quite meet her eyes, for which she was thankful. Now was not the time to get lost in those ocean-colored depths. "Let's go grab the next one," he said, leaving for the hallway.

Cassie followed, hoping the heat in her cheeks would go away before they looked at each other again.

Brock was glad to return to the open air of the living room. Even though the master bedroom in the Wilson house was large, the presence of Cassie and her bed made him feel short of breath and a little claustrophobic.

But that wasn't the way his thoughts should be turning, he knew.

They made quick work of the second shelf, and without pausing in Cassie's room, for which Brock was grateful, moved onto the third. As Brock picked up his end, he could feel the strain in his back, a holdover from an old rodeo injury. If he was tired, he imagined Cassie must be exhausted. He almost set down the shelf again to propose they take a break, but before he could, Cassie had lifted her end and begun moving toward the hallway with dogged determination on her face.

Brock couldn't help but be impressed. She didn't shirk the work it was going to take to get this place running, that was for sure. They carried the thing into the boys' room, where they set it up against the wall as the two boys watched from where they'd been playing on the floor. When it was in place, Cassie leaned against it to catch her breath. Brock took the chance to stretch his back.

"Did you boys finish putting all your clothes away before playing?" Cassie asked after a few moments.

The children nodded, but Brock noticed they seemed a little hesitant. He glanced over at the chest of drawers. From the look of the bursting bottom drawer, Cassie's earlier prediction seemed to have come true. She noticed, too, and she opened it wider. "I don't think you'll be able to find anything in here," she told them, with an impressive amount of patience. "How about we work on this together?"

Brock could see this might take a while, so he left Cassie with her kids and went back to the library. This woman just kept getting more and more attractive. A beautiful, hardworking doctor with the patience of a saint. He shook his head in amazement.

He wanted to ask her out. What harm could a date do? He imagined she could use an evening being pampered.

There was one big flaw with that idea, though: What if she said no? He didn't want the next couple of weeks to be awkward as they worked on her house and ranch together. Or worse, she felt so uncomfortable that she insisted on doing it all by herself, even though it was clearly too big a job for just one person.

So he wouldn't ask her out yet, then. Not until he was sure she'd say yes, or until enough work was finished that he wouldn't feel guilty if he got turned down and was asked to never see her again.

He hoped to God that wouldn't happen.

What about her kids? A small voice inside him piped up.

Well, it would just be a date. Nothing serious. He wasn't going to turn everything in his life upside down because of a passing attraction. They'd go on a few dates, have a nice time and then he'd leave. If they both agreed to nothing permanent, neither of them could get hurt, right?

Brock felt a twinge of uncertainty but dismissed it. If he had to choose between a temporary relationship with Cassie or no relationship at all, he knew which side he fell on. The thought lifted his spirits, and he looked around eagerly for something to accomplish.

Near the library, leaning against a wall, were some boxes with pictures of small white shelves on them. They were clearly pieces of furniture for her future doctor's office, and would need to be assembled before she could start seeing patients.

He immediately set to work on the first one.

The task went quickly, and by the time Cassie appeared, he was halfway through the second, with instructions and pieces surrounding where he sat on the floor. Seeing her made his heart beat harder, and he found it difficult to remember what it was he'd been doing. She caressed the top of the completed piece in such a way that it took every bit of his self-control to not ask her out right then and there.

"Thank you for your help," she said, so sincerely that it squeezed at his heart. It was clear from her tone that she'd desperately needed an extra pair of hands.

"I imagine it's hard to get much done with two young boys around," he commented.

She let out a sigh of agreement and nodded. "They're putting things on their new shelf now, so that should give them something to do for a little while, at least," she said, sitting down beside him and leaning close to look at the instructions.

For a moment, she was too close, and he wanted more than ever to do something about the feelings crowding in him. As he opened his mouth to say something stupid, she moved away again, and his mind cleared enough to keep quiet. She didn't seem to notice, and before he could get out of his daze enough to get back to the task at hand, she was grabbing pieces and fitting them together with nimble, quick movements.

With some effort, Brock turned back to his own work, and they flew through the rest of the low-lying shelves, two cabinets and several small drawers. He imagined them holding cotton swabs, latex gloves and myriad other items that a doctor would need in order to care for the people who came to her. From the way Cassie was smiling as she touched each completed piece, she could, too.

When they were finished with the last drawer, Cassie sat back and looked around her at all they'd done. Brock could only stare at her. She was endlessly fascinating. They had worked almost entirely without speaking, anticipating each other's motions in a way he couldn't describe. They had been assembling a few inexpensive pieces of furniture, but it had felt more like a dance where they moved in harmony together.

He stood and started placing the completed items against the wall, out of the way until they could be placed into the new office. The silence that had been comfortable a few minutes before became thick, and he grasped for something to talk about. "What's the next big task on your to-do list?" he said, hoping she didn't notice the strained sound of his voice.

"Until I have paint, we've done about as much on the office as we can. I guess the next big part—"

He hoped she wouldn't say her bedroom. He'd noticed the boxes and incomplete bedframe, but boy howdy, an hour in her bedroom seemed much more dangerous than jumping out of an airplane or climbing on the back of a bull right now.

"—would be the fence, or maybe the barn," she finished.

Brock exhaled with relief.

"Well," he started, considering the best plan of action, "we should probably take a walk along the perimeter, see where the fence needs to be fixed or replaced."

Brock wasn't sure if he really thought the entire fence needed to be checked or if he was just torturing himself with a long, private stroll with Cassie. He didn't need to worry about the latter, though, because Cassie immediately stood and said, "I'll go get Zach and Carter.

They'll be happy to get out of the house," before disappearing down the hall toward the boys' room.

Cassie was glad for the twins' company as they all walked out into the late-morning sun. The hours she had spent with Brock already that day made her very aware that she needed chaperones, if only to keep herself from doing something stupid like kissing him.

Luckily, her children were excellent distractions.

As soon as they were out of the house, the boys were tearing around like two tiny dust storms, creating havoc wherever they went and only stopping occasionally to ask Brock questions about life as a cowboy.

Through his answers, she learned that he was visiting his parents for two weeks and that he worked on the circuit—though she wasn't entirely sure what that meant. The boys were thrilled to discover that he owned a truck *and* a motorcycle. And that he liked horses and owned lots of cowboy hats and boots.

From the way he answered each question without a sign of irritation, she also realized that Brock was patient, good-natured and kind. She wished he was just a little bit worse of a human being, so she'd have something to grasp to that might help her get over her overwhelming attraction to him.

Finally, she cut into the questions, both because she wanted to save Brock from the unending list the boys seemed to have, and because she was curious what he was doing as he examined a fence post.

"Boys, why don't you race each other to that tree?" she suggested, pointing out a small oak a hundred yards or so in the distance. Zach and Carter ran off, their excess energy seeming to burst out of every seam.

Cassie turned to Brock. "What are you checking for?" she asked, wondering if she sounded like the young boys.

"To see if the wood is rotten or not. If you have rot, you'll need to replace those sections, or they might come down not long from now. It'll be a lot of extra work, though."

"And money, I'm sure," Cassie said, biting her lip.

She would need to get her doctor's office going, and soon, or at this rate she and the boys would be living off peanut butter sandwiches for the foreseeable future.

Brock nodded. "But the fence can wait, if you aren't planning on keeping animals out here, in which case we could just fix the paddock and barn."

Cassie gazed across the land covered in tall grass the color of gold. What would she do with the crops? She had just wanted a ranch with some horses, but it was becoming more and more obvious that she didn't know the first thing about ranching...

Maybe her mother was right: she was getting in way over her head. She was just a city girl playing rancher, and she didn't know the game.

"Everything okay?" Brock asked, pulling her out of her reverie.

She started to nod but couldn't bring herself to pretend. "There's just so much I need to figure out," she answered, looking at him.

The sympathy in his dark blue eyes made her heart thump heavily, and she had difficulty keeping control of herself.

He looked out over her ranch and she took the chance

to catch her breath. After a few moments, he nodded. "It'll be a lot of work, but it's a good piece of land. Do you have a buyer for the hay you won't use?"

She shook her head, feeling stupid. She didn't even have any idea how to turn the grass waving in front of her into hay bales, let alone what to do with it. "I don't—"

Cassie stopped talking, her voice catching in her throat. She had been told that the farm was growing grass to turn into hay, but she hadn't thought about what to do with it until she'd actually gotten here and seen it.

The enormity of the tasks before her threatened to overwhelm her. She could only imagine what Brock must think about her, purchasing this whole place without knowing how to do a single thing.

"This is my lucky day," Brock replied.

Cassie looked at Brock, surprised at the enthusiasm in his voice. Was he being sarcastic?

Brock hitched his thumb back toward his parents' ranch. "Pop could use a good chunk for their horses, and my brothers would be happy to buy the rest, I'm sure. And they'll pay to get the baling machine out here, too, if you don't already have one lined up. It's my lucky day because this means almost my entire family will owe me, which can be useful in the McNeal house."

Cassie laughed, more out of astonishment than anything. "Do you really think your brothers would do all that?" she asked, trying not to get her hopes up too high, but unable to suppress the grin that came to her lips.

Brock nodded, smiling back. "They just started a business working with rodeo stock, and I'm sure they could use it. They'll give you a fair price."

A weight lifted off Cassie, and she felt some of the

tension in her shoulders ease. She would be able to sell the hay. If she could do that, start seeing patients, mend the fence and make the barn livable for her horses, maybe everything would be all right. It was a big if, but it was something.

"You'll want to keep a bit of it for your own horses, right? I know the Wilsons had a couple."

She nodded, picturing Rosalind and Diamond, the two mares that had come with the property. "If I can get the barn and fencing in shape enough to keep them here, yes. For now, they're being kept at a place a few miles away."

"Well, we can figure out what lumber you need for the fence and paddock, but mend the paddock first. That way, you can move the horses here sooner. They don't need a perfect barn in this weather, so those little fixes can wait."

She didn't say anything about the boarding costs, yet another worry on her plate. Cassie suddenly felt embarrassed, as if every shortcoming and difficulty of hers was being laid bare in front of this man she'd known less than twenty-four hours.

Despite how much she appreciated his help, she also felt slightly uncomfortable with how much she needed it. She'd always been self-sufficient, smart and able to do whatever she put her mind to. This whole thing wasn't great for her ego, that was for sure.

Still, she'd gotten herself into this mess, and right now she just needed to worry about surviving it with as much of her dignity intact as she could manage. As long as nothing else landed on her plate, she would be able to handle it.

She hoped.

Chapter 4

Brock looked at Cassie, his heart going out to her. He could tell she was anxious, with her lips pinched so tightly together. It seemed like a world of worries was swirling about in her head.

"So, with the hay issue settled and our next job planned, we can get back to checking the fence," he said, hoping to get her attention on the here and now, and away from her thoughts. "With the perimeter fence, if you're only growing crops, we can just repair it a bit, but if you plan to have any animals roaming around, we'll need to make sure it's perfectly solid. Do you think you'll have stock out here, or just crops?"

Apparently his question didn't help at all, because she only looked more worried, and he could see that tears were threatening to fall. Even though they had only met the day before, he couldn't stand by and watch without doing something. As if on the same impulse, he pulled her into a hug as she threw herself against him. "I don't know what I'm doing here," she said, her voice muffled against his chest.

"Momma? You okay?" Carter asked.

Brock looked down, startled to see the boys. They had finished the race apparently, and were standing side by side with expressions of concern on their identical faces.

Cassie broke away from his chest and smiled down at her children. "I'm fine, honey. I was giving Mr. McNeal a hug. Because he's being so nice to help us."

Brock stood there, not sure what to say. The moment had been so raw, so pained, and yet she was able to put it all aside for her little boys. He had to wonder if she'd done the same thing when her husband died, burying her hurt in order to stay strong for her children. He was almost sure she had.

He was truly amazed by this woman.

"Let's keep walking," Brock said at last, trying to bring himself out of his own thoughts. "I'll check for rot, and we can figure it all out once we know what we're looking at. How does that sound?"

Cassie flashed him a grateful look, and they all continued along the perimeter of the land.

The boys immediately filled the silence with their questions and whatever else seemed to pop into their heads. Brock couldn't help but like them. His ma was right: they were sweet kids.

Zach grabbed Cassie's arm. "Momma! Tell about Daddy!"

Brock was glad he was already looking at a fence post and the lumber nailed to it—it gave him a chance to hide his reactions. Curiosity mixed with a little embarrassment, and maybe even some jealousy. The man had, after all, been married to Cassie, been father to these two boys. He couldn't help wanting to stack himself up against him, even if his good sense told him it was a bad idea in more ways than one.

Once he'd mastered his expression, Brock turned back to Cassie and the boys, hoping he seemed nonchalant. He was surprised to see the slight flush of red in Cassie's cheeks, and wondered if his presence was causing her to feel uncomfortable.

He moved ahead of the other three, just in case the distance might make her feel better. He couldn't help listening, though.

"Your daddy," she began, in a tone that made Brock sure she'd said these same words many times, "was one of the hardest workers in our precinct. He worked lots of hours trying to keep the city safe for everyone."

"He was a good policeman," Carter added, as if he held that knowledge close to his heart.

Brock felt heartbroken for these two boys, who had lost their father at such a young age. It brought back his own painful memories.

He didn't look at Cassie, kept his eyes on the fence, but he imagined her nodding and smiling at her son, remembering her brave police officer husband. Asking her out suddenly seemed like little more than a pipe dream.

"One time, he was driving along in his squad car," Cassie went on, "and he saw a man yelling at a woman, who was crying."

"That man was mean!" Zach shouted, angry.

"He was mean," Cassie agreed. "Your daddy went up and helped the woman, and the man couldn't hurt her anymore because your daddy was there to protect her. It's good to help and protect people who need it," she concluded.

The boys gabbled happily about the story, running on ahead. Brock stood with Cassie, unsure what to say. Complimenting her deceased husband didn't seem right, but neither did asking questions or completely ignoring what just happened.

Before he could figure out what to say, Cassie spoke to him, her voice quiet enough to keep the boys from overhearing. "Sorry. About before."

With the image of her husband looming large over Brock, he had almost forgotten her tears from just a few minutes ago.

He waved away the apology. "None of us know what we're doing all the time," he said.

She made a noise that could have been a snort, or perhaps a small sob. "It's not just a small case of indecision. I made all these choices, moving us all the way out here, without really thinking things through. I was so desperate to get away from—well, it doesn't matter. So I followed a silly childhood dream, and now the reality of it all is a bit much. My mom was right," she said with a small, sad laugh, "I was being too impulsive, too stubborn."

Brock smiled. "My ma says that about me all the time, too."

"Is she right?" Cassie asked, her voice quiet.

Brock could see she was hoping for something to hold on to. He shrugged. "Yeah, but I've got to make choices for myself, right? You can't be happy living the way other people want you to."

He watched her absorb his words. Finally, she nodded, wiping away a stray tear, and turned to the fence. "Is much of it decayed?" she asked.

He half wanted to bring the subject back to why she had come here, what she was running away from, but decided to let it lie. It probably had to do with her husband's death, and if she moved here because the memory of her lost love was too painful, he'd rather not know. Brock knocked on the fence board in front of him. "It seems like most of it is okay. It just needs some new nails and a fresh coat of paint. You'll need a few hundred bucks' worth of lumber, at most, if the rest of it is like this," he said, gesturing at the expanse of fence behind them.

Cassie seemed relieved, and they continued walking in silence. After a short while, Brock said, "You might want to consider raising a small herd of cows out here. It would cost a bit at first, but you can buy them as you can afford them, and they'll be more lucrative than selling bales of hay in the long run."

Brock wasn't sure if the information was helpful or more to add to her plate, but he felt sure, despite how little he knew about her, that she would appreciate knowing his opinion on the subject.

Cassie smiled. "Owning cows to go along with my horses, huh? That would make me a real country girl," she said, hooking her thumbs in her jean pockets.

He laughed. "Get some boots instead of those sneakers and a good hat, and nobody will know you're a city slicker."

She nodded, raising her hand to shade her face from the sun's powerful rays. "I'll definitely need a hat, if it's always this sunny. I'm not used to the weather here."

"Where are you from?" he asked without thinking.

It was only after he said it that he remembered her earlier words. Wherever she was from, she had run to the country to get away from it. Brock felt like an ass for bringing it up, but it was too late now.

"Minneapolis," she said, without elaborating further.

Still, she didn't seem devastated by the question, and he was curious about her. *In for a penny, in for a pound*, he thought. "That's a pretty big city," he commented.

"Smaller than you might think," she answered in a light tone, but the expression on her face hardened slightly.

Something within him pushed to keep the conversation going as they continued along the fence. They were over halfway done, and he felt like this was an opportunity to get to know her. Something about the wide-open land and sky around them made it easier. "I can see why you haven't had much experience with land and fences up there. It's not exactly a ranching area. The winters are brutal there, aren't they?"

She rolled her eyes, and his heart jumped when she gave him a genuine smile. "Like you wouldn't believe. That's one of the reasons I picked Spring Valley. I'll be just fine if I never see snow again."

He wanted to keep her smiling. "Well, this is the place to be if you hate snow. It's a rare winter that we get more than an inch or two."

She nodded and looked fondly across the hot brown grass. Before the silence could stretch too long, he said, "I'm surprised you even managed to find this place. Spring Valley doesn't show up on many maps."

"Hank, my—my late husband—his parents live in Glen Rock, not too far from here. I fell in love with the area the first time we visited. It seemed just like the place I wanted to live when I was a kid. Somewhere far away from the busy city life, with land and animals to tend…"

Her voice drifted away, as if she was picturing the ranch, not as it was, but as she must have imagined it when she was little. She seemed so sincere, so hopeful, that he knew he'd do whatever he could to help make that dream a reality.

Then she started walking again and he followed. In what felt like too short a time, they had finished most of the fence and then just had the paddock left. He wished there were more fence to saunter along, some other reason to dawdle outside. There was something calming, *right*, about strolling out there with Cassie and her boys.

"Have you lived here your whole life?" she asked, pulling him out of his reverie.

That simple question was always a difficult one to

answer, and even though he felt like Cassie was a person he could confide in, he wasn't ready to explain the whole situation to her. He stuck with his honest-but-short response, hoping she wouldn't ask for more details. "No. I lived in San Diego for a while when I was little."

"Surfer-turned-cowboy, huh?" she said with a smile.

Her fun tone made him want to joke with her, but he couldn't bring himself to do more than give her a small smile. The image of his father teaching him to surf always brought with it an unpleasant ache in his chest. Despite all the extreme sports he'd tried as an adult, he'd never been able to get back on a surfboard. "Something like that" was all he said.

She seemed to sense his unwillingness to discuss his life in San Diego, because she didn't ask him anything more about his childhood.

Cassie wasn't sure if she was happy or not that the walk was over as they finished the loop around the paddock. It was hot, and she was looking forward to the cool and shade of the house, and to an icy drink, but she couldn't help but wish she and Brock were still ambling on beside each other. He somehow managed to set her on fire and soothe her soul at the same time, and she worried the feeling would disappear once they were back in the house, away from the great expanse of land that surrounded them.

They stopped walking, and Cassie lingered an extra moment. Brock made no move toward the house, either, and they stood there quietly as the boys ran inside.

"So, what's the verdict? How much do I need to re-place?" she asked, not yet ready to go inside.

Brock smiled at her, and she felt her heart thump. "Not much, actually. It's better than I would have ex-pected, and the paddock shouldn't take more than a bit of lumber and a few hours' work before it's ready to hold your horses."

Cassie felt relief course through her. Maybe she would be able to make this work, prove to herself that she could do it.

She looked into his eyes, and the heat around them grew even thicker with unsaid thoughts. Cassie was wondering what it would be like to kiss him when the slam of the screen door came as a welcome diversion. She turned toward the house, creating distance between her and the smoldering man beside her.

Both of her boys were running across the golden grass toward her, leaving a woman standing on the back porch. Cassie squinted in the bright sunlight to see who it was.

Carter skidded in front of her, already talking. "Momma, Miss Emma is here. She brought a pie. She said it was for dessert, but can we have some now? Please?"

"Is that Emmaline Reynolds?" Brock asked from behind her.

Something like jealousy popped up in Cassie, but she quickly tamped it down. She had no call to feel posses-sive about Brock, she reminded herself. He could date Emma all he wanted.

She couldn't stop herself from saying a quick prayer that he wouldn't, though.

"I haven't seen her since grade school. Didn't even know she still lived here. You sure make friends fast," Brock commented.

Her mood suddenly lifted, she flashed him a smile. "When you have a sweet tooth and two young kids and you move to a town with one bakery, you get to know the owner of said bakery very quickly. Especially when the boxes of kitchen supplies go missing for a week. We've also made friends with the owners of the pizza place and the café."

Brock chuckled, the sound reverberating through her body, and his grin caught her off-guard, turning her legs to jelly. She started to regret saying something amusing, looking at him and having a sex drive at all, because this man was certain to be her downfall if a laugh and a smile could do all that to her. Apparently not noticing her discomfiture, he said, "I'm going to go do another check of the paddock real quick, just to be sure we didn't miss anything, and then it's probably best we take a break anyway. You'd be surprised how fast the heat can get to you."

It wasn't the heat that was getting to her, but she wasn't about to say that.

"I'll go see what Emma wants. Come on in when-ever you're done," she said to him as she turned away.

She was going to need to be very careful around Brock McNeal.

At the back porch, Emma smiled at her friend. "I came to tell you that I need some more of your business cards to put by the register, because people have been taking them left and right. You should expect to start getting calls for appointments any time now. My neighbor, Mrs. Edelman, asked me to bring her in just as soon as you're open for business. In fact, I'm not working the day after tomorrow, if you'll be ready by then"

Cassie couldn't believe it. "I may not have my office perfect yet, but I'd be happy to meet her then, if that works for you."

Emma nodded, satisfied. "And you really ran through all those cards?" Cassie couldn't help but asking.

"What can I say? People here are excited to have a doctor in town," Emma responded.

Cassie had given Emma a stack of cards only a few days before, in the hopes that she could start meeting with patients as soon as the office was completed. If they were gone already, and if she had her first appointment lined up, her practice might get a running start after all, and she would be able to pay for whatever new expenses cropped up.

Emma's voice broke through her thoughts, bringing her back to reality. "Also, I brought you an official 'welcome to the neighborhood' pie. And it's a 'thanks for treating my burns' pie and an 'I'm glad to have a friend who's also the town doctor and plan to keep her very happy' pie, too."

Emma tilted the pie in her hands so Cassie could see the laced top, beautifully browned with dark berries peeking out and sugar crystals sprinkled on top. The sight made Cassie's mouth water. She laughed. "Pies convey a lot of meaning, huh?"

Emma shrugged. "I just want you to know that I'm glad you moved here, Doc. You have great timing."

When Emma had burned her arm badly the week before while Cassie and the boys were at the bakery, Cassie was happy to help treat the wound. That and Emma's amazing cinnamon rolls had started a quick friendship, one that Cassie was very grateful for in her new life.

"Your very meaningful pie looks amazing, Emma," she responded, inhaling the wafting smell of pastry and berries.

"I thought you could probably use a treat, but," Emma added, nodding her head toward Brock in the distance, "it seems like you already have a sweet treat here. Who is that?" she asked in a gossipy whisper.

Cassie looked toward Brock, whose muscles looked almost heavenly in the bright sunshine as he moved about the paddock that would one day hold her horses. "It's Brock McNeal. His parents live next door and he's giving me a little help fixing this place up. He said he knew you from school."

Emma whistled a low note and leaned back against the doorjamb. "Brock McNeal. I haven't seen him since we were kids. He did a great job growing up."

Cassie ushered Emma into the cool, dim kitchen, where they put the pie on the counter. Emma kept looking out the window at Brock, leaving Cassie feeling more agitated than she'd like. "Did you two date in high school? I imagine everyone in such a small town must've gone out with each other at some point. Unless you're related, of course," Cassie said as nonchalantly as she could.

Emma's head whipped around to stare at Cassie, and she gave her a conspiratorial smile. "No, we never dated. I moved away in middle school and only came back two years ago to start the bakery. I missed my chance, I guess."

Cassie tried to pretend she didn't hear what her friend was implying. "Let me take a look at your burn. I want to make sure it's healing."

Emma's expression made it very clear she wasn't fooled by the change of subject. Cassie couldn't help but laugh when Emma rolled her eyes and crossed her arms, refusing to cooperate until she was given more details. "He's attractive," Cassie admitted, "but I've got my boys and too much to do around here as it is. Brock's just helping me fix up the ranch. Nothing romantic going on. I'm not about to start any messy relationships."

"A messy relationship could be really fun," Emma said, slipping Cassie a wink and rolling up her sleeve. Cassie inspected the nearly healed burn, happy with its progress and that Emma didn't push the subject of Brock McNeal any further. Cassie was quite aware of how fun a messy relationship with the man could be, and she was determined not to allow that thought to go any further than it already had.

After ensuring herself that Emma had taken care of the burn as directed, Cassie released Emma's arm as Brock came in the door, carrying a couple short planks of wood and a hammer. "Hey, Brock. Long time no see," Emma said.

Brock smiled at her. "Good to see you, Emma. I'd shake your hand, but—" He trailed off, gesturing at the lumber in his arms. "How's your brother?"

"Oh, he's fine," Emma said, leaning against the counter. Cassie couldn't say for sure if Emma was being casual or flirty, and immediately wanted to smack herself on the forehead for even caring. "He's saving lives in Cambodia. Making the rest of us look bad. You know how it is."

Brock chuckled, but this time the feelings it created in Cassie's belly weren't nearly as nice as before. She wished Emma wasn't quite so tall and leggy. Next to her, Cassie felt tiny, almost invisible.

"I know how that is. My sister's the same way," Brock said before turning to Cassie.

When his eyes locked to hers, Cassie's heart began to pound. She suddenly felt anything but invisible. "I'm just going to fix that bunk bed real quick, then I'm going to go home and get cleaned up. Is it okay if I come by in a few hours, though? Once it cools down a bit, I can bring over a crowbar from our place and start tearing out boards in the paddock that need to be replaced."

Cassie felt nearly breathless with his generosity. "You don't have to do all that," she answered, aware that Emma was standing right beside her. "It's too much to ask."

Brock shrugged. "I'm not doing much else but getting in my ma's way. It's nice to feel useful. And those kids won't be able to properly settle into their room until that bed's safe enough to withstand a hurricane. I'm guessing they'll push that furniture to the limits as much as the Wilson boys did."

Cassie returned his smile. She had been worried about the same thing, and her heart filled with gratitude. "Thank you so much, Brock," she said, putting a hand to her chest in a show of earnestness.

It was only when Brock's ears reddened slightly that she realized where her unconscious gesture directed his gaze, and she quickly dropped her hand to her side. Intensely aware that Emma was watching, Cassie tried to lighten the mood. "I'll need to make another stack of pancakes to thank you. And you're welcome to a slice of delicious pie, thanks to Emma," she finished, pointing toward the dessert.

Brock smiled at her. "Can't say no to that," he responded. "I'll just go take care of that bunk bed and then I'll be out of your hair for a few hours."

With that, he was out of the kitchen. Cassie waited, listening for Brock's footsteps to fade.

It was only after he was definitely out of earshot that Cassie turned to Emma, hoping her friend had missed that short moment of tension—if that was what it was, which Cassie had probably misinterpreted anyway—and had only seen an innocent conversation. Cassie was proud of herself. Really, she thought, Emma couldn't possibly have cause to think their relationship was anything but neighborly.

Which is all it is and will ever be, a stern voice inside her scolded. The reminder didn't cheer her.

Emma looked at Cassie and shrugged. "Fair enough,"

she said. "I've never had luck with love anyway. Maybe you will."

"What does that mean?" Cassie asked, praying Emma didn't mean what Cassie knew she meant.

"Don't even try that," Emma responded, wagging her finger at Cassie. "I know when a guy's hooked. His eyes were locked on your face that whole time, except for when he was distracted by your...hand," she said, wiggling her eyebrows suggestively. "He could hardly manage a glance at me, and he didn't even look at my pie, which is a first."

"Maybe he doesn't like pie," Cassie suggested, trying to brush away Emma's insinuations.

Her friend snorted in response, as if the very idea was preposterous. "Well, I need to get back to the shop, but I expect to hear more about Brock McNeal the next time I see you."

After giving Emma another stack of business cards and saying goodbye, Cassie went to Zach and Carter's room. She walked in to find the boys at opposite ends of the bunk bed, pushing and pulling at it with all their might, giggling hysterically in the process. Brock was standing a few feet away, watching with his hands on his hips.

None of them seemed to notice her arrival, so she stood in the doorway and watched as the boys collapsed on the floor, laughing breathlessly.

"I told you that it wouldn't budge an inch," Brock told the boys.

Cassie moved forward into the room and looked closely at the bed, noting the boards Brock had used to steady the wobbling top bunk. Before she could think of what to say, Zach and Carter were on her, pulling her over to show her exactly what Brock had done to make their bed safe.

She allowed herself a quick glance in his direction to find him suddenly looking slightly awkward, and before she could say anything he hooked his thumb toward the door. "I'm going to go home to wash up and change, but I'll be back this afternoon."

Hardly waiting for a nod from her, he strolled out of the bedroom. She faintly heard the front door open and close, and he was gone.

Why had he disappeared so quickly? She hadn't even been able to express her thanks for what he had done for Zach and Carter.

"He's nice," Carter commented, climbing up into his new bed. Cassie had to agree.

Nice, and sexy. And a little bit confusing.

With a deep exhale, she headed to the shower to wash off the sweat from the heat of the day. It also gave her time to think.

Her first thoughts as she stepped into the water strayed to Brock. Showering. With her. Emma's words rang in her head. *I know when a guy's hooked...*

The idea made her stomach flutter with excitement. She immediately shoved her head under the cool spray, biting back her sexual frustration.

Why, why did the man willing to help her need to be quite so perfect?

Men weren't an option right now, Cassie knew, but oh, man, if they were, she knew right where she'd go.

Cassie sighed and turned off the water, feeling cleaner but still very unsatisfied.

She would need to be careful if she was going to avoid rumors getting around town that she and Brock were an item. She didn't want the boys to hear anyone suggesting that she might be replacing their daddy.

She could just imagine the whispered talk, the way people would look at her, wondering how much was true…

She'd been through that too recently for the idea of it starting all over again to sit well.

And if she knew Emma at all from their short friendship, she guessed talk would be all around town in a matter of days. The thought made her skin crawl.

This time, though, she could at least make sure the rumors had no truth behind them, no teeth to sink into her and hurt her.

Chapter 5

"Thanks, Diego," Brock said into his phone as he sat on his childhood bed. "I'll let Cassie know you guys will buy the hay."

"No problem. She's doing us a favor, really," Brock's adopted brother answered. "Tomorrow when we get into town, Jose and I will drop by to meet her and hammer out the details."

They said their goodbyes and Brock hung up. Since he'd been home, he had eaten, showered and called his brothers about the hay. He looked at the clock and knew he should kill some more time before heading back to Cassie's.

Brock glanced around the room, at his high school rodeo trophies, snapshots of him with his friends and siblings, and a picture of him bungee jumping when he was seventeen—Ma had been so mad when she'd found out, but she still didn't have the heart to get rid of the picture, apparently. All these relics of his life in this home hardly registered, though. His mind was listening to the slow ticking of the clock, and thinking of the woman a house away.

After deciding to wait another half hour, Brock stood and paced as best he could in the cramped room. He probably wouldn't have lasted another thirty seconds, but luckily, his phone buzzed in his pocket. He looked at the screen to see that Jay, one of his rodeo buddies, was calling him.

He swiped the screen and put his phone to his ear. "Hey, Jay. Did you make it in the money?"

He had left too early from the last rodeo to see Jay ride, but his friend was one of the best bull riders on the circuit, and he was sure the man had done well.

"Second place," Jay said. "Your uncle was hopping mad that you didn't get a chunk of the purse."

Brock shrugged, even though his friend couldn't see it. He'd expected as much. "Uncle Joe is hopping mad about half the time. I'll do better in the next one," he added, more for himself than anything.

"Speaking of the next one," Jay said, no doubt getting down to his reason for calling, "you're going to the rodeo in Glen Rock, right?"

That was the one coming up in two weeks. It was about the closest big rodeo Spring Valley had all year. "Yeah, I'll be there," Brock said, wondering where this was going.

"Well, I found out there are some abandoned mines

about an hour out of town, and I've been looking into mining exploration. How about a group of us head there and check them out on our way out of town the day after the rodeo? I'll bring rappelling gear and flashlights. I've been reading up on it, and we might be able to find something down there. I've heard of people stumbling onto rubies the size of your fist in abandoned mines."

Brock seriously doubted they'd be finding any giant rubies, but Jay's plans always turned into great stories, and it would give Brock something to do after the rodeo. He had a feeling he might need something big to keep his mind off leaving Spring Valley. And the people that resided there. "Sounds like a plan," Brock responded.

"Great!" Jay said. "I'll see you at the rodeo!"

"See you," Brock said, hanging up and sliding his phone into his back pocket.

He sat back down on the bed, resolved to follow through with this new, likely dangerous, plan. It was good to have a reminder about what kind of life he was living. Anything that happened between him and Cassie couldn't last. He'd have to move on eventually, and what better way to show that than to jump into a mine the day after he left town?

Sure, Cassie was beautiful, and interesting, and seemed to have an amount of inner strength that intrigued him. Something about her pulled at him with an intense attraction he'd never experienced before. But she also had children and the kind of settled home life he wasn't looking for and didn't want. He'd worked so hard for so long to keep all that out of his future, and he couldn't just chuck it away now.

He was a rodeo bull rider, a thrill-seeker, a free spirit.

Even though it had only been five minutes since his decision to wait another thirty, Brock gave up and pushed his cowboy hat onto his head as he went downstairs. After grabbing a crowbar from the storage shed beside his parents' barn, Brock set off for the ranch next door.

As he tromped across the lush expanse that separated his parents' home from Cassie's, Brock took a deep breath of the warm air, the smell of dust and grass as familiar as an old friend. The old Wilson place stood out against the mountain backdrop like something in a painting: the cozy ranch in the Texas countryside.

Cassie's smile disrupted his thoughts once more. Despite his reservations, maybe he would ask her out… He couldn't offer her more than a nice night out or two, but he wasn't sure he could withstand the pull between them altogether. But, he reminded himself, he really should wait a bit longer. Make sure she knew that he was there to help her, whether or not they were having fun on the side. That would give him a bit more time to think this through.

Brock knocked on the door, confident that he had a solid game plan, only for everything to fall away the moment the door opened.

Cassie stood there, her hair still slightly damp from her own shower, so fresh and enticing. "Thanks for coming over again. Do you mind if we go get paint instead of starting on the paddock? I'm going to meet a patient the day after tomorrow, so I'll need to paint it tonight or tomorrow morning."

It was as if, in the small space of time they were apart, he'd convinced himself he could be patient around her. But seeing her now, the attraction was hitting him full force. The look of excitement on her face just added to it.

Before his brain could stop him, he stepped forward and kissed her, his lips touching hers lightly at first, then harder when she responded. Her hand slipped around his neck to pull him against her. For a long moment, they melted together. When they finally broke apart, though, the expression on her face wasn't promising. "Go out with me tonight," Brock blurted out.

Her expression only worsened, but there was nothing he could do now except continue on. "Nothing serious. I'm going back on the circuit in a couple weeks. I just thought that we…"

He trailed off. Before she said anything, he knew what her answer would be. "I can't," she said, shaking her head. "Not with the boys, and Hank—"

She paused, as if searching for the right words, but he knew he didn't want to hear them. She was still in love with her valiant police officer husband, and any physical attraction she had for him wasn't going to change that. He didn't need to make her say it. Before she could speak again, he shrugged and smiled, trying to hide his disappointment. "Hey, it's no big deal. We can be friends, right?"

"Right," she responded, but she still looked uncomfortable.

He wanted to do something to *show* her he was still willing to help her fix up her place. "We should get to the hardware store. If we don't dawdle, we can get your office painted today, and then you'd be able to see patients tomorrow, if you want."

Cassie nodded, though she still seemed lost in thought.

"Let's take my truck so we can haul the lumber you'll need for the fence and paddock, too," he told her.

Cassie finally seemed to come back around, though her eyes wouldn't exactly meet his. "That sounds like a great idea. Does your truck have a backseat for the boys?" she asked.

At least she wasn't mad at him, he thought with relief. "Yep, plenty of room," he said.

"I'll get the boys ready, then," she said, half turning away from him, back toward the dim interior of the house.

Brock looked back to his parents' house, where his truck shone in the driveway. "I'll go get my truck and meet you back here in a few minutes."

Cassie nodded and disappeared into the house. Brock started down the steps after setting the crowbar out of the way on the porch. With the change of plans, he wouldn't be using it quite yet, but it didn't make sense to carry it all the way back when they would need it another day.

Brock strode quickly back the way he had just come a few minutes before, steering himself toward the driveway this time. He berated himself the whole way. What had he been thinking, kissing her like that?

Brock knew the answer. He'd been thinking she was interesting and smart and all kinds of sexy. But that didn't change the fact that he'd known better than to do that. It seemed Cassie wasn't the only one who was impulsive. She bought a ranch, he kissed women without thinking.

Well, one woman.

At least now he knew he didn't have a shot with her, even if she seemed to feel the same electricity he did. She may have gotten caught in the moment, but the look of instant regret on her face was all he needed to know that it wouldn't be happening again. If she was still loyal to her husband's memory, he couldn't begrudge her that. So they would just be friends.

Brock hopped in his truck and drove the short stretch of road to Cassie's house. By the time he got there, she and the boys were bustling down the porch steps.

As soon as he opened the vehicle door, he could hear the boys chattering excitedly about the prospect of riding in a big cowboy truck. He smiled as they tried to climb in, struggling with the height of the cab.

"Here," he said, lacing his fingers together and kneeling down to create an extra step for them.

Once the boys were in, he looked at Cassie, who was standing there. She was giving him a small smile that he couldn't interpret. "Thanks for this," she said to him.

He wasn't sure what to say. Would things be too awkward between them now?

Brock felt a little sheepish. "I want you to know that I'm not a jerk, and I'm sorry if I came off as one earlier."

Cassie moved as if she was going to put her hand on his arm, then seemed to rethink it and dropped her arm to her side. "I don't think that, Brock."

God, he wanted to kiss her again. He turned to the truck to get away from her beautiful eyes and realized the boys were crowded with his duffel bags from time on the rodeo circuit. By the time he'd moved the bags into the truck bed, Cassie had already gotten in and closed the door. He wasn't sure if he was grateful or disappointed that their moment was over.

Cassie settled into the passenger seat of Brock's car, her heart pounding. She still felt aflutter from the scene at the door, though dissatisfied at the same time. That kiss. Oh my. And then he had asked her out.

And she'd said no.

Oh, she wished she could have said yes. She wanted nothing more than to kiss him again, press her body against his. As she sat beside him in the front seat, she could almost feel the energy between them, hot and thick. She could imagine laughing with him at a restaurant, touching his hand, talking with him as he walked her to her door, kissing him again and again in the country moonlight.

But her boys jabbering excitedly in the backseat reminded her again that now just wasn't the time to start dating. They were still so young, and they'd lost their father so recently. She had to be a mother first, a doctor second and a rancher third. Being a single woman was so far down on the list it didn't even rate a mention.

"I spoke with my brothers," Brock said, breaking the silence and dragging her back into the moment. "They're happy to buy your hay. They wanted to know if they could drop by tomorrow to see it and talk to you about prices."

Relief washed through Cassie, both for a safe topic of conversation and the possibility of one big worry to be solved so quickly. "Absolutely. Thanks for calling them," she responded, not sure what else to say.

Brock shrugged, though he seemed pleased. "They were planning on visiting anyway, and you'll be doing them a service, really. Getting a new business off the ground is no easy feat."

"What did you say their business was? Selling animals?" She was interested, but mostly she just wanted to keep the conversation light and flowing.

"Sort of," he answered. "They own stock—bulls, broncs, a few calves—and they rent them out on the rodeo circuit."

Cassie's eyes widened at the news. She'd never been to a rodeo, but was looking forward to changing that very soon. She was a cowgirl now, after all.

"I imagine you and your siblings have been to quite a few rodeos, living around here," she said.

Brock chuckled. "More than you can imagine. Amy, my sister, rode in the junior rodeo. She only gave it up when she became a journalist and started traveling the world."

"And you?" she prompted.

He had said he was on the circuit when the boys asked what his job was, and again during the recent scene on the porch that she was trying to forget. She wasn't positive, but she thought she'd heard that phrase in connection to rodeos.

"I ride bulls on the circuit. I travel around from one rodeo to the next and compete," he explained, his eyes on the road.

Cassie hadn't expected that. She was aware of the fact that some people out there hopped on the back of giant twisting animals for a living, but she'd never actually met one.

She tried to focus on the danger of it, to remind herself to keep her distance from this man.

But she could just imagine him, using every one of his very noticeable muscles as he defeated a crazed bull in a battle of strength and wills. The picture sent a thrill through her.

Cassie shook her head slightly at her own silly imagination. If they were going to be friends, she would need to avoid picturing him in that romantic way. Or maybe theirs would need to be a very distant friendship. Just close enough to work together on her house and barn. After that, it would probably be best if they didn't see each other much. Like a mantra, she repeated the important things: children, patients and horses.

Horses. "Oh, shoot," she said aloud, "we were planning to go and visit our horses tomorrow morning. Will your brothers be able to come in the afternoon?"

Brock nodded. "That should be fine." Then he added. "Since we're getting the lumber today, I can work on the paddock while you're out, if that's okay."

She melted a little. Even though she'd turned him down, he was still willing to work so hard to help her.

She had spent years married to someone selfish, and

now she'd finally found a nice man she couldn't have. Thanks, Destiny.

"That would be wonderful," she said. Before she could think things through, she blurted out, "Unless you want to come with us?"

She wanted to slap her forehead. Why was she putting herself into these situations? She should be spending *less* time with him, not *more*!

But it was too late now. Her impulsiveness had gotten the better of her once again, so she might as well go all in. "I don't know much about horses and would appreciate having them looked over by someone with a practiced eye," she said.

He gave her a little smile that wiped away the nagging voices inside her. She knew exactly why she asked him to come—she couldn't help but want to be around him.

"Can't say no to spending some time around horses," he answered.

Cassie spent the rest of the drive amazed at the human capacity for conflicting emotions.

Finally, they reached the hardware store, to Cassie's relief. The large building was a reminder that she had more important things to do than fight herself over Brock. They all climbed out of the truck and headed inside.

Now she could think about those other things: paint for her doctor's office, lumber for her fences, and plenty of other items she didn't even know she needed. Even the worries at the cost of it all seemed preferable to thinking about Brock.

Zach and Carter looked around them at the large store, and Cassie could see their fingers itching to touch everything they could reach, the more dangerous the better. "How about we go pick out paint?" she asked. When they seemed disappointed, she added, "You two can paint your room any color you can both agree on."

With that, they were hopping excitedly toward the paint swatches, already arguing about what color to choose. Cassie followed them, feeling Brock beside her, but not looking at him. "You're really going to let them pick *any* color they want?" Brock asked, sounding amazed.

Cassie nodded, keeping her eyes trained on her sons. "They'll have a hard time agreeing, and Zach will keep Carter from choosing something too crazy. He won't want anything too bright."

At least she could feel confident about one aspect of her life right now. She knew her boys.

They walked through the store, looking like a happy family on an outing, Cassie knew. She tried to brush the idea away. This was time for work. She turned her mind, instead, to choosing exactly the right color for her office.

Cassie followed the boys into the paint section and felt immediately overwhelmed at the number of choices. Giant sections of hundreds of colors surrounded her, each section a different name brand. She didn't even know where to start, and the only name she recognized was some of the brands boasted ultra-expensive collections.

Beside her, Brock pointed out a name she didn't recognize. "I suggest getting one of these ones. They make good paint at a decent price. We can find the right one to spruce up the fencing and keep it water-tight here, too."

With her choices narrowed to a much more manageable hundred-or-so options, Cassie followed Brock and started pulling out paint cards to consider. Soon she had a dozen or more in her hands, from periwinkle to sky blue to mocha to gentle fawn. She could hear Zach and Carter arguing over colors, and she could see Brock out of the corner of her eye considering which dark brown would match best, but she was mostly, blessedly, absorbed in the choices in front of her.

"Hmm. Tough choice," Brock said, sidling so close to her that she could smell his cologne or aftershave or whatever it was that made him smell so darn good.

Damn. Her mind was now 100 percent on him, her libido firing up and demanding action, the memory of them on the porch only compounding the problem. She forced herself to stay still, her eyes on the colors in front of her, even though she was no longer really seeing them.

As if Brock could feel the intensity of her desire, he stepped back a little and cleared his throat.

Cassie kept her eyes on the squares of color, purposely avoiding looking at him. "I'm just not sure what would be best."

Brock leaned back for a second, putting his hand on his chin as he considered. Then he leaned forward and plucked out two of the colors: a buttery yellow and a bold blue. As he did so, his fingers grazed hers, and she pulled back as if singed and looked up at him, the absolute wrong thing to do, she realized. The dark blue of his eyes threatened to suck her in.

He held up the colors he'd chosen as if they were a type of protection from her, and she reined in her thoughts, turning her attention to the swatches.

"I think either of these would go particularly well with the furniture," he said, his voice sounding strained. "But any of the colors you picked would be fine, honestly."

She had to agree with him. After a quick inner debate, she chose the blue. "The yellow reminds me too much of a nursery," she explained, not mentioning that the blue reminded her of his entrancing eyes.

Brock didn't respond, and when she saw how awkward he'd become once again, she scolded herself for bringing up babies with a man who didn't particularly like children.

It didn't stop her from picturing him in a butter-yellow nursery, holding a little baby in his arms, though. She gave herself a little shake and spoke, hoping to clear the air. "Did you find something for the fence?"

He held up the brown swatch and she smiled. It might not have been too exciting for some people, but it was the color a fence and paddock on a working ranch should be, and that made her happy. They brought the colors up to the paint-mixer and placed the orders. When they finished, Brock said, "You should also think about what color you want the barn to be. You'll need to repaint the whole thing at some point."

He didn't have to say that it would need to wait until after he was gone. There simply wasn't time while he was in town to get that done on top of everything else. The thought made her sad, but she tried to ignore it. "Hmm… I might go for a white barn," she said, picturing the beautiful white against the deep greens and browns of the surrounding landscape.

Brock nodded. "It would be a pain to keep looking bright, but white barns are nice," he said.

Before she could comment again, Zach and Carter ran up, smiles on their faces.

"We chose a color!" Zach said, holding out the chosen swatch.

Cassie looked down at the lurid green and groaned. "Really?" she asked. "This is what you both want?"

"Look at the name!" Carter said, "The nice man helped us read the names," he explained, pointing to the tiny words on the bottom of the swatch.

Dragon scales.

Cassie looked over to see the clerk who had helped them. He gave her a pained smile—apparently he realized too late the problem with letting two little boys know that a color had the word "dragon" in the name. She could hear Brock laughing behind her. "Well, that backfired," she said to him, handing the color swatch over to be mixed. She had promised, after all.

After the paint, it was quick work to walk into the lumber area and find the right size boards, then get a small crew of workers to haul the lumber to Brock's truck. Cassie went to the checkout line with several cans and buckets of paint, the necessary accompanying items, plus a ticket for the lumber. Thankfully, the purchase went through without too hard a hit on her bank account.

When she slid into Brock's truck, a feeling of triumph washed over her. She hadn't done anything too stupid, like kiss him again, and her finances were working out better than she'd hoped. She was going to make it through all this.

She could see herself and her boys, snug in their new home, with the horses in the barn and her patients getting the help they needed in her little examination room. They would all be just fine, even when Brock left for his rodeo circuit.

But first, they would paint her doctor's office together, and she held on to that thought as they drove back home.

Chapter 6

Brock and Cassie looked around the little office with pride. The walls shone with wet paint, and they were both splattered head to toe in it, too, but the task was complete.

Brock knew he should leave now that the job was done, but he waited a few extra seconds anyway.

Zach and Carter, whom Cassie had sent to work in their room rather than have them make an even bigger mess of the paint than the grown-ups, rushed into the room and started tugging at their mother's arms. "Momma, come see all the work we did!" Carter shouted, trying to get her out of the room.

"All our toys are put away and everything," Zach added.

Cassie groaned and leaned against the doorjamb.

"Give me a second, boys. Mom's been working very hard all day."

"What're we going to have for dinner?" Zach asked, sounding concerned.

Carter nodded. "I'm hungry."

Cassie ran her hands over her face and through her hair, and Brock's heart went out to her. She seemed even more weary than he felt. "Okay," she said at last, "first I'll figure out food, then you can show me all the work you did. Sound good?"

The boys looked disappointed, and Brock could sense that they really wanted her to see what they had done. "If you're happy with sandwiches or pasta, I can work on food while you go with the boys," he suggested.

Cassie looked as if she was about to object, so he said, "It's purely selfish, I assure you. I'm starving and you promised me dinner and that pie, which is sounding mighty delicious right about now." He continued, "We need to have a meal before we have dessert, right?"

Cassie gave him a half smile, making it clear she saw right through him, but all she said was, "That's right. No dessert before dinner in this house."

Brock smiled. "Well, then, I best rustle up some grub."

"You talk like cowboys on TV," Zach said, looking at Brock in awe.

Brock tipped the cowboy hat he'd just placed on his head after retrieving it from the living room, where he'd stowed it for safety earlier in the day. "You stick around here for a bit, pardner, and you'll start talking like that, too."

Zach's eyes widened in amazement. He stared at Brock for another moment, trying to absorb the idea of him speaking like a cowboy, before following his mother and twin toward his bedroom. Brock chuckled and went to the kitchen. They were good kids, all right.

After a quick inventory of ingredients, he got a pot of water and an oiled pan heating on the stove, then gathered tomatoes, an onion and some cloves of garlic, and started chopping.

He dropped spaghetti noodles into the boiling water and slid a pile of chopped onion and tomato into the hot pan, where they sizzled as they began to cook. Cassie walked in, telling the boys how impressed she was with their progress. The boys beamed.

When she came up beside Brock to look into the pot on the stove, he risked a glance at her before going back to chopping more tomatoes. She just looked so damn *kissable*, even when she was worn out from a hard day's work, her dark hair in disarray around her face, and a smudge of blue paint on her chin.

Brock shifted, uncomfortable as Cassie leaned in even closer, sniffing the tomatoes in the pan. "Smells great," she commented.

"Pasta pomodoro, or, in layman's terms, spaghetti and tomato sauce."

Cassie chuckled low in her throat, sending a thrill through him. "Not exactly cowboy fare," she said.

He smiled, but kept his eyes on the tomatoes as he finished chopping. "Well, you don't have any chicken to fry or ribs to barbecue, so I fell back on bachelor fare. Easy, cheap and good."

"I'm *so* hungry!" Carter exclaimed, breaking into their tête-à-tête.

Cassie turned to her son, "That was a little rude, buddy," she said.

"Sorry," he responded, sounding so contrite that Brock wanted to laugh.

"I'm hungry, too, but we need to wait for everything to cook. What can we do while we wait?" she asked.

The boys jumped up, shouting over each other about plates and washing hands, and suddenly there was a flurry of activity behind him.

Cassie came back to where Brock stood, stirring the sauce. "Sorry about that," she told him as she pulled out a noodle to check.

Brock shook his head. "Nothing to apologize for."

He was actually amazed. Cassie made raising children look so easy.

She took the pot of noodles off the stove and strained out the water, dumping them in a large bowl and bringing it over to Brock so he could put the sauce on top. Just as they had with the bookshelves and the painting, the two of them worked together seamlessly. In no time, they were all sitting around the table, everyone eating with the speed of the hungry and tired.

"'S'good," Carter mumbled through a mouthful of noodles.

The rest of the family grunted in agreement.

Once the spaghetti was gone and their hunger abated, Brock leaned back, letting his body relax. He could see the pinks of the sky through the windows, and knew the sun had gone down and he'd spent nearly the entire day with Cassie, despite his inward insistence that he help her while having as little contact with her as possible.

Well, at least if he worked longer days, he could always finish early and spend the last days of his visit to Spring Valley Cassie-free, right?

He couldn't fool himself into believing that was a possibility, though. He knew that he would find *something* around that place to fix up until the day of the rodeo. Even then, it would probably feel like it was too soon.

But for today, at least, he had gone beyond an acceptable visit, and he should leave Cassie and her children in peace to spend the rest of their evening as a family. Without him.

"How about some pie?" Cassie asked him.

"Sure," Brock answered as he began to clear the table.

Well, he couldn't leave until after pie, right?

Cassie stood in the doorway as Brock walked out. "I'm going to leave my truck here so we can take the lumber out of the bed tomorrow," he said, gesturing to the vehicle piled high with planks of wood.

They'd been so busy with painting that she had totally forgotten about the lumber. "Sounds good," she told him.

With an awkward little wave, as if he wasn't quite ready to leave, Brock turned toward his parents' home and walked away, eventually disappearing into the inky night. Even then she lingered, though she couldn't have explained why. Knowing he would be back tomorrow didn't quite erase the desire to run out into the darkness and bring him back.

The more time she spent around this man, the more things she discovered about him that she liked. Her decision not to date was the right one, of course, but she couldn't stop herself from wishing they had met when the boys were a little older, their father's memory a little more faded.

Cassie shook her head, annoyed with her own train of thought. It was obvious enough to her that he didn't lead a settled life, and never planned to, either. He was a wanderer. Even if the boys were old enough for her to go on dates, Brock would still only be in it for a quick fling, no strings attached.

She came with lots of strings. Two identical strings in particular.

Cassie sighed. There was no hope for it. Brock McNeal was something she wanted that she simply couldn't have.

She shut the door, but it didn't shut out the picture of him kissing her. Or the one of them sitting around the table, eating pie like a family…

She found Zach and Carter in a sleepy heap on the couch and her heart jumped. Even if she couldn't have that picture, she had her boys. "Come on, guys. Time for bed," she said, prodding them gently.

They raised their arms to her, and she lifted them both up, trying to ignore her aching muscles. It wasn't *that* late, but they'd had a long day and were clearly feeling as weary as she was. She carried them to their room and settled Zach onto the lower bunk and Carter onto the upper. She took off their shoes but didn't bother with the rest. The twins curled into their brand-new bed and slept on, oblivious to the world.

Brock walked slowly through the dark country night. The sun had set long before, and a slice of coolness cut the warm summer air. Exhaustion kept him from noticing it much, though.

He tromped upstairs and went immediately into the bathroom, where he scrubbed at the splatters of blue on his hands and arms. Impatient as he was to get to bed, he still wiped down the sink, trying not to leave a trace of paint anywhere. He was a grown man, but he had a healthy fear of his ma's wrath, and nothing could set it off quite like leaving a mess for her to clean.

Brock was so tired. Not just from the day full of fixing and painting and hauling, though that was draining, but from spending the entire time in Cassie's presence.

It wasn't that she was difficult to be around—in fact, it was the exact opposite. He felt *too* comfortable with Cassie. His mind and body yearned for impossible scenarios, which set him constantly on edge around her. After all, he knew that even if she was magically cured of her loyalty for her lost husband and she suddenly decided she wanted nothing more than to be in his arms, there was still the problem of the twins.

Kids made everything more complicated, and he knew he couldn't take over any type of a fatherly role. Not with the kind of life he led.

He thought of Jay and the abandoned mines, and the idea of having children waiting for him to come home sent a shudder through him. What if he never came back?

It was better to have no ties, nobody to hurt.

So all Brock and Cassie could have was a temporary fling, and even that seemed astronomically unlikely at this point. He knew all that. So why was he picturing waking up beside her day after day? Why did he let the twins steal a little bit of his heart when they begged to help their momma prepare her doctor's office?

Brock splashed cold water onto his face, trying to rid himself of those thoughts. It was all moot, anyway, so he might as well let it go. He'd seen her expression after their kiss.

The kiss where she pulled us closer together, a small voice reminded him. Even if she didn't want to date him, she *did* kiss him back. He could still taste her, feel the energy that radiated from her as she responded to him.

Brock walked down the hall to his room, wishing he'd stayed away from Spring Valley and the woman who had so quickly taken over his mind.

"G'night, Brock," Ma called down the hall. "Don't forget, Amy and your brothers will be here tomorrow, so I'll need you home early for a nice big family dinner. No lollygagging over at Dr. Stanford's, you hear?"

Brock felt a retort rise in his throat, but he bit it back. It was certainly true that his mother had been the one to orchestrate his acquaintance with Cassie and offer his help to her, but he didn't need to point that out to her.

There was no reason to snip at his ma anyway. Just because he was grumpy about the unfortunate circumstances that kept him from what he wanted and desired didn't mean he should take it out on the woman who had cared for him nearly all his life.

"Yes, ma'am," he said instead, tilting his hat to her. "G'night."

Ma kept looking at him, and for a moment he thought she was going to ask about how her matchmaking between him and Cassie was going, but instead she simply nodded and disappeared into the master bedroom. Brock turned to his own room, feeling relieved; he didn't have an answer to that question.

Right now, the one and only thing he needed was a good night's sleep.

Cassie woke up and stretched, feeling aches in muscles all along her arms and back. With the all the chores from the day before, she'd expected as much.

What she hadn't expected was the hours of tossing and turning as she fought a war about Brock McNeal. No matter how many times she'd told herself nothing would happen with him, it didn't stop her body from complaining about the decision. The more time she spent around him, the more longing she felt, and their kiss kept repeating itself over and over in her head. Not only was that moment mind-blowing and a promise of so much more to be had, Brock was kind and funny, not to mention attractive as all get-out.

All she wanted was to keep her hands off him, yet at the same time, she desired him more than anyone she'd ever met. Thoughts like that had made it nearly impossible to sleep.

Cassie felt lighter this morning, however. By the time the sun had come up, she'd finally decided to allow herself to accept her feelings for Brock. He wouldn't be kissing her or asking her out again after already being shot down, and there was no reason to be stiff and distant with him, so long as she never went any further again. They had agreed to be friends.

So long as she had too many responsibilities to start up something with the sexy bull rider, why not enjoy light banter with her helpful neighbor?

And speaking of responsibilities…

It was nearly eight, and the fact that she hadn't heard from her sons could either be very good or very bad. Normally they would be banging down the door by now in their excitement to start the day. Cassie groaned and stood up, even though she badly wanted to curl back under her covers.

She slipped on panties and bra—not her sexiest ones, because that would be taking things too far—but on the slinkier side. She told herself it was because the silk felt good against her sore and tired body. Then she dressed in jeans and a blouse that hugged her curves nicely, because it felt good to look good sometimes.

Then she went searching for her sons. She discovered the reason for the twins' absence quickly enough, when she heard thumps and giggles from their bedroom and went to investigate. She opened the door to find Zach hanging on to the railing of the top bunk and swinging himself into the bottom bunk as Carter attacked his brother's legs from the shadows of the lower bunk.

For a second, Cassie considered just closing the door

and pretending she hadn't seen what she'd seen. She was sleepy and aching, and being a good parent seemed like a lot of work.

But the doctor in her wouldn't let her walk away. "What are you two doing?" she asked pointedly, knowing she wasn't going to like the answer.

"Playing on our new bed," Zach explained matter-of-factly.

Cassie softened at their worry-free expressions. "Well, stop playing in ways that might send you to the emergency room. How about we go make some breakfast?"

The boys jumped up and raced past Cassie toward the kitchen. She followed, her heart filled with love for the two rascals.

"Are we going to have pancakes again?" Carter asked once she joined them.

"Cereal today," she answered, glancing at her watch.

They had gotten a late start, and she wanted to get to the horse barn before too much longer. If Brock's brothers were going to be over that afternoon, she wanted to make sure they were back in plenty of time. Plus, she needed to spend some time preparing her office, since Emma had sent a text confirming she'd come by with her neighbor bright and early the next day.

Cassie poured cereal for herself and the boys, then sat down to eat, wondering if Brock would be arriving soon to see the horses with her.

Part of her hoped he would decide not to, but most of her jumped with joy when a familiar knock sounded at the door, as if her thoughts had conjured Brock out of thin air.

"I'll get it!" Carter shouted as he jumped out of his seat and ran to the door.

Cassie put another spoonful of cereal into her mouth to hide the smile she couldn't stop from spreading across her lips.

Carter came back to his seat. "Brock is here!" he announced unnecessarily, as Brock stepped into the room right behind him.

Cassie looked up from her bowl, trying to keep her face as serious as she could make it, though inside she was grinning like a Cheshire cat. "Back for more punishment, huh?" she asked, thankful she'd decided to let herself flirt without feeling guilty so there was no inward scolding.

Brock gave her the kind of smile that could turn a woman to mush. "I was told we were going to see some horses today. What kind of a cowboy would I be if I passed that up?"

She laughed, unable to contain her glee any longer. She couldn't help how good she felt when he was around, and for the moment the impulsive side of her was winning. She would hate to admit how nice it was to give it free rein.

"Sit down and have some cereal, if you're hungry," she told him, gesturing to the empty seat at the table.

"Oh, I'm fine. Don't trouble yourself," he said, but Zach had already hopped up and grabbed him a bowl and spoon.

She said nothing, just gestured to the empty seat

again. He conceded without any more argument. Soon they were all eating, the only sound the clink of spoons on ceramic bowls. Cassie felt more at ease than she had since first meeting Brock. She couldn't pinpoint what, exactly, had happened overnight to so change her attitude toward him.

Perhaps it was that her soreness and exhaustion, along with the excitement of her first patient's looming appointment, had all combined to weaken the tight grip she'd been keeping and made her temporarily foolish. Perhaps the kiss from yesterday had worked some magic on her during the night, creating this newfound inner quiet. Either way, this new, relaxed version of her was exactly what she'd needed.

Cassie smiled down at her bowl again before looking up at the boys and Brock. "Should we go visit some horses?"

Brock wasn't sure what it was, but Cassie seemed different today. More at ease. Was it because she was sure he'd gotten the message when she turned him down yesterday and no longer needed to worry about him making advances? If so, she was right about that, and he was glad the air between them seemed clear.

Brock led the way out the door as Cassie helped the boys put on shoes, but he stopped when he stepped off the porch. His truck was still parked in front of Cassie's house, the back still full of the lumber they'd purchased the day before.

He and Cassie would need to unload it once they got back from the horses, and then they could start on the paddock. Then Brock remembered the crowbar he'd left on the porch, and he decided to grab it and toss it into the truck bed so the boys wouldn't trip over it or anything.

Brock ran up the porch steps to grab it, only to find that Cassie was rushing down them at the same time, the boys right behind her. Brock stopped in his tracks and Cassie came to a halt, too, but the boys weren't paying attention and bowled into her legs, propelling her forward into Brock.

He put his arms out to steady her, catching her before they could tumble down the stairs together. His heart thumped so hard he was sure she could feel it where their chests met. She looked up into his eyes, and without thinking, he leaned toward her. Luckily, she turned away from him to check on Zach and Carter, and he was able to catch himself before doing something phenomenally stupid like kiss her. Again.

Brock forced his gaze from Cassie and instead looked to where her children had been only seconds before. Now they were in a heap on the floor of the porch. Brock started to go to their aid, worried they had gotten injured in the collision or hurt themselves on the crowbar somehow, but then he noticed that they were both doubled up, laughing hysterically.

Cassie put her hands on her hips, but she was smiling. "Now just what exactly is so funny? You're not laughing at *me*, are you?"

The teasing lilt in her voice made Brock grin. He loved seeing Cassie being silly with her boys.

"Carter said we made you into a Momma-sandwich," Zach said at last, gulping for air.

Brock couldn't help but laugh at the humor of four-year-olds. Cassie gave her sons another falsely stern look. "Well, making me into a Momma-sandwich has suddenly turned me into a tickle monster!"

And with that she was on the floor with the boys, all three of them laughing as Cassie grasped at her children, who rolled desperately to evade her fingers.

Brock was laughing so hard his side hurt. He couldn't remember a time he'd laughed that much. Cassie glanced at him with a conspiratorial smile, and for a moment he felt as if he were a part of the scene instead of an outsider.

He didn't want to admit how good that felt.

Cassie stood up, her cheeks red from exertion and amusement, her hair wild and her eyes shining. She was so pretty it hurt.

She looked up at Brock, and his heart stuttered. "You ready?" she asked.

Oh, he was ready, all right. For all sorts of things. It took him a moment to realize that she was asking if he was ready to go visit the ranch where the horses were being stabled. Once he understood, he nodded and followed her down the steps to her SUV. For the moment, he didn't trust himself to speak.

Chapter 7

Cassie glanced at the back seat to make sure her sons were buckled in, then started the car. As she turned in her seat while she reversed out of the driveway, carefully maneuvering around Brock's loaded-down silver truck, her arm brushed against Brock's muscular bicep. His large frame made the front of the SUV feel too small for comfort, and she was grateful the moment she could settle back into her seat, as far from him as she could manage. In the truck the day before they hadn't felt quite so close, but in her car it was almost…intimate.

And however much leeway she was giving herself to chat and be friendly, intimate was definitely *not* good. She'd tried to hide it, but that moment when she'd been pressed against his chest was almost more than she could handle.

"Where are the horses being stabled?" Brock asked her as they drove away from town, toward some of the larger ranches that dotted this part of the country.

"Stuart Ranch," she answered. "Tom Stuart gave us a good price and won't make me pay if I move them home earlier than expected."

She didn't need to say what needed to get done for that to happen. Brock knew, and she was sure he would do everything in his power to get her animals settled as soon as possible. Another smile touched her lips.

"I've known the Stuarts forever. One of the boys dated my sister for a while. They're good people," he said.

She waited a moment for him to add more details, but the only sounds in the car came from the two boys playing in the back seat. The casual ease at the kitchen table shortly before was threatening to disappear completely, and she wasn't sure what to do to save it.

Luckily, the ranch was close, and soon Cassie gratefully left the confining vehicle. After a quick word with Grandma Stuart—who insisted she watch the twins while Cassie and Brock see to the horses—the pair headed to the large barn.

Horses of all different types walked around the paddocks, munching on hay and relaxing in the morning sunshine.

Tom Stuart was just inside the barn, working with a mare that seemed to be limping slightly. Cassie hoped the animal wasn't too badly injured.

"Brock! Haven't seen you around in a long while," Tom said, moving to shake hands with Brock. "It seems you've met your new neighbor," he added, nodding toward Cassie.

"Came to take a look at her horses. They in here somewhere?" Brock responded.

Cassie couldn't help but compare the two men. Though Tom was handsome in his own right, he couldn't hold a candle to Brock. While both were muscular, Tom was taller, with a more wiry look to him, where Brock was more compact and solid. But that didn't explain what made Brock stand out. He had a spark, a subtle inner liveliness, that called out to her.

Cassie tuned back into reality and the two men before her.

Tom pointed down the length of stalls along one side of the barn. "Cassie can show you where they're stabled, if you don't mind. I need to stay with Sadie here," he said, patting the side of the large mare.

Brock took a step toward the injured animal. "Any idea what's bothering her?" he asked, rubbing the animal's neck, then sliding his hand down to her leg, lifting the hoof and inspecting it.

Cassie watched as Brock and Tom conferred over the horse's hoof. Then Brock let go of Sadie's leg and patted her one last time before turning to Cassie.

She had been so absorbed watching him care for the horse, the concern he showed filling her with if-onlys, that his eyes on her sent a jolt of surprise through her. It took a long moment before she realized he was waiting for her to show him to her horses.

With effort, she tore her gaze from his and, after a

quick wave to Tom, turned to the stalls where Rosalind and Diamond were waiting.

"Was it a very serious injury?" she asked.

To her relief, Brock shook his head. "A bruised sole. Not fun, but she'll be right as rain soon enough."

Cassie nodded as she walked up to her horses, turning her attention to the beautiful beasts before her. She was still amazed that they were hers. She'd only visited them twice, and every time she saw the two regal animals, she could hardly believe it.

Before becoming a doctor, she'd wanted to be a veterinarian. Her childhood dream had been to live in the country and own and care for horses. Her mother had disagreed—and while her mother's pushes toward a career as a doctor had been ultimately successful, Cassie had never given up her country dreams. She didn't regret not becoming a vet, but she knew she would have always felt like she'd missed out if she hadn't bought the ranch.

Cassie pressed her face into Diamond's neck, breathing in the scent. Horses of her own, a ranch that was actually coming together and a new life for her and her boys.

If she could keep her nose to the grindstone, she and her boys would be settled and happy here. Then they could be a content little family.

Just the three of them.

Cassie didn't like that there was a drop of sadness in that thought, and she tried to ignore how her heart thumped harder when she saw how kind Brock was to her horses.

She walked up beside him, hoping to learn from him. "Do they have a smooth gait when you ride them?"

Brock asked as he rubbed the legs of the sleek chestnut mare.

Cassie felt her cheeks flush with embarrassment. "I've never ridden them," she said. She hated to admit the truth, but she said it anyway. "I haven't ever actually been on a horse."

Brock gave her the look of disbelief she expected, but it quickly shifted to determination. "Well, then, we better saddle them up and take them for a quick ride," he said, moving toward the saddles and tack hanging along the side of the barn. "Tom, you think your ma would be fine with watching the boys for twenty minutes while we let these ladies stretch their legs?" Brock called out to where Cassie could just see Tom in the dim light, still working with Sadie on the far side of the barn.

"She'd keep those two for good and all if she had half the chance," Tom replied.

Brock nodded, as if that settled it, and picked up the first saddle. He made no mention of Cassie's admission, just got to work, for which she was immensely grateful.

Cassie watched carefully as Brock saddled each of the horses, explaining exactly what he was doing as he went. Once he had everything cinched tight and secure, Brock stepped up to Rosalind. "You should take Rosy," he said. "Diamond seems like she might be a little skittish."

He explained to Cassie how to put her foot in the stirrup and swing her other leg over to get onto the horse.

He stood holding the reins, keeping the large animal steady while Cassie attempted to mount her. As she swung herself into the air, she wobbled and instinctively grabbed at Brock's shoulder to steady herself. She could feel his hand on her waist, helping her into the saddle.

By the time Cassie was settled atop the horse and Brock's hand had moved away, she was breathless, and not from the effort to get up there. It was the second time that day they'd had far too much physical contact, and it proved to Cassie that she certainly shouldn't let it happen again if she wanted to keep her sanity. And her heart.

She took the reins from him, careful not to touch him, and instead marveled at the sleek neck of the animal she was now sitting on, touching the horse's mane with wonder. For the first time in her life, Cassie was on a horse, reins in hand. This had been a dream of hers since she was a little girl, and it was finally happening. Excitement and gratitude washed through her.

"Thank you," Cassie told him once he was mounted on Diamond and leading Rosalind toward the edge of the ranch.

Brock shrugged, but she could see from his solemnity that he understood how important this was to her. "I was a greenhorn once, too" was all he said.

She sat quietly, reveling in the feel of the large animal shifting beneath her.

Once they were out of the property's fenced enclosure, Brock turned Diamond toward a dirt trail that wound its way into the distance. Cassie turned Rosy the same direction to follow him, the way Brock showed her. When the horse did as directed, Cassie's pride soared.

"So…" he said.

She knew what he was going to say. "Why did I buy

a ranch and move all the way out here if I'd never even ridden a horse before?"

He nodded, smiling at her perception.

Cassie sighed and patted Rosy's neck. "I've always lived in the city, and my mother was dead set against me getting on a horse, no matter how much I wanted to, so there was no chance to learn as a kid. When I was an adult and finally had the money, I bought tickets out to Dallas and planned to go for a week at a dude ranch so I could learn how to ride. I was all set to go when I found out I was pregnant. No horses for me. Since then, I'd always been so busy with the twins that the chance never came up again."

Cassie glanced at Brock to see his reaction. He nodded sympathetically. "Well, let's make sure you get comfortable. You'll be doing plenty of riding from now on," he said.

Cassie's heart warmed at the thought.

Brock watched Cassie carefully as they first set out, but it quickly became clear that she was a natural on a horse. Soon, he had to avoid looking at her because the swaying of her hips with the horse's gait was more than his body could take. His admiration of her tenacity and refusal to give up on her dream despite the years and obstacles only made her more attractive, and he was having a difficult time resisting her.

"These are good animals," Brock told her. "The Wilsons may have let the place go a little, but they had good taste in horses."

Cassie's smile was such a mix of relief, thankfulness

and hope that Brock felt both embarrassed and pleased by her confidence in his assessment. He had seen the look in her eyes the day before, too, when he'd told her the fence didn't need as much lumber and expense as they'd thought.

She clearly had been worrying about finances and her choice to purchase the ranch and move so far from her home, and he was glad he could be the one to ease her concerns. He knew she would fit into her ranch and Spring Valley better than she might give herself credit for.

Their eyes met and held for a moment. Then another.

Brock felt the intimacy settle in around them and instinctively recoiled, shifting his eyes back to Diamond. She had turned him down once before, and he wasn't prepared to get shot down again, so it was best to keep from getting his hopes up. This could easily turn into a romantic horse ride in his mind, and he couldn't allow that. It was important to keep things friendly.

He was starting to hate that word.

"Your top three movies. Go!" he said.

There was a silence, and for a moment he thought she wasn't going to accept the change of mood. Part of him hoped that was true.

Then she said, "Okay, first is *The Count of Monte Cristo*, then *The Terminator* and for the third—" she paused for a second, then spoke all in a rush "—*CuriousGeorgeAVeryMonkeyChristmas*."

"What was that third one?" he asked, risking a glance in her direction.

Her face was red, but she looked at him defiantly. *"Curious George: A Very Monkey Christmas."*

He started to laugh, more at the look on her face than anything else.

"What?" she demanded. "The songs are catchy. And I have little kids."

She laughed, too, and he delighted in the sound of it. "Now it's your turn," she said to him. "And no lying. If *Sleepless in Seattle* is one of your favorite movies, you need to own up to it."

Brock shrugged, still chuckling. "*Sleepless in Seattle* is overrated. I'm a *You've Got Mail* guy myself."

For the next half hour, they talked and laughed about Brock's favorite movies, what they would do if they won the lottery, and what each would bring with them to a desert island.

All too soon, they arrived back at the ranch. Brock hopped off Diamond and moved to help Cassie get down, but before he could, she had dismounted and was standing beside Rosalind, patting the horse with affection. "You're really looking like a cowgirl," he told her.

"Thanks, but don't try to change the topic. You need to give an answer. *One* item to bring to a desert island."

He grinned. "A premade emergency backpack full of food and gear counts as one item. I've bought one before, so I know it exists. Don't get mad at me because my answer was so much better than yours. How would you survive if you just brought a book with you?"

She shook her head at him as they led the horses onto the property. "That's not the point of the question," she said. And, because she was curious, "Why did you need a backpack full of food and gear?"

"I went trekking and mountain climbing with some

buddies at the last minute and needed supplies to last a couple of days," he answered.

He didn't mention that the bag had slipped from his arm and smashed on rocks hundreds of feet below on their first ascent, nor how miserable the following days were because of it.

Before she could ask more questions, one of the twins ran out of the house. "I saw you riding the horses from the window! You were gone a long time," he commented.

Brock turned to him, glad he wouldn't need to recount some of his less successful adventures. "Carter, if you were going to an island with no food or water on it, what would you bring in your backpack?"

Carter thought for a moment. "Pancakes," he said.

"Smart man," Brock said, looking at Cassie in triumph.

"Or a boat so I could leave," the boy added.

Cassie grinned at him. "The four-year-old beat you at your own game. You realize that, right?"

Brock shrugged, enjoying the conversation. "He really did. But both of our answers were still way better than a book."

"Who would bring a book?" Carter asked, scrunching up his face to better show his distaste at the idea.

"Okay, smarty-pants," his mom told him, turning him back to the house, "you go back inside. We'll get the horses settled in and be there in a few minutes."

"Can I help with the horses?" he asked, turning to Brock.

Brock was taken aback that the boy was asking him instead of Cassie, but he answered, "Not this time. We want to get them brushed down quickly so we can get back to work on the ranch. Another time, okay?"

Carter nodded excitedly and took off for the house.

Cassie continued to lead Rosalind toward the open barn door, amazed that Carter had asked Brock instead of her. Brock seemed to be thinking the same thing, because as they entered the dim light of the barn, he commented, "I hope what I said was okay with you. I wasn't really expecting Carter to ask me that."

Watching Brock interact in such a comfortable way with Carter had made her heart flip-flop around in her chest, but she tried to keep that out of her voice when she answered. "It was exactly what I would have said."

It was what the father they deserve to have would've said, she thought to herself. She wiped that notion out of her mind as quickly as she could. The twins had her and all the best memories of their dad, and that would need to be enough.

"They're good kids," Brock told her as he led the horses into their stalls, a small smile on his lips.

Diamond and Rosalind settled in, munching happily on the hay.

As Brock handed Cassie a brush and got his own to groom Diamond, he said, "I think Carter is going to be hopping up on one of these horses in no time. Did you see the way he looked at Diamond?"

Cassie had her brush against Rosalind's silky neck, but stopped to turn and looked at Brock. She had suddenly realized something. "How did you know that was Carter and not Zach?"

Brock seemed oblivious to her eyes on him. She could see the smile grow wider across his lips as he brushed down Diamond. "Zach will grow to like them, too, but he's a bit more hesitant, which is probably why he stayed inside. That seems to be a personality trait, don't you think?"

She did, but that didn't answer her question. "No. I mean, how can you tell them apart? You knew it was Carter without anyone telling you."

He turned to look at her, surprised. "They're two different people. They look similar, sure, but they're unique." He hesitated for a moment, then said, "You can tell them apart, can't you?"

Cassie realized she had been staring at Brock like he was crazy and blushed. "I can, but almost nobody else is able to. Even their grandparents and Hank—well, most people can't tell which is which. I was just surprised you were able to."

Brock went back to grooming Diamond, and Cassie got started on Rosalind. After a few seconds of silence, Brock said, "I think people don't really look at identical twins very closely. They just expect them to be the same, so they don't worry about finding their differences."

Cassie found herself nodding, even though she knew he couldn't see her. She had noticed the very same thing.

"My brothers are twins," he went on, "and when we were kids, I noticed that adults didn't try to tell them apart, even though they're separate individuals."

Cassie knew Brock had brothers, obviously, but he'd never mentioned that they were twins. Trying not to imagine a pair of girls sporting her curly hair and Brock's beautiful eyes, she asked, "Do twins run in your family?"

Brock knew he could answer without explaining the entire story, but something inside him told him to tell the whole truth. Cassie was bound to find out at some point that he and his siblings were adopted, and he felt like she should hear it from him.

"Actually, they're my adopted brothers," Brock said, keeping his eyes on Diamond's mane. "Ma and Pop never had any kids of their own. They're actually my aunt and uncle."

The repetitive sound of the brush against Rosalind stopped. He didn't turn, but waited for her questions.

After a short silence, Cassie asked, "Do you want to talk about it? You don't have to."

He was so surprised he turned from his task and met her eyes. They were serious but lacked any expression of pity. He knew she must be curious, and he appreciated her ability to not pry. Few people managed that.

Suddenly, without him making the conscious decision to do so, he began talking to her about things he rarely discussed with anyone. "My parents died when I was a kid. A car crash. I moved out here from San Diego to live with my aunt Sarah and uncle Howard right after that. They had adopted Amy, Diego and Jose years before but immediately brought me into the family as if I'd always been a part of it. They saved me, Ma and Pop. Even when things were tough—"

He paused there, not quite sure what he wanted to

say. Was he going to tell her about the guilt he'd felt over his parents' death? The dark days he'd never have survived if not for the caring people who treated him with such kindness?

Cassie nodded, seeming to understand, and Brock felt lighter somehow. "Anyway, they gave all of us a home. They're as good a family as I could wish for," he finished lamely.

"I can see that," Cassie agreed, her voice soft, before turning back to her task.

Neither spoke as they finished with the horses then went to find Tom and his mother inside the house. Even when Mrs. Stuart insisted they stay for lunch, Brock and Cassie hardly looked at one another. Finally, they said goodbye to the Stuarts and left with Zach and Carter in tow, each sucking on a candy from their time in the hands of Grandma Stuart.

Brock had known from the first day he'd worked with Cassie that she was a kind, helpful sort of person. Finding out she was a doctor had only confirmed his suspicions. Now, he hoped her big heart wouldn't stop her from treating him the same way she always had. He didn't want or need sympathy or anything else when it came to the death of his parents. He'd had plenty of that growing up.

Mostly, he didn't want to lose the easy way they'd spoken before, and the worry of that possibility made him nervous to say anything at all. Even when he was fighting his attraction for her, there was something about the way they were able to converse that he'd hate to lose. He realized for the first time that they truly had become friends, beyond all the sexual tension and desire, and he didn't want anything to hurt that friendship.

Cassie's voice broke into his thoughts. "Should we start unloading the truck when we get back?"

He said a quick prayer of thanks for the change of topic. "Sure. We can make a pile of the boards out back near the corner of the fence for now, and separate out what we need for the paddock once we start on that. Maybe we'll even be able to get a few sections of it completed before it gets too late, or we could spend some time setting up your office. When did you say you're meeting your first patient?" he asked.

Cassie smiled a little. "Early tomorrow morning. Emma's bringing over her neighbor."

"That's great," Brock said, feeling genuinely happy for her.

She would be up to her ears in patients by the time he left, at that rate.

Cassie didn't look away from the road, but he could see she was happy with the prospect of her first patient. Brock was once again struck with her courage, moving so far away from everything she'd known and starting from scratch.

He imagined her husband's memory played no small part in the decision. If she loved him as much as he suspected, everything in her old life probably reminded her of her loss.

He wasn't sure if he was sympathetic or jealous of a deceased person, but either way it didn't bode well for him.

Chapter 8

Cassie tried to keep her mind on the road, but her thoughts kept straying back to what Brock had said back in the barn about his past. She ached for the young boy who had lost his parents and everything he'd known, and it gave her a newfound wonder at the strength and humor she found in this handsome cowboy.

She could tell Brock didn't want to hear any of that, though, and she could understand why. He'd probably gotten more sympathy from people than he knew what to do with, and she'd had enough sympathy after Hank's death to last her a lifetime. Just being able to talk about normal life without that pity hovering around the edges was all she'd wanted after his crash, and she bet Brock felt the same way.

So normal was exactly what she'd give him.

Once she parked the car, she enlisted the boys to carry a single piece of lumber between them and readied herself for another bout of heavy lifting. She and Brock gathered the boards and began moving them, load by load, from the bed of the truck, around the side of the house and finally to a growing pile of lumber near the corner of the fence closest to the paddock while the boys "helped" as much as they could.

Cassie's still-sore muscles began to protest almost immediately, but she ignored them. Brock pushed himself, and she didn't complain, happy to be working so hard she couldn't fixate on the way his muscles looked under his shirt or think about the way his lips felt against hers, or how he had opened up and shared his past with her.

None of that was helpful here. She just needed to concentrate on what she was doing.

Once all the lumber was out of the truck and in a big pile, she sat on the boards and sucked in a few slow breaths while the boys dropped their last piece on the ground with a thunk. Brock sat beside her to rest, too, and they watched as the energetic boys tried to make their few boards into a respectable pile like that of the adults. There was a faint ding from Brock's pocket, and he shifted his weight as he attempted to extricate his phone from his jeans.

Cassie could feel the wood heap move beneath her, but it was too late to hop off, and she tumbled to the ground along with the lumber. She heard Brock thud beside her and swear under his breath. She turned toward him, worried he was injured.

He had fallen so close to her that her movements brought her to rest with her chest pressed against his arm. She scrambled away as if he was too hot to touch—which in a way, he was. As if she wasn't having a difficult enough time already. Then she noticed that he was still on the floor, and she dropped to her knees beside him. "Brock? Are you okay?"

He grimaced as he tried to sit up. "Yeah, it's just my back. I tweaked it when I fell."

Cassie offered him her hand, and with her help he was able to stand, though he was obviously still in pain. "It just does this sometimes. Has for years," he said through gritted teeth.

"I think we should take you in for a scan, just to be sure you're fine," she said, her training as a doctor taking over.

Brock shook his head. "I promise, it's not a big deal, Doc. A bit of aspirin and some stretches and I'll be right as rain."

"Can I at least take a look?" she asked, though part of her objected to the idea of seeing more of his body than she absolutely needed to.

She was a doctor, and now was the time to be professional.

Brock glanced at her for just a moment, as if he had some idea what she was thinking, then turned his back to her. She pulled up his shirt and looked at his back, running her hands over his skin, trying to ignore the way his obvious strength made her stomach melt into a puddle.

They were just friends, that was all, she told herself.

Yes, he was fit. Yes, if she slid her hands around to his stomach she would likely find six-pack abs that would make her knees go weak. Yes, he could lift her up and pin her against a wall like she'd pictured in her fantasies.

Whoa, Nelly.

She put her hands in her pockets in order to keep herself from touching him any more. "Nothing seems out of place or anything. Likely just a muscle spasm, though you really should get it checked out if it happens often."

Brock pulled down his shirt as he turned, giving her just a glimpse of those abs. Lord, what had she done to deserve this type of punishment? "Sorry about that. You could've been hurt."

She waved away his apology. "It was an accident. You were just checking your phone."

Apparently he'd forgotten about his phone until then, and he pulled it out of his pocket. After a few seconds, he looked up. "My brothers. They were texting to say they're almost here. I should go out and meet them."

Cassie nodded. "Head through the house and get some aspirin. There's a bottle in the cabinet above the kitchen sink. I'll work on stacking the lumber a bit more securely than before," she said, giving him a little smile, which he returned.

She watched him, trying to focus her thoughts and energy into his health and getting the hay turned into bales and sold. The stuff that mattered. Instead, though, her mind kept returning to the feeling of sliding her hands along Brock's skin. When his eyes caught hers, they held for a long moment, and she wondered if he was thinking of the same thing. She waited for him to say something, do something.

Without saying anything, he turned and walked to the back door of the house. She sat down on what was left of the lumber pile, trying to catch her breath.

"What should we do, Momma?" Zach and Carter asked in unison, clearly itching to help more.

Cassie looked at her hands as she tried to think of something for them to do. The splinters in her palm gave her all the inspiration she needed. "Go grab the tweezers from the drawer under my bathroom sink. I have some splinters, and you probably do, too."

The two boys looked at their hands for a moment, nodded, and took off for the back door. Cassie closed her eyes for a moment, enjoying the moment of silence and calm.

Brock took a few gulps of water to get down the aspirin and watched as Zach and Carter sprinted past him, bouncing off the walls in their hurry to do whatever mission they were on. Then he walked through the house and out the front door, unsure if he was happy or not to be away from Cassie's stare. As Brock moved carefully down the steps, his brothers Jose and Diego stepped out of their black truck.

"Hey, Broccoli," Jose said, giving Brock a big trademark grin.

Brock rolled his eyes at the dumb nickname and hugged each of the identical men. "Glad you two could make it. How's the business going?"

Diego just shrugged, but Jose slapped Brock on the

back, making pain flare through his body for a moment. Jose didn't notice. "Couldn't be better. We'll be millionaires by the time we're thirty. Soon you'll be part of the family we've forgotten during our rise to fame and fortune."

Jose had always been the joker of the family, and most people were only able to tell him and Diego apart because Jose was the one who always had a smart-ass comment and a wide grin. Diego, the more serious of the two, got down to business. "You've got some fields for us to check out?"

Brock beckoned them to follow, and he walked back into Cassie's home with the two trailing him. "Is your back giving you trouble again?" Diego asked, more aware than his twin, as usual.

Brock nodded. "I fell just a couple of minutes ago. Should be fine soon enough."

He brought Jose and Diego into the kitchen. He could see Cassie from the window, dragging the boards back into a pile. He should've known she wouldn't waste any time waiting for him, though he wasn't sure how much he'd be able to do with his back the way it was.

He turned back to the kitchen, about to tell his brothers to follow him outside, only to find a strange sight behind him: Zach and Carter, standing side-by-side, staring up at Jose and Diego. The two pairs of twins gave each other a once-over. A twice-over? Brock didn't think that was a thing, but it definitely applied to this moment.

"You look the same," Zach commented.

Jose and Diego glanced at each other. "So do you," Diego said.

Zach and Carter shook their heads in unison. "Nuh-uh," Carter said.

"Carter has more freckles on his nose," Zach added.

"And Zach's eyes are darker," Carter finished.

Jose and Diego nodded, as if this made perfect sense. "Diego has a scar next to his ear," Jose said.

"And Jose is more obnoxious," Diego said.

Jose smiled. "Very true."

Zach and Carter seemed to accept all this. They ran out the back door together.

Jose and Diego turned back to Brock, who'd watched the proceedings with enjoyment.

"Hay?" Diego prompted.

Brock nodded and they went through the back door as well, shielding their eyes from the afternoon sunlight. Cassie looked up from the two young boys, who seemed to be in the middle of a long and hurried story, and Brock's heart jumped at the sight of her. If she wasn't just so damned beautiful...

Jose walked up to her, hand outstretched. "Hello. I'm Brock's much more attractive and successful younger brother."

Jose gave Brock a wink as he shook hands with Cassie. Normally, Brock would wink back, or at least roll his eyes at his brother's antics, but this time was different, and the best he could do was try not to scowl at him. What did Jose think he was playing at? He was here to check out some hay, *not* the owner.

Diego walked up and gave Cassie a quick handshake

before starting in on questions about the acreage of crops she had to sell. Brock always thought Diego was the smarter of the two.

Before Cassie could answer, Carter tugged on her shirt. "Momma! What about the splinters?"

Cassie leaned down to him. "If you couldn't find the tweezers, they must still be in a box somewhere. Once I finish what I'm doing, I'll go help you search, and then we'll be able to get out all the splinters."

"Do you have a bad one? I can get it out using a credit card," Brock offered.

Cassie gave him a skeptical look. "You can get splinters out using a credit card?"

Brock smiled, carefully extricated his wallet from his back pocket and pulled out a credit card. "Sure. They didn't teach you that in your big-city college?" he asked, glad to clear the air from their earlier heated moment.

"I must've missed that day," she said. "Carter, do you want to show Brock your splinter?"

Brock took the young boy's hand in his, stretching the skin around the splinter. In a few moments, he had used the corner of the card to push the splinter out.

"Cool!" Carter exclaimed, his eyes wide.

Brock looked up to Cassie, who nodded in agreement. "That *was* pretty cool. I'll need to remember that trick."

Diego cleared his throat, bringing Brock out of the moment. "I'll keep an eye on the boys. You three go talk business," he said.

Soon, Cassie was walking with Jose and Diego out into the fields and Brock was directing the boys on the final additions to the lumber pile while he stretched his back. If he could loosen it up some, he and Cassie would be able to get her doctor's office all ready before he needed to leave for the evening. Amy had flown in that morning and, with Jose and Diego now in town, he'd be expected at the family dinner Ma had mentioned.

Brock reached toward his toes as far as he could until the scream of pain quieted. When he straightened, his eyes sought out Cassie and his brothers, who had moved a good distance away, and he could only see the backs of their heads as they talked and gestured. He tried not to imagine Cassie laughing at Jose's jokes, smiling back at him when he gave her his patented thousand-watt grin.

Brock kept stretching, getting more and more annoyed at the efforts he was sure Jose was putting into seducing Cassie. Luckily, they were back before Brock's imagination could run away with him too much, and Jose and Diego shook Cassie's hand once more. Jose said, "It was so nice to meet you, Cass. Everything will be baled and out of your hair by the end of next week. And please think about the dinner invitation, okay?"

Cassie nodded and smiled back, but before she could say anything more to Jose, Brock broke in. "I'll see you two out."

With that he stomped toward the side of the house, knowing the two would need to follow before Jose could say anything else. In a flash and despite the still-prominent ache in his back, he had made his way through a broken section of fence and around the side of the house, until he could see his brothers' truck waiting beside his in the driveway.

"Whoa, what's the rush?" Jose asked as Brock ushered them toward the vehicle.

Brock thought he might hit his brother, but Diego got there first, smacking Jose on the back of the head. "You're lucky Brock's not killing you right now," he said.

"What? Why?" Jose asked, rubbing the back of his head.

"Cass? Dinner? What's with the smooth talk, Jose?" Brock said, folding his arms in front of him.

"I was just being polite," Jose said in his defense.

"You were being fresh," Brock shot back.

Diego jumped in. "Brock, nobody says 'fresh.' Stop acting like an old man. Jose, brothers don't go after the same girls. Brock was here first, and if he has a thing going with Cassie—"

"I don't have a *thing* with her," denied Brock. "It's just that…" He searched for an explanation that didn't involve the story of how she'd shot him down when he asked her out. "She's our parents' new neighbor, and a very nice widow, and she doesn't need to fend off your flirtations."

Diego raised an eyebrow. "Nothing's going on with you two? Seriously?"

Brock wasn't sure what to say to that. "We're friends" sounded like a lie, but what else were they? If he was being honest with himself, he had no answer. No answer he liked, anyway.

The silence lengthened between them until Jose burst out, "Fine, I will no longer be, um, *polite* to Cass. I mean, Mrs. Stanford," he added after seeing the look on Brock's face.

Brock nodded and walked them the last few steps to their truck.

"In my defense, though," Jose continued, "I wasn't asking her *out* to dinner. I was inviting her to dinner at home. Ma told me to. So don't worry so much about me getting too fresh, Grandpa."

With that and another big smile, Jose hopped into the passenger side of the truck. Diego shook his head. "I'll keep him under control. See you in a few hours?"

Brock nodded and Diego got into the driver's seat and started the engine. Brock turned around, feeling equal parts annoyed and ashamed.

He had jumped down his brother's throat for flirting with Cassie. If they were just going to be friends, why should he get to say who flirted with her? Brock knew that wasn't fair to her, or to Jose, or to any guy who liked her. If she didn't want to date because of her husband's memory, that was fine, but he should leave that decision to her. She could decide to go out with anybody she liked.

Still, the thought of Cassie with someone else bothered him more than he wanted to admit.

Brock ran his fingers through his hair. If he could survive another ten days around her, it wouldn't matter, anyway. He'd go back to his regular life and that would be it for this whole thing.

Brock sighed and went back to where Cassie was standing, the pile of boards back to the state it had been before it tumbled. The boys were nowhere to be seen.

Her eyes lit up when she saw him in a way he was sure Jose would never experience, and in that moment of triumph, he threw caution to the wind and kissed her again, hoping that this time…

Any thought after that disappeared as her body and lips met his, sending bursts of electricity flowing through his veins. He wrapped his arms around her and held her close, though she needed no urging.

Then she pulled away, and in a flash his arms were empty and she was standing beside the dilapidated fence, not looking at him and shaking her head.

Brock laughed ruefully. "If that kiss did anything near to you what it did to me, then your husband must've been some amazing guy for you to be so loyal to him."

It was Cassie's turn to laugh, though hers was bitter and hinted at struggles beyond her young years. "Hank? If he'd survived the car crash, we would be divorced and I would probably still be kissing you right now. He was…not a very good husband."

Brock was confused. Everything he'd heard about the man painted him as a saint. Cassie seemed to know what he was thinking. "I don't want the boys to know the darker sides of their father. For now at least, they should think of him as a heroic police officer."

"Instead of…" Brock prompted.

He could see the pain in her eyes, and thought she might want to share the story. When she didn't speak at first, though, he opened his mouth to change the subject. Before he could say anything she began speaking, all in a rush, as if the words had been walled up and the dam had just burst.

"Hank was a cop back in Minneapolis. I got pregnant when we had only been dating for a few months, and we got married. Things started to fall apart even before the boys were born, and we had a lot of arguments about me going back to school to finish getting my MD. Still, I tried to stick it out."

Brock watched her intently. Cassie took a deep breath and continued. "He was gone a lot—working extra shifts, he said—which meant we didn't see much of each other those last couple of years. It was probably the reason we stayed together as long as we did. But—"

She paused. Brock wasn't sure she was going to continue. When she spoke again, her voice was quiet.

"But I had no idea what was really going on. It was only after the accident that I found out. He got in a car crash in the middle of the night. He'd crashed into a pole. He died..."

She grimaced, either in hurt or disgust, Brock wasn't sure. "The woman in the passenger seat survived."

Brock moved forward and stood beside her, aching with the betrayal she must have felt. "She was—"

"His girlfriend," Cassie said, the calmness of her voice belied by the sparkle of a tear in her eye. "One of many, it turned out."

Brock wasn't sure what to say, but before he could find words, Cassie continued, "And they found drugs in the car, too. I had been so busy with the twins and finishing my residency that I had no idea any of this was going on. I felt so stupid."

Cassie covered her face with her hands and fell silent for a moment. Brock wanted to hug her, but held himself back, only looping a single arm around her back as a show of support. She dropped her hands back to her side and forced herself to continue.

"The rumors about Hank were everywhere. He was a cop, after all. A 'pillar of the community' sort of thing. Every person we talked to would look at us with pity, and I hated it. I didn't want the scandal of it to ruin the boys' memories of their dad. So I packed them up and moved them across the country to keep them safe and happy. Sometimes I'm not so sure it was a great idea, but here we are," she said, standing and looking out the barn toward the ranch house.

"Anyway, that's why nothing can happen between us. I'm not loyal to Hank's memory. I'm loyal to Zach and Carter and the memories of their father that they hold so dear. They've been through so much, and we're finally getting into a good place. I don't want to do *anything* to jeopardize that. That means no dating, no kissing, no flings, regardless of the man."

Brock could see in her face and hear in her voice how much she desired him, and if it didn't give him what he really wanted, at least it soothed the feeling of rejection. Before he could do more than nod, the twins came running up to their mom, chattering excitedly about their adventures searching for the tool chest.

Cassie looked up at Brock, none of the emotions she had experienced so recently showing on her face. "I sent Zach and Carter to find the toolbox so we can work on the office, unless you need to get home and be with your family?" she asked.

She was giving him an out, a chance to slink away

without discussing all that had happened in the past few minutes. He knew she would understand if he walked away now and never came back. "I've got enough time to help. And if we have that out of the way, we can get started on the paddock tomorrow."

Cassie's smile transmitted her relief without the need for words, and Brock walked with her and the boys into the house. He wished there was something he could do to convince her that she deserved to be happy as much as her children did.

But if he couldn't do that, at least he could respect her wishes and do whatever possible to make her life a little easier. If anyone deserved a helping hand, it was Cassie.

An hour and a half later, Cassie watched from her doorway as Brock walked to his parents' house. She wasn't sure if she was relieved or disappointed that they'd never had a chance to speak privately after her confession by the fence. The boys had been so eager to help as they hung her diplomas and organized the furniture, there was no opportunity for her and Brock to be alone.

So Cassie couldn't help but wonder what he thought about everything she'd said. It was clear Brock was still willing to help her, but that was all she knew.

Once he was out of sight, Cassie walked into the kitchen and took a long drink of cold water. She had just put the glass down and started to consider what to do with the rest of the afternoon when her phone buzzed. She glanced at it to find a message from Brock: Ma wanted me to make sure you were coming to dinner. Will you be coming? She wants you here by 6.

Dinner with the McNeals. An entire night of unsatisfied lust for Brock and fending off Jose's flirtations didn't sound all that appealing, but she couldn't find it in her to say no. Mrs. McNeal was so nice, after all, and she didn't want to disappoint the old woman.

Cassie knew it was a lie to say she was going for any reason besides Brock. She might not be able to have him, but she still couldn't stop herself from spending what time around him she could. Even when she engineered ways to stay away from him, she still managed to sabotage them.

She cut off the internal monologue and texted back. We'll be there.

Once the decision was made, Cassie went to tell Zach and Carter. Then they needed to decide what to bring their hosts, and she would need to go through the long process of agonizing over what to wear so it wasn't flirtatious, yet attractive enough that the little voice inside her still hoping for some impossible romance didn't shout too loudly.

A quick trip to the bakery solved one of her problems, and an hour in front of the mirror solved the other, and by that time it was nearly six o'clock and she had to hustle Zach and Carter out the door.

Cassie watched her boys run ahead of her through the late-afternoon sunshine toward the McNeal home. The lights shone through the windows, creating an inviting scene, but it did nothing to ease Cassie's nerves. She told herself that she was just nervous because she was planning to spend the evening with a bunch of people she hardly knew, not because of anything to do with Brock McNeal.

She didn't believe it, but it was better than admitting the alternative: that her feelings toward Brock were getting more confusing all the time. She couldn't forget the way her body reacted to his kisses, or the way her heart melted at his smile.

All Cassie wanted to do was get her ranch finished and keep her heart unscathed, and instead she was planning to spend an entire evening in Brock's presence under the eyes of his whole family, who also happened to be her neighbors in her new hometown. She really had a knack for creating the perfect recipe for disaster.

Zach and Carter hopped onto the porch, then waited for their mother to catch up. For one crazy second, Cassie considered calling them back to her and turning around. They could just go home and send their apologies.

The door opened and Mrs. McNeal, an older woman with a head of white curls and a wide smile, greeted the two boys. "Come in! My, but it's good to see young boys in my home again. If I'm not mistaken, you've grown taller since you moved here. 'Fore I know it, you'll be as tall as my boy Brock."

Cassie walked up the porch steps and saw the look of astonishment on the boys' faces. "I'm going to be *that* tall?" Carter asked with wide eyes.

Mrs. McNeal nodded confidently. "Taller, if I'm not mistaken. And I'm never mistaken. Now come in off the porch, you three."

"Thank you for inviting us, Mrs. McNeal," Cassie said as she entered the large, well-kept ranch home.

Brock's mother waved her hands as if getting rid of a bad smell. "Sarah, if you please. We're neighbors, after all. We don't put on any airs here, Cassie."

Before Cassie could reply, Sarah had her arms wrapped around the boys and was leading them through the house. "You two will call me Nana Sarah, won't you? My children haven't given me any grandbabies to spoil yet, so I'll need to spoil you instead."

Cassie followed Sarah and the boys, trying to gird herself for the jolt of electricity she felt every time she saw Brock. Even so, there was no way she could have been prepared for the wash of emotions she felt when she walked into the kitchen, where Brock stood with his arm around the waist of a beautiful, tall blonde woman.

Cassie couldn't believe what she was seeing. Did Brock have a girlfriend he'd never told her about? The pain she'd felt when she discovered the truth about her husband came washing back over her, taking her breath away. Was Brock taken and simply trying to have some extra fun on the side with her? Cassie's heart ached at the thought.

Brock turned toward her, giving her a smile that cut right through her. It hurt to realize that she wasn't as special to him as she'd believed, that he was another cheating man like Hank. She considered running out the door right then and there, but she stopped herself. She wouldn't let another man embarrass her like that.

Chapter 9

Brock felt his heart speed up at the sight of Cassie standing in the doorway, holding what looked to be another of Emma's pies, which his ma smelled with glee. When Brock smiled at Cassie, though, he was surprised to see her give him a stony expression. He wondered if something had changed since he'd seen her a few hours before. Maybe she was mad about the kiss and regretted telling him about her husband. Or maybe, despite her determination to stay single, she had fallen for Jose's smooth talk after all and had decided to create a cool distance between them before pursuing something with his little brother.

He knew that didn't make sense, but even so, it was difficult to push the thought away.

"Brock, why don't you introduce Cassie to everyone

while I take this pie and the boys into the kitchen? I need a couple of taste-testers to help make sure everything's ready," his ma urged, breaking the silence before disappearing through the doorway to the kitchen, boys in tow.

"I know everyone except—" Cassie paused, looking at Amy.

Brock used the arm around Amy's waist to turn her toward Cassie. He tried to grin at her again, hoping he was just reading too much into things. "Cassie, this is Amy, my sister."

"Oh!" Cassie exclaimed, her eyes wide in surprise and maybe something else. Relief?

Cassie shook hands with Amy, her friendly manner completely restored. Brock decided he must have just imagined her previous hesitation. He guided Amy to a chair, where she sat down with a sigh.

"Sorry," Amy said to Cassie's questioning gaze. "I rolled my ankle getting out of the truck earlier today, and it's pretty painful. I'll need to get it checked tomorrow. I can't even make it to the dinner table without help, but I guess that's what big brothers are for," she finished with a wave in Brock's direction.

Jose, who had been lounging against the wall on the other side of the dining room, spoke up. "Amy can climb Mount Fuji without a problem, but getting out of a truck in Spring Valley is apparently a little more than she can handle."

Cassie didn't seem to notice Jose—she was too busy staring at Amy's ankle in concern. It made Brock happy to see how little attention she gave Jose. Even though he knew she wasn't planning on dating anyone, it was still nice to be sure he wouldn't need to watch Jose and Cassie become an item.

"Cassie, would you be willing to take a look at it?" Brock asked, sure that her fingers were itching to help.

It was just the kind of person Cassie was.

She nodded and knelt by Amy's foot. "Do you mind? I'm a doctor."

"You're a *doctor*?" Jose said, clearly surprised.

Brock knew what his brother was thinking: What was a doctor doing buying a ranch in a tiny place like this?

He felt a touch of pride for Cassie and the good work she planned to do in the little town she had decided to call home. "She's turning the old library in the Wilson place into a doctor's office. We'll have a genuine doctor in town, so people won't need to go all the way to the hospital."

Brock's siblings all nodded, clearly seeing the advantages of having Cassie move in. The closest hospital was in the next town over, a pretty long drive. They'd all experienced that interminable trip as children with ear infections or when a cut was so deep that it warranted stitches.

"It'll just be for checkups and minor injuries. Big problems will still need to be examined at the hospital," Cassie amended in her casual, humble way that Brock had grown to love. Like.

As friends.

"Spring Valley will be lucky to have a doctor," Brock told her.

Any town would be lucky to have her, he added silently, glad Cassie couldn't read his thoughts.

She continued to assess Amy's ankle, but he saw a light flush creep up her neck and hoped his affection for her hadn't been blatant. Since her confession, he had resolved to put a little distance between them, both physically and metaphorically, and already it was a difficult promise to keep.

Cassie seemed willing to let the moment pass, though, so he said nothing more. She looked up from Amy's ankle, but kept her eyes on his sister and didn't look Brock's way, for which he was grateful. He was pretty sure any eye contact between them would be send a clear signal about his feelings to his hawk-eyed family.

He couldn't say what it was, but being with her around his family changed things, somehow. Watching her help Amy, greet his mother with a pie. She just fit.

He took a small step back, as if hoping he could force himself to fade into the background.

"It doesn't seem to be broken," she said at last. "But it's a pretty bad sprain. I'd like to wrap it and put some ice on it to reduce swelling."

"Beautiful *and* smart? I may have stayed in Spring Valley if I'd known someone like you would turn up," Jose commented from his corner.

Before Brock could do more than glare at his brother, Diego stood up. "I'll go find the first-aid kit for you," he said to Cassie, heading toward the kitchen. "Jose, you come help me."

Jose slunk over to his twin and followed him into the next room. Brock was sure Diego was going to give

Jose a quick reminder to back off, and he couldn't pretend to be displeased.

Cassie nodded her thanks to them, then turned back to Amy. "Keep it elevated as much as you can for the next couple of days. I'll check it again in a day or two to make sure it's healing, if that's okay with you."

Amy nodded. "Thanks. Hopefully it'll be fine by Tuesday. That's when I'm flying out."

As if on cue, Ma walked into the room, her hands on her hips. "Why you need to leave so soon is beyond me, Amy dear. You just got home."

Amy shrugged. "Sorry, Ma. I need to be in Marrakech by Wednesday."

Ma harrumphed and walked back into the kitchen, passing a confused Diego as he returned with the kit. Cassie began rummaging around for the necessary bandage while Jose gave her a bag of ice, very clearly avoiding making eye contact with her.

Amy turned back to Cassie. "Sorry about that. Families, you know. And thanks for looking at my ankle."

Cassie finished wrapping Amy's ankle with practiced hands and stood. "Any time. I owe your family a pretty large debt, what with Brock helping me fix up the place and Jose and Diego agreeing to buy my bales of hay. Your ankle balances out the scales a little."

Before anyone could say another word, Zach and Carter walked into the room carrying plates and silverware. "Nana Sarah said for you lazybones to get to work like us," Carter announced, dropping a handful of cutlery onto the table with a clatter.

"Carter!" Cassie admonished, shaking her head disapprovingly.

Brock tried to hold in the laughter at the look of surprise on Carter's face. The kid clearly had no idea why his mom was so shocked at him.

Ma peeked her head into the room. "Did you call them lazybones like I said?" she asked Carter.

"Yes, Nana Sarah," Carter said, still looking slightly distressed.

Ma nodded approvingly. "Well that's all right, then. And you—" she said, pointing at Brock accusingly. "Stop your snorting over there and get to work. You heard the boy."

"Yes, Ma," Brock answered, grinning widely.

Sarah McNeal didn't pull any punches, that was for sure. He glanced over at Cassie. She turned to him and their eyes met. He shrugged, hoping she would be understanding about his slightly eccentric mother. Cassie laughed. "Get to work, lazybones," she told him.

Without thinking, Brock laughed, too, threw his arm around her shoulders and kissed her playfully on the cheek.

Brock wasn't sure if the rest of the house suddenly got silent, or if it was just that he had stopped caring about anything else going on. Cassie looked up at him, and for a second he was sure she was going to lean in and kiss him. His heart stuttered.

Then she looked away. "I'll go get napkins," she said, and without another glance in his direction, she walked into the kitchen.

"Smooth," Amy said, rolling her eyes.

Jose started setting the table. "Oh, like you're so great at love, Ames. How many years has it been since the last time you were with a guy?"

"That wasn't cool, Jose," Amy responded, turning red from either anger or embarrassment.

Brock left the room, ignoring the argument starting between his siblings. Why couldn't he control himself around Cassie? He knew she was determined to avoid even so much as a brief relationship, and yet he still found he was unable to stop himself.

The living room was much quieter, which suited him just fine. He needed time to think. He sat down on the old couch, an ugly patterned thing that must have dated from the sixties. The springs creaked as they took his weight.

Brock battled with his frustration. There was only one thing he could do, it seemed, to be sure he didn't attempt to kiss Cassie again: no more trying to be friends. And no more close encounters. He'd go over to her place and work as far away from her as he could.

He wished there was some other way, because he truly enjoyed spending time with her, but it didn't seem like he had any other option.

That shock of electricity, the pure joy of the moment, didn't feel like a light, casual nothing to him. It felt like a big, definite, something. It wasn't a passionate kiss full of lust like the others. It was…sweet. And loving. And that broke all his rules, too.

Brock sighed and put his head in his hands, wishing things could be different.

After a few seconds of silence, Brock felt a small tap

on his shoulder and looked up. Zach was standing there staring at him. He looked nervous.

Brock knew just what had the boy so worried, and couldn't help but smile despite his other thoughts. "What did Nana Sarah call me?"

"A laggard."

"All right, I'm coming," Brock said as he stood up, resolving to act natural when he saw Cassie.

"Brock, what's a laggard?" Zach asked, almost in a whisper. "Is it a bad word?"

Brock chuckled at the concern in Zach's voice. "It's just another word for lazy."

Zach looked visibly relieved as he ran back to the kitchen shouting, "Nana Sarah! I told him just like you said!"

Back in the dining room, platters of food covered the large table. His ma had apparently made enough to feed a small army. "You might've outdone yourself this time, Ma," he said as he surveyed the steaming chicken fried steak and pile of mashed potatoes.

Sarah looked at the spread with pride. "I wanted our new neighbors to have some good ol' Southern food. Everybody sit down and tuck in while it's hot."

Brock took his usual seat, only to find Cassie seated next to him. A glance at Ma's face was enough to tell him she had orchestrated the seating arrangements. Brock decided to enjoy these last few minutes this close to her.

"Your ma sure knows how to cook," Cassie said, though the way she kept her eyes trained away from him belied her relaxed tone.

Brock nodded, unable to bring himself to share in much conversation. As he bit a green bean in half, Amy caught his eye. She was clearly still sore about Jose's comment, but she raised her eyebrows at him, silently asking if he was okay. Brock gave her a little nod, though he wasn't sure if that was the truth.

Cassie was glad the food in front of her gave her a reason not to look at Brock, since she wasn't sure she could do so without making a simpering fool of herself. That kiss on the cheek, though so much tamer than the other kisses they had shared, made her melt in an entirely different way. It was...sweet.

That scared her.

So she kept her head down and ate, glad that the silence of everyone tucking in meant she didn't need to try to make conversation. And that lasted a short while, at least.

"Cass—Dr. Stanford," Jose said, in a formal way that struck her as odd. "How are you settling in?"

Everyone's eyes turned to her as they waited for her answer.

Cassie swallowed and answered honestly, "This town already feels like home."

She didn't mention how much Brock's help had been a part of that.

"So you're adjusting to small-town life okay? You don't wish you were working in a big hospital?" Diego asked.

Cassie nodded, thinking of her horses and ranch, and of the cowboy who had become a part of all that so quickly. Small-town life suited her just fine. "I love my little office," she said. "And I'm going to see my first patient tomorrow morning, actually. This is the kind of doctor I always wanted to be."

"I bet Brock can't wait to be examined by you," Jose said quietly, but not quietly enough.

Diego smacked him on the head, and Howard said a warning, *"Jose!"* from the other side of the table.

All at once, Jose calling her Dr. Stanford instead of "Cass" made sense. Brock must have told his brother something about what had happened between them, probably to get Jose to back off. Why else would Jose change his behavior toward her so quickly?

And judging by everyone's reaction, he'd told them, too. They all seemed to believe she and Brock were some kind of an item.

What had he told them, exactly? Did they know about the kisses? About Hank?

A picture of the whole family sitting around dissecting everything she'd said and done with Brock made her stomach churn. And what if it all got around town, twisting and morphing until she couldn't show her face in Spring Valley?

It was Minneapolis all over again.

"How about we have some pie?" Sarah said, standing from her place at the table.

Cassie felt claustrophobic. She needed to get out of there. She stood as well, grasping for some excuse to leave. "Actually, we need to leave," she said, hoping she sounded calm. "I didn't realize how late it was, and Zach and Carter need to go to bed."

The boys looked up, distressed. "We don't get dessert?" Carter asked.

"Diego was going to let me wear his cowboy hat after dinner," Zach added.

Cassie was in no mood to stick around. "Not this time. Go get your shoes on," she told them, and the two boys left the table without another word.

Before Cassie could rush her children out the door, Brock appeared. He was the last person she wanted to see.

"I'll walk you home," Brock offered.

"No," Cassie almost shouted before regaining control of herself. "We can manage, thanks."

As Cassie opened the door to let herself out, Sarah came running in from the dining room, a plate of pie in her hands. "I'll be darned if I'm going to let my unruly children eat all the delicious pie you brought over without your sweethearts getting some," she insisted, shoving the plate into Cassie's hands.

Cassie hardly had the sense of mind to thank the older woman before she was out the door, her two boys hurrying to keep up. She wanted to get away from there as fast as she could. Before she could leave the pool of light created by the ranch house's windows, though, she heard Brock rushing up behind her. "Cassie, wait."

She turned toward him, her irritation boiling inside her.

"Jose—" he started.

She cut him off before he could say another word. "I don't want to talk about this. I just…" She trailed off.

I just thought you were different, she wanted to say,

but she could feel tears of frustration welling in her eyes. She turned and continued on her way home before she could let them fall.

It was only after Cassie had given Zach and Carter their pie and tucked them into bed—then taken a long bath to try to soothe her muscles and thoughts—that she glanced at her phone as she placed it on her bedside table.

A few minutes after she'd left the McNeal house hours before, Brock had sent her a text. Jose was making a joke at my expense. Because it's obvious to everyone who knows me how much I like you. I set them all straight and they hope you aren't too mad. I'm sorry.

Cassie understood her mistake immediately and looked out her window, which faced the McNeal house. The entire place was dark. It was too late to go talk to Brock.

He hadn't told them anything about her, obviously. Since when had she gotten so suspicious of other people, so ready to see the worst in men?

She knew the answer to that, of course. Since the day she'd learned about Hank's affairs.

Cassie resolved to go see Brock right after her morning appointment. She needed to apologize, and it needed to be in person. He deserved that much.

She turned off the light, even though she knew it would be a long time until she'd be able to fall asleep. She had a lot to think over.

She awoke the next morning to her alarm beeping at her, and opened her bleary eyes to the sun streaming in through the window. It looked to be another bright, hot day, though at this point in the summer, that came as no surprise.

Cassie turned off the alarm, thankful she'd set one to be sure she didn't sleep too late. She'd had a nearly sleepless night, and would likely have slept until noon if she could.

Then her two human alarm clocks came running in, reminding her that it'd be a long time until she'd be able to sleep until noon, regardless of appointments with patients.

"Momma!" Carter called as he and Zach pounced on her. "Are we going to paint our room today?"

Cassie grimaced. The prospect of painting alone was unpleasant, but she'd need to apologize before she could even think about asking Brock to do more work on her house. "Maybe later, honey," she said. "I have a patient coming this morning, remember? And Brock might not be coming over today."

Zach looked worried. "Why isn't Brock coming today? Is it because I called him a laggard? Nana Sarah told me to!"

Cassie's heart ached at the distress on his face. She gathered her sons into a tight hug. "Brock isn't mad at you, I promise. You did nothing wrong. I just haven't asked him if he'll be around today, yet. I'll do that right after the appointment"

And eat a little crow, she added silently.

Cassie rose and dressed quickly, throwing a doctor's smock on over scrubs, and while the boys ate breakfast, she went into her office for one final check before her first patient arrived.

She put the last item into place none too soon, because the doorbell rang as she closed the cupboard. With one last backward glance, Cassie rushed to the door and opened it to find Emma and a friendly-looking old woman on the other side.

Emma gave Cassie a broad smile. "Mrs. Edelman, meet the town's new resident doctor. Dr. Stanford."

Despite everything going on with Brock, Cassie's mood lifted. She'd missed being a doctor and was excited to meet her first patient. The older woman gave her a strong handshake and a huge smile. In her thick Texas drawl, she said, "Oh, dear, am I ever glad to meet you. Spring Valley has needed a doctor. You, honey, are a godsend."

Cassie blushed. "I'm happy to be of help. Would you like to come into my examination room?" she asked, gesturing Mrs. Edelman through the door to the library-turned-office.

"I have a couple of cuties to feed and entertain," Emma said, holding up a bag that clearly held treats from her bakery. "You two holler if you need me."

With that, Emma was gone and her neighbor was settling herself onto the examination table. "What can I help you with today, Mrs. Edelman?" Cassie asked, realizing that in all the rush to get everything ready in time, she'd never asked what exactly her patient wanted to see her about.

The older woman's grin grew even wider, if that were possible. "I need vaccinations. I'll be leaving to see the world, and it wouldn't do to die of malaria as soon as I leave. This is my itinerary," she said, handing Cassie a couple of folded sheets filled with travel details.

Cassie read through the list of cities, amazed at the variety. It seemed Mrs. Edelman was planning a round-the-world trip that any twenty-year-old nomad would be proud of. "You are quite the adventurer," she commented.

"Oh, my dear, I've never been outside of Texas. I've wanted to see the world my entire life, and now I'm going to do it, come hell or high water," she said, the ferocity in her voice surprising.

"I don't doubt you will," Cassie said. "I'll need to go through this list of places and see what vaccinations you should get, and then I'll order them. Would you mind coming back for another visit before you leave so I can administer them?"

Mrs. Edelman nodded. "That would be perfectly lovely."

"Since you're already here, would you like to have a quick checkup to make sure you're ready to trek across the globe?" Cassie asked, pulling out a pair of gloves.

"So long as you don't tell me I should stay home, poke and prod away," the older woman responded.

Cassie smiled as she pulled out a blood pressure cuff. "I wouldn't dream of doing that. You seem so determined that I doubt it would do any good if I did, anyway."

"Well," Mrs. Edelman said, looking at Cassie thoughtfully, "I should have gone long ago, but I was too busy being a wife and a mother to do what I wanted for myself. If I could go back and change things, I would. I'd have lovely memories of the pyramids and the Taj Mahal, and what's the worst that could've happened? Fred and the kids might've needed to cook a dinner or two. It would have done us all some good if I was a bit more selfish back then. But it's too late to change that now, so I'll just need to start from here and see what I can while I have any juice left in this old body of mine."

Cassie shook her head in amazement at her first patient and completed a careful examination, happy to declare that the woman seemed to be in fine health. Mrs. Edelman gathered her purse and scooted off the table. Cassie showed her into the living room as she went in search of the old woman's ride home, the idea that had been formulating since her conversation with Mrs. Edelman still in the forefront of her mind.

When she saw Emma playing trucks with the boys, she came to a decision. "Emma, Mrs. Edelman is ready whenever you are."

Emma stood up, stretched, and went to her friend. "Your boys are wonderful, Cassie."

"I'm glad you think so, because I have a favor to ask," Cassie said. "Would you take them with you and watch them for a couple of hours? I need them out of the house for a bit."

Cassie expected her nosy friend to ask what she had planned, but luckily Emma just nodded. "No problem! I don't need to be at the bakery until two this afternoon. Is it okay if I bring them back about an hour before that?"

Cassie agreed, relieved. "That's perfect. Thanks. I owe you one."

Emma pulled up her sleeve to reveal the nearly healed scar from her burn. "Already paid in full. Come on, boys! Your momma says I get to take you home and feed you more delicious sweets!"

The boys jumped up, excited. Emma turned to Cassie, noting the slight frown on her face. "Hey, if you don't want them eating dessert for lunch, don't let a baker babysit."

With that and a laugh, the four of them left the room, and a few minutes later, Cassie was waving goodbye as they disappeared into the distance. As soon as the car was out of sight, she turned back to the house, intending to change out of her scrubs quickly before heading over to Brock's.

Before she could put a foot onto the porch, however, Cassie paused and listened. It took her a few seconds to realize that what she was hearing was hammering, and it seemed to be coming from behind her house.

Curious, Cassie followed the noise to find Brock working on her paddock, nailing a new piece of lumber into place. Based on the pile of lumber beside him, he'd been at it for quite a while despite how early it was.

Cassie walked up to Brock without him noticing, and when he stopped to examine the board he'd just nailed in place, she said, "Decided to get an early start, huh?"

He jumped slightly and turned to her, giving her a grin that made her weak at the knees. He shrugged. "Yeah, well, I figured I had a readymade metaphor here, so I came over to mend some fences. Metaphorically and—" he gestured at the paddock "—literally."

Cassie smiled at the terrible pun. "I'm sorry I over-reacted last night. I'm still not quite over what happened in Minneapolis, and I let it get to my head," she told him.

Her heart pounded as she gathered her courage.

Brock shook his head. "You don't need to apologize—"

Before he could say another word, Cassie pulled him into a kiss.

Brock seemed stunned for a moment, but then his arms wrapped around her and he kissed her back enthusiastically. After a long, long kiss that neither of them seemed willing to break, they finally came up for air. Brock gave Cassie a pained smile and pressed his forehead against hers. "It seems we're both terrible at controlling ourselves, huh?" he asked.

Cassie shook her head, and moved even closer to him. "I'm done controlling myself," she said.

Brock moved back just enough to look her straight in the eyes, a surprised look on her face.

"I got some good advice today. If I wait until the boys are grown to do anything for myself, it might be too late, and I don't want that. It won't hurt them if I'm a little selfish and impulsive for the next nine days."

"Nine days," Brock repeated, though Cassie couldn't quite tell what emotion he was feeling when he said it.

She nodded resolutely, as much for herself as for him. "Until the rodeo. We can work on the house, and in the small snatches of time when the boys aren't around, we can do…more grown-up activities."

Brock smiled. "We better make them a good nine days," he commented.

Cassie kept talking, anxiety building now that she knew what might come next. "Plus, I need some help if I'm ever going to get over what happened with Hank. It affected me more than I realized. I need to practice being in a relationship again, even if it's only a short one."

"So I'm your training wheels?" Brock asked, tipping her head up with a single finger.

"Not exactly," Cassie backpedaled, trying not to blush.

But Brock said nothing, just leaned in for another kiss.

Chapter 10

When they separated this time, Brock could hardly think straight. That morning he had woken up expecting little more than to hopefully smooth things out with Cassie and continue working on her ranch while also staying as far from her as possible. Now he was kissing her, touching her, and had even more to look forward to in the future.

Well, for the next nine days.

He didn't want to waste any of it. "Where are Zach and Carter?" he asked.

"Emma's watching them," Cassie said, still breathless. "She's bringing them back around one."

Plenty of time. On to the next important question. "Have you eaten yet today?"

"No," she answered. "I didn't have time before—

where are we going?" she asked as he grabbed her hand and began pulling her away from the paddock.

"We need breakfast," he replied, not slowing down. "We're going on a date!"

"Oh!" Cassie exclaimed, and Brock paused and looked back at her.

In the rush to get the most out of every second, he was getting ahead of himself. "Do you want to go on a breakfast date with me?"

"Absolutely," she answered, so emphatically that it made him grin. Or maybe a grin was just permanently plastered on his face after what had happened during the past ten minutes. "I just thought we'd be…"

She looked at the house, and when he realized what she'd been thinking, he needed to take a deep breath to calm himself down. As much as he wanted to, that wasn't how he did things. "You deserve a delicious breakfast, don't you think?"

"I should just change," she said, waving a hand at her scrub and smock.

Brock didn't think he'd ever seen her in anything so sexy. "If you want to," he said, "but I think you look just perfect."

"Two minutes," she said, running into the house.

Brock paced in front of his truck, which was still parked beside her house, his stomach in knots. He was going on a date with Cassie. And after that, well, he could hardly allow his mind to go there.

Cassie came back out of the house all in a rush, slipping low flats onto her feet as she went. She had changed into a knee-length dress that nearly killed him, made of some shiny brown material that set off the fiery accents in her hair.

"It's been a long time since I've been on a date," she said breathlessly once she reached him. "I want to be dressed for it."

He managed to unglue his tongue enough to tell her how beautiful she was and give her another deep kiss before helping her into his truck.

In moments, they were out of her driveway and heading to his favorite little restaurant. "I hope you don't mind cheesy diners with delicious food," he told her. "It's one of my favorite places, and it's a little ways out of town."

He wasn't sure if she wanted to keep everything, even them going to eat together, a secret, but if she did, this was the best location. People in town usually went to one of the two restaurants on the main drag, not fifteen minutes out into the middle of nowhere.

"Sounds perfect," she answered, and he settled into the drive.

The silence between them felt charged and tense as they went. After a few minutes, Cassie said his name in a serious voice that made him worry she was rethinking her earlier decision.

"You should know, before we go any further," she started.

He waited for the bomb to drop.

"I'm a mother first. This can be a fun thing, but we need to keep it from affecting my kids in any way," Cassie finished.

Brock laughed in relief. There was no new information there. "I'd never do anything to hurt Zach and Carter," he told her truthfully.

Cassie leaned back. "Then let's go have a date," she said.

The little restaurant Brock took her to reminded Cassie of diners in movies, complete with a cherry pie under glass and a large pottery cowboy boot painted with desert scenes in dusky reds and yellows. Brock maneuvered her through the place to a small corner booth. "Best spot in the restaurant," he said.

He didn't need to tell her that. It was secluded, almost private, and small enough that they were sitting nearly shoulder-to-shoulder. Her heart raced as he waited for her to sit before seating himself. "You are quite the gentleman on a date," she commented.

He smiled. "My ma raised me right," he said.

Cassie looked through the menu, but the combination of nerves and the variety of options made it difficult to choose. The diner seemed to serve pretty much everything under the sun.

Finally, she settled on the French toast. Brock ordered a corned beef skillet and a side of dumplings.

"Dumplings?" Cassie asked as soon as the waitress was gone.

"Their dumplings are fantastic," Brock answered. "You need to try them. If that means you're eating dumplings before ten, well, then, so be it."

She was skeptical, but said nothing. Brock seemed so happy to be out with her that she couldn't spoil any part of it, even if it involved having a pan-fried treat with her French toast.

Luckily, the meal ended up being fantastic, dumplings and all. Almost as good as the conversation and sexual tension.

By the time they'd finished eating, she wanted nothing more than to take Brock home and fulfill a few of her fantasies. So when they were both in his car and he asked, "Do you want to go see a movie or something?" she put her foot down.

"You're killing me, Brock!" she said, exasperated.

He laughed. "This is how I treat ladies I'm dating," he said. "Would you rather we just go back to your place?"

"Yes!"

"Thank God," he said and turned the truck in the direction of her ranch.

The drive felt far too long for Cassie, and she wished they'd gone to eat somewhere in town, despite the chances of gossip and missing out on amazing dumplings. She could feel the time dwindling away, even though she knew they still had a couple of hours before the boys came home.

Brock seemed to be thinking the same thing, because the moment the truck was parked in front of her home, he leaned over and pulled her into a kiss ripe with urgency, as if every moment counted.

That could've just been desperate need, though. She felt that, too, as all the pent-up desire from the past few days took over, and she nearly crawled into his lap to get closer. The heat of the day quickly warmed the car to an almost unbearable temperature, and finally they broke apart, gasping. They looked one another in the eye, and as if by silent agreement, they opened their doors and rushed for the house.

Inside the dim, cool house, Brock seemed to feel the need to slow things down. After the door closed behind them, he took her in his arms and ran one hand over her face, moving her hair out of her eyes. She nearly melted from his tender touch.

Just as he leaned in toward her with agonizing slowness, the tinkling music of Cassie's phone broke through the moment, making her want to scream with frustration. She briefly considered letting the phone go to voice mail, but reminded herself that it could be Emma or a patient and they came first, and she dug it out of her purse.

"Dr. Stanford speaking," she said, hoping it would be quick.

"Dr. Stanford, my name is Melody. I live in town. Got your card from the bakery."

Cassie could hear a baby wailing in the background. "Hi, Melody. What can I do for you?" she asked, even though she had a guess, based on the strength of the cries.

"It's my daughter, Lizzie. She's sick and won't stop crying. Is there any way you can see her?"

Cassie could hear the worry in the woman's voice—one that sounded quite young. She knew that anything between her and Brock would need to wait. "Bring her over as soon as you can. You still have my card with the address?"

"I do. Thank you, Doctor," Melody replied, and the gratitude in her voice tugged at Cassie's heartstrings.

After Cassie had hung up, she kept looking at her phone. She didn't want to see the disappointment in Brock's face.

"Is there something wrong with Lizzie?" he asked, catching her by surprise.

"How did you know?" she asked.

Brock didn't look disappointed like she'd expected. Only worried. He said, "Melody had a baby girl six months or so ago. My ma says she's a sweet little thing. She's helped Melody out some when she can. Her fiancée up and left when she was a few months pregnant, and she's been working herself to the bone to provide for Lizzie. She's Melody's whole world."

Cassie put her hand on his arm. "I'll do everything I can for her. She'll be here any minute."

Brock nodded. "How about I work on getting Zach and Carter's room ready for painting? If you're still with Lizzie when the boys get here, I'll keep an eye on them. And if you finish up in time…" he said, brushing his lips against hers in a way that both excited and frustrated her.

He seemed to sense her mood and chuckled. "Hey, worst-case scenario, you can always hide me under your bed until the kids are asleep, and I can sneak out the window in the middle of the night. Real clandestine secret-affair type stuff."

She laughed, though she wasn't completely sure he was kidding. The idea didn't sound half-bad, either.

Cassie hardly had time to change into her scrubs before the doorbell rang. By the time she got to the door, Brock was there, holding a screaming baby and talking to the anxious-looking mother. She only caught the end of what he was saying, "—will do everything she can to help."

Melody's forehead smoothed a little at his words, and Cassie put her hand to her heart at the sentiment. She quickly gathered her wits and walked up to the small group. "Hi, Melody, I'm Dr. Stanford. This is Lizzie?"

Brock handed over the squalling infant. "She's been sick the past couple of days, but just a runny nose and a little fever. A couple of hours ago, she started screaming. I've tried everything," Melody explained.

The poor woman looked so frazzled and upset, Cassie gently patted her arm. "Let's go into my office and I'll examine her."

She led Melody into her office and set Lizzie down on the examination table. As she started checking the baby head to toe, she asked Melody questions to determine what could have prompted such a quick change of behavior.

Cassie checked the baby's ears, mouth and nose, listened to her heart and prodded her stomach for lumps. Nothing struck her as a possible cause for the screaming, and she was starting to worry that Melody and Lizzie might need to go to the emergency room. As Cassie checked the child's legs, though, her eyes landed on Lizzie's right pinkie toe, and she let out a quiet sigh of relief.

The toe was an angry reddish purple, and when Cassie looked closely, she found the culprit: a single strand of hair had become wound around the toe, cutting off the circulation and causing Lizzie's distress.

As soon as Cassie removed the hair, Lizzie quieted into sniffly sobs. Cassie held up the hair to the baby's mother, expecting her to be as relieved as Cassie was.

To Cassie's surprise, Melody burst into tears. Cassie sat down beside her, Lizzie on her lap. The baby gurgled and reached out for her mama.

Melody grasped the baby and held her close, continuing to cry. "I never thought to look at her toes. I should have checked everywhere," Melody sobbed.

Cassie rubbed her shoulder lightly. "You did nothing wrong, Melody. You called a doctor as soon as you realized something was really off, which was the best thing you could do."

Melody's tears subsided at Cassie's words. "I'm sorry, Dr. Stanford," she said.

"Call me Cassie," Cassie said.

Melody smiled at her and wiped her eyes with a tissue Cassie offered her. "Cassie. I don't usually act like this. It's just… Lizzie's my everything. It broke my heart to see her cry like that."

Melody held her baby tight to her chest, where Lizzie gurgled happily, her good mood entirely restored.

"You're a caring mother," Cassie said.

Melody breathed out a long sigh. "It's difficult sometimes. I'm usually at work right now, but I stayed home today when she started screaming and panicked when it didn't get better. I thought maybe her cold was something worse, and I'd just ignored it."

Cassie could see that Lizzie's nose was running.

"How about I check her now that she's calm so you can be sure it's just a cold?"

Melody's expression held such gratitude that Cassie took the baby without another word. After a careful examination of Lizzie, Cassie declared her healthy apart from a little cold. "Nothing to worry about," Cassie assured the young mother.

By the time Melody and Lizzie were gone, Cassie knew the boys must be home, though she'd been so absorbed with the appointment she hadn't heard anything outside of her office.

Cassie went in search of her children and Brock. It didn't take long to find them, though, as they were all sitting quietly on the living room floor, studying playing cards. Marshmallows were strewn about between them. What could they possibly be doing?

Before she could ask, Brock said, "I see your three and raise you three more," as he tossed six mini-marshmallows into the center of their little circle.

"You're playing poker? With marshmallows?" Cassie said in disbelief.

She couldn't decide if she was angry or not. She felt like she should be upset about her young boys gambling with little balls of sugar, but something about seeing the three of them together, clearly enjoying themselves, made it impossible.

Brock looked up at her from where he sat, his smile begging her not to be mad. "They wanted to learn how to play," he explained.

The boys looked up from their cards, faces still serious from concentration. Normally when she walked in after being away, they tackled her as soon as she entered. This time, though, they didn't budge from their spots, they were so intent on the game.

"They're *four*, you know," she reminded him, the corners of her lips sliding up involuntarily.

Brock shrugged. "Zach's got a great poker face," he said, as if that settled the matter.

"Me, too! I have a poker face!" Carter chirped.

Brock smiled at him, making Cassie's heart thump hard in her chest. "You've got Lady Luck on your side. I've never seen anyone get so many pairs," Brock told Carter, making the boy beam.

Cassie tried to reel in her emotions. "And the marshmallows?"

"We had to bet something," Brock said, as if it was the most obvious answer. "I figured using real money might make you mad."

"So marshmallows were clearly the best choice," she said, grinning so widely that her words couldn't possibly carry any bite to them.

"*Mini*-marshmallows. They're practically a vegetable. Plus, I'm planning to wipe them out before they get to eat any. I promise."

Cassie shook her head, but didn't say anything else. "You have ten more minutes to play and then we're having a *healthy* snack."

Cassie went into the kitchen and started slicing celery and carrots. She couldn't regret helping Melody, but she did wish she'd had a little more time alone with Brock. Just thinking about what could have happened sent shivers of excitement down her spine.

Well, they'd just have to wait. Though with only eight days left after this one, she was starting to wonder how they would ever manage to find another moment alone. Maybe having him hide under the bed wasn't such a bad idea—

Heavy footsteps behind her stopped her thoughts. Brock moved close, and when he leaned in to see what she was doing, his arm looped around her waist. "What are you making?" he asked, though she was sure he could very well see what it was.

She smiled and leaned into him for just a moment. Then another one. "Just your standard veggie plate," she told him. Finally she moved away. "Where are the boys?"

"Putting the cards away," he said, not stepping any closer, but not falling back, either.

She tried to think of something to talk about. Anything to keep her mind off how near he was. "The game ended pretty quickly. You cleaned out the four-year-olds already?" she asked.

His silence in response made her turn to look at him. His face was sheepish. "You didn't…lose, did you?" she asked, laughing.

"They kept going all-in, and when I called them, they'd hit the best hands. It was the most ridiculous luck I've ever seen."

Cassie just raised an eyebrow at him.

Brock grimaced. "I think your kids hustled me."

They both laughed, and were still laughing when Zach and Carter joined them, eager to tell their mother about their triumph.

As they all dug into the snack, the conversation turned to paint. "Can we paint our room now, Momma? Please!" Carter implored.

Cassie looked over at Brock. He said, "While you were in with Melody, I got just about everything ready, so we can if you're up for it."

"It's decided," she told the twins. "Let's finish eating and then we'll paint your room the color of dragon scales."

Brock opened the paint cans while Cassie changed out of her scrubs. He wished she was still wearing her date dress, but even her grungiest paint-splattered jeans made her look so good, he wondered if she'd actually let him hide under the bed. The idea was sounding more and more reasonable.

To distract himself, Brock decided to mention the idea he'd gotten while playing poker with the boys. Once Cassie had them occupied outside of the room, as far from the paint as she could get them, he decided to talk to her about it.

"I don't know if you've ever considered getting a dog, but I think Zach and Carter would really love one," he commented as he began slathering one wall in the lurid green paint.

Cassie looked up at him from where she stood with her own roller, her eyebrows raised in surprise. "Did they say something to you about wanting a dog?"

"No," he said, "but dogs are great for kids on ranches. Though you don't need to if you think it'd be too much work."

"Actually, I think it's a great idea," she replied, turning back to her task.

"I bet my ma will watch the boys tomorrow for a few hours so we can go down to the shelter and pick one out without them knowing. I bet they'd love the surprise of coming home to find a dog waiting for them," he told her.

He could think of lots of amazing ways to spend a few hours alone with Cassie, but picking out a pet for her little boys seemed more important. For Cassie as well as Zach and Carter.

Cassie nodded, a small smile on her lips that he couldn't read. "What're you thinking?" he asked.

"It's just odd. You don't seem to dislike kids," Cassie said, not taking her eyes off the wall in front of her, "but I get the feeling you don't want any of your own."

Brock figured it was best to be as open as possible, just to be sure neither of them got any ideas about what could happen beyond the rodeo. "My life doesn't really work with children," he explained. "I like free-climbing cliffs and snowboarding down unmarked trails and skydiving, and I'd need to give all that up if I had a kid at home to worry about. I don't want any children of mine to go through what I did when my parents died."

Cassie nodded, but she didn't say anything. Clearly she had some thoughts on the subject.

"You can say it," Brock prompted her. "I've heard it all before from my ma."

Cassie shrugged. "I have no call to judge your lifestyle. I'm just a nine-day romance," she said, bumping him with her hip to show she was teasing.

"And I'm just your training wheels," he responded, bumping her back.

They glanced at each other, and Brock wasn't sure if they would start laughing or kissing. Neither happened, though, as Zach and Carter ran in at just that moment, looking around the room in amazement.

"You boys shouldn't be in here," Cassie warned.

"It's so cool!" Carter shouted.

"It smells bad," Zach said. "Is it always going to smell like that?"

Brock ruffled the boy's hair. "The smell will go away soon," Brock explained. "It's extra strong right now because the paint is still wet. Once we finish and let it dry, it won't be so strong."

"I don't want to sleep in here if it smells so bad," Zach said, looking upset.

"Once we're finished painting, I'll help you two get sleeping bags and you can sleep in the living room tonight. How does that sound?" Cassie asked Zach.

He still seemed concerned. "Can we sleep in your room?" he asked his mother.

Cassie paused for a moment before agreeing, and the boys raced off happily.

So much for hiding under the bed, Brock thought. Cassie must've been thinking the same thing, because she caught his eye, and when they grimaced at each other, they both burst into laughter.

Once the room was finished, Brock knew he needed to go home, as little as he wanted to. He consoled himself with the thought that he and Cassie would be alone the next day, even if they were spending that time picking out a dog. They'd manage a few kisses, and maybe…

Brock cleared his throat at the thought. Cassie looked at him expectantly. "I should go," he told her. "With my siblings over and everything—"

"Of course," she said, though she sounded reluctant. "I don't have any patients tomorrow or anything, so as soon as you want to go on our errand, the boys will be ready."

Brock said goodbye to Zach and Carter and walked home. He looked back a couple of times, wishing he had an excuse to stay.

Before he walked in to his parents' house, Brock took stock of himself. He didn't want to give his siblings any hint as to what had happened that day. It was better if nobody knew, not even his family.

Which was why he felt so annoyed with Amy when he walked through the door and she immediately asked, "When's the wedding?"

Jose and Diego, who were sitting across from her on the couch, gave him twin smiles. "You didn't tell us you were getting married. Congratulations!" Jose said.

"I call best man," Diego added.

Jose looked scandalized and was clearly about to start an argument when Brock cut him off. "None of that. Don't any of you start rumors about me and Cassie."

He looked so fierce that Diego held up his hands. "We were just joking, Brock. We're your family—you know we won't do anything to hurt whatever it is you two have going on."

"Here's a pro-tip, though," Jose said. "If you want to keep a secret, maybe don't make out outside." He gestured out the window near where Amy sat with her foot propped on pillows.

"Inside your truck isn't super sneaky, either," Amy added.

Brock glanced out the window and saw immediately what they meant. From there, his siblings had a great view of Cassie's paddock and the driveway, too.

Brock shook his head, annoyed at himself. He should have thought of that, but it was too late now.

"Swear you won't say anything to anyone, not even Ma," Brock told them.

Amy rolled her eyes. "What are the chances Ma doesn't know already? I'm guessing around zero percent."

"Seriously, does being in love really make you that stupid?" Jose asked, which earned him a shove from his twin.

Jose fell off the couch with an "oomph!"

"I'm *not* in love, and you need to keep your mouth shut, Jose," Brock said aggressively, standing over his brother for a moment before stalking out of the room.

He found his ma and, to his relief, she said nothing about his and Cassie's apparently very public display of affection. All she did was agree to take care of the twins while Brock and Cassie went to the animal shelter. "I love those two boys. You let Cassie know that I'm happy to watch them anytime," she told Brock.

He wasn't sure if her comment was completely innocent or not, but he decided it was better not to ask.

Chapter 11

The next morning, when Brock and his ma prepared to go pick up the boys, Brock noticed that Amy was yet again sitting in front of the window, despite the early hour. There was a book in her lap, but her eyes were trained out the window, as if she was watching for someone or something. Had she been spying on him on purpose the day before, or was she standing vigil for another reason?

She didn't seem to be looking over at Cassie's house. Her eyes were on the street and their parents' driveway.

Now that he thought about it, that was where she would sit most of the time she was home, on the few occasions they had both been home at the same time in the past decade. "What're you watching for?" he asked her.

For a moment, Amy gave him a slightly panicked look, which just raised further questions, but she quickly controlled her expression and denied watching for anything. Their ma slapped Brock's arm. "You leave your sister alone and take me over to the Stanfords'. I've got some young children to spoil."

So Brock went with his mother, leaving Amy sitting beside the window. He considered trying to get his sister alone to figure out what she was doing, but the farther he got from the house, the more likely it seemed that he'd just imagined things. He dismissed the thoughts and focused on the task ahead of him.

"Thanks for taking the boys, Ma," Brock said as they tromped through the grass.

Sarah dismissed his gratitude with a wave of her hand. "Well, of course. Every young boy should have a dog. I'm proud of you for thinking of it."

"How do you know it wasn't Cassie's idea?" Brock asked.

His ma gave him a frown. "You don't think I know you well enough by now, boy?" she asked.

Brock laughed and put up his hands in surrender. "Sorry I questioned your clairvoyance."

She smacked him on the arm again and followed him onto Cassie's porch. Before he could knock, the door opened and Zach and Carter came tumbling out. "Nana Sarah" laughed in delight as she hugged them. "Do I ever have a fun day planned for you two," she said as she hustled them back toward her house.

"Be good!" Cassie called after them from inside the house.

"Should we get going?" Brock asked as he turned toward her.

He stopped, confused, when he noticed she was still wearing a bathrobe. Had she not expected him to be there so early?

Before he could ask, she grabbed his arm and pulled him into the house, closing the door behind him. At the same time, she tugged at the belt of the bathrobe, causing it to fall open and reveal black silk and lace beneath.

Brock's jaw dropped. "On the other hand," he said, wrapping his arms around her, "I think we have a few minutes."

When they parked in front of the animal shelter a long while later, Cassie knew she was still grinning like an idiot, but she just couldn't get herself to stop. After what had happened that morning, she doubted she'd be able to stop smiling for a week.

Well, eight days to be exact. After that, Brock would be out of her life for good.

That thought was enough to bring down her mood a little. She reached for the truck door, but Brock was there opening it for her before she could, and he helped her down so gallantly that she blushed.

She needed to remind herself, for perhaps the tenth time that day, that this was all short-term. Not something she should get used to.

Cassie put her hands in her pockets to avoid the temptation to hold his, and together they walked into the animal shelter.

After speaking briefly with an employee, Cassie and Brock were ushered into a large area full of dozens of barking dogs in search of homes. Cassie wandered past the canines, trying to concentrate on finding the right one for Zach and Carter, not on the cowboy beside her who was cooing at the animals in a way that tugged at her heartstrings. If she let herself watch that, she might just fall for him, and *that* was certainly not allowed.

Temporary. Eight Days.

"How about this fella?" Brock asked her, bringing Cassie out of her thoughts.

He had stopped in front of a brown-and-white dog that was licking his fingers. After a few final kisses for Brock, the dog started running in circles, apparently proud of himself for completing his objective. She couldn't help but laugh.

"This is Freckles," the worker explained. "He's mostly beagle. A very happy dog, and he probably won't get much bigger. Good for young children."

Cassie agreed. The boys would love Freckles. The worker opened the cage and Freckles jumped into her arms, his tongue all over her face and every part he could get at. She hugged him close, then turned to Brock.

"He looks like a winner to me," Brock said, rubbing the furry little head.

Freckles wiggled in Cassie's arms, trying to get close enough to Brock to give him another thorough licking.

After signing enough documents to make her question if she was adopting a dog or a child, Cassie paid for a final vet check and vaccinations and was told she'd be able to pick up Freckles the next day.

Finally, Cassie and Brock left the animal shelter. Cassie wondered what time it was, and if she should go pick up Zach and Carter right away. She wasn't sure if she wanted more time with Brock alone or to have her young chaperones back as soon as possible.

If she was being honest, she was a little nervous. Now that things between them had finally gotten physical—*really* physical—she knew it would be hard to give it all up in only one short week. It almost seemed easier and smarter to stop it now, before she completely fell for him.

Cassie knew she wouldn't stop their relationship, though, regardless of how smart it might be. She'd enjoy every second of it, whatever it did to her once he'd left.

As soon as they buckled in, Brock asked, "So, how are you going to get free long enough to pick up Freckles tomorrow?"

"I spoke with Jack Stuart this morning, actually, and planned on Zach and Carter going over to his ranch for a half-day horse camp. Your brothers are going to have their equipment over to cut and bale the hay," she explained.

She didn't say that she'd only decided to send the boys to camp *after* her date with Brock in order to give them another opportunity to be alone. Judging by the sly look on his face, he seemed to guess as much.

"Jose and Diego will want us to stay out of the way while that's going on," he said, not explaining where they could be or what they could do while the machinery operated in the yard.

He didn't need to.

"So, are we heading straight to my house to pick up Zach and Carter?" Brock asked.

Cassie wanted to say no, but their morning trip had

lasted well into the afternoon, in no small part to her black negligee. "Yeah," she said, trying not to sound deflated.

It was silly, of course, to want Brock again so soon. It had just been a few hours since they'd been together in her bed, creating memories she was sure would last her many lonely nights.

Still, she couldn't help but desire him even more, now that she knew what she'd been missing. It wasn't just that he was good in bed—though that certainly seemed to be the case—it was the two of them together that made it spectacular. Just as they worked well together when painting a room or making repairs, they worked well together in all physical aspects, apparently.

If only their lives harmonized, too, she thought with a silent sigh. Unfortunately, their lives were halves of two very different jigsaw puzzles, and trying to shove them together would be an impossible task.

How had she gotten on that topic again? Cassie had found herself going over the same well-worn tracks of thinking again and again, and it was getting wearisome; they had a week left together, end of story.

"Don't tell Pop you're taking Zach and Carter to the Stuarts' for horse camp," Brock said, breaking into her thoughts.

Cassie was confused for a second before realizing what he meant. Brock's adopted father ran his own horse camp. "Whoops. I completely forgot. Is that a problem?"

"No, probably not, but it's best not to bring it up. We've been telling him for a while now that he should hire more help, that the camp is too much for him. He's a little sensitive about it. Thinks we're calling him old."

Cassie agreed not to say anything, then looked out the window to see her home as they passed. For one wild moment, she considered telling Brock to stop and turn in. Another half hour together before they picked up the boys couldn't hurt, could it?

They continued on and parked in front of his parents' without her saying anything, though. As they climbed out of Brock's truck, Cassie felt a twinge of regret. Not only for deciding to collect the boys immediately, but also because Brock's truck would no longer be parked in front of her house. It was silly, she knew, but she liked having it there. It was a reminder that he would be coming back.

Before she could dive down that hole any further, her sons ran out the door. She braced herself for a high-speed hug, but the boys veered from her and went straight to Brock.

"Did you really ride a bull when you were twelve years old?" Carter asked.

Brock looked up at his ma, Jose and Diego, who were all standing in the doorway. "What have you been telling them?" he asked.

"Only the truth," Diego answered. "They asked what you were like when you were a kid, so we told them."

Brock wondered if anything had been mentioned about his parents' death—he could easily imagine Jose saying something without really thinking about it—but there was no way to ask at the moment. Not with Zach and Carter right there.

"We should go," Cassie said, breaking into the moment.

Brock automatically turned to go with her before he realized he should probably stay home. His whole family rarely got together, and everyone would be leaving in a couple days. Plus, it might seem suspicious to everyone if he left, and he didn't need any more of that going on. "I'll come by tomorrow morning for…"

Brock trailed off, not able to say where the boys were going nor bring up the errand he'd run with Cassie. Cassie nodded. "We'll be leaving a little before nine. Just come in whenever. The door will be unlocked."

Brock wondered if she was giving him a coded message, telling him to sneak over that night after Zach and Carter were asleep.

No, she couldn't mean that, could she? She *had* surprised him that morning with that sexy black outfit.

Then again, Cassie had made it plenty clear that her kids came first, and that might include keeping their distance from each other when the boys were nearby, even if they were asleep.

Brock didn't know, which meant he wouldn't be going over there tonight, much as he might want to. It was best to err on the side of caution, to avoid stepping on her toes and ruining the whole thing. Even if it wouldn't last beyond a few more days, he didn't want to do anything to spoil it for either of them.

Finally, when Cassie and her boys had disappeared into their house, Brock turned back to his family. They all acted as if they hadn't been watching him, but they were doing a bad job of it. A little reluctantly, he followed them into the house.

Chapter 12

Cassie tucked Zach and Carter into bed that night with excitement pooling in her belly, even though she knew the chances that Brock would come over were slim. She couldn't be sure that he'd understood what she meant when she said the door would be unlocked, or that even if he did, he'd be able or willing to sneak out of his parents' house.

All of it made her feel like a teenager trying to arrange an illicit tryst, and she loved it. The entire afternoon, even when she was on the phone making appointments for two more new patients, she could hardly focus on anything but to wish for night to come faster.

Cassie had never been one for this sort of behavior as a teen, and she didn't even start dating until she was in college. Even then it was all fairly rational and well-behaved. This time, she didn't want to be well-behaved. If she was going to have this once-in-a-lifetime kind of connection for a limited time, by God, she wanted to get as much out of it as she could.

Cassie turned out Zach and Carter's light and closed the door. She went and checked once more that the front door was unlocked, though she'd already made sure at least five times, and then she went to her room.

After sifting through her pajama options carefully, Cassie settled on a long-ish shirt—no pants—and climbed into bed with a book. She tried to read, but it was nearly impossible. What if she ended up sitting there pretending to read and he never showed up?

What if he did?

Cassie was almost starting to regret this situation for herself when she heard a very quiet *click*. Her heart stopped in anticipation.

Maybe it was one of the boys getting up to go to the bathroom.

Still, she set down her book and waited eagerly.

Brock appeared in the doorway, cowboy hat on his head and boots in his hand, looking a little unsure. "If you don't want me to be here—"

Before he could finish the sentence, she had jumped out of bed and closed the distance between them. In short order, the door was closed and the light was off, and the butterflies in Cassie's stomach changed to molten ecstasy.

When Cassie awoke, it was still dark, but she could hear small noises coming from a few feet away. She picked up her phone and looked at it blearily. It was just past four in the morning. Brock knelt beside her and brushed her hair out of her face. "Hey," he whispered softly.

She pressed her cheek against his hand like a cat and smiled, even though he wouldn't be able to see it in the dark. "I didn't want to wake you, but I should get back before anybody gets up. You still have a couple more hours before you need to be up, though."

She wanted him to stay. What if he just stayed? For the next day and the night after that and the night after that—

No, that wouldn't work, of course.

So Cassie just nodded, enjoyed one last kiss that she could feel all the way to her toes and then said goodbye.

After he was gone, her bed felt unpleasantly empty, and Cassie wondered if this romance was such a good idea after all. Just as with every time that thought had come up before, she knew she would take every second with Brock McNeal she could get.

Even if it was only for another seven days.

Brock walked into Cassie's house the next morning after checking to see that the door was still unlocked. Though it felt a little odd, it was nice, too, and the memories of the night before flooded through him pleasantly. He pushed them away, though, because today would be about Zach and Carter, not him and Cassie.

The living room was empty, so he went to the kitchen in search of the home's occupants. Nobody was there, either, but it also felt cool and inviting, and he lingered there for a moment, enjoying the atmosphere of a quiet country home. His tiny apartment in Dallas lacked any feeling of home—though a good deal of that probably had to do with how little he was there. Being out on the rodeo circuit for months at a time kept him from ever feeling really settled. Heck, he'd probably slept in his truck more times than he'd slept in his own bed.

But there was more to it than that. This wasn't just a kitchen in anybody's house. This was Cassie's kitchen, which already showed signs of her personality despite the boxes still sitting in the corner. A blue spoon rest with painted daisies all over it sat beside the stove, and an oven mitt that looked like a dinosaur's mouth, complete with cloth teeth, hung on the wall. He could imagine her attacking Carter with it before pulling something out of the oven.

He felt a sudden twinge of wistfulness and walked out of the kitchen toward the hallway. He needed to find Cassie, so he started walking toward her bedroom. Just the thought of being alone in there with her again sent adrenaline through his veins, but he knew the boys were somewhere close by, and that fantasy was going to need to wait.

As he walked down the hall, he stopped when he heard murmuring through the open doorway of the twins' room. Glancing inside, he saw Cassie, Zach and Carter on the floor, driving toy cars around on a rug covered in street designs, each one occasionally screeching to a halt or flipping over in dramatic car crashes. Cassie looked beautiful, the lack of sleep from the night before undetectable. It even seemed like her smile was brighter than usual, and there was a glitter in her eye that he liked to think was his doing.

Or maybe she was just enjoying playing with her sons, he thought when he saw her car fly into the air as she laughed. That sound rolled through him as only her laugh could. He watched the little family, not wanting to spoil the moment.

Then Carter saw him and ran over with a car in his hand. "Here," he told Brock, handing him the tiny car. "You can use the red one."

"Momma said we could play cars until it was time to go because we got ready early," Zach said.

Brock understood he was expected to play cars with them, though it was a strange thing, to drive tiny cars along tiny streets. Still, he dutifully knelt down on the floor and started running the car along one of the streets, feeling a little foolish.

"This isn't really your thing, is it?" Cassie asked him under her breath.

No good answer came to him, so he simply replied, "I usually drive a truck, myself."

"Here's a truck!" Zach said, dropping a small silver truck in front of Brock.

Brock picked up the truck and studied it. "This is actually pretty similar to mine," he commented.

"Yeah," Zach said. "I got it with Aunt Emma. She said we could have one car each, but I picked a truck instead because it looks like yours."

Brock stared at the young boy for a few seconds, astonished. These two kids constantly surprised him.

"There you go," Cassie said, her voice soft. "Now you have a truck to drive that's just like yours."

Brock could only nod, and for several seconds, the only sounds were the explosions the boys created as they slammed vehicles together.

"Where is your truck going?" Carter asked Brock as he drove along the street. "To the rodeo to ride bulls?"

He sounded so excited about the prospect of bull riding that Brock's mind whirred quickly. There was no way he was going to encourage Carter's newfound obsession with riding bulls. "Nope," he told Carter. "My truck is going to the carnival to ride the Ferris wheel and eat cotton candy. Maybe while he's there he'll play one of the games and try to win your momma a stuffed animal."

Carter's car pulled up alongside Brock's. "Me, too! I want to go to the carnival, too!"

"We like carnivals, don't we?" Cassie asked her sons, who both nodded.

"Well, you missed the spring fair, which is big and not too far away. But the Halloween carnival will be here before you know it."

"Will you take us?" Zach asked, looking straight at Brock.

"I…" he started, but he didn't know what to say.

He was leaving town soon, but he could come back for the Halloween carnival. Brock could just imagine Zach and Carter picking out pumpkins and screaming at the top of their lungs as they all whirled around on the teacups.

Or would it just be better to make a clean break and

avoid all three of them as much as possible? His heart and his brain had two very different answers.

And none of that addressed the fact that Cassie might not even want him around after these few days were over. Once she was done with her training wheels, she might be ready for something more permanent with somebody else.

Cassie looked Zach in the eye, her face serious. "Remember what we talked about? How Brock needs to go back to work and won't be around anymore?"

Zach looked glum, but he nodded. Brock couldn't feel worse if he tried.

Cassie looked at the man and two boys. They were all still moving their vehicles around, but none of them seemed very happy at the prospect of Brock moving on.

He didn't contradict her, though, so it was clear that was still the plan. Seven more days together, and then he'd be off for the rodeo.

"We should get going," Cassie said as she stood, pushing away her unpleasant thoughts. "It's time for horse camp!"

Zach and Carter jumped up, their good moods restored at the thought of horses. "Will we get to ride one?" Carter asked eagerly.

"I don't know. What do you think, Brock?" she asked, trying to turn his mood around, too.

Brock seemed to think carefully about the question, the way people often did around very young children. It was clear he was catching on quick. "I'm not sure how the Stuarts run their camp, but I'm guessing you'll meet the horses first, pet them, learn about them, and after all that you *might* ride them. But only if you feel ready for it."

Cassie could tell his last sentence was directed toward Zach, who seemed a little nervous at the prospect of hopping onto a horse's back. For all his agreement with Carter's talk about bull riding, Zach would need a bit of time before he was ready to ride any large animal.

Soon they were all settled into Cassie's SUV and on their way to the Stuart Ranch. While the boys discussed camp noisily in the back, Brock sat quietly in the passenger seat. Cassie redirected her thoughts away from the cowboy beside her and onto the tasks for the day. Buy bedding, toys and food for Freckles; then get him from the shelter. By the time he was settled at home, it would likely be time to pick up the boys.

She tried not to feel too disappointed about that. She'd had more amazing times in Brock's arms than most people got in their entire lives, so could she really complain if they had no opportunity to be alone that day?

Cassie knew the answer to that. Of course she could complain, as long as she was the only one to hear it.

When she pulled onto the dirt driveway of the Stuart Ranch, Zach and Carter climbed out. They shouted their goodbyes and thundered toward the small group of young children surrounding Grandma Stuart. Cassie waved to their retreating backs and put her car in reverse.

"I wish we had time to say hi to Rosalind and Diamond," Cassie said, "but we have too much to do to get the dog settled before camp is over."

Cassie hoped Brock wouldn't say anything about the boys being sad he was leaving. Frankly, she was, too, and she didn't want to talk about it. Better to enjoy the little time they had.

"I think they're going to be over the moon about Freckles," Brock said.

Cassie was relieved, and they talked about the silly dog the entire way to the pet shop. As they walked through the giant store, Cassie and Brock laughed and argued good-naturedly as they chose the perfect bedding, food and collar for little Freckles. "This pup is going to be pretty spoiled for a ranch dog, I imagine," Brock commented as they dropped a half-dozen toys into their already full cart.

Cassie knew she should watch her spending more carefully, but now that the hay was being baled and she had a few patients, she couldn't help but feel more secure, and she was willing to splurge on the adorable mutt. "I think he'll prefer relaxing in his bed and terrorizing the house over herding cattle. Maybe I'll need to get another dog someday just for that purpose."

Brock smiled at her. "You're going to have cattle?"

"A pretty smart cowboy mentioned it to me once, and I think it's a good idea," she said, thinking back to the day they'd walked along the fences.

It had been only a few days before, but so much had happened since then.

"I think we can get your paddock finished in a day or two if we really put in the time, and then Diamond and Rosalind can come home," Brock told her, clearly thinking about that walk, too.

With the rush to finish her office, that had been

pushed to the wayside. If they could get it done, though, her ranch would be on its way to matching her dream.

And they only had seven days before he left, so time was not her friend.

Brock picked up a container of dog biscuits and tossed it in the heaping cart on their way to the cashier.

"How about we buckle down on that tomorrow? Amy's leaving in the morning, but after that, I've got the entire day free. We should be able to fix it and paint it, if we're quick about it, and maybe even pick up the horses the day after," he said.

Cassie agreed, then turned to her current objective: becoming a dog owner.

And that seemed to be a much more expensive task than she'd previously thought, judging by the numbers jumping up on the cash register. She was starting to re-think the dozen top-of-the-line dog bones and the collar with the studs when Brock whipped out his credit card.

"Got a splinter there, Brock?" she asked, blocking the credit card machine with her hand.

Brock rolled his eyes at her attempt to keep him from paying. "It was my idea for you to get a dog. You'll have to clean up his poop every day. I should at least pay for his bedding, even if you decided against the one with the horseshoe pattern."

After a brief argument, she relented, secretly happy she didn't need to put anything back in order to pay for it. Soon, the items were packed into the back of her car and they were off to get Freckles.

When they parked in front of the shelter, Cassie turned to Brock. "Ready to pick up a dog?" she asked.

Then she noticed that he was distracted, looking out the window back the way they'd just driven. Before she could ask him what he'd seen, he turned back to her and gave her a kiss that made her toes curl. "You grab Freckles. I'll meet you back here faster than green grass through a goose."

He got out of the car and was gone before she could recover her wits and understand what he'd said enough to find out where he was going.

All Cassie could do was wonder at his behavior, as well as his choice in idioms, and smile because of the kiss as she greeted Freckles, who seemed even more excited and loving than the day before, if that was possible.

By the time Freckles was secured in his crate in the back seat of the car, Brock was back, a large box in his arms. "Don't ask," he said the moment she opened her mouth.

Cassie closed her mouth again and got in the car. Brock seemed very happy with himself, so she could only imagine he'd purchased something ridiculous for the dog and wanted it to be a surprise. Probably something cowboy-themed to make up for her vetoing his choice of dog bed.

They got back to her place and unloaded all the purchases, except for one. Brock left the mystery box in the car, warning her not to touch it.

As Cassie had feared, by the time Freckles was settled in, it was time to pick up the boys. She started to say goodbye to the dog when Brock shook his head. "How about I go get the boys? That way you can be here waiting for them with Freckles."

Cassie loved the idea, so she tossed Brock her keys and settled in to wait, petting the sweet little animal, whom she already considered part of the family. Freckles scrambled into her lap and snuggled close, licking her hand at every opportunity.

Almost as soon as Brock left, Cassie's phone rang. A quick glance told her it was Emma.

"Hello?" she said.

"Hey Cassie, Daniel Forrester needs to come in for a doctor's appointment."

Cassie could hear bickering in the background and Emma say, "Yes, you do, so stop being a baby, Danny."

The name sounded familiar. "Danny's your cousin, right?"

Emma had told Cassie about her cousin who was currently staying in the tiny apartment above her bakery until he "got settled in town," in Emma's words.

"Yep, my cousin. He has some weird pain in his leg every once in a while, and despite what he says, he should get it checked out," Emma explained, though it sounded like she was talking more to her cousin than to Cassie.

"Is it something he should go to the hospital about?" Cassie asked.

"Listen," Emma said quietly, "I'll be lucky if I can get him to go see you. There's no way he's going to the hospital unless you tell him it's life-or-death. Which it could be!" she exclaimed much louder, likely in the direction of Danny.

Cassie tried not to laugh. "Do you want to bring him in right away, or can it wait until after Mrs. Edelman's appointment next week?"

"Next week would be great. He will see you then."
Emma said.

Cassie laughed as she heard Emma say, "Yes, you
will!" to her cousin as she shut off the phone.

That was going to be an interesting appointment.

Good. Anything to keep her mind off Brock leaving.

She had already scheduled three other appointments
for the same day as Mrs. Edelman's. The day after the
rodeo.

It just seemed best to keep herself busy.

Luckily, she heard the car pull up and was able to
get her mind onto Freckles and her children. Better
topics, for sure.

The door opened and Freckles jumped out of her lap,
running toward the noise as Zach and Carter ran into the
house. They entered the living room with Brock behind
them, amazed at the dog that came up to greet them.

"A puppy!" Zach shouted as he and Carter kneeled
down to meet Freckles.

Cassie was just as surprised as they were. "Where
did you get those hats?" she asked.

The boys were both sporting child-size cowboy hats.
They were so enthralled in the dog that they didn't hear
her question, but the answer became obvious when she
saw that Brock was holding another hat. He held it out
to her. "I thought they should have cowboy hats after
their first real horse experience. And you should have
one, too, now that you're a rancher."

She no longer had any doubt about what his mys-
terious box contained. She didn't know what to say as

he placed the hat on her head, and it took everything in her not to pull him into a kiss right then and there.

"Thank you," she said, her voice soft as she held back happy tears.

He just smiled back and tipped his own hat, the grown-up version of Zach and Carter's, at her. Then he turned to watch the boys play with their new dog. Cassie did after a moment, too.

"Is he ours forever?" Zach asked, looking at her with wide eyes, his hands low so Freckles could lick them.

Cassie nodded. "Yep, he's our dog now. We adopted him. His name's Freckles."

"Freckles is a silly name," Carter commented.

Cassie worried there was going to be a whole argument over the pup's name, but Brock kneeled down next to them and said, "There's a rodeo bull with the same name. Crazy fella. I've been lucky enough that I haven't ever tried to ride him. He'd chew me up and spit me out."

Zach and Carter's eyes grew wide, "Really?" Zach asked.

"A bull named Freckles?" Carter added.

He nodded. "Yep. Freckles."

"Cool!" they said in unison, then bent back down to the dog.

Brock stood again and smiled at Cassie. Once he was close enough that they wouldn't be overheard, she whispered, "There isn't really a scary bull named Freckles, right?"

Brock put a hand over his heart. "God's honest truth."

Cassie laughed.

The rest of the evening was spent gathered around

the new puppy, exclaiming at every wag of his tail, and the boys chattering excitedly about horse camp. Finally, though, she saw that the boys' eyes were drooping and she looked at the clock. "It's past your bedtime, guys. Go brush your teeth and I'll put Freckles away in his crate."

Zach and Carter protested, but once they saw that their mother wasn't going to budge, they got up and did as she said. On their way out of the room, Carter walked up to Brock and craned his head so he could look the grown man in the eyes. "Will you tell us a bedtime story about riding in the rodeo?" Carter asked.

Cassie was about to cut in, reassuring Brock he didn't need to and placating Carter with a bedtime story about their father, but before she could say anything, Brock was ruffling Carter's hair. "Sure, buddy," he said.

Carter and Zach ran off to brush their teeth, looking excited.

Cassie said nothing as she settled Freckles down for the night, but her heart felt twisted tight inside her. She was touched by her boys' attachment to Brock, but at the same time saddened that in just a few days they would need to say goodbye.

In only a few short minutes, the two boys lay in their bunks, looking expectantly at Brock. For a moment he felt a kind of stage fright. They were just so attentive. At least he had some good stories.

"One time a few years back," he began, "I was all set to ride a bull named Whirlwind. He was the biggest, meanest bull I'd ever had to ride."

"Were you scared?" Zach asked in a whisper, his eyes the size of saucers.

Brock wanted to laugh at how serious the boy was, but he held it in. "Sure I was scared. Wouldn't you be?"

Zach nodded solemnly.

"But I'd prepared and practiced, and I wasn't about to give up just because I was scared."

"Did you get hurt?" Carter asked, leaning forward in his bed.

"No, but it was a close thing. I thought I was going to get thrown the moment they opened the chute, but I managed to stay on for the whole eight seconds."

"Did you win?" Cassie asked.

Brock looked over to see her leaning against the green wall of the room, listening to the story. He smiled at her. "Yep. Biggest purse I ever got."

"I want to ride bulls!" Carter exclaimed.

"Me, too!" Zach said.

As much as Brock enjoyed riding on the circuit, the idea of these sweet little boys jumping on the back of a crazy bull was too much for him. "Whoa, pardners," he said. "My story isn't over yet."

The two settled down as Brock tried to come up with something to add that might keep them from bull riding. His most recent ride came back to him, and he told the boys, "After I jumped off the bull and was waving to the crowd, Whirlwind got free and came after me!"

"Oh, no!" Zach shouted.

"Oh, yes," Brock said as seriously as he could. "He stomped his big scary hoof this close to my head." He held up his finger and thumb an inch apart. "And I learned that riding bulls can be very very dangerous and should only be done by people who practice a lot."

Zach and Carter seemed satisfied with the ending and snuggled down in their beds. Cassie went over and kissed each of them good-night, and then she walked with Brock down the hallway, toward the door. "Whirlwind didn't *really* almost kill you, right?" she asked.

"Nah. I just added that at the end," he said, feeling a twinge of guilt at the omission that it had happened with another bull just a few days ago.

Cassie seemed relieved. At the door, Cassie put her hand against his chest and they shared a long, lingering kiss. Brock almost asked to stay, but he knew she would say yes and he wasn't sure if he could make himself leave in the middle of the night again. Plus, his sister had her flight out of the country early in the morning. He needed to be home.

Still, he didn't want to go. If he went home, the next time he saw her, they'd only have six more days left.

But he said good-night and turned away, pausing for a long moment to wait for the click of the lock that never came, and then he walked slowly back to his parents' house, his mind whirling between Cassie, her unlocked door and his interactions with the twins.

He'd always said he didn't want children, but Zach and Carter made something tug inside him he hadn't felt before. Was he willing to make children a part of his life, even if it meant leaving them without a father?

He pictured a bull's hoof slamming down next to his head, a slip of his hand while rock climbing that nearly dropped him a thousand feet, his motorcycle sliding around cars at breakneck speeds.

No. He couldn't do that to kids. He *knew* that, so why was this suddenly a question for him?

Brock reached the dark house and closed the door behind him, wishing he could shut out the feelings that had followed him home. He took off his cowboy hat, leaned against the door and drew in a deep breath, letting it out slowly.

"What's going on, Brock?" Amy asked.

Brock looked around, surprised. He'd thought he was alone and hadn't noticed his sister sitting in the corner of the room, working on her laptop, her foot propped high as usual. She closed her computer. "You aren't really falling in love with her, are you?" she asked, her voice worried.

He wanted to answer that he wasn't, but he knew it would sound like a lie. "Maybe," he said. "But it doesn't matter. Neither of us is looking for anything long-term."

He didn't want to really examine his feelings for Cassie. "She has kids, which is the main problem," he said.

"Oh, yeah, your no-kids rule," Amy responded.

"I just don't want to leave some kids without a father, okay?" he said.

He knew he was sounding defensive, but it was true.

He thought it best to change the topic. "Do you do dangerous stuff while you're out there in the world?" he asked, thinking back to a conversation he'd had with their ma a few days before.

Amy looked at him thoughtfully. "I don't hide in my hotel room, if that's what you mean. But dangerous? Not particularly. I like to travel, but that doesn't mean

I have a death wish or anything. I write about interesting places, not about free-climbing cliffs or jumping out of airplanes."

Brock tried to hide his grimace. He'd done both of those things in the last couple of years. Did that mean he had a death wish?

It wasn't a question he wanted to know the answer to.

"Listen, Brock, do you *want* to have kids?" Amy asked.

Brock's answer a few days before was a firm no. Now, though...

"Do you?" he asked, more to delay answering than anything else.

"We're not talking about me here," she said.

Brock knew Amy well enough to know when she was holding something back, and this was definitely one of those times. He was about to ask her what it was when she stood up, careful to keep her weight off her sore ankle. "I'm going to bed," she said, grabbing a crutch that their pop had found somewhere in the attic.

Brock guessed she'd known what he was going to ask and considered stopping her, but he just said goodnight and let her leave the room. If she didn't want to tell him, that was her choice.

Brock glanced out the window and saw that Cassie's bedroom light was still on, and he put his hat back on. Whatever self-control he had left him, and he knew he'd need to find some way to leave Cassie's arms before morning.

What else could he do?

Chapter 13

Brock felt bleary-eyed and sleepy when he woke up in his bed the next day, which wasn't surprising since he'd now gone two nights with only a few hours' sleep. But he needed to get up to say goodbye to Amy, and then he had a paddock to fix.

He wasn't sure whether or not to ask Amy about their conversation the night before, but ultimately he decided not to say anything. His sister had always played her cards close to the chest, and he'd learned long ago not to push her to talk about something she wasn't ready to share.

Brock knocked lightly on her bedroom door. She opened it, and he could see her backpack and suitcase ready to go behind her. "Want some help?" he asked.

Normally, she'd punch him on the arm and explain

how she managed to haul her belongings across the globe, and she could probably make it down the stairs, too. But hobbling as she was, she just nodded and he grabbed her things.

Brock went first down the stairs, carrying Amy's bags, ready to help if she had trouble, but between the crutch and the handrail she was able to maneuver them just fine. Pop was waiting at the bottom of the steps and took her things out to the truck. Amy and Brock went to the dining room, where Ma had laid out quite a feast for breakfast, including waffles and syrup. He wasn't sure if Ma did that as a treat for his sister, or if it was more of a last-ditch effort to bribe her to stay longer with the promise of sweets.

Soon, the whole family was gathered around the table. With the twins about to leave for Dallas to work on their business and Amy heading to Morocco, Brock's parents seemed quieter than usual. He felt for them and vowed to spend more time at home from now on. He could probably come visit every couple of weeks, if he put in the effort.

He tried to believe this thought had nothing to do with Cassie, but it wasn't easy to convince himself that he didn't want more time with her.

Six days just didn't seem long enough.

Brock turned his thoughts back to his family. "When are you coming back, Ames?" he asked.

She swallowed, but didn't look up from her plate. "Actually, I'll be back in the fall, I think."

There was a clatter as their ma dropped her fork. "So soon? For how long?"

Brock could see that Ma was trying not to get her hopes up. Amy still kept her eyes on her plate, not looking at their mother. She looked pale. "I'm not sure. It's still up in the air."

Everyone around the table waited for her to say more, for Ma to prod her, but both women remained quiet. Finally, Pop said, "We love having you here, you know that. Stay as long as you can."

With that, the conversation was finished. Brock wondered what could be bringing his sister back to Spring Valley after so short a time, when for the past decade she'd made a habit of visiting once a year or less.

But, as usual, Amy didn't say anything else and Brock didn't ask. There was no point pressing her about it and the entire family knew it.

After breakfast, Amy said goodbye to Jose, Diego and Ma. Brock walked out with her as Pop started up the truck. Brock could hear Ma sniffing behind him, and she knew the woman was unsuccessfully holding back tears. From the expression on Amy's face, she knew it, too.

Brock was glad his brothers were staying the rest of the day, or he knew Ma would be nearly inconsolable.

At the truck, Brock kissed Amy on the cheek. "I'll miss you," he told her. "If you're back in the fall, I'll try to be here. We can spend a little more time just you and me, what do you say?"

Brock knew that if given the chance, he would spend time with Cassie then, too, but he didn't say it aloud.

"It's been a long time since we hung out, hasn't it?" Amy said, wiping away a quick tear.

Brock hadn't really thought about it, but it was true. In middle and high school, they had been good friends. Even when he left for the circuit as she finished her senior year, they had stayed in touch.

It must've been the summer after she graduated, when she left for college, that things had changed. How had he not noticed that?

Brock wished he had realized it sooner, that he and Amy could talk before she needed to leave, but she was already climbing gingerly into Pop's truck. Next time, he vowed.

"Bye, sis," he said.

Amy opened her window and gave him one last searching gaze. "Be careful with Cassie," she told him, her eyes serious and a little sad.

Did she think Cassie was dangerous somehow? He didn't know what to say to that. Amy seemed to realize he was confused, because she added, "With your heart, I mean. Love isn't always what it's cracked up to be."

Then she rolled the window up and turned to their pop, and the truck started moving. Brock watched, trying to absorb what she'd said. What had happened to Amy to make her say something like that? It was too late to ask, though. All he could do was wave.

She waved back, and then they were gone.

Brock walked back inside to find his ma sitting at the table with Diego. He had no idea where Jose was, but Brock guessed he was out at the barn or something. He never did well with emotions. That was Diego's job.

"Hey, Ma," Brock said, sitting on the other side of her.

The woman looked up at him and brushed away a

tear. "What are you still doing here, Brock? Didn't you say you and Cassie would be fixing the paddock today so she could get her horses home for good and all?"

"Well, yes, but—" he started.

Surely she didn't expect him to leave her there in tears?

Apparently, she did. "You get along, then. That woman needs your help much more than I do. Go on, get!"

Brock stood, simultaneously concerned for his ma and happy to be going to see Cassie. Even though it had only been a few hours since he'd held her, it felt like much too long.

Along the short walk between the two houses, Brock's mind wandered back to his sister and the rest of his family.

The concept of family had never been something super important to Brock—he loved his siblings and the parents who raised him, but it had never mattered much if he saw them twice a month or twice a year. Now, suddenly, he felt an ache for that kind of closeness he never quite got on the circuit, even with his uncle Joe coaching him.

Or maybe he was feeling the desire for a family of his own.

If so, it was just a temporary feeling, brought on by the amount of time he was spending with Cassie and her children. Nothing could come of it in the end, he knew. Even if he could convince Cassie to see him occasionally when he was in town, eventually she would find someone who could be the husband and father she and the boys deserved.

She was too kind and loving, and the boys were too wonderful in their own right for her to stay single for very long.

Brock didn't like that thought one bit, and he was relieved to feel his phone buzz as a welcome distraction. It was Jay, texting him about the mines.

I've got five guys who want to go with us and all the rope we might need. Do you have your climbing gear with you? It could come in handy.

Brock's climbing gear was piled in a duffel with his rodeo stuff, gathering dust since he got to Spring Valley. Just like everything else not connected to working on Cassie's ranch.

Brock sent a quick affirmative, then put his phone away. He was walking up the porch by that point and didn't want Cassie or the boys to see. He was worried Cassie would find out what he had planned and be disapproving, but he was even more concerned the twins would think it was cool and exciting and try something like that themselves.

He'd never forgive himself if they got hurt doing something foolish like that.

Inside the house, he quickly found the little family on the floor doting over their new pet. He was glad to see them all wearing their new cowboy hats. He'd bought them on a whim, and it gave him a good feeling to know all three of them liked the gift.

Something to remember him by. He quickly dismissed that depressing thought. He'd see them again.

Even if it wasn't the same, even if Cassie *did* find someone who would be a good husband and father, they would still be his parents' neighbors.

The knowledge didn't help much.

Cassie looked up and saw him, and the way her expression brightened as their eyes connected made his heart thump.

He was going to make these six days count. Solid fencing, a repaired barn, mended house and as many nights in each other's arms as he could get.

"Are we working on the paddock today?" Cassie asked, standing.

"You bet," Brock replied, and soon the four people and one rambunctious puppy were outside in the morning heat.

While the boys tried unsuccessfully to teach Freckles to fetch, Brock and Cassie began working on the fencing around the paddock, checking each piece of wood, using the crowbar to pull off any that needed to be replaced and nailing up new ones. Cassie never once complained about the hard work, and it went quickly.

Just like in every other situation, Brock and Cassie worked seamlessly together. In just under three hours, they had managed to do what Brock had thought would take an entire day or more.

By the time they were finished, everyone was starving and Brock was happier than ever about purchasing hats for everyone, since the sun had been beating down on them relentlessly the entire time.

After food and time to cool off, they once more braved the heat to paint the paddock so it would be completely ready for Rosalind and Diamond, who they'd decided should come home the next day.

Zach and Carter were reluctant to go back out in the heat, so Brock sent a quick text to his ma, who scurried over to take Freckles and the twins to her house for ice cream—and general spoiling—while their mother and Brock labored in the sun.

By the time they were done, neither of them wanted anything more than a cool shower. And, since the boys were still secure in Nana Sarah's clutches, that was just what they did.

That night, when Brock returned after the twins were asleep, he found Cassie dozing on her bed, the light still on. He was about to leave when she woke up enough to hold her arms out to him, so he turned out the light, slid into bed with her and slept hard until just before dawn.

And then there were only five days left.

The next day rushed by in a flurry of activity as Rosalind and Diamond got settled in. Brock helped Cassie prepare stalls for them in the barn, and they repaired anything in the barn they could get their hands on, all while Brock instructed Cassie on everything he knew about horse care and maintenance.

Another sunset, another late-night entrance, another few hours in Cassie's arms.

Four days left.

Cassie felt the days speeding up as the rodeo loomed closer and closer. They worked on the ranch and house at breakneck speed, as if Brock wanted everything to be absolutely perfect before he disappeared from their lives.

They continued fixing the perimeter fence and she met another new patient, and suddenly another day was gone.

Three days left.

Another day on the fence, and then they only had two days until the rodeo.

Brock went around the house repairing every stuck window, squeaky hinge and unyielding kitchen drawer while Cassie unloaded the last few boxes scattered around the house.

One day left.

The last day they spent doing little things and discussing a plan for purchasing cattle over the next few years. Neither of them mentioned that it was their final day before the rodeo.

When the sun began to set, Brock asked, "Do you mind if I tuck the boys in and tell them their story?"

Cassie understood why and left the room, unable to watch Brock say not only good-night, but also goodbye. She was sure the twins would need her once he was done, but at the moment she wasn't sure she'd be able to keep her tears at bay, let alone comfort them.

As many times as she'd reminded herself about the number of days they had left and what would happen at the end of them, she still couldn't wrap her mind around the thought that she wouldn't be seeing Brock anymore.

After a while, Cassie felt composed enough to go check on the boys. In the dim room, Zach and Carter were sleeping peacefully. Brock was sitting in a chair in the corner watching them. Cassie couldn't see his face, but she knew he was as sad about their time ending as she was.

Brock stood and walked over to where she waited in the hall, shaking his head. "I just couldn't say goodbye to them," he told her.

Cassie felt hope rise in her chest. Was he saying what she thought he was saying?

"Is it okay if I come by the morning after the rodeo? Before I leave town I need to let them know I won't be around anymore. You know?" he said.

The hope she'd started to feel deflated into nothingness. He really was leaving.

Brock looked at her, and his eyes seemed to be asking her for something, but she didn't know what. Consolation? She didn't think she had it in her.

She nodded. "They'll be staying at Hank's parents' house in Glen Rock while I go to the rodeo—"

His eyes lit up and he smiled. "You're going to the rodeo?"

Cassie blushed a little. "I've never been to one, and I have a cowboy hat now. And, well…"

I needed to see you one more time.

I'm not ready to say goodbye.

I love you.

She let the sentence drift away. He could fill in the blank with whatever he liked.

"And you'll wait for me after? I'll be busy most of the day, but I can come find you as soon as my ride's over."

She didn't need to answer. Of course she would wait.

He seemed lighter, more relieved, but she couldn't

share in those emotions. Whether they said goodbye right now or tomorrow or the day after, the end was the same. He would leave and she and the boys would need to pick up the pieces of their hearts.

"But the boys will be at their grandparents'?" he asked.

Cassie nodded. She didn't want her boys watching, getting ideas about bull riding if Brock did well. And if he didn't, well, she didn't want them to see that, either. Also, selfishly, she wanted her last little bit of time with him alone. "But we should probably be back by eight or so the next morning, if you're coming back here."

"I will," Brock said.

They stood there, silent. What else was there to say?

"I better get going," Brock said, not moving from where he stood.

"You have a big day tomorrow," Cassie added, hating the inanity as it came out of her mouth.

Then, as if by mutual agreement, they rushed into each other's arms, holding each other close, their lips pressed together as if they needed to concentrate hundreds of kisses in that one.

Brock awoke the next morning, more tired than he'd ever felt, as his alarm beeped incessantly. He'd come home only as the sun rose, when he finally convinced himself that it was time to leave Cassie's embrace.

He stayed in bed a few extra seconds, wishing it was a different day. It was fruitless, however, and he knew it. This was the day of the rodeo. It was going to be a painful day, he was absolutely sure, and that was because he had two big problems: he was out of shape for his ride, and he wasn't ready to say goodbye to Cassie and the twins. The thought of not being able to see the twins every day, in fact, was turning out to be harder to accept than he'd anticipated.

After this, he'd be off on his adventures and back on the circuit, and the boys would go back to life without him.

Well, he could still drop by and see them, be neighborly, that sort of thing. It was little consolation when he knew what he was giving up, but there was no way around it unless he wanted to leave behind everything in his life that he enjoyed doing.

Brock had planned to ask Cassie about seeing each other again, even if it was just for a day or two the next time he was in town, but he'd chickened out. He wasn't ready to hear her say no, and he knew that she would.

Brock sighed and sat up. At least he would see Cassie again that night, and Zach and Carter the next morning. If he held on to those thoughts and ignored the rest, he could make it through okay.

Brock drove to Glen Rock early to register for the bull-riding competition, and then he spent the next several hours with his uncle Joe. The old man growled about how out of shape he was, and how did Brock ever expect to make it to the NFR in Vegas in this condition?

Brock had no answer. He hadn't thought about the NFR in nearly two weeks. His mind had been occupied with other things.

Once he was limbered up a bit, stretching his back to try and prevent his old injury from flaring up on him at the wrong moment, there wasn't much to do but wait and chat with the other competitors. Jay came up to him immediately. "Brock! You haven't been much help planning the mine exploration. It's been like pulling teeth to get anything from you."

Brock shrugged. "I was busy," he said.

Every time he'd gotten a message from Jay, he either ignored it or gave a single-word response. He felt a little guilty every time Jay wrote, as if he was sneaking behind Cassie's back, though he knew that didn't make much sense.

"Busy? What've you been doing?" Jay asked.

Brock paused, not sure what to say. "I've been helping a neighbor," he responded finally.

Jay raised his eyebrows and smiled in a way Brock didn't care for. "*Oh.* I guess I should've asked *who* you've been doing."

"Watch it, Jay," Brock said, his jaw clenching.

All of the guys ribbed each other about their buckle bunnies, but Brock wasn't about to let that go on about Cassie.

Jay's expression didn't change one bit. "Is that why your uncle is so pissed at you? Were you so 'busy' screwing—"

For all his bulk, Brock was not a violent guy, which was why he was as surprised as anybody when his fist collided with Jay's jaw.

Brock stood there dumbfounded, not believing what he'd done, as Jay sat up from where he'd landed on the floor, rubbing at the place where Brock had hit him. The other cowboys closed in, and Brock knew that they were preparing to separate them if either one threw another punch.

"Sorry about that," he told Jay, holding out his hand.

Jay looked at the proffered hand for a second, and Brock thought he might have lost a good friend, but then Jay just laughed, took the hand and pulled himself to his feet. "Okay," he said good-humoredly. "Point taken. No more comments about the neighbor."

Jay moved on to the topic of the mines, and Brock half listened. What had gotten into him? Sure, he never participated in that particular type of talk—his ma had raised him to always speak respectfully of women—but he'd never gotten so wound up about it before.

Of course, it had never been about Cassie.

Brock ran his fingers through his hair and stood up. "I need to go find Uncle Joe," he said, more for a reason to leave than anything else.

Jay nodded, though he still looked a little confused about Brock's behavior. Brock found it hard to care too much at that moment. All he wanted to do was go look out in the stands and see if he could find a certain woman with curly brown hair underneath a white cowboy hat.

Brock found a good spot where he could see all of the stands, but before he could scan much of the crowd, Uncle Joe walked up to him, scowling. Brock couldn't believe his uncle was still that upset about his lack of preparation, but his uncle cleared things up immediately. "I just got the lineup," Brock's uncle told him. "You're tangling with Freckles today."

Brock couldn't help but laugh. Of course he would be riding Freckles with Cassie watching. He gave up any hope of doing well in front of her. He'd settle for surviving the encounter.

Brock took a deep breath and looked at the audience again, sweeping his eyes across for the wild, curly hair, the face he'd grown to know so well.

There. She'd made it. And she *was* wearing her hat, just like she said.

He wasn't sure if he was glad she was there or not, now. But just seeing her bolstered his spirits. She was even more beautiful than she'd been the night before. He soaked in the sight of her, wishing he could go to her.

As soon as he was done with his ride, he vowed, he would go into the stands. Hug her. Tell her he didn't want this thing between them to end. Not yet.

Brock's uncle started talking to him again, and Brock turned his attention back to the old rodeo pro, trying to keep his mind on the coming ride. He knew he would need all the help he could get if he was going to survive this thing.

Cassie sat in the stands, waiting for Brock's turn. Each cowboy's ride filled her with more and more worry. Some seemed so close to danger, a split second from being trampled. She thought of Brock's bedtime story and wondered if there was more truth to it than she'd originally thought. Her heart stuck in her throat.

"Brock McNeal riding Freckles," a voice announced over the loudspeaker.

Cassie almost laughed when she heard the name of her silly dog, but then she remembered what Brock had told the boys about Freckles, and her worries increased tenfold. He had said he was happy he'd never ridden Freckles, that the animal was crazy.

The buzz of conversation around her didn't help, either. "Last time I saw Freckles, he 'bout killed the cowboy riding him," said a lady sitting near her.

"I hope for Brock's sake he can manage to hold on," muttered a man in a large cowboy hat.

Cassie crossed her arms, hugging herself to keep the fear at bay.

The buzzer sounded and the chute opened, and there was Brock on top of a mean-looking bull. Whoever named him must've had a terrible sense of humor, Cassie thought.

Each second went by with incredible slowness.

One, two...

Brock was holding on, moving well with the bull, and Cassie's spirits lifted.

Three, four, five...

She was watching so intently she could see the exact moment when something went wrong. Suddenly Brock was out of sync with the bull, and Cassie wanted to close her eyes, but she couldn't look away.

Six...

Brock's head slammed into Freckles's back and he slid off, lifeless. As he fell, bullfighters rushed into the arena, trying to pull the bull away from where Brock lay.

Then Freckles was gone and it was just Brock on the ground, not moving.

Cassie stared, unable to comprehend what had just happened.

Chapter 14

Brock woke up slowly. He felt as if he was swimming up through an ocean of black. When he finally broke the surface and opened his eyes, he closed them again immediately to shut out the light of early morning sunshine. He didn't remember anything of the bull ride or the time that had passed since. His head pounded.

"What happened?" he asked the room, though he wasn't even sure if anyone was there with him.

"You hit your head on the bull's back and got a concussion," a voice answered.

It was Cassie. Just hearing her voice soothed him, and his head seemed to hurt less. He opened his eyes a little so he could see her. She was sitting beside his bed in what had to be a hospital room. Her cheeks were pale, but she still looked incredibly beautiful.

When their eyes met, she asked, "Who was the first president of the United States?"

Brock had gotten a couple of concussions in his life, so he knew why she asked. "George Washington. Was I pretty bad?"

"You were out of it for quite a while, but you seem to be better," Cassie said, looking into each of his eyes carefully. Brock felt lucky to be dating a doctor. "You should be up and about in time for your trip to the mines this afternoon."

Brock felt a rush of dread. How did she know about that?

"Your cowboy friends came by to check on you last night," Cassie said, responding to his unasked question.

Brock waited for her to tell him it was a stupid, dangerous idea. He almost welcomed it. Anything would be better than this sad, quiet calmness that he couldn't interpret.

Cassie stood up and slipped her purse over her shoulder. "Your family is waiting outside to see you. The last two weeks have been amazing, Brock. You've helped me more than you know. But I think it's best if things end now, for good. I'll tell Zach and Carter you said goodbye."

Brock finally got his tongue unstuck. "Goodbye?" he asked.

This couldn't be it for them, could it? Cassie shrugged. "We've always said it wasn't a permanent thing, Brock. Now that I'm sure you'll be okay, it's time for me to go."

"I don't want it to be over," he said. "I could visit—"

Cassie shook her head. "We shouldn't see each other anymore. Jay and I chatted for quite a while, and it's clear that my boys and I don't fit into your life. I'd always known that, but I can't lie to myself about it anymore. Zach and Carter need someone stable, who'll be there for them. I can't put them through another father's death. And I love you too much to watch you try to kill yourself."

She wiped away a single tear, the only sign of emotion from her.

He couldn't think what to say. His brain seemed jumbled, unable to organize his thoughts into coherent sentences. He wasn't sure if it was from the concussion or the fact that Cassie was leaving for good.

She turned away from him and walked to the door. Once there, she hesitated, and he felt hope rise in him. But then she was gone, the door shutting slowly behind her.

Cassie left the hospital as quickly as she could, only stopping for a brief moment to say goodbye to her neighbors, Brock's parents. Once she was in the privacy of her car, she let her sobs take over. It had taken all her strength to keep herself calm while he had babbled nonsense due to the concussion, while Jay explained to her about their mine exploration plan and their past adventures, and then finally while speaking to Brock. Now, however, she could allow all the worry and sadness to wash over her.

After her tears had lessened enough so she could see, Cassie buckled her seat belt and started up her car.

She made the quiet drive to pick up Zach and Carter, her mind constantly running in circles, though always with the same conclusion.

She couldn't be with Brock. She'd known it from the beginning, and the information about the mines and the other daredevil stunts he and his friends participated in was just a reminder of that fact.

As soon as she saw Zach and Carter, she pulled them into a tight hug. If nothing else, she had them. They would always be enough. "I missed you boys," she said into Carter's hair.

"Did Brock ride a bull?" Zach asked.

"He did," Cassie said, dancing a fine line between telling the truth and protecting her children. "Let's go home." She settled them into the SUV.

"Is Brock going to come tell us about riding the bull? I want to hear it as a bedtime story," Carter explained.

Cassie's heart went out to her two boys. "Actually, Brock won't be able to come by anymore. Remember when we talked about how he would be leaving Spring Valley for his job? Well," she said, trying to hold back the tears that threatened, "he won't be coming over anymore. He wanted me to say goodbye to you for him."

The looks on the boys' faces were almost more than she could bear. They looked devastated. "He's not going to tell us about the rodeo?" Zach asked.

"Can we go with him?" Carter asked.

Cassie put her head in her hands, wishing this were easier, then began to drive, hoping she would come up with something to make the pain her children were feeling hurt less.

* * *

Brock watched as his friends put on lamp helmets and climbing gear, but he didn't make a move toward the pile of equipment. He just couldn't get himself excited about exploring the mines, even though his buddies all seemed energized and ready to go.

Brock walked toward the mine entrance and peered into the darkness, but his mind wandered to a mass of curly brown hair and green eyes, and to two matched grinning faces. He understood why Cassie had asked him to keep his distance—he didn't want to hurt the boys any more than she did, and as long as he was doing stuff like climbing into mines, that was all too real a possibility.

Brock pulled at his phone and looked at the screen, even though he knew he had no messages. Who would have sent him one?

The phone buzzed in his hand, and he had a moment of hope before he saw that he'd received a text from Ma. Cassie might be moving away. I saw her packing. Thought you'd want to know.

The blood drained out of Brock's face as he absorbed the words. She was packing?

Then he realized what that meant. If he didn't do something quickly, he was going to lose her for good.

Brock looked toward his friends, who were geared up and ready to walk into the dark, abandoned entrance and he knew what he had to do. There was someplace he needed to be, and it had nothing to do with mines.

"Where are you going?" Jay asked, but Brock didn't

have time to answer. As he opened his truck door, Jay called out, "Is it the neighbor?"

"I'll let you know how it goes!" Brock shouted back.

He heard Jay yell, "Good luck!" as he started down the dirt road that would lead him to the highway and Spring Valley.

Brock parked in front of Cassie's house and hopped out of his truck. He hardly had a chance to wonder why the front door was open as he bolted through it and to Cassie's office, where she was standing with an older woman he recognized from town. Probably a patient.

Neither noticed him.

Cassie and the woman hugged, and Cassie said, "I'll miss you, Mrs. Edelman."

His heart tightened painfully. "Please don't leave Spring Valley," he said, knowing he was begging but unable to care.

The older woman glared at him. "I will so leave Spring Valley, young man, and no green rascal is going to stop me," she said, pointing her finger at him.

Brock was confused, but he couldn't deal with that right now. There was too much at risk to lose focus. He rushed up to Cassie and gave her a kiss. He couldn't help himself. She seemed at a loss for words, but the way her body molded to his gave him hope. "I don't want to lose you and the boys, Cassie. I love you. All three of you. I'd rather be a husband and a father than a lonely thrill-seeker." He rubbed his thumb along her bottom lip, memorizing its shape. "Please don't go back to Minneapolis. I can't say goodbye to you."

Her expression went through several changes, from surprise to what he hoped was love, then to confusion. "Who told you I was leaving?"

"Ma saw you packing. The moment I thought I might never see you again, I knew I wanted to be with you forever. You and Zach and Carter give me something to live for."

This time, she initiated the kiss, and he wrapped his arms around her. For a long moment, they stood entwined.

Then the patter of tiny feet heralded the entrance of the twins, who shouted Brock's name in excitement. Brock knelt to the floor and accepted their hugs. He didn't think he'd ever felt happier than at that moment.

His ma poked her head into the room. "I'll be taking the boys now, Cassie. We'll be back in a couple of hours, after I've spoiled them properly." She turned to Brock, a satisfied smile on her face. "Came to your senses, did you?"

"Why did you tell Brock I was leaving?" Cassie asked the older woman.

"Technically, I said I saw you packing, dear. Which was true—you packed toys into these backpacks," Sarah explained, pointing at the backpacks the twins were wearing. "And it wasn't all my idea."

"Did it work?" Emmaline Reynolds asked, coming in from the other room.

"Emma?" Cassie asked her friend.

Emma shrugged, and Brock's ma smirked. "I knew he'd figure things out eventually, but it seemed best to light a fire under him. Now the boys and I will get out of your hair."

"And I'll take Mrs. Edelman home. She leaves for her big trip tomorrow, you know. Sorry again about Danny canceling his appointment, but I assume you can find some way to fill the time," Emma said, giving her friend a wink before walking out.

The hall cleared out as quickly as it had filled, and Brock turned to Cassie, who was shaking her head and laughing. It took him a moment to fully register what had happened. "You were never planning to leave," he said. It wasn't a question.

Cassie shook her head. "Want to take back anything you said now that you know I'm not giving up on my dream because of you?"

He moved close to her, reveling in her vanilla scent. "Not one bit," he said, happy.

"I thought you loved your thrill-seeking life," she said.

"Funny thing," he said thoughtfully. "I always thought that if I had kids, I would need to give up everything I enjoy because I didn't want them to grow up without a father.

"But I had it backward," he continued. "I don't want to do dangerous things anymore because I don't want to miss a single minute of them growing up. Risking your life doesn't seem as much fun when you have that at stake."

They heard the front door close, and silence surrounded them, Brock realized they were alone. Cassie seemed to notice the same thing. "I have another patient coming later today," she said.

Brock brushed the hair out of her face. "Would you be able to make a little time for me first, Doc? I've had a recent head injury."

Cassie knitted her eyebrows. "That's right. How are you feeling?" she asked as she placed her palm against his cheek and looked in his eyes.

Brock smiled. "Better than ever," he said, leaning down for another kiss.

* * * * *

SPECIAL EXCERPT FROM

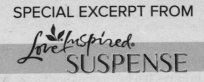
Love Inspired.
SUSPENSE

*A K-9 cop must keep his childhood friend alive
when she finds herself in the crosshairs of a
drug-smuggling operation.*

Read on for a sneak preview of
Act of Valor *by Dana Mentink,*
the next exciting installment in the
True Blue K-9 Unit *miniseries, available in May 2019*
from Love Inspired Suspense.

Officer Zach Jameson surveyed the throng of people
congregated around the ticket counter at LaGuardia
Airport. Most ignored Zach and K-9 partner, Eddie,
and that suited him just fine. Two months earlier he
would have greeted people with a smile, or at least a
polite nod while he and Eddie did their work of scanning
for potential drug smugglers. These days he struggled
to keep his mind on his duty while the ever-present
darkness nibbled at the edges of his soul.

Eddie plopped himself on Zach's boot. He stroked
the dog's ears, trying to clear away the fog that had
descended the moment he heard of his brother's death.

Zach hadn't had so much as a whiff of suspicion that
his brother was in danger. His brain knew he should talk
to somebody, somebody like Violet Griffin, his friend
from childhood who'd reached out so many times, but
his heart would not let him pass through the dark curtain

"Just get to work," he muttered to himself as his phone rang. He checked the number.

Violet.

He considered ignoring it, but Violet didn't ever call unless she needed help, and she rarely needed anyone. Strong enough to run a ticket counter at LaGuardia and have enough energy left over to help out at Griffin's, her family's diner. She could handle belligerent customers in both arenas and bake the best apple pie he'd ever had the privilege to chow down.

It almost made him smile as he accepted the call.

"Someone's after me, Zach."

Panic rippled through their connection. Panic, from a woman who was tough as they came. "Who? Where are you?"

Her breath was shallow as if she was running.

"I'm trying to get to the break room. I can lock myself in, but I don't… I can't…" There was a clatter.

"Violet?" he shouted.

But there was no answer.

Don't miss
Act of Valor *by Dana Mentink,*
available May 2019 wherever
Love Inspired® Suspense *books and ebooks are sold.*

www.LoveInspired.com

Need an adrenaline rush from nail-biting tales
(and irresistible males)?

Check out **Harlequin Intrigue®**,
Harlequin® Romantic Suspense and
Love Inspired® Suspense books!

New books available every month!

CONNECT WITH US AT:

Facebook.com/groups/HarlequinConnection

 Facebook.com/HarlequinBooks

 Twitter.com/HarlequinBooks

 Instagram.com/HarlequinBooks

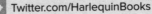 Pinterest.com/HarlequinBooks

ReaderService.com

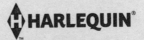 **HARLEQUIN®**

**ROMANCE WHEN
YOU NEED IT**

SGENRE20

Looking for inspiration in tales
of hope, faith and heartfelt romance?

Check out **Love Inspired**® and
Love Inspired® **Suspense** books!

New books available every month!

CONNECT WITH US AT:

Facebook.com/groups/HarlequinConnection

 Facebook.com/HarlequinBooks

 Twitter.com/HarlequinBooks

 Instagram.com/HarlequinBooks

 Pinterest.com/HarlequinBooks

ReaderService.com

Love Harlequin romance?

DISCOVER.

Be the first to find out about promotions,
news and exclusive content!

EXPLORE.

Sign up for the Harlequin e-newsletter and
download a free book from any series at
TryHarlequin.com.

CONNECT.

Join our Harlequin community to share
your thoughts and connect with other
romance readers!
Facebook.com/groups/HarlequinConnectio

**ROMANCE WHEN
YOU NEED IT**

HSOCIAL20